Igniting the Darkness

Ashes of the Past Saga, Volume 3

Christina Dickinson

Published by Christina Dickinson, 2024.

IGNITING THE DARKNESS

First edition. December 2, 2024.

Copyright © 2024 Christina Dickinson.

ISBN: 978-1952009143

Written by Christina Dickinson.

Table of Contents

In memory of Ronan,

A better friend than they believed.

In memory of Sabine,

A better mother-in-law than I could've imagined.

For everyone out there who isn't what they were told they had to be.

1

~Travin~

FEAR WORMED ITS WAY through Travin Esk's fingers as they trailed over the lists on his desk. There was a pattern emerging. His people, those he'd cultivated for the last ten years, were disappearing. Some had died. Some had disappeared. Others he'd had taken care of when they'd gotten sloppy. Secrets only stayed secrets when they were kept. The Gray Army was a very big secret.

His secret.

Twenty years ago, when Irrellian Thornne had been defeated in the Great War, Travin had been the one to hold the forces together. He had founded Harish to keep an eye on Irrellian's tomb. He'd been the one to recognize the weakness in Temple Hill. Without the gods to tell friend from foe, it had been easy to trickle into their power base and turn the houses of worship into a base camp for his best soldiers. For the first decade, he kept things in order for the return of the Flayer Mage. After ten years of keeping the faith, things started to change. Travin liked his role as the underground ruler of Mytana.

Irrellian's creed had been about changing the world. He wanted to scrape the face of Arra clean and start again. Travin had signed on for that vision as a young man with nothing to lose. Now, he had his own power at stake.

But Travin's comfort wouldn't delay Irrellian Thornne from enacting his original vision.

Travin shook his head, hoping to shake his concerns aside. The number sheets and letters on his desk seemed to swim in the murky candlelight. He'd been at this too long, trying to figure out exactly when his people had started being pruned. Reports from all over Eerilor confirmed that Irrellian was back. Had he awakened as recently as the Solstice? Or had he awakened when Harish burned and his tomb had been reported empty?

Why wouldn't Irrellian have sought Travin out that first night?

Unless...

Travin rubbed a gloved hand over his head and pushed his once-auburn hair away from his gray-green eyes. His beard had gone ragged and untrimmed. He glared hard at his paunch, riding over top of his belt. It was more obvious sitting in this chair than when he stood up but, even standing, he now carried a belly. His skin had once been firm and uniformly tan from many hours of training in the sun. It was now pale, blotchy, and loose. The years of excess had made him soft. Weak. The man Travin had been twenty summers ago would've despised this version of himself.

His physical prowess wasn't the problem, though.

How much did Irrellian know? And how long had he known it?

Travin walked to the fountain in the corner of his office and took his copper mug off the wall hook. He could slake his thirst and get back to the reports. It wasn't like worrying about the Flayer Mage would let him sleep tonight anyway.

Running a hand under the water, he splashed the crisp, cool liquid across his face. The fountain had Eerilorian rune-work, so it was always as cold as melted snow. It soothed his skin, almost like his fears were burns, branded across his features. He had to get himself under control soon. Fear could be lethal in the Gray Army. One of his underlings might kill him as readily as Irrellian Thorne would, should the Flayer Mage find out how much Travin had strayed.

Travin sat down again. He picked up a random sheet out of a stack of papers and shuddered. There was definitely a pattern forming. He needed to call the remaining knights back from the Eerilorian border dispute and send out the call to action for those still in hiding. Perhaps if he made the right moves, Irrellian might spare him a bit longer.

With a bit more time, Travin Esk might find a way back to the Flayer Mage's side. Then, Travin could sink the dagger himself. If he became the hero credited with defeating the Flayer Mage to some, and the man in charge to the rest, Travin could continue the life he'd built. Only he wouldn't have to hide anymore. No more stealing children for indoctrination from neighboring cities. He could demand them outright. Children raised to fear and love him were so much easier to command than adults. Aside from the mistake made with Sir Estan of the Protective Hand, the others brought up within the temples were turning out quite biddable.

But something had disrupted that operation as well. Saving children didn't seem like Irrellian's work though. Irrellian might even have appreciated it, if Travin was able to convince the Flayer Mage it had been attempted with him in mind.

No matter.

Jarelton belonged to Arad Rhidel and the Venom Guild. Travin had too much to deal with in Seirane and his side of Mytana at present. He had to get his troops ready for war. Not this silly conflict with Eerilor, but the real battle for Arra's future.

Assuming Arra survived what was to come.

2

~Khiri~

KHIRIELLEN NO-LONGER-Fortiva watched Kal's back move as he climbed the face of the mountain in front of her. On even footing, Khiri usually faced mid-torso on the silvery mage. Tall for an elf. Short for a human. She felt like she'd barely seen more than his ankles for hours. Her strawberry blonde hair, normally tied back with a strip of leather, whipped around her face in the mountain winds. It was getting much too long, but she hadn't felt like cutting it since her arrival in the Eerilorian palace. The last time she'd seen her reflection in a stream, her delicate features were sharper, almost gaunt. Normally, her olive-toned skin held a youthful sheen, but it was dulled. Her blue eyes looked haunted. Despite how slowly elves were supposed to age, Khiri had lost years, as though they'd been drained out of her.

They hadn't spoken much since leaving Eerilor. Khiri wasn't sure what to say. Her father had disowned her, Ullen had abandoned her, and the gods had gone quiet. Maybe they'd left her too. She wasn't really sure.

"You've still got me," Micah said, breaking through her rising gloom. *"And Kal's here. He's more than ready to talk any time you're ready. I asked him about the silence and he said he's giving you space. But I think you've had enough space at this point."*

Khiri bit back a sharp retort. If it had been anyone else, she might've let fly with a verbal slap. This was Micah, though. Micah Ulimani, her sworn brother who'd died and become her Lifewood bow. No one had lost as much on this journey as Micah, no matter how far she'd sunk in her father's esteem. And he was right, as loath as Khiri was to admit it. Their silence had lasted far too long.

"Kal..."

"Yes, *laska*?" Kal actually paused and turned, allowing her to catch up, rather than forcing her to have this conversation with his backside.

There was a part of her that wished he would let her stay behind him. It was much easier to focus without his mirrored owl eyes focusing on her. Despite his declaration of love, all they'd shared was a single kiss. So much had occurred since that kiss. There were always distractions it seemed. Not the least of which was Khiri's bond with the Flayer Mage.

Telgan Korsborn. It strummed through her core like an iron bell. Their brush with Irrellian Thornne had only strengthened the name's grip on her. For a brief, shining moment, Kal's kiss had weakened the name's hold. Khiri had thought there would be more time to explore what that meant. Now, she wasn't sure.

"Thank you," Khiri said.

His gray eyebrows rose, wrinkling his pale, glimmering skin into an expression of surprise. Kal reminded her so much of a moon's reflection on the surface of a lake. She'd caused a ripple on his surface.

"You're welcome," Kal responded. His cadence was cautious, almost a question. "What am I being thanked for?"

"For standing by me," Khiri said. "Very few others have."

"Your father was posing for the crowd," Kal said. "Some of those courtiers saw Irrellian grab you, speak with you. Genovar Fortiva can't be seen as someone who would compromise his loyalty, even for his own daughter."

Tears burst from a dam Khiri hadn't realized she was building. She crumpled to the ground and Kal's arms were around her an instant later. "He's... He always... I can't..." Khiri sobbed maybe a dozen half-formed sentences against the silk shirt covering Kal's chest. She was getting him wet, and despite the sun, the mountains were freezing.

"He's always been hard on you, but he does love you," Micah said. *"I remember. I was there too. Your father knew better than any of us that you weren't going to live a sheltered life, tucked away in the Life Trees."*

"You have more reasons to resent him than defend him," Khiri replied.

Micah gave her a mental shrug. She felt like if she focused hard enough, she might be able to see his golden hair brushing his equally golden cheeks, the tattoo around his brown eyes crinkling as he grinned at her. *"Maybe. But I chose to follow you. I chose this form to stay with you, even when you couldn't hear me. I know how hard it is to let go of you, Khiri. Your father isn't heartless. He's feeling this every bit as strongly. Trust me."*

Kal didn't interrupt. Khiri wasn't sure if he'd even heard. They hadn't spoken mind-to-mind since the Winter Solstice. Granted, she'd barely spoken to him for anything other than what was needed to facilitate their daily making and breaking of camp. He held her close, letting her sob herself dry.

"Could you hear any of that?" she asked, still pressing her cheek into his chest.

"I could tell you were talking to Micah, but I couldn't actually make out the conversation," Kal said. "My mind-speech has faded in and out since Shydan left."

"Shydan's gone?" Khiri asked. The news that Kal wasn't an avatar any longer distracted her despite her continued grief.

"Left on the Solstice. Their plan to break through to the heavens seems to have worked. Is Imyn still with you?" Kal asked.

Khiri sent a mental call out for the Goddess of Power and Change that had ridden within her skull since the release of the Flayer Mage. There was no answer, but she hadn't been fond of answering Khiri anyway. They got along out of necessity more than affection. Not like Estan and Taymahr. Assessing the spot where Imyn had curled up inside her was useless. Khiri couldn't remember what normal felt like anymore.

"I don't know," Khiri said at last. "But I hear Micah as strongly as I ever did."

"Can't get rid of me, now," Micah teased.

"Shyden told me as he was leaving that some gifts last longer than others, and even the gods don't know when those gifts fade entirely. It could be that my mind-speech won't even last the winter." Kal rubbed Khiri's back with his free hand. The staff he clutched with his other glowed orange as heat coursed through Khiri like she'd plunged into a warm bath. "A shame. It's been useful. But the two of us weren't without our own talents before."

For emphasis, Kal thumped his staff on the stones and caused the intricate rune work to glow like embers.

Khiri gave Kal as much of a smile as she could muster. This talk had made her feel better. It hadn't fixed anything, but she no longer felt like a walking ghost. For the first time in days, she really took in her surroundings. If she wasn't mistaken, they were in the Eissessi Mountains. They'd taken the same path out of Eerilor that they'd followed in all those weeks ago. But if they were following the same course, that meant they'd eventually make it back to the Burning Valley and Harish. "Where are we headed?"

"I wasn't really headed anywhere other than *back*," Kal admitted. "I'm not exactly a wayfinder. Most of our guides have been left behind or..."

With a shudder, Khiri remembered the glassy eyes and gruesome smile of Fennick as his life drained away, freeing the Flayer Mage. The first life she'd taken on this journey, but not the last. So many mistakes she'd made in less than a year. She had to start setting things right. Without her father's guidance, there was only other person she could think to turn to for counsel.

Leyani Fortiva—her mother.

A human hidden among the elves.

There were so many questions, Khiri wasn't even sure where to start.

"It's time to go home," Khiri said. "I may not be welcome to stay, but I have to go back."

"The road home will take us through Jarelton," Micah reminded her. *"We should see how our friends are doing while we're in town."*

A nervous flutter tickled Khiri's stomach. Estan had kissed her and asked her to go with him when he'd left. She had no interest in rekindling his ardor, but she liked the idea of seeing him again. Him, Resmine, Dewin, and Catapult. Things hadn't been the same since they had all parted ways. If she was lucky, maybe she'd even get to see Dewin's siblings again. Corianne and Evic had saved her life once—and though Khiri hadn't gotten to know them well, she'd liked them.

With a sense of renewed vigor, Khiri untangled herself from Kal's arms. They had a long way to go, and she didn't want to camp on the barren side of a mountain. Tonight she was determined to have a proper meal and bed down in a well situated camp. She would trim her hair back into something manageable and regain some control over her own destiny.

Telgan Korsborn or Irrellian Thornne or whatever he called himself be damned.

KHIRI HAD BROUGHT DOWN two partridges and a grouse while hunting. Kal was tending the spit, roasting the birds slowly over an open flame. He'd also sliced some of their travel bread and was letting it toast on a flat stone next to the fire. Every so often, Kal picked up one of the bread slices and dabbed the birds as they started to drip fat into the fire.

"Whatever you do, don't let Khiri take over," Micah cautioned.

Kal chuckled. "We've traveled together long enough that I don't need the warning."

With an exaggerated sigh, Khiri let them tease her. Kal's mind-speech was working well enough to give the two men some bonding time. It was important that Kal get along with her brother. Kal was important to her in ways she still struggled with, and Micah was family. Occasionally, she thought she might even love the lanky mage. It was hard to tell though, with all of her Destined business getting in the way.

Telgan Korsborn, her Destined name agreed.

Khiri tugged a few strands of hair against the enchanted knife her father had gifted her. It was a masterwork with runes etched along the single-sided blade. A hawk in flight was cleverly designed to function as the hilt guard. Genovar had assured her it would never go dull nor break. She'd since learned that her father had given it to her for other reasons. It carried the agreement he'd made with the gods to repay them for a forbidden magic. A secret her parents had never seen fit to warn her about.

He'd given it to her the day before her Name-Breathing. The day she and Micah would've been married in the eyes of their people if all had gone according to plan. In that sense, the name of her Destined altering had actually been a blessing. She and Micah wouldn't have been happy together. Not that way. Micah had never made her blood sing. Kal was the closest she'd come to something like that.

As though he could sense her thoughts, Kal turned to meet Khiri's gaze and smiled. Khiri's pulse caught in her throat. She shifted her focus back to her hair and the knife. Snick. Another lock on the ground. Snick, snick, snick.

"You know, we've never really talked about my father's people. My grandfather didn't want me to be raised with them, but that didn't stop me from sneaking to the lake every chance I got. I managed to run away for a whole week once," Kal said.

"We discussed how your people recognized their soul mates..." It was like the fire had transferred all of its heat directly into Khiri's cheeks. She concentrated on breathing normally. In and out. In. And out.

"Yes, but not much beyond that. Would you like to hear about the Odlesk?"

Khiri wasn't sure if she was relieved or disappointed. She was curious though. The Odlesk had intrigued her for a while. "Yes."

Picking himself up, Kal moved to Khiri's side and extended his hand toward the knife in a gentle request. Handing the knife to him, Khiri scooted forward so he could sit on the stump she'd been using as a back rest. Using his long fingers to coax out a tangle, Kal began to work on her hair. Glancing at the spit, Khiri saw that he'd worked some kind of spell onto the handle to keep it rotating. It had been a minor enough enchantment that her ears hadn't registered it past the tingles she'd already felt from handling the knife.

Her sensitivity to magic hadn't been as strong recently in general. Not since Kal had started teaching her how to use her own abilities. She tucked that thought away for later.

"It's said that Lake Echar was born of Arra's tears. Though it's called a lake, and has been for time out of mind, Lake Echar is really more of an inland sea. The Odlesk, children of the water, are made up of three tribes—roughly translated, these are the Tribe of Moonlight Shallows, the Tribe of the Twilight Current, and the Tribe of the Nightwater Reef. My father was a member of the Nightwater Reef, though the tribes are all very friendly and the lines between them are thin."

Khiri began to nod, but then thought better of it. Moving her head could be hazardous when Kal was trimming her hair. "The Life Tree Clans are very close, too."

"The tribes of Lake Echar migrate from city to city throughout the year. There are four cities down below the water to rival the beauty of Taman. They are Coral Grove, Sand Flat, Algae Field, and Crevasse Edge. Each is named for the closest landmark. While no one tribe is allowed to lay claim to any one city, there are those that choose not to move with the turning of the tides. They favor one city and stay there for one year or many. My father became one of these when he first saw my mother. She was swimming on the beach with friends. His tribe had only arrived in the nearest city that very day. He hadn't even chosen his house, but he knew he wouldn't leave. One of my uncles told me they'd been reluctant to leave him, despite it being the way of the Odlesk not to interfere. My mother's people had long been prejudiced against my father's. My parents' union was taboo in her village. Obviously that didn't stop her."

Khiri rubbed a hand over Kal's boot, saying a silent thank you to Kal's parents for being stubborn enough to defy the wishes of his mother's village. It seemed odd to recall her own path had intersected with Kal's when he was an assassin with the Venom Guild. Part of a team sent to kill her. Part of a team responsible for Micah's death.

Kal had more than proven himself loyal to Khiri and her friends since then. If he'd been any good as an assassin, he wouldn't be here with her now. Khiri wasn't sure she'd be here herself.

"Tell me more about the Odlesk," Khiri said. "How do they cook beneath water? What kind of celebrations do they have? What do they wear?"

With a laugh, Kal brushed his fingers through her hair. The strands slid apart like they were made of wind. Khiri leaned into the warmth of his hand against her scalp before she caught herself.

"As to your first question, there are thermal vents. They roast fish and algaes into pies and wraps over these vents. They have magic sigils, not unlike the runes favored by Eerilor, to filter out toxins, although there are few poisons our people can't comfortably ingest. It's not uncommon to prepare foods with knife-work alone. A properly sliced fish is delicious. Celebrations—there are a few. Moving-in day is one that occurs three or four times a year. A child's fifteenth name day is when they are considered a full tribe member and they're allowed to choose their own home and expected to contribute to the city's needs. Normally this means adding to the communal food supply, but there are also builders and artisans. Those with exceptional magical ability are generally encouraged to seek the surface, where there is better training for such things. Not that the Odlesk lack magical traditions. They just don't view it as being as important as other things."

"Wait," Khiri said. "So, even if you hadn't been discovered by the Mage College and taken from your grandfather..."

"I likely would've found myself there eventually, yes."

Khiri found her thoughts drifting toward Irrellian Thornne. If he was of the Odlesk, as she suspected, he'd grown up in a society that didn't find his defining talent as anything important. Had she isolated another thread in the tapestry that made up the Flayer Mage?

She was afraid of bringing up Irrellian Thornne right now. Kal's fingers curling through her hair and the firelight bouncing off the surrounding snow banks created a cocoon of warmth and safety. Kal had placed a ward around their camp, so the two of them didn't even need to keep watch tonight. This tiny camp, filled with the aroma of roasting game birds, was an oasis of calm. Khiri could practically feel bits of her shattered soul drawing together.

But it was so rare for Kal to bring up his heritage. If Khiri didn't ask now, she thought she might not get another chance.

"Was Irrellian Thornne originally an Odlesk mage?"

Despite the quiet that followed her question, Khiri felt like her heartbeat could be heard over the crackle of the fire. The spit continued to turn and the flames continued to dance, but there was no movement behind her. She couldn't even hear Kal breathing. If it weren't for the foot beneath her palm, Khiri might've thought he'd been abducted from behind her by some magical means.

"He was," Kal said. Her friend's voice was thick with emotion, but she couldn't place it. "It's not something that my people are proud of, but he came from the lost tribe—the Tribe of Dawning Waves. There was an accident involving a surface ship and an unfortunate mix of magic and those thermal vents I spoke of. I don't know all of the details, because I was very young when I last saw my relatives, and they were reluctant to talk about it. But they felt I should know why some people might look at me funny. And that our people still grieved. From what I understand, the Dawning Waves tragedy happened a few years before Irrellian left Lake Echar. He was one of only five survivors, and the only one of his family."

Another silence took them, but this one was less tense. After a few moments, Kal returned to the task of trimming Khiri's hair, but the gentle caresses were gone for the night.

Khiri lamented her need to ask about the Flayer Mage. It was vital to learn all she could about Irrellian Thornne, though. Her destiny was set on a collision course with the man she'd released from his crystal coffin, and she didn't know what information could mean her survival.

She was only alive now because Irrellian Thornne had let her go—twice. Khiri wasn't sure he'd do it a third time.

3

~Estan~

THE EVENTS OF THE SOLSTICE had led to two different power vacuums opening in Jarelton at the worst possible time. With the Thieves' Guild leaderless, the Venom Guild was attempting to take over the city's shadows. Literally, in some cases. Guild-contracted Flayers could seep into Jarelton through any unprotected darkness of appropriate size. Enchanters were being contracted to lay protective runes on the richer streets, but much of Jarelton's population couldn't afford the expense.

What the city needed was a new Lord or Lady Ilamar, but the public demise of Orin Treag had seemingly put off even his once-ambitious siblings. The Council of Nobles, whose primary duties were to recognize and work with the Illamar, refused to meet for fear of being targeted by assassins.

Estan sighed as he tugged on his helmet. There was no use in pretending not to walk down the streets of Jarelton fully armed these days. City guards, who would've normally stopped a man with an unsheathed sword, merely nodded at him yesterday—as though passing by a fellow peacekeeper. It was the most respect Estan had been afforded since giving up his knightly armor.

He had an appointment to see one of Orin's siblings this afternoon. With the continued presence of Arad Rhidel and the Venom Guild, Estan still wasn't able to travel the streets without a disguise. As careful as he'd been, he wasn't sure if the Venom Guild's leader still believed him dead or not. Catapult's ability to make illusions hadn't faded in the slightest since the High Ones had returned to the heavens, but Estan was reluctant to test his healing abilities. If Estan took another dagger to the chest, it might be the last.

Not an experience I'd like to make a habit of anyway, Estan grimaced to himself. He was fully healed but, if he thought about it too hard, he still remembered the pain.

The ruse of his death meant he hadn't been able to return to Ren and Adela, the keepers of the Talon Acre Inn, and make his apologies. He missed his room at the Talon Acre Inn. Sleeping alone in the chambers formerly occupied by his departed lover felt wrong. Dirty.

Corianne assured him it was safe, though. Until a new guild leader was accepted, no one else had access to the apartment. The passing of the title imparted a new code into the new leader's head. They could share that code with trusted individuals. Once someone knew the code, they could share it too. But Estan was the only bed-friend Ysinda had named as her consort. He should be the only one who could still enter the Pit's Royal Suite.

Ysinda's cute and deadly collection of armor, weapons, and figurines were a constant reminder of the woman. They hadn't been in love. Not really. But they'd desired each other, respected each other, been intimate with both their bodies and their secrets. She'd hidden her softer side in these rooms, away from the eyes of her court. The pastel mugs hung in Ysinda's cozy kitchen, waiting to hold hot peppermint tea for a woman that wasn't coming back. Estan thought maybe he should clean out the cute, soft bits of her collection before the next leader took power. Even if Resmine succeeded in her bid for Queen of Thieves, Estan wanted to keep Ysinda's secrets. She had entrusted him with her innermost self. These things weren't for other people's eyes.

Estan made himself shut the door and waited for the wall to slide back into place. If he didn't get moving, he'd be late. It wasn't good to make one of the nobility wait. Tak and Catapult fell in beside him from seemingly nowhere. Catapult likely had kept them hidden just to see if he could make Estan jump. The war horse had always possessed a mischievous nature and his time spent as avatar to Numyri, Goddess of Mirth and Mayhem, had only elevated things.

"Good to see you too, my friend," Estan said, patting the blue roan on his dappled shoulder.

"It's no fun when you don't jump," Catapult complained, using his current favorite borrowed voice. It sounded vaguely like Ullen, if the dwarf were of a sunnier disposition. Better by far than when he'd used Evic's voice—Corianne and Dewin practically refused to come near the warhorse anymore. It had taken almost a week to explain why using the voices of dead friends upset his living friends. Catapult had told Estan that he missed their voices, so he thought everyone else might too.

Explaining loss to a horse... Estan almost missed his days on Temple Hill. Those he'd looked up to had been lying traitors, but he hadn't known that. Life had seemed pretty simple back then.

"Disguise, please," Estan said.

Catapult snorted and tossed his head in the horse equivalent of an eyeroll, but obliged. Holding up a hand mirror that he kept in his pocket, Estan watched his lustrous brown skin fade into something slightly more sallow. His softly curved nose sharpened into a long beak, hooked and broken. Wide cheeks thinned, the strong jaw loosened, and full lips stretched. Hard earned muscles became less defined and lanky. Catapult's illusion left Estan's scalp bare. Shaving every day had become something of a ritual for Estan since he'd moved into Ysinda's former residence, and the roan seemed to think it suited his knight. Estan couldn't check his disguised height with his mirror, but Tak's gaze still met his own still-brown eyes.

"Looks good on you," Tak said with a wink.

"You say that when he drops the disguise, too," Estan reminded the trader.

"Because that looks better," Tak grinned.

Estan couldn't help grinning back. Tharkern Anverin, or Tak as he preferred to be called, was a flirt, but a happily married one. Being only slightly smaller than Estan's knightly build, with dark brown hair that hugged his cheekbones, eyes like chips of amber, and boyish features, Estan had no doubt Tak could break a few hearts if he ever felt the need. His clothes were usually very casual, but colored to compliment the olive undertones of his complexion. Tak never pressed for more than a smile and he didn't flirt with anyone that didn't appreciate it. Estan's tastes didn't run towards men, but he liked Tak. For a random stranger found in the woods when Dewin and Estan had been sparring, Tak made for a very good, if very odd, friend. As usual, Tak was completely unarmed. It was hard to believe how deadly a fighter the trader could be, until he was seen in action.

"Ready for your meeting with Araylia Treag?"

Grimacing, Estan shook his head. His hand rested on his hilt as he walked next to Tak down the largely empty cobbled streets. The sun was still rising, casting small shadows off of every pavestone. Prime Flayer conditions. The only thing the demons liked better was cloud cover. Jarelton was protected against Flayer fogs, for which Estan thanked Taymahr. Catapult, disguised as a dun mule with an illusory lead hooked to Tak's waist, kept watch from the rear.

"I approached Orin at Taymahr's behest with the full knowledge that I had my goddess backing me. This is different on every single level. Orin told me that if he and his siblings didn't agree by the Winter Solstice, the title would fall on a cousin with only sixteen summers under her belt. The poor girl's never even seen Jarelton. But Orin thought Araylia and Holt would let the council elevate her just to spite him if he decided to try for the seat. Orin's death staved off the council's decision for another year, but now I have to convince someone to take the mantle of Ilamar against the Venom Guild's open animosity without knowing who Taymahr would prefer."

Tak listened as Estan ranted. The information trader had heard most of this before, and would probably hear it again the next time they went drinking together. "It's a tough situation. Even if the lot of you were still avatars, are you certain your goddess would have guidance for you?"

Before Estan had the chance to respond, he heard it. The scratch of something like claws on stone and the low, hissing, whisper-like chant.

"Blood, rend, tearing flesh, fear, death..."

A Flayer.

He drew his sword and twisted on his heel, scanning the gray stone city for nearby pockets of darkness. A Flayer nearby meant there were also, potentially, victims. Estan was a Knight of the Protective Hand for a reason. He couldn't let Flayers attack innocent people—and everyone was innocent, compared to the demon-bound.

In a nearby alleyway, the surrounding buildings too close together for sunlight to penetrate the shade, Estan spotted movement. Without thinking, Estan drew his sword and charged toward the struggling blob.

"Gushing, feasting, dripping..."

"Please! Let me go!"

The grotesque mask of something that had been human stopped its chanting as Estan entered the shadows. Mottled flesh, purpled like bruised skin, had begun to crack and peel. In life, this Flayer had been little more than a teenage girl when she'd made her bargain, with a wiry build and the remnants of freckles on what was left of her bleached skin. Dull ringlets drooped over the creature's bloodshot, cloudy eyes. Its hands were stretched into deformed, elongated things with talon-like claws jutting out from the tip of each finger.

Grappled in the creature's arms was a small boy with black hair and tawny skin. From what Estan could make out, the child's clothes were rags and he hadn't seen a good meal in a few weeks. An urchin. Maybe orphaned during the Solstice or in the weeks since. The boy's face was scrunched up in terrified sobs, but the Flayer hadn't actually drawn blood yet.

"Let him go!" Estan demanded.

With an evil grin, the Flayer looked up from its captive. *"...Kill"*

A cold gust rushed in from all sides as Flayers stepped out of their realm and joined Estan and his adversary.

It was a trap.

Of course it was a trap...

Estan silently cursed his own hubris. One of these days, he'd learn to look before he leapt. Possibly.

As new Flayers arrived, the teenage Flayer girl started to step back, attempting to take the boy with her.

"No!" Estan lunged forward, trusting his years of training to guide his sword. He didn't want to hit the boy but, if it was a choice between Estan's sword and whatever awaited the child in the hellscape beyond, death might be kinder. The Flayers surrounding Estan dove to intercept him. None of them were fast enough to prevent his blade from finding its mark, though.

The boy screamed as the creature holding him flailed, its claws striking him across the cheek. It crumpled into a steaming, seething mass as the demon-tainted blood boiled and burned its way free of the mortal remains.

Estan didn't have time to relish the brief victory. His limbs were tangled in a mass of Flayers. Despite his armor, it felt like their claws were pressing against his skin. The sensation made his stomach curdle. He wrenched his torso and both arms, attempting to free himself from the foul creatures.

An angry whinny sounded from behind him and one of the Flayers on his right side crumpled into a sizzling heap. Tak appeared on his left, jumping off of the nearest wall and kicking one of the clinging Flayers in its head. The thing lost its grip as it spun to the ground with the momentum of Tak's body behind it. Tak landed in a crouch over the Flayer, his wry grin no more than a memory. Twisting the thing's neck with a sickening crunch, Tak placed himself between the remaining horde and the boy.

Two fewer Flayers made the difference Estan needed to rip his arms loose. With another slash of his sword, another body fell into a jittering, searing pile. Catapult trampled down a second of their enemies, nearly kicking Estan's face in the process. Ducking away from his horse's well-meaning hooves, Estan plunged his sword into yet another demon. The thing let out a wail as it began to vibrate, still skewered on the knight's blade.

Those that remained fled through the shadows. Whether they scattered to report to their keeper or embark for places unknown, Estan neither knew nor cared. At the moment, he was just happy they were gone. This little venture had definitely made him late to his meeting with Araylia Treag.

Tak scooped the crying boy up into his arms and questioned the child about his family. Estan knew Tak had noticed the boy's clothing and near-starved physique. As a trader of information, there wasn't much Tak missed. The questions were meant to distract the child from what he'd witnessed.

"No parents, huh. My friend there doesn't have any parents either. Can you tell us your name?"

Big, deep brown eyes, like wells, looked up at Estan. "Did they get your parents too?"

Estan pulled a clean cloth out of one of his pockets and wiped down his sword before resheathing it. Despite their rumble, Catapult still looked like a dun mule. Given that Catapult's illusions tended to drop if the disguised person did something unbelievable, the knight made a mental note never to tangle with a mule. "I never knew my parents," Estan said. "I don't know what happened to them."

"Oh," the boy said. "That's sad."

"Do you have a name, kid?" Estan asked. He'd never really dealt with children outside of breaking up the Venom Guild's kidnapping ring. This encounter was awkward and uncomfortable. He'd almost rather already be at his meeting.

"Hilaf...But Ma always called me Hil."

"Would you rather we call you Hil or Hilaf?" Tak asked.

"Hil."

"We're running late," Estan reminded the trader.

"We had an errand," Tak said. "We needed to make sure our new friend Hil made it somewhere safe."

Estan wasn't sure where Tak intended to drop the boy off, but he was sure their meeting with Araylia Treag wouldn't go any smoother for the delay. Still, he'd been the one to charge into the alleyway to save Hil in the first place, so Estan let himself be led away from the ambush site.

How much longer could this take anyway? Estan thought with a sigh.

"YOU WERE EXPECTED THREE hours ago," Araylia Treag's butler informed them. Gray eyes attempted to stab their way through the two interlopers darkening his lady's stoop. The man's hair was like rust against his parchment-white skin with a dusting of iron in his manicured facial hair. Every thread of his clothes was crisp and hung impeccably. He was not an imposing man, being an even height with Resmine and Dewin, but Estan's war training told him this was someone with combat skill. In a pinch, the servant probably functioned as a bodyguard as much as a butler.

"Our lady isn't a patient woman. If it weren't for your reputation Master Anverin, I'm quite sure you wouldn't be meeting with Lady Treag ever again."

"Please, call me Tak. Most of my friends do. I apologize for the delay, Caspen. We were unavoidably detained. We did not wish to entangle your good lady with any disputes we may have with the Venom Guild," Tak said, his enigmatic grin giving nothing away. At least, nothing more than the servant's name, which Estan hadn't caught before.

They'd walked little Hil all the way across Jarelton, stopped for lunch at a pub, and deposited him with a blacksmith who'd lost her son in the Winter Solstice carnage. While Estan was happy to know the child would grow up with a strong protector, he'd also balked at the delay. Tak had asked Estan to trust him, so Estan remained silent while they waited to be let in to see Araylia.

It was a long wait. Araylia Treag was not above wasting time to prove she was more important than those coming to see her. She made them sit on a padded bench in a lavishly appointed antechamber for two hours. A painting of the lady in her prime took up an entire wall. She was draped in a purple gown with a pale green surcoat. The portrait's hair was as red as the leaves in fall, and her eyes were a gentle, thoughtful hazel. Her face was long with a pointed chin and the artist had left the hints of dimples next to her soft smile. Estan thought she was fetching enough to have courted her fair share of suitors, but there was also something familiar about her. Painfully familiar. He stared at the painting hard enough that he lost all track of time.

"Lady Treag will see you now," the servant announced. Tak dipped his head. It wasn't quite a bow, but it was enough for the servant. Estan's attempt to mimic Tak was a little too late. He got a stern look and disdainful sniff from the man in livery. "This way, gentlemen."

They were led up a flight of wooden stairs which had been polished until they were nearly as reflective as glass. From the crystal chandeliers to the plush rugs, signs of wealth and affluence were scattered over Lady Treag's house as though to remind everyone lucky enough to see it that she was a scion of the Ilamar line.

If Estan recalled correctly from his historical studies, the title Ilamar was drawn from the name of the first recorded lord of Jarelton. Jarel Ilamar had started the tradition when he'd handed the title to an adopted daughter rather than his birth son. She was the first of the Treag line to inherit. When her children were born, she bestowed them with her own last name, declaring only those who succeeded her would bear the title of Ilamar. Lord Brens Ilamar was forced to relinquish his name as well as his birthright. He'd fought against his adopted sister's right to do either, but she'd won over the people and Lord Brens was found dead in his bed chambers only a week later. It had been recorded as a suicide, though Estan wondered how accurate the historic annals were.

This was so much easier with Orin, he thought.

Following Tak into the most decorative library he'd ever seen, Estan bowed at the waist as they waited to be acknowledged by the woman sitting behind the desk. Lady Treag dismissed her servant without looking up from the document in front of her, her tone brisk, but not unkind. "Thank you, Caspen. Shut the door behind you, please."

"Very good, my lady." Caspen stepped out of the door backwards and pulled the door shut hard enough for an audible snap.

Lady Treag continued to write with a quill on the sheet of paper spread out on her desk. The silence extended for long enough Estan started to wonder if she'd forgotten she wasn't alone in the room. Trained as he was for the Knighthood, the extended bow was hardly taxing, but Estan had never been asked to show this much deference to a mortal. Only seconds before his patience with noble posturing waned, she said, "Master Tak, your request for this meeting left much to the imagination. I wasn't sure whether to chance seeing you or not, given your support of my late brother. Now, you've left me waiting for a good portion of the day and I do have other business. What was so pressing that you and your associate felt it was more important than our appointment?"

"We rescued a child from the Flayers," Tak said. "He was only maybe six or seven years old."

From the corner of his eye, Estan saw the trader was still holding his bow with all his normal ease. Taymahr's knight tried not to sigh as his back urged him to straighten.

The scratch of the quill halted. "A child?"

Something had changed in the library's atmosphere. Estan couldn't be sure without looking up, but Araylia Treag's voice held a note of wistfulness. Or maybe longing?

"An orphan. I placed him with a blacksmith who'd recently lost her own boy."

Another pause.

"Well, stand up. Both of you. Anyone who'd save a child can have a seat in my presence." Lady Treag rang a bell on her desk.

Estan straightened and got his first look at Orin Treag's older sister. She had aged since the portrait in the antechamber was painted. Her red hair was duller, threaded through with gray. The slimness of her youth had given way to a much more matronly build. Lines crinkled the edges of her eyes, though her cheeks were still smooth and her skin unblemished. She wore a simple long-sleeved gown, black for mourning. The sense of familiarity was even stronger now that Estan saw her in person.

Caspen opened the door as though he'd never moved away from it. "Yes, my lady?"

"Have chairs and refreshments brought for my guests," Lady Treag instructed. "And Master Tak, if you'd be so kind as to give me the name of this blacksmith, I might send someone to drop off an order or two."

Estan wanted to ask why rescuing an orphan made such a difference, but he knew enough to save his questions for later. He needed to concentrate on the meeting. They still had to convince one of the Treags to take the mantle of Ilamar. But between Estan's compulsive need to rescue everyone and Tak's stockpile of secrets, they'd stumbled their way into making an excellent impression on Araylia.

4

~Ullen~

STARING ACROSS THE snowy landscape, Prince Ut'evullen Dormidiir wished he could see the slopes and swirls of Taman from his current perch. It was odd how much Ullen missed the palace, considering how little he'd desired his title for most of his life. He'd been called nothing but Ullen for so long that his full name felt like it belonged to a different dwarf. But ever since Hon'idar had killed their mother and joined his forces with those of Irrellian Thornne, Ullen had yearned to go home. While Queen Di'eli lived, all she'd wanted was to place her younger son on the throne. It had only been after she was gone that Ullen finally agreed with her.

It was time for him to accept the crown of Eerilor.

The acknowledgement made his shoulders sag with unseen weight. He'd been running from it for so long. Giving in allowed a long-unacknowledged weariness to seep into his bones.

After the events of the Solstice, Genovar's people had retreated to Earl Tolen Terilles's estate. Despite being one of Eerilor's oldest dwarven families, his estate was very modern in design. All the buildings were above ground, and largely built of timber. The outer perimeter of his grounds was protected by a more traditional stone wall, complete with towers and battlements. Tents took up two fields normally set aside for growing animal feed, while Ullen and Genovar's other generals were housed in guest quarters of the main hall. Most of the other nobles they'd escaped with had gone home with promises to rally their own troops. Ullen had his doubts that many would be ousted from their homes until the weather started to warm again. Whether human or dwarf, Eerilorians all knew snow made for miserable marching.

Ullen missed his young friends. He wondered how Estan, Resmine, and Dewin fared in Jarelton. He was curious how Kal and Khiri were doing, after their ugly dismissal. If things had been different, if Eerilor could've been safely handed to another heir, Ullen would've gone with them in a heartbeat—especially Khiri. The poor girl had been heartbroken, and Ullen's shoulders bore the burden of guilt for his hand in things more than twenty years prior. But Khiri and Kal's investigation into the armed bands of Flayers leaving Eerilor's borders had uncovered Hon'idar's treachery. Eerilor's problems were bigger than the civil war brewing within her boundaries. Hon'idar's choice to ally with the Flayer Mage meant that the Gray Army was tangled up with Eerilorian forces. Genovar had called together alliances forged twenty years ago, during the last war, to fight against their old enemy. And the elf had drawn a hard line between his allies and his own daughter.

Irrellian Thornne's plans were as hard to untangle as Eerilor's troops. It was unclear what the Flayer Mage had in mind. Was he using Eerilor as a base? Or was he merely sowing chaos to undermine a former rival?

Ultimately, it would all amount to the same thing. More Eerilorian blood watering the battlefields. Ullen worried about his people. How many of those fighting for his brother were Gray Army advocates, and how many were merely loyal to the older prince? Neither Ullen nor Honi'dar had been affirmed as the rightful ruler, and there were plenty of commoners that didn't believe the rumors about the Flayer Mage's return. As far as they were concerned, the younger son had disappeared for fifty years only to raise a stink and demand the crown right as their queen died.

In their place, Ullen would've been suspicious too.

Maybe that was why he tossed and turned so often in his sleep these days.

"So this is where you've been hiding," Lady Terilles—Jaspar—said. Her crest of chestnut curls fell over her face as she made her way up the ladder—the only access point to top of the lookout tower Ullen had all but commandeered. She tossed her curls back in one fluid motion. As always,

Ullen lost himself in her violet eyes, tilted like a cat's. Her button nose and strong jaw caught the sun at an angle that pulled at memories of their younger days—days when Ullen would've greeted her by wrapping her in his arms and kissing her until they were both breathless. Her soft copper skin would be pressed against his in all the right places.

Ullen had never really understood why Jaspar, the most beautiful dwarf he'd ever laid eyes on, had taken any interest in the dark, broody second son of the royal family. Hon'idar was always the handsome one. Burnished golden hair, golden skin, golden tongue. Compared with his personable brother, Ullen had always been self-conscious of his shorter stature, his lankier build, his hooked nose, the sharpness of his cheekbones, his inky hair, and unruly mustache and beard. Ullen hadn't really come into his own until he'd been on the road a while, which was after his romance with Jaspar was cut short by her father's ambition. He'd shaved the beard, tamed the mustache with ribbons, all while his muscles filled out. While Ullen's confidence had risen, he still felt unworthy when he looked at the vision in front of him.

In the palace, Jaspar wore dresses befitting a lady of her station, but she'd switched to black or dark brown trousers almost as soon as they'd arrived at her father's estate. She was stuffed into a fitted jacket, dyed the same violet as her eyes, and had an even deeper purple silk sash wrapped around her waist.

"I'm not exactly hiding, Jaspar," Ullen said, gesturing to the lack of roof overhead. He was struggling to completely drop the casual Eerilorian speech patterns now that he meant to take the throne, but they still snuck out from time to time. Especially when he was either tired or emotional, as he was currently. "Anyone with a scry rune could fair see me."

"Don't be obtuse. You know you're avoiding the war council meeting right now."

"I ain't avoiding the meeting," Ullen grumbled. "I'm avoiding them what's in the meeting."

"Ullen..."

With a sigh, Ullen turned back to the snowy landscape. "I know. I can't continue to do this and be worthy to lead our people. There's a lot of history between Genovar and me. He didn't want Khiri to know things. Ages before I ever met the lass, hells, it were before she was even born, he told me not to go following his daughter about. I was to avoid her if at all possible. I know his gift, and I still went seeking her out the first chance I got. When Genovar sent the young knight out to guard his daughter, I knew who it was we were looking for. I knew I was doing exactly the thing Genovar had warned me against. And he's mad at me for it, and I'm mad at him for asking it of me. Khiri's a sweet lass. Deserves much better than the hand fate dealt her, and Genovar knows he's responsible for most of it. Which makes him all the madder, because I know it and he knows I know it."

Jaspar joined Ullen in leaning against the parapet, looking over the powder white hills. "Sounds complicated."

"Aye," Ullen agreed.

"But no one can change the past. All you can do is move forward. It sounds like you're both mad because you love Khiri. While she's his daughter, you've definitely got a fatherly affection of your own. Might have started when he warned you not to interfere. You can be contrary like that," Jaspar said, smiling over her shoulder. "So rather than huffing at each other like angry kittens, why don't you two talk. You started as friends at some point."

Dragging himself off of the wall, Ullen let out a dramatic sigh of exasperation. "It's been fifty-odd years, Lady Terilles. Why must you still be right about everything?"

"It's what I'm good at, my prince." Jaspar leaned forward and gave Ullen the lightest peck on the cheek. "And Genovar needn't be the only old friend you reacquaint with. But first, the meeting with the war council."

"OUR NETWORK HAS SPOTTED a great deal of activity outside of Seirane recently." Sir Quinton Ilyani, Knight of the Protective Hand and a former avatar of Taymahr, placed a handful of soldier pieces on the map of Arra they'd draped over a former dining table someone had pulled out of storage for the makeshift war room. His ruddy face and iron-gray hair were as stern as Ullen had ever seen them.

Their war room had been a ballroom in years past. There were scuffs on the floor—caused by a great many shoes—and a large collection of drums, lutes, flutes, and other instruments hung on pegs in one corner of the spacious hall. It took Ullen quite a few steps to get across the cavernous space.

"Sorry I'm late," the dwarven prince said. "I was on the lookout tower and lost track of time."

Quinton gave Ullen a brief nod, though Genovar's mouth tightened noticeably. Ullen hoped Jaspar was right about them being able to move forward. It didn't look like the elven man was going to make it easy.

Genovar had always been larger in personality than stature. He was only taller than Ullen by a handspan or so. His long hair, the color of beech tree bark, was pulled back from his face in a simple braid. Like Khiri, he had delicate, olive-hued features and large blue eyes—midnight rather than azure, but still blue. Unlike his daughter, he was still dressed in the leather armor of his people, designed to blend into the leafy canopies of their native forest. He stood in a position at the middle of the table, with Quinton on his left and Vess Lorrei on his right.

Vess was a former avatar of Shyden and another member of the original team to stop Irrellian Thornne. A diminutive human woman with hickory-brown hair, eyes the color of slate, a constant layer of soot and grease obscuring her features—Vess was one of the most brilliant engineers Ullen had ever met. She regarded the cold greeting between Ullen and Genovar with indifference. Vess hadn't bothered to get involved much in group squabbles in the past, either. Unless someone was letting their emotions get in the way of a mission, Vess rarely interfered with other people's affairs. It had been something of a surprise when Kal and Khiri mentioned they'd gotten her to agree to take a friend of theirs on as an apprentice. Khiri did have a genuineness about her that made it hard to refuse her, though.

Maleck Dorell, who'd been neither a general nor an avatar, but one of the only mages to join Genovar in the war against the Flayer Mage, sat on a stool on one end of the war table. He'd been in the chamber with them during the binding of Irrellian Thornne, and his blood had been offered during the contract with the High Ones. Maleck's old staff, imbued with a good deal of the mage's knowledge and power, was currently in Kal's hands. Ignoring the rift between his two friends, the squat and stodgy blonde man gave Ullen a genial smile. The mage's round face hadn't changed much in the two decades since Ullen had last seen him.

There were others seated around the table, but Ullen didn't recognize all of them. Earl Tiennes was on the end of the table opposite Maleck, but the rest were newcomers to the fight. Two decades had seen the numbers of original avatars and generals halved. Ullen sent a brief prayer of remembrance to both Tharothet and the Stone for the lost friends and commanders, but quickly reined his thoughts back to the present.

"Brief summary so far: between Taman and Seirane, the enemy currently outnumbers us by almost four to one," Vess said. "Mytana ceded their claim to the river, but it hardly seems to matter. Mytana's central leadership is housed in Seirane. They do nothing without the approval of Temple Hill. Jarelton's more or less a separate entity. It'll be something of a surprise if Mytana hasn't dissolved into city states by the end of this."

"Four to one," Ullen repeated. He'd known things were bad, but not this bad. "Has there been any word from our former allies?"

"Gyth and Verem requested proof of Irrellian Thornne's involvement. Chultha responded that they cannot side with us until the matter of Eerilor's rightful ruler is settled. Firinia's dual kingship is split. We may get a handful of soldiers there, but nothing like their full support. Our messengers to Ochel and Ethica haven't returned yet," one of the new faces around the war table reported. She seemed young to be a general, maybe sixteen or seventeen summers. She was quite stout in build, with more freckles than skin. Her fiery orange hair was cropped short around her ears and her nose was lumped onto her face like a potter had forgotten his clay. There was a fierce intelligence burning behind her green eyes and she stared at Ullen as though challenging him to argue with her.

"What's your name, lass?" Ullen asked.

"Jathy," she said. "Jathy Ettleway. I've been appointed as first commander of scouts by General Fortiva."

"Thank you, Commander Ettleway," Ullen said formally.

Jathy opened her mouth angrily, as though prepared for a different response. When she realized Ullen hadn't been goading her, her mouth closed with a click and she gave him a stern nod.

Whether other people had commented on her age, or there was something else bothering her, Ullen made a mental note that Jathy was out to prove herself. He'd try to get to know her better later, and maybe ease that chip off her shoulder. Maybe Genovar had said something in passing, or on purpose, to make things harder on Ullen. Or perhaps Jathy had been there on the night of the Solstice, when Genovar had publicly denounced Khiri and those that followed her. Ullen had given the elf girl a parting hug despite the label of traitor.

A few of the other fresh faces had turned similar looks of assessment toward Ullen. The dwarven prince let a sigh out through his nostrils. It looked like he had a long slog ahead of him. His rift with Genovar was no longer a private matter.

5

~Resmine~

STRETCHING HER ARM onto Dewin's empty side of the bed, Resmine groggily opened her hazel eyes. They'd been up late, discussing Dewin's plans to begin turning Dothernam Square into a real place of worship rather than a walled courtyard which *happened* to be consecrated. Being the former avatar and deity-tapped priestess of Adari, Dewin had taken it upon herself to make the courtyard into a temple for the Goddess of Greed and Guile.

Resmine had pointed out the irony of Adari's holy ground being a place the Thieves' Guild was technically not allowed to go.

The moonlight blazing in through the uncurtained window had given enough light for Resmine to clearly see Dewin's raven-wing bangs draped over her fine eyebrows. Dewin's copper skin had been shadowed blue in the night's soft glow, while the tilt of her chin, her thin nose and round face etched themselves into Resmine's heart. Time had seemingly paused as Resmine drank in the view.

Rolling her big brown eyes at her lover, Dewin had responded with, "Being on the brink of leading the Thieves' Guild, you should know that makes it perfect for Adari's followers, love. Sneaking in is part o' paying tribute."

"Beauty and battle, love," Resmine had responded. Her smile was wide enough she could almost feel her dimples showing. With her heart-shaped face, head of chestnut curls, lustrous pale skin, and her willowy frame, Resmine was well aware of her natural allure. "I was always meant to be beholden to Locke."

Dewin had responded by pressing her delicate lips against Resmine's, then pulling her face back just enough to tease. "Beauty, true enough, but battle may as well be bullshit, love."

With a laugh, Resmine had tackled Dewin to the bed. That had been really the end of their planning. But apparently Dewin had enough thoughts of her own to venture out into the cold morning air.

Sighing, Resmine shifted herself up off the pillows. Her idea of a proper morning started at noon. Not that she'd ever had much luck getting any of her companions to agree. Still, without Dewin's warmth pressing against her, Resmine decided she may as well get up. There was plenty to be done, after all. Corianne had agreed to meet her in the taproom downstairs for breakfast.

Staying at the Talon Acre Inn after Arad Rhidel's attack on Estan was risky, but Ren and Adela had paid for some extra enchantments against intruders. Of course, they hadn't wanted Ysinda to make the Talon Acre home to her court of thieves, so Resmine doubted she'd be allowed to hold court there either. Out of respect for the couple, Resmine didn't even intend to ask. They'd been put through enough on behalf of their group already. Ren was an amazing cook, though, so even after they moved out of the inn, Resmine fully intended to stop by often for meals.

Assuming she passed the tests.

Resmine wasn't sure what these tests for becoming the ruler of the Thieves' Guild entailed but, given that the normal method of inheritance involved a duel to the death, she was sure it was nothing good. She'd been trying her best not to think about it. Dewin had been avoiding the subject whenever it was brought up. Which was why Resmine was meeting with Corianne today. As hard as it could be to decipher Corianne's cant, Dewin's sister would give her straight answers.

Dressing in her warmest red woolen shirt—donning her armor and weapons on principle—and throwing on a dusty gray cloak for added warmth, Resmine headed down the stairs. This winter promised to be bitter enough without suffering through the cold.

Corianne was waiting for her. Ysinda's most trusted lieutenant, next to Evic—brother to Dewin and Corianne, sadly lost during the raids on the kidnapping ring—Corianne was decked out in black. Black trousers, black blouse, black bracers, black boots, black cloak... Even the rune pouch hanging off her belt and the hilts of her various daggers were all black.

Her hair was the same raven black, though more wavy, as Dewin's. If Corianne felt like it, it seemed like she could become a shadow. Her chin was more stubborn than her sister's, and her eyes were an even darker brown. With the same thin nose and copper skin shared between all three siblings, there was more than a passing family resemblance. But somehow, where Resmine found Dewin's beauty intoxicating, Corianne's she merely appreciated.

Resmine wondered privately if that was because the woman had such a long-standing interest in Estan. Estan was Resmine's brother in all the ways which counted, and they'd never knowingly be romantic rivals.

"So, love, what's on your mind that you're callin' the likes of me in? You and my sister about to make each other more honest, or is this 'bout things on the other side of the curtain?" Corianne asked. She'd propped herself lengthwise, with her legs crossed at the ankles, over an entire bench she'd pulled up against the wall next to the taproom fireplace.

It took Resmine a moment to realize Corianne's implications. She blushed a bit as she shook her head. "We're not engaged yet."

"Oh, ho! But there's the ember of it there! I fair meant only to jest, not to squirrel a nugget of truth out! Well done, me. Fret not, love. I'll not toss the rune on your courting."

"I was hoping you could tell me more about what I'd be facing in the test to take leadership of the guild," Resmine said. She had enough practice with matters of intrigue to lower her voice without leaning in like she was trying to hide something. It didn't matter that she was alone in the taproom with Corianne. There was no such thing as going off duty for someone on the wrong side of the law. Corianne clocked it with a meager nod of approval.

"Well, sure enough Shiv can spot a talent," Corianne said. The grin didn't leave her face, but her attitude was much less jovial. "While I can't say I'd be sad to serve, for Dewin's sake, I hope you've more on offer."

"More than talent?" Resmine asked.

"Takes talent, wit, moxie, a fair wink o' tenacity... A handful of things that ain't rightly quantified. Anyway, I can't tell you about the test, love. It's not been taken since well before her previous Majesty's ascension. Mayhap even afore I joined, though I was slitting purses as long as my memory spans," Corianne said.

The sounds of Ren thumping around in the kitchen heralded the coming of breakfast. Depending on what the tavern keeper's husband was making, Resmine and Corianne's conversation time was running short. "If you don't remember anyone taking it, but it's an established test within your guild, are there some sort of guidelines? Anything you can tell me at all?"

Leveling Resmine with a measuring look, Corianne pinched her bottom lip between her fingers and pulled it to one side. It was the first time Resmine had ever seen the thief woman look so torn. "I can't tell you more, love. But might be we could take a peek. Fair certain we're not gonna be the only two what look."

"Who else?" Resmine asked.

"A few of the others what propped their shoes under Ysinda's mattress had ambitions toward unthroning, and I do believe there's another outsider's nose in the crock."

Arad Rhidel. The name popped into Resmine's head unbidden, but it was unlikely Corianne meant anyone else. What other outsider would benefit more from gaining leadership of the Thieves' Guild? If Arad Rhidel managed to take over from the inside, the Venom Guild would go unchecked in Jarelton's underbelly. He could easily take out whatever opponents raised their voices against him. As King of Thieves, there wouldn't be any bolt holes he didn't have access to. Dewin might be safe if she never ventured out of Adari's holy courtyard—but staying there indefinitely was impossible. No sustainable food or water lay within the walls and, while Flayers couldn't get to her, she'd be alone against two combined guilds of thieves and assassins.

What had seemed high stakes before had scaled up to being absolutely vital. Resmine steeled her nerves, reminding herself of the countless years she'd spent disguised as a simple stablehand to pass unnoticed by the Gray Army. They'd taken over the temples of Mytana, killed her lover, and only left her alone because she'd outwitted them. Resmine was adaptable. She was fierce and loyal. Most of all, Resmine was a survivor. She would take anything the Thieves' Guild could throw at her, and she would do it before Arad Rhidel got the chance.

"Show me."

AS MUCH AS RESMINE would've liked to leave the Talon Acre Inn right then and there, Corianne refused to leave before they partook of Ren's cooking. It was worth waiting, as the large man had wrapped hard boiled hen eggs in a shell of sausage, cased the entire thing in bread crumbs, and then fried them until the outer crumbs were crispy. He'd paired the things with sweet berry preserves for spreading or dipping. It was easy to comprehend why neither Ren nor Adela were anything like lean. The tavern usually served whatever Ren himself felt like eating.

As much as Resmine would've liked to tuck away a second egg, one was already making her belt a tad snug. Against the protests of her taste buds, she pushed away from the table, leaving a few extra silver pieces behind for Ren. While the Talon Acre was often empty of residents, Adela and Ren never seemed pressed for coin. At some point in the future, Resmine might actually ask one of them about it.

Her own store of pocket money came from a few fenced items she'd acquired from the kidnappers' warehouse. She and Dewin had picked the place clean with the help of the children they'd rescued. The money they'd brought in was enough to cover a tab with the Talon Acre for a few months.

Corianne polished off her own plate of egg and sausage, wiping up the leftover preserves with a bread slice. She too left a handful of silver on the table before getting to her feet. "We're gonna burn the lot of that out of our bellies before we even get halfway 'cross the queendom. You'll be thanking me for the delay, no doubt."

"No doubt," Resmine echoed. "Lead on."

They walked out of the Talon Acre, donning the hoods of their cloaks as they entered the cold. Despite the dangers presented by Flayers, Corianne guided Resmine through a labyrinth of alleyways and sidestreets, deep into the heart of Jarelton. It was midafternoon by the time Corianne approached a flight of stairs cut into the side of a street, like any other walk-in basement. The steps led down to a heavy, wooden door with enough iron rods and fittings to resemble one of the city's massive gates. Despite the locked-down appearance, it swung open almost before Corianne even touched it.

Without speaking, Corianne beckoned Resmine forward.

Crossing the threshold, Resmine felt a chill run through her body that had nothing to do with the winter winds outside. It penetrated her bones and nestled itself inside her chest. Dread. This was a cold born of fear. Despite the repulsing thrum, Resmine had known much deeper fear. She'd lived with it hanging over her head for more than a dozen years. Pushing past the frost building inside of her, Resmine continued forward as both she and Corianne were swallowed by darkness.

Corianne waited until the door swung shut to pull out a runestone. The stone's steady blue light illuminated the same gray stone walls that made up the entire city of Jarelton. In front of them, even more stairs crawled deeper into the depths of Arra.

"How far down are we going?" Resmine asked. Her voice was barely more than a whisper, despite her intention to sound nonchalant.

"All the way, love."

Swallowing back the hand of fear clutching at her tongue, Resmine nodded. *I can do this,* she told herself. *I can face whatever is down there.*

As Corianne turned and the blue light of the rune receded, Resmine hoped she was right. There was something about this place that made her skin crawl. She wasn't sure where Corianne was leading her, but the thief woman's silence was adding to the uncanny nature of this outing. Anyone who'd spent much time with Dewin's sister knew how much Corianne liked to talk, whether or not she could be understood.

In an effort to distract herself, Resmine began counting the steps. One, two, ten, eleven, fifteen, twenty-seven, thirty-nine... She stopped counting after fifty. There was still no sign of the bottom and Corianne seemed unconcerned.

The gray stone of the walls gave way to darker materials. It became harder and harder to see the stairs the deeper they went, as though the stairwell was draining the light from Corianne's rune. Finally, right before Resmine's courage found its breaking point, they reached an archway of polished jet.

"Right impressed, love. Took me three tries to make the stairs my first run," Corianne said. "The Below knocks it out of the best of us."

"What is this place?" Resmine asked.

"Ancient," Corianne said. "Past that, not sure who rightly knows. It's home to what tests the thieves, though. When you're ready to be put through the trials, this is where'n you'll enter. First to emerge alive, the chambers Estan's squattin' in will open to yer touch. That's about all there be to it. Excepting for what happens inside, o' course."

"First through to come out alive?" Resmine said. "Is there a set date or do we all have to enter at the same time or anything?"

Corianne actually laughed. "No such rules could bind this sort of band, love. We're thieves. We're barely bound as it is."

"Fair point," Resmine said. She took a deep breath, chiding herself for what she was about to do. It was the kind of thing Estan would do if he were down here. And she would've given him a thorough tongue lashing for his trouble. "If I don't make it back, tell Dewin I love her and I'm sorry!"

With no more warning than that, Resmine sprinted through the archway, leaving Corianne to return up the stairs alone.

6

~Irrellian~

THE FLAYER MAGE'S ICE blue eyes narrowed as he looked down over the former courtyard in the center of Jarelton. A single lock of his pitch hair defied its restraints and obscured his vision. Despite it being the dead of night, golden trails of light flickered across his glassy, obsidian skin. Irrellian Thornne stood, letting his full height silhouette against the holy glow for the few eyes that could see it. To most, he'd likely just be a column of darkness, an unremarkable shadow in a city under siege.

The unwelcome holy aura pulsed in waves over Jarelton. It wasn't strong enough to keep Flayers from entering the city. In fact, Flayers were here en masse. Like moths drawn to a flame—his demon kin craved the holy energy. Even more than they desired to be on the face of Arra, they wished to return to the heavens. And somehow, despite the blocks he'd left in place, the High Ones had made it back.

A surge of fresh rage shot through Irrellian. Though he tried to keep his statuesque face as still as stagnant water, he could feel the anger causing the pointed tips of his ears to quiver. He'd meant to ascend into an empty heavenly court. Enough belief would've opened the gate for him before the High Ones had time to realize they'd been deposed. Compared to the power base he was building, Arra's minor gods wouldn't have been able to stand against him. Seirane's temples would've been abandoned and crumbled into ruins as the Flayer Mage made sure his former jailors were forgotten, joining the ranks of the countless unremembered gods they'd followed to power—turning their so-called avatars into unwitting Flayers and placing some of Irrellian's greatest enemies directly under his control.

Because that was the secret behind Arra's demons. The wish-granting horde, vying to bind themselves to mortal shells, were merely trying to regain what they'd lost. Belief, worship, accolades. It was the ambrosia of the immortal. When it was taken away, gods became ravenous. They turned into that which they feared and loathed most.

There was more to it, though. Demons were what the gods became, but the larger secret of Arra's pantheons was that almost all of them started as mortals. Arra's very first gods were all born of human parents. This was the secret Irrellian Thornne had discovered before making his bargain with Telgan Korsborn. He'd been the first to bind a contract with the mortal name of a demon, a former god. One of the original heroes of Arra. Telgan Korsborn wouldn't consume Irrellian for fear of returning to obscurity.

No Odlesk, elf, or dwarf had ascended before, being bound by their birth elements to the face of Arra. But those bindings were weakening. The dwarves could no longer hear the Stone. His people, the Odlesk, were no longer protected by the Lake. Soon, Mother Arra would even lose her connection with the elves of the Life Tree clans. His bond with Khiriellen Fortiva was its own proof. Rather than sit by and wait for the Arra-bound power of his heritage to dwindle, he'd severed it—committing himself fully to the magic of belief. Once Irrellian ascended to godhood, he intended to end the cycle. He would close the doors on the ever-shifting heavens. No more demons, no new gods. And then he'd remake the face of the world. Put an end to the decay.

Irrellian still questioned how Telgan Korsborn had fused his name to a ring and set it out to drift across Arra. Perhaps the demon had hoped to make itself a lifeboat in case Irrellian failed in his mission to take over the heavens. Despite Irrellian's technical immortality, the Flayer Mage would remain vulnerable until his ascension.

Irrellian trailed his fingers over the edge of the holy barrier. It stung to linger in this place, but he was as drawn to it as any other Flayer. However, other Flayers would burn out if they got as close as he was. His name was being spoken by a thousand different mouths all over Arra. Once the war began in earnest, it would only be a matter of time before he could use this gate himself.

It wasn't the easy victory he'd envisioned. But perhaps this wasn't the failure he'd feared. A grim smile stretched over Irrellian's thin lips.

After all, the game was only beginning.

7

~Khiri~

SILVER MISTS PARTED *beneath her feet, revealing dark cobblestones. Khiri reached for the familiar comfort of Micah's grip before recalling her brother was no longer at her side in any form. Her heart ached, even though she understood. Resting her hand on the hilt of her father's knife instead, Khiri tried not to think about how useless the broken blade would be in a fight.*

"Come to me," Irrellian Thornne said. His voice carried through the mist like an intimate whisper. The silver light she followed seemed to be emanating from his obsidian skin like trapped moonbeams. It beckoned her forward.

And it was time to end this.

"Meet your Destiny."

Khiri's eyes popped open and she released a groan as she sat up. The dream was hardly a dream at this point. It was more like a vision, one that got more vivid every time she saw it. Which was happening more and more frequently. She'd had the dream every night for the last three days.

A series of soft snores came from the lanky mage sleeping in the roll next to hers. Even though his warding magic provided both protection and warmth, they'd been sleeping closer and closer to each other recently. Something about their proximity seemed as inevitable as her vision, but Khiri didn't mind as much where Kal was concerned. If she were someone else, maybe she would've leaned into it by now. Even Micah had advised her not to let her ties to the Flayer Mage keep her from happiness where it was offered. But something continued to hold Khiri back.

Maybe she was broken inside. All of her friends seemed to think about pairing constantly. But, even when she liked someone, she couldn't even picture being with them physically. While the idea could make her blush, it sparked little to no interest.

Maybe it was because Irrellian Thornne could sometimes tell what she was experiencing. She could sense his emotions occasionally, especially when they were near each other or he emoted hard enough. Not too long ago, she'd experienced a blast of rage from him just as she'd been drifting to sleep. If Irrellian could tell when something made her insanely happy or pleased her excessively, what was to keep him from using that information against the people she cared about?

Khiri still remembered the Flayer Mage reaching through Kal's shield to grab her by the arm, like the magical barrier had been little more than a soap bubble. How much of their protection could Irrellian swat away? How much did he allow them to get away with just for show? Khiri's father had fought against the Flayer Mage by raising an army... But it seemed like the more Genovar fought, the stronger Irrellian became.

When she really thought about it, Irrellian Thornne had let her friends go after he'd been awakened. None of the people killed on the Solstice had been on the side opposing him. He'd left the actual killing to Hon'idar and his people. Again, he'd let the witnesses run away. But to what purpose? To rally more troops?

Despite these thoughts, Khiri wasn't sure how to stop people from fighting. Or if she should even try.

It had been months ago, but she still remembered stepping into a realm that wasn't a part of the Arra as she knew it. Petora, a minor goddess of fertility and the moon, had pulled Khiri through the barrier to advise her that the only way forward was to ignite the darkness. At the time, Khiri hadn't a clue what Petora was talking about. Later, in Irrellian Thornne's tomb, Khiri thought she understood. She doubted herself after the Flayer Mage was released, but that mistake had also freed the Council of Gods, the one people sometimes called the Higher Ones. Khiri was becoming more and more certain she hadn't misunderstood anything. She had to let the darkness continue to build.

Darkness had to win before she could light it on fire.

Khiri watched Kal's chest rise and fall in the morning light, hoping she and her friends would make it through the deepening shadows.

"FROM BEHIND!" Micah warned.

Ducking beneath a mottled arm as it swept through the space her head had been, Khiri reeled as she got an open mouth full of Flayer stench. She'd inhaled at the wrong time. A new hunter's mistake. She should've known better.

If Khiri were using something sensible, like a bow, it wouldn't have happened.

"...blood?...death?...tear?..." The usual Flayer chant was little more than a hiss. Individual words still rose over the sizzle of their combined whispers, but they almost sounded like questions. Flayer fogs were caused by a number of Flayers gathering as their mortal bodies deteriorated. The demon-bound would then hunt as a group. As more Flayers joined, the fog maintained integrity. This particular fog was the weakest Khiri had ever encountered, though. It seemed that even the newly weakened had deemed this fog a lost cause.

Kal struck down three Flayers with balls of fire he shot from his fingers. "Don't try to force it, *laska*. Let the magic happen naturally."

"If your people are born of water, how are you so good with fire?" Khiri muttered darkly. She was beyond frustrated, especially since she'd asked for this. They'd spotted a Flayer fog on the foothills and she'd thought they could use the weakened Flayers as target practice. It was a chance to hone her magic. The continued visions where she lost her two main weapons made her desire to harness her magical skills sharper than ever.

As long as Kal kept one of his fire spells at the ready, there wasn't much chance of being overwhelmed. These Flayers could barely manage a shamble. It was more embarrassing than scary that Khiri had needed to dodge one.

"Because I study and practice. The time I spend communing with my staff teaches me how to tap into things I couldn't before. If you'll recall, I needed a whole pouch of components and was still barely more powerful than a novice when we first met. Keep trying and you will get the hang of it," Kal said. "On your right. Try to immobilize those two. Doesn't have to be a fire spell."

"Immobilize? Not kill?"

"Pretend they're not Flayers," Kal said. "How would you stop someone you didn't want to hurt?"

It didn't take much for Khiri to remember facing off against Fennick in the cavernous tomb of Irrellian Thornne; the pulsing green glow of the crystal, the iridescent sheen of poison coating the two knives, and Fennick's scruffy jaw jutting forward as he leered at her. She hadn't wanted to kill him, even in self-defense. At the time, she'd had no other choice. Her magic was untapped, little more than a warning buzz in the tips of her ears. If she'd been able to shield her mind properly, maybe Fennick wouldn't have succeeded in luring her away from the rest of her friends. She also recalled the man who'd jumped her in an alley during her first night in Jarelton. If Corianne and Evic hadn't shown up, she may have been forced to do something drastic there too. A proper spell to hold someone until help came...

Khiri's hand rose to the level of her deeply blue eyes, her fingers loose and splayed. She felt the ribbons of power flowing through her body. No, not ribbons. Vines. They coursed through her like blood. And they were rooted deep within Arra's soil. She sensed similar vines of power all around her. The Flayers were like rotten, thorny brambles. They were as tainted and grotesque as their scent. Micah was a shining beacon of Lifewood. Kal's power was different—tangled? No, woven. There were still vines... But there were also threads of water, fire, shadow, lightning, mist, and things she had no names for.

This was a far cry from that first venture through a Flayer fog where she could only sense blurry figures while her eyes were squeezed tightly shut.

"*Hold*," Khiri told the Flayers. The power in her voice made the word more of a compulsion than a request. The two Flayers slowed in their shambling. They appeared to consider the command for a few moments before continuing forward. Two flames blossomed in their chests before Khiri even had a chance to curse.

What she'd considered a failure, Kal responded to with a huge smile. "Excellent work, Khiri! You almost stopped them for a full thirty-count!"

"They barely paused!" she protested.

"Are you ready to finish off this fog?" he asked. "We can practice more another time."

In response, Khiri swung Micah off her back. He was strung with an arrow loosed before Kal's next wave of fire balls mowed down another handful of the damned. Khiri was going to have to move fast if she wanted to catch up.

Arrow to the eye, arrow through the temple, fireball to the chest, fireball to the legs and trampled by another Flayer. Khiri started to run low on arrows, so she switched to her knife. She sprinted toward the line of approaching demons, meeting them head on. Their mortality was so far gone they barely had enough blood left to burn their corpses away. Dodging slow-moving arms and slashing throats as she went, Khiri felt this was less a fight than a mercy. The smell was deadlier than any force these Flayers could muster. For the first time in her life, Khiri found herself feeling sorry for Flayers.

WHEN THEY FOUND THE road, Khiri's instinct was to shy away from it. Most of her travels had cut away from things like roads for fear of being discovered by assassins or worse. Kal reminded her that roads meant things like villages and inns would be easier to find. He also reminded her they weren't currently being hunted.

Her awareness of Irrellian Thornne agreed. The Flayer Mage was currently engaged in some other scheme or project. Whatever he was doing, his attention was not focused on her at all at the moment. Unless something had changed since their first day in Taman, Arad Rhidel's personal war against Khiri was still at a cease fire. The Gray Army was busy fighting her father. For the first time since she'd left the Life Trees, Khiri wasn't on the run.

Not on the run didn't necessarily mean she wasn't in a hurry. Khiri still had to talk to her mother about the secrets she'd uncovered in Eerilor—her mother's former name, Elithania Haud, exchanging it with the original Leyani, while knowing their future daughter would have to pay for the choice. There hadn't been a chance to talk to Genovar about any of it before he'd disavowed her. Leyani would surely make sense of it, though. She had to tell Khiri something. Like exactly what the price on her soul was that her parents had agreed to. They'd signed Khiri's name on a contract she'd never read, and then neglected to even tell her about it.

No use dwelling, Khiri thought with a sigh. They still had a long road ahead. An actual road. With inns. Which meant baths. And new foods she'd never encountered. Who could dwell on secrets when such experiences were close at hand?

A sign with an arrow promised *The Grumpy Old Bastard Died So Now I Can Call It What I Want Inn* was only a few miles further down the road. Khiri didn't care what it was called, as long as they had hot baths and warm, ready food.

The sun was drifting toward the mountainous horizon as they rounded a bend and the inn came into view. It was a stately old building, one of the largest Khiri had seen in Mytana. It was three stories tall with shutters on every window. Its walls were painted as orange as butterfly weed and its roof was covered in burgundy tiles. Khiri wondered if the owner was trying to stand out or blend in with the region's sunsets. On the side of the building facing the road, a large porch jutted out like the inn had a sore jaw. There were attached stables with four carts parked outside. This little hub seemed very popular. A sign with a shiny orange mug proclaimed this to be The Copper Mug Inn and, despite herself, Khiri wondered about the name change.

Nestled across the road were a handful of houses and a small market. While this town wasn't quite large enough to be much more than a village yet, it was an active, thriving community. Children chased each other across a snowy open field, laughing and chucking snowballs as they ran. A warmly dressed young woman with her head wrapped in a blue scarf knocked on a door. She held a basket filled with steaming rolls. With a smile and a wave, she acknowledged the strangers entering her neighborhood.

Khiri waved back, her own smile hesitant. People being friendly made her nervous after all of her adventures. After a lot of bad choices, she was starting to doubt her ability to judge anyone's character. But Rigger had been nice. And Corianne and Evic. Estan, Resmine, Dewin, Ullen, Catapult, and Kal... All of them she'd met since leaving the Life Trees. Granted, Estan and Resmine were sent after her by her father. Her father, whom she'd misjudged horribly.

"Let's call it even odds," Micah said.

"Don't start," Khiri responded out loud without thinking.

"Talking to Micah?" Kal asked.

"Yes, sorry. You can't hear him right now?"

"Not since breakfast," Kal sighed. "I do miss being an avatar."

They trotted up the steps to the wide porch. A few tables and benches were set up, but currently unused. Kal showed her how to use the boot scraper next to the door and then they made their way inside.

Warm air escaped like a wave, the cold air from outdoors rushing to fill the space. A few patrons sitting close to the entryway grumbled as the frost nipped at them. Half of the taproom was taken up by a massive trough of burning wood. A chimney was built into the ceiling while a thin metal mesh, like chainmail but easier to see through, hung from the bottom and surrounded a round trough of fire in the center of the taproom, protecting patrons from sparks. Servers walked to and from the bar, carrying foaming tankards and plates of roasted meat, carrots, onions, and potatoes. Most of the rectangular wooden tables being waited on only had two or three customers. Several people surrounded a round table, drinking from heavy tankards and laughing as loudly as the children outside. There were cards and coins scattered in front of them.

"Gracelin! Gracelin, love! Another round! I'm winning tonight!" A talking mountain of muscle and curly red hair shouted. He had thick, meaty lips and a massive forehead. He was sweating so hard his sheen almost matched Kal's.

"Does that mean you'll pay your tab for a change?"

"You wound me, lass!"

"I'm about to!"

Despite the verbal banter, the woman behind the bar, presumably Gracelin, headed over to the card table with a full pitcher of dark brown ale. She filled the red headed giant's mug first and then topped off anyone else raising their cups. Gracelin was a tall, solidly-built woman with skin the color of pinecones and a genial air. Her black hair was ashy with age, though the only creases on her face were laugh lines. As she walked back toward the bar with her pitcher now empty, she seemed to notice her new guests for the first time.

"Hello there! Welcome to the Copper Mug! My name's Gracelin. Is there anything I can get you two? Have a seat! Have a seat!" Gracelin waved them toward three empty or mostly empty tables, well away from the raucous card players. "Here! You must be absolutely freezing. Let me check the kitchen and see what Fressa has ready."

"She seems nice enough," Micah said.

"You also liked Fennick," Khiri reminded him. She leaned in close to Kal and whispered, "What do you think?"

"Seems nice enough," Kal shrugged. "Hard to tell just yet, but I'd rather take our chances here than stay outdoors again. We've been relying on my magic for warmth a lot lately, and that storm the other night drained me."

Khiri had nearly forgotten there was a storm recently. She'd come to trust Kal's ward so thoroughly that she'd slept through the worst of it. It had been morning, when they crawled out of a dome of snow, that she'd noticed fallen tree limbs and other debris. If Estan were still traveling with them, he'd have been shocked at how much she was relying on Kal, and not just because of his rivalry with the former assassin.

"Okay," Khiri said. "We can stay. Let's ask if there's any chance of a hot bath."

8

~Estan~

EVEN WITH TAK'S BOOST, Estan hadn't gotten Araylia Treag to agree to anything. The most she'd allowed was a nebulous promise to consider the matter. But it was still less hostile than anything Estan had gotten from her brother, Holt—who'd made a somewhat veiled threat to feed them to Flayers for having supported Orin.

Once they were well out of earshot of Lady Treag's house, Estan asked Catapult to use his illusionary noises to make sure no one on the street could overhear his conversation with Tak. "Even me?" the horse asked.

Estan raised an eyebrow at Tak. Catapult could keep secrets when he wanted to, but there wasn't a guarantee he'd want to keep whatever it was from the larger group. For that matter, Estan wasn't sure if Tak even wanted to tell him what was going on. "Depends on how much you're willing to trade," Tak said.

"I can trade," the roan offered. "Resmine told me a lot of secrets when I was just a horse."

"What are you now?" Estan asked. While Catapult had been an avatar and a valuable asset to their party, it hadn't occurred to him to think of Catapult as anything other than a very talented horse.

"Well, I'm still a horse," Catapult said, flicking his tail as though to gesture at his own flanks. The gesture lost something with his disguise as a mule, but Estan understood. "But I'm not *just* a horse."

Tak appeared to consider the horse's offer, but shook his head. "That wouldn't work. Most of the secrets she would've shared during that time have either already come into play or would be too personal to find a buyer. This requires something with a bit more heft."

"Okay. I don't have to hear," Catapult said. "Estan can just tell me later."

Estan didn't bother to correct the war horse. Odds were good he would confide in Catapult at some point, whether it was soon or in a few weeks. It was so ingrained in him that a knight could talk to his horse about anything, it may be as soon as this evening. They waited until Catapult nodded his large head before they resumed talking.

"I'll never get accustomed to this talking in the streets during broad daylight business," Tak said. They were still in the nicer, richer neighborhoods of Jarelton. Even though this part of the city was built with the same gray stone as the poorer streets, the roads were broader and the houses had planter boxes with shrubs, flowers, even the occasional tree. Enchantments against Flayers were painted or etched along nearly every corner. Servants were running errands and well dressed merchants and nobles both were much more at ease than their lower city counterparts.

Of course, the enchantments wouldn't protect people from other people. This area was a favorite haunt for the Thieves' Guild. Estan wondered if he might catch a glimpse of Corianne if he looked hard enough.

"What would be a big enough exchange for this?" Estan asked, trying to pull his mind back from wherever it was wandering. There would be another time to think about the thief woman.

Later, later, later, his own mind protested. *Always later. You know better than most... Later may never happen.*

He pushed the thought away.

Tak tapped his chin thoughtfully. "I know you don't have the kind of coin needed for a secret of this magnitude. A trade in kind... I already have the knowledge of your faked death, and I will not sell that. I may be a trader, but I am first and foremost your friend. Let's see... Dewin's more or less retired as my apprentice since sanctifying Dothernam Square, but you don't really have her talent for information harvesting. How about we trade for... A favor?"

"You want me to do you a favor?" Estan repeated. "What kind of favor? What couldn't you ask of me already, as a friend?"

"That's a fair question. But sometimes even a friend says no if a favor is against their wishes or ethics." Tak's face was impossible to read behind his carefully honed mask of boyish foolishness. Even his amber eyes were neutral, if amused.

"Is this a favor against my wishes or ethics?" Estan asked.

"Most assuredly."

Estan glanced over his shoulder at Catapult, but the horse wasn't paying any attention to the trader or the knight. While the horse was still following them, he'd begun to create illusory butterflies and was playfully nipping at them as they fluttered around his face. Life seemed much easier for a horse, even if he wasn't just a horse.

"Will it require me to hurt anyone?" Estan asked.

"Not physically. I'm not asking you to go kill someone for me or act as my bodyguard or anything," Tak said. He was walking along the street, appearing as easy and carefree as ever. It occurred to Estan that when they'd arrived in Jarelton, Tak had walked into the Pit and Orin Treag's home with seemingly equal unconcern. Tak didn't share Estan's views. Estan wasn't even sure what Tak's views were. It hadn't seemed that important until they'd decided to barter.

"Is it worth it?"

"Really only one way to find out," Tak shrugged. "Do we have a deal?"

Replaying the scene in his head, Estan thought about their strange reception. Lady Treag had been livid when they'd arrived late, but the moment she found out they'd saved a child from Flayers, things had changed. It was obvious the secret had something to do with a child. Trying to piece it together on his own was hopeless. Estan didn't have enough clues to understand. Did he need to understand? Wasn't it enough that Tak knew? Estan knew he was grasping at straws, trying to talk himself out of shaking Tak's extended hand.

But Tak was an expert when it came to making bargains.

When they shook hands, Estan felt it like a thunder clap in his soul. There was some kind of binding magic within their agreement. Perhaps the interior of Tak's bracers had some sort of enchantments or rune work to enforce his deals. Whatever now bound them made Estan's skin crawl.

"Are you ready to hear what you agreed to?" Tak asked.

Estan nodded, though he was still scowling down at their clasped hands. He already had a feeling he wasn't going to like this.

"The favor I ask is that you not repeat a word of this to anyone until I give you the go ahead," Tak said.

"That's it?" Estan reeled. After all that build up, he wasn't sure what he'd expected. But it hadn't been the request not to spread the knowledge around.

"Not a single person, or animal, within the whole of your acquaintance. Especially not Resmine. That's it. The whole of your task is to keep your mouth shut," Tak grinned. "And I'm glad I take precautions because, as much as I trust you to be a man of your word, I don't think your promise would survive the night otherwise."

Though Estan could feel his temper rising, he punched it back down. Tak wasn't the sort to casually insult his friends. If the trader had roped Estan into bargaining his silence, there had to be a reason for it. "So what's this big secret?"

Despite Catapult's seeming unconcern with whatever his human friends were discussing, Tak shook his head. "When we get back to the Pit. There are protections in place in those quarters that beat anything the three of us can do while walking through the city."

It was a long, silent walk through Jarelton, aside from the occasional clack of horse teeth as Catapult continued to amuse himself.

AS ESTAN INPUT THE code to let himself back into Ysinda's rooms, he couldn't help feeling like this was the bigger price of bargaining for information. This was an invasion of Ysinda's privacy, one he'd hoped to spare her by cleaning the rooms out himself. Eventually. Soon. There was no telling how much longer he'd have access. Every time he left, Estan wondered if he'd be able to return.

Silently, the wall slid open.

Catapult slowly walked away, a false Tak riding on his saddle. Sparing a brief moment to wonder how much his horse was wandering the city streets without accompaniment, Estan waved Tak to follow him into the hidden door.

There was the barest rumble underfoot as the wall shifted back into place behind them. Letting his eyes adjust to the darkness, Estan used his hands to guide himself to the end of the hall, where skylights let natural sunshine into the cozily appointed kitchen. When he saw the wall of pastel mugs, with the sea foam, cream, and blue hung in no particular pattern, Estan's chest hurt. He expected Tak to start poking around or comment on the unexpected softness on display within the late queen's chambers, but Tak merely took a seat at the tiny two person table.

Rushing forward, Estan performed a cursory check of the remaining rooms to ensure there was no one waiting to ambush him. Despite Corianne's assurances that he was the only person Ysinda had told the code for access to these quarters, he didn't want to risk taking another dagger to the heart for lack of foresight. He still rushed, hoping Tak wouldn't be curious enough to follow him.

"Would you care for some tea?" Estan asked as he came back to the kitchen. He hoped he could find something other than the peppermint Ysinda had favored.

"No need to hover, Estan. We already made a bargain. I'm not looking to discover anything about Ysinda that you'd rather keep hidden."

Relief coursed through Estan, easing tensions he hadn't even been aware of. He'd felt the pangs in his chest, but now his shoulders loosened, his legs wobbled and even his eyebrows relaxed. "Thank you."

Tak nodded, his face more serious than Estan had ever seen it. "You and I have gone on a few visits together, but we've never really talked in depth about my profession. While I do glean from all over, unless there is something crucial to a living person, I try to leave the dead to their own business. I understand what it is to lose someone, and I wouldn't want people poking around in the secrets of my loved ones."

Estan sank down into the empty chair on the other side of the table. From Tak's position, there wasn't a clear view of the bedchamber, and while the display of mugs was pretty, they weren't really in and of themselves damning evidence of Ysinda's hidden depths. He let himself relax the rest of the way. "I do miss her, you know," the knight admitted. "I'm not entirely sure what we were to each other. But she cried for me, when I died."

"It was an odd situation. Leaders of the Thieves' Guild don't often choose total strangers for the role of Consort. Let alone men of honor," Tak said. "Now, on to the secret you purchased."

Even though he knew they were alone, Estan found himself leaning forward.

Tak leaned back, tucking one foot under the opposite knee on the seat of his chair and intertwined his fingers behind his head. "This secret is a bit of a story, so I hope you're comfortable."

"I'm fine. Please, just tell me already!"

Estan's response drew a wry smirk out Tak, but the trader finally capitulated.

"It was a few years before the War of the Burning Valley broke out. Somewhere between twenty-two and twenty-four summers ago... Right around the time that portrait you were staring at was commissioned. Lady Araylia and her brother, Holt, were in high social demand. With only a year difference in age, they were the two most likely heirs. Orin, being more than ten years younger and seemingly disinterested in learning about Jarelton's political landscape, didn't bear much thought at the time.

"Lord Holt Treag was slowly earning himself a sordid reputation, patronizing many of Jarelton's less reputable institutions. And while there's nothing wrong with visiting a brothel from time to time, the nobles were starting to worry about the frequency of Holt's visits and the rumblings of misconduct within. No doubt they were envisioning scads of illegitimate Treags making a march for the title of Ilamar someday—or worse scandals.

"Araylia became very fond of one of her mother's footmen. It was a very secret courtship; it didn't seem like anything more serious than a young dalliance, or perhaps a minor act of teenage rebellion. He was a servant, and Araylia was still flirting with all the young nobles at the balls. Her mother still believed her daughter would find a match that solidified their power base. Maybe even broaden it.

"When Araylia was suddenly unable to make party appearances, her mother made excuses about a sudden illness. She was kept out of sight for six months. It took me ages to confirm the true reason for her seclusion was pregnancy. Her belly had swelled past the point of disguise.

"Now, Lady Ilamar wasn't a total monster. She would've acknowledged the match given time. She actually had plans in motion to elevate the footman's status to a minor landed noble. Land transfers were already signed, ready to be presented. For unknown reasons, the footman chose not to wait. Two nights after Araylia birthed their child, she found a letter demanding a ransom. She recognized her lover's handwriting. According to city records, Jarelton still has a bounty out for both him and the child he took—a bounty handled by an office of solicitors favored by Holt. I can't find any other evidence of Holt's involvement, but I don't believe in coincidence.

"Araylia sent out soldiers for weeks, but under her mother's orders, they were only to search as far as Jarelton's county borders. Word was not sent to any of Mytana's other provinces. I think Lady Ilamar wanted to keep the embarrassment of a missing Treag close to the chest. When Araylia learned of her mother's interference, she tried to hire private citizens to search out her former love and their child. He was found dead at a campsite, with no sign of the child.

"After a full year of fruitless inquiries, Araylia ran out of her own money. Lady Ilamar threatened to cut her off entirely unless she gave up her baby for dead. Araylia agreed on the condition that the child's papers remained active—she still has them somewhere, not trusting the archivists with her secret. Unsurprisingly, Araylia never really forgave her mother. She became a much different woman during court functions. Harder, more cynical, less trusting and friendly. Before the child went missing, Araylia had been on the verge of being made heir. If the footman had waited, he would've found himself wed to the next Ilamar. And the child, a daughter, would be around twenty-three summers now."

Estan blinked. Twenty-three summers... The hazel eyes and dimples. Lady Treag had roughly the same body-type as his bond-sister. His jaw worked loosely a few times before he managed to utter a single word. "Resmine?"

"I believe so," Tak said. "I've dug into all the angles just to be sure, but our sweet little Queen of Thieves-to-be looks to be a possible candidate for Ilamar. Which is why you can't say anything just yet."

A flare of rage burned through Estan. He didn't realize he was on his feet until he heard the chair hit the floor behind him. "You don't think Resmine's good enough to sit on the Ilamar's throne? Is that why you want to hide the fact you knew exactly who her mother was this whole ash-forsaken time?"

"No," Tak said. Despite Estan's threatening posture, Tak didn't even ease his feet onto the ground. He seemed just as relaxed as he had when he'd first begun speaking. "I don't want to let her, her mother, or her uncle, know just yet because I want the same thing Orin wanted. Stability for Jarelton. If we tell Resmine, do you think she'd risk becoming the Queen of Thieves to battle the Venom Guild incursion? Do you think her mother would let her take on such a dangerous task if they were suddenly reunited? Or is it more likely that the Thieves' Guild would find themselves battling a raging mother with the full backing of her noble house on top of a bunch of assassins? Right now, for the two of them, nothing has changed. If we all live through this, it'll be a nice reunion. If we don't, they're no worse off."

"Except they'll probably kill both of us on principle," Estan growled. He sank to his knees and lowered his head to the table. "I should've just let it go. I was better off not knowing this... And what about Holt? He seems like the strike-first type."

"And now you know why I felt your silence was a fair price," Tak said.

A rapid hammering knock sounded on the inner door. Estan rose slowly to his feet with Tak only a moment behind him. When they'd entered, Estan hadn't wanted Tak following him into Ysinda's quarters, but now he was glad to have the trader at his back. Only a handful of people knew Estan was in residence down here, and he wouldn't have expected any of them to sound that frantic.

"Estan, you lout! Be a love and jimmy this portal quick-like!"

Well, that was undoubtedly Corianne. But he'd never heard her that frantic before. Unbolting the door and sliding it open, Corianne pushed through as soon as it was wide enough. "Resmine... She jumped in the arch... I don't rightly know how long we've got, but time to clear out!"

"What arch?" Estan asked.

But Corianne wasn't in the mood to answer questions. She shoved a bag at each of them and began stuffing pieces off the shelves into her own satchel. "Grab anything what looks useful and then we bolt, loves. This place will shift itself over to make room for a new ruler. Anything left gets ashed! So move!"

Estan got moving.

9

~Ullen~

"WE KNOW WHAT THE GRAY Army can do if left unchecked! If we hit them with something like this before they ever make it to the fight, they'll know—"

"They'll know we're desperate enough to care as little about casualties as they do," Genovar said, cutting off Quinton's argument.

It wasn't the first time they'd heard Quinton's proposal to fight the Gray Army using their own tactics, but even thinking about it made Ullen sick to his stomach. He was glad he and Genovar were on the same page when it came to this... If Genovar Fortiva approved the plans to blow up Temple Row in the middle of Seirane, Ullen wasn't sure he could talk anyone out of it.

"By Taymahr, we're going to get slaughtered if we don't figure out something soon," Quinton muttered. A storm cloud roiled behind his stern features.

They'd argued for the better part of the day. Even now, the ballroom-turned-war room's rune lamps were snapping on. Seeing the sweat and frustration on every face at the table in keener detail did little to alleviate the pressure they were all feeling. Servants had arranged a cold lunch on the room's side tables. Ullen was picking at a plate of smoked pork and jam rolls. He may as well have been eating sand. Sand would've sat in his stomach better.

"Rigger and I have made four of his barrel-walkers so far," Vess said. "We'll have two more up before the week is out."

The barrel-walkers—odd contraptions—each consisted of a large, armored barrel lined with runestones mounted on two mechanical bird legs, and powered by a series of rune-fueled pistons. Ullen had seen one of the things in motion and still wasn't entirely sure how it worked. There was a mirrored scry plate affixed to the barrel's closure to allow the person inside a view of their surroundings. Rigger had been teaching volunteers how to control the things. Hopefully the volunteers were getting better at it than their teacher. While Vess' apprentice was brilliant at making these contraptions, he was very clumsy when it came to demonstrating his creations.

"What we need is more recruits," Ullen sighed. "The unfortunate truth is, even with heroes of the last war leading the charge, people don't want to see that this is the same Gray Army we fought the last time. They'd like to just ignore us until the problem wanders off on its own. Despite our number of noble witnesses, the common people are sick of fighting."

"So we need to recruit from cities that will believe the Gray Army is rising," Genovar said. "If they won't believe us in Eerilor, maybe they'll believe us in Mytana. Jarelton is still filled with veterans. I'll raise the call myself."

There was a hush at the war table meeting this proclamation. No one wanted to be the one to voice the objections to their foremost leader leaving the main war camp, but someone had to do it. "Are you sure we shouldn't be sending someone else?" Ullen asked.

"I'm the most recognizable face of our army, but that doesn't mean I'm our only face. This is your kingdom, Ullen. I think it's time you took the reins here." Genovar's expression was set. There was very little chance of changing his mind when he got that look.

"He's leaving the traitor in charge?" someone whispered. Ullen was willing to believe it was Jathy Ettleway. The commander of their scouts still hadn't warmed to him.

But there was something bigger at play behind this decision. Ullen saw it in Genovar's eyes. His old friend had received another vision. Ullen wouldn't ask again, not here in front of everyone. Instead, Ullen promised the group to send out another wave of letters to the Eerilor's other neighbors to ask again for aid.

Later, though, before Genovar left, Ullen meant to talk to the elder Fortiva about what he had seen and why he was really leaving on the cusp of the second war against the Flayer Mage.

"GENOVAR?" ULLEN ASKED, knocking on the already open door. "Can I talk to ya a moment?"

With a heavy sigh, Genovar stuffed his mending kit into his travel sack. He'd been darning socks in preparation for his trip, but the moment Ullen came in, he switched to sharpening his knives. The message wasn't lost on Ullen. Despite leaving the dwarven prince in charge, Genovar was no less angry. "Go on then. Make whatever excuses you need to, just do it quickly."

"That's right-friendly," Ullen said, his own temper flaring. "I come to mend bridges and you're good and ready to throw away everything we were 'fore I even start."

"No, Ullen. You came to mend your own conscience. Our friendship ended the moment you decided to follow my daughter across Mytana," Genovar seethed. "In the past, when I asked you to trust me and not do something, you listened because you believed in my visions. And I warned you, well before she was even born, when the chance to meet my daughter came along you weren't to interfere with her. 'If you think the girl might be a Fortiva, walk away and don't look back.' Those were my precise instructions, yes?"

"Aye," Ullen agreed. He was still standing in the doorway. With a glance over his shoulder to make sure no one had overheard, Ullen came the rest of the way in and shut the door. Despite Genovar's hostility, it seemed prudent to keep the conversation as private as possible. "I canna pretend I misunderstood. Might be I forgot at the beginning, being a good twenty summers ago, but I remembered right enough the moment I saw her."

Genovar turned his midnight blue eyes on Ullen, his mouth pressed into a stern line. "Sometimes our actions seem insignificant but, by leading her down the path she's taken, you've helped cause far more destruction than you can possibly conceive. I've done my best to mitigate things, but I've more than played my own part in what's to come."

Turning this over in his head, Ullen crossed his arms. "So you knew the end of this path and all you told me was: *don't*? And you're blamin' the whole of what's to come on something that weren't at all clear more than twenty years ago?"

"I didn't know the outcome until the path was chosen," Genovar admitted. He dropped the knife he was working on, spread his palms on either side of his work kit, and lowered his head. The elf was the picture of absolute grief. "All I knew for certain was dark things lay down that road. Now that I've seen it... Ullen, I'm sorry for how much anger I've laid at your feet. This, all of this, it was my doing. If Leyani and I hadn't sought to change our fate, none of this would even be possible."

Now Ullen was glad he'd closed the door. It would do nothing for the morale of the already struggling troops to see the great Genovar Fortiva crumbling. Ullen laid a heavy hand on his friend's shoulder in a solid grip of commiseration. "Surely there'd still be a Flayer Mage out there. This doesn't all land on our stoop. Would you have been out here to fight him if you hadn't sought a solution to your ill-fated match?"

"It doesn't matter. I couldn't change things now if I wanted to. It's all about moving forward. Our last hope is that Khiri can still see something I can't," Genovar sighed. "I'm sorry I said we're not friends. You've got a good heart, Ut'evullen Dormidiir. When... Well, you'll know when. Make sure these make it to my wife and daughter." Walking over to the far side of the room, Genovar opened a drawer and withdrew two envelopes. One had Leyani's name scrawled across it, and the other was addressed to Khiri.

Ullen recognized final letters when he saw them. He also knew what his being entrusted with them meant. Genovar Fortiva didn't believe he was coming back.

"What did you see?"

Genovar didn't answer, but went back to his packing. After a few moments, Ullen left his friend's room feeling even heavier than he had before they'd spoken.

10

~Resmine~

DARKNESS SHOULD'VE been all Resmine could see this far below ground. It had taken ages to go down the steps with Corianne, and the thief woman had been the one holding their light. Resmine had charged through the arch expecting a blind run through a maze or perhaps a pit fight against an unknown assailant. She thought she'd been ready for anything the strange arch could throw at her.

This wasn't anything like what she'd been expecting. In fact, the arch, Corianne, the stairwell... It all felt like a dream. She tried to focus on the task at hand.

"I told you! This gown is absolutely made for you, my dear!" Lady Gresha Esser raved. She was taller than Resmine, gorgeous waves of amber hair, golden-brown skin, and a dazzling citrine brooch arranged so Resmine was having a hard time not eyeing the woman's assets. "Most girls can't wear this shade of yellow, but you've got the coloring for it! You're going to spark so many flames tonight!"

Dewin! The name sparked something in Resmine's mind.

"I'm all but engaged already," Resmine insisted. She'd already been towed to three different establishments looking for *the* dress, *the* shoes, and *the* jacket for her ensemble to some sort of dance.

"Tsk! As though I wouldn't know about anyone you were fixed on!" Gresha gushed. "You've been awfully sly, not telling your oldest, dearest friend. You wouldn't do that to me, would you, Rezzy? Please, tell me you haven't cast me aside!"

"Don't call me Rezzy," Resmine said. She wasn't sure what this world was supposed to be. For the first few shops, she hadn't remembered anything but the life she'd found herself in. Her name was Lady Resmine Treag, and her best friend was this dandelion fluff. She was bedecked in a dress fancier than anything she'd worn in her life. Thin, finely woven layers of burgundy created a bell around her legs all the way to her ankles, only permitting her half her normal stride. The top of the garment was artfully draped so it teased hints of her own modest cleavage, with fastens at the shoulders, slit sleeves, and a cinched waist. And this was supposed to be a shopping outfit! Resmine wanted to tear the thing off right here in the street. She wanted her armor, with its woven leather legs and firm support around her curves. More than that, Resmine wanted her whip. "I've got to get out of here."

"What's gotten into you, darling? We've been talking about this ball for months and months!"

Resmine looked around, desperate to find a way out of this waking nightmare. There were two servants right on her heels, carrying several dozen parcels for her and Gresha so the ladies wouldn't have to strain themselves. It was tempting to rip the boxes from their hands and throw them across the cobblestones. This world felt like a cage. She was good at blending in, but this wasn't her. This life had been a daydream once, perhaps, when she was young. But she wasn't a lost, little orphan stuck in the Temple of Locke anymore.

Then she spotted the weapons stall. Odd that she hadn't seen it before she reached her breaking point, but it was every bit as real as the rest of this place. A cart horse was approaching from the opposite end of the road. Gresha was about to lead her right through a group of children playing a pebble tossing game. Resmine palmed one of the pebbles as they passed. If she timed this right, she'd be able to make a run for it.

One afternoon with Gresha was enough to know the woman wouldn't be interested in stopping at the weapon stall, but there was a window with an assortment of bags and boots near enough to suit Resmine's purposes.

"Let's look at these, shall we?" Resmine suggested. As expected, Gresha began to simper over one of the bags. Glancing at the two servants, Resmine made sure her throwing arm wasn't in their line of sight. Taking careful aim, Resmine popped the cart horse in the flank with her pilfered stone. It wasn't enough to hurt the creature, but it was enough to make the horse lunge forward. The cart driver let out a yelp and the kids playing pebbles shrieked. During the commotion, Resmine snagged a dagger and a whip off of the stall's table. She had them hidden before anyone around them noticed.

When Gresha pushed her way into the next shop, Resmine spotted another woman about her height and build going in the same door. She ran into the woman on purpose, jostling her about and making apologies as she slid the girl in between Gresha and the two servants. Resmine stood outside the shop, alone and triumphant. Before anyone could discover her ruse, she ducked into a nearby back alley and used the dagger to cut slits into her many layers of skirt so she could run unimpeded.

Resmine wasn't entirely sure where she was going, but she knew something was watching her. She ran through the streets of Jarelton and climbed through the back alleys. Finally, she found herself on a roof. There was nothing seemingly special about this place. One roof in a sea of rooftops. But she knew she'd made it to wherever it was she needed to be.

"I'm Resmine, Daughter of Locke, next Queen of Thieves!" Resmine shouted at no one in particular.

Dark clouds blotted out the sky and ribbons of black mist swarmed out of the streets around her. Where the mists touched, her skin became deathly cold, but Resmine wasn't afraid. This was also as it was supposed to be.

Whatever came next, she was ready.

"YOU CARRY THE SHIELD well, Sister." Estan smiled at Resmine from Catapult's back. The shining plate armor of Taymahr covered him like a second skin. He'd been nearly unbearable for the last two years, constantly rubbing in that he'd been the youngest shield-carrier of the generation, but now he wasn't alone. "Congratulations on your elevation!"

The cool autumn breeze whipped past as they rode, only carrying the vaguest whiff of dusty horse. Resmine's own mount, a big brute of a destrier, coal black from nose to tail, gleamed in the afternoon sun. If knights got to name their own mounts, she would have named him something suitably intimidating like Avalanche, Shadow, or maybe even Harbinger. Instead, the monument of muscle beneath her was named Timid. Maybe Timid had been shy as a colt, or maybe someone thought it was funny. Either way, Resmine was tired of the jests.

"Any idea where we're heading?" she asked.

"Rumor is there's trouble on the border. Shouldn't be anything major though. Ser Quinton Ilyani says this joint scouting venture is to give those of us without any real battle experience some field practice," Estan said. "How's the new plate? Feeling heavy yet?"

Resmine hefted her shield. Her armor was built a bit differently, but Taymahr and Locke were very close deities, being the Goddess of Protection and Loyalty and the God of Beauty and Battle. Where Estan's plate was built to take a beating, Resmine's was built for ease of movement. Knights of the two temples often sparred together, and even held tournaments. It would be good to get Estan into the arena where she could teach him how well she'd taken to the sword.

"It looks good on you, sweets," a soft purring voice came from behind. The crunching of hooves approaching from her open flank made Resmine's heartbeat quicken and her cheeks flush red despite the gentle weather.

Syara, Resmine's fellow Knight of the Bold Blade and the love of her life, trotted her own horse, Brick—named for his red clay coloring—up beside the two greener knights. While Estan's armor suited him to the point Resmine couldn't imagine him as anything but a knight, Syara glowed so brightly it seemed like her plate could barely contain her. Any moment, she might gallop Brick straight into the heavens and take her place amongst the gods. Estan was tall, but Syara was taller. Her flaxen hair sparkled as much as her aqua eyes. A scar marred her right eyebrow and cheek, but Resmine thought it added character to a face in danger of achieving perfection. High, pronounced cheekbones and skin like alabaster. Resmine had always felt the slightly older woman was a creature out of legend. What she saw in the gangly teen Resmine had been when they first fell into bed was a mystery. Even more perplexing was why she'd chosen to continue the courtship. But Resmine had never been happier.

Dewin, a small, faraway voice said.

Resmine scowled. Where had that thought come from?

"Seriously though," Syara cautioned, "be on the lookout, you two. I have a feeling we weren't given the full brief on what to expect out here."

As though it had been waiting for someone to notice, a sliver of gray began to build on the horizon. Resmine thought the sun was too strong for fog, but the cloud only seemed to get larger as they approached.

"Weapons ready!" Quinton's voice called from the front. "It's a Flayer fog!"

Resmine braced herself, but wasn't prepared for the wave of terror the fog brought with it. The crisp, clean breeze was overpowered with the heavy, sickly sweet rot of decay. From the front of the line, she heard the clashing of weapons and the hissing of *something*. Whatever those sounds were, they came from nothing natural or holy.

"Ripping, gushing, lapping, viscera, pooling, blood, carnage..."

Shapes started to form in the mist. They looked human but horribly deformed and blotchy with ripened bruises. Where there should've been fingernails, there were sometimes talons or claws. Some of the creatures had bits of charred flesh around the worst of their wounds.

You've fought Flayers many times with Dewin, Khiri, and the others, the same faraway voice as before whispered.

The voice was right. She had done this. But the sword felt wrong in her hand. Tossing it away, she pulled a whip from Timid's saddle. Weird how she hadn't noticed the whip before. Her armor was also wrong. She began shedding pieces as quickly as she could. There was still time before the Flayers were on her.

"What are you doing?!" Estan cried.

Resmine ignored him. He wasn't the right Estan anyway. This Estan had too much hair and still thought too highly of himself. The Estan she knew had been through a lot, and even if he still did dumb-ass things, he knew they were dumb. Much like she was doing now. Less armor and a weaker weapon might not be smart, but they were essential to who she was.

"Resmine! Please, my love! You don't know what you're throwing away!" Syara cried.

Meeting those aqua eyes, Resmine felt a welling of tears burning down her face. She wasn't going to see those eyes again in her lifetime if she continued. There was a surety in Resmine's deepest soul—this was her last chance to spend her days with her warrior queen. "I'm sorry," Resmine said, dropping off Timid's side and rushing to meet the line of Flayers.

Brandishing the whip, Resmine caught the first Flayer by the throat. "I am Resmine! I am the former avatar of Locke, enemy of the Venom Guild, lover of Dewin! And I will be the next Queen of Thieves!"

As the Flayer's neck cracked, the gray of the Flayer fog was overtaken by ribbons of freezing darkness. The ribbons wrapped their way around Resmine's ankles and up her torso, closing over her head, until darkness was once more all she knew.

RESMINE'S EYES FLUTTERED open. She couldn't make out much in the darkness. The floor beneath her was the same gray stone that made up most of Jarelton. Shivering, she pulled herself into a ball to huddle against the frosty nip in the air. For some reason she was clad in little more than a threadbare rag. It was too long to be a shirt, and too short to be a dress. That and her under clothes were all she seemed to own in the world. A smell hung around her like she hadn't washed in almost a month. She winced away from her own armpits, wishing there were some way to move her nose farther from her own body.

"Prisoner! Food!" a voice called from behind the opposite wall.

Now that Resmine knew to look for it, she could make out the faint outlines of a door with torchlight blazing on the other side. She scrambled forward to grab at a tray slid through a flap at the door's base. There was a small clay bowl with something she chose to believe was soup, though it smelled rancid and had gone cold well before it was brought to her. A small hunk of stale bread with a bite taken out of it was meant as much to be her utensil as her supper was barely in her hand before the tray itself was yanked back out of her cell.

"Where am I?" Resmine yelled. Her voice was rough and thin, like she hadn't used it in days.

"They get like that sometimes," she heard through the door. "Can't remember where they are or what they did. Best to just ignore 'em though. You start talking to this lot, you may end up in here your own self."

Well, the accent was definitely Mytanan. Between that and the familiar stone, Resmine felt it was safe to assume this was Jarelton. What *had* she done to get here? The last thing she recalled... Ysinda. Ysinda had sent her to retrieve Orin Treag's papers of nobility. Because Orin Treag had declared war on the Thieves' Guild to solidify his power grab.

But why would he do that? It made no sense to Resmine. He was smart enough to know the Thieves' Guild was a stabilizing entity in Jarelton's underworld. They didn't allow too much to be fleeced from any given neighborhood. If people couldn't pay their bills, there was less for the pickpockets and cutpurses to harvest. He'd claimed crime was on the rise, but if that were true, it meant someone was undermining the Guild's policies.

Resmine shifted herself off the floor and began to walk in laps around the mostly empty room. She had to figure out how to get out of this place first. Then she could report back to Ysinda.

Ysinda's gone, an inner voice hissed. *You report to no one.*

Even if that were true, Resmine needed to start by getting out of this cell. She paced the length of the room one way, counting as she went. Ten. The other direction. Nine. In one corner, she had collected a pile of scrap cloth. It wasn't much. From the amount and material, she guessed the pile had once been her pants. Had she already been formulating a plan? Or had something happened to her clothing?

It was a big blank space in her memory. No matter. It only made sense to press onward.

Her bedding was a pile of straw, none too fresh. While there was a blanket, it was barely enough to wrap over her knees. So far, that made small scraps of fabric, a clay bowl, and one big scrap of fabric. If she had been forming a plan, Resmine hadn't left herself much to go on.

More light would help, but Resmine had never possessed even a flicker of magic. There was probably a bit of sunlight during the day, as she'd identified a few vents of fresh air drilled into the wall she'd been laying next to, but morning seemed a long way off.

There had to be something she was missing. Resmine hadn't made it for so many years as a stablehand under the Gray Army's nose without knowing how to improvise. *Wait, when did I...?*

Yes, she had been a stablehand. She'd pretended to be much slower and clumsier for years, waiting for a chance to escape. When Estan had gotten himself labeled a traitor to Temple Hill, she'd made a break for it.

As Resmine was working on the memory like a seed wedged in her teeth, her fingers found something more substantial hidden in the straw under her blanket scrap. It was a long, slender iron rod. Now she was getting somewhere! The rod on its own might not be much, but if she found a small hook to go with it, she'd have a basic lockpick set. That was why she'd pulled the pants to bits... It hadn't made sense when she was only looking at scraps, but if the lock was magical in some way, tying the fabric scraps around her hands might provide her with a small amount of protection.

The rod had been easier to find when she wasn't thinking about escape, so Resmine made herself go back to her fleeting thought about Ysinda's disappearance. No, not disappearance—death. Ysinda was dead. She'd died... On the Solstice. The very same night as Orin Treag... And the two of them had never been at war. They'd been allies against the growing threat of the Venom Guild. With both of them gone, Jarelton was in greater danger than ever. The Thieves' Guild needed a leader, and so did the nobility.

Would've been interesting if they'd made a political marriage, combining the two sides of the city like nobles merge provinces, Resmine thought. *A bit hard to manage with Ysinda being an actual fugitive, but worth some thought. What could straddling those two spheres achieve?*

And there it was! Her fingernail caught on something worked into the mortar between the stones, underneath the clay chamber pot in the corner opposite her bedding. A sharp sliver of something metal. Tweezing it between her thumb and forefinger, she extracted a long, delicate wire with a firm curve on one end.

She hadn't recalled seeing a keyhole in the door's torch-lit outline earlier, but it was definitely there. Sloppy work for a prison cell, honestly. Even as careful as this lot had been not to give her access to sharp objects or metal, Resmine had scraped together enough tools to pick a simple lock.

Listening at the door, Resmine heard the sound she'd secretly been hoping for—soft, lilting snores. Her guard was asleep at his post. As quietly as she possibly could, Resmine got to work with her rod and pick. Tumblers shifted into place and the door gave a soft groan as it swung open.

Peeking out of her cell and as far down the hall as she could in either direction, the only thing Resmine saw was the sleeping guard. She crept over to him and relieved him of his weapons: a whip and a dagger. Odd for a prison guard, but they felt entirely natural in her hands. She closed her door and locked it again. With any luck, it would be a few evenings before they thought to check.

But if Ysinda and Orin are dead, what am I doing here?

Resmine turned the question over in her head as she dodged guards making their rounds through the dank, dim corridors. It wasn't until she reached the door to the outer world that she pieced it together. "This is the test. Ability, self, and desire. Each time, I have to demonstrate skill, remember who I am, and what I want..."

Ribbons of darkness came from the shadows around her and wrapped her in their freezing embrace. Resmine waited for her consciousness to reset, as it had during the previous test iterations, but she remained floating in the void.

"What do *you want?"* This was not her inner voice speaking. Nor was it Locke's. Resmine didn't recognize it at all, but it held the same coldness as the enveloping darkness.

The easy answer, to be the Queen of Thieves, played on her tongue. But it felt wrong. Gaining the title was a necessary step toward a larger goal. She was being judged by someone or something, and it would know if her answer was false. Resmine wasn't sure where her certainty about its judgment came from, but it was there. One chance.

"I want to protect Jarelton and the people in it. All of them. It's my home."

Very well.

And then Resmine found herself laying on the gray stone floor outside the archway. The stones that had been black in Corianne's runelight were still swirling with an otherworldly amaranthine glow. Firmly implanted in Resmine's head was the knowledge that she'd been accepted as the new Queen of Thieves. Along with codes to enter every safehaven and crash space belonging to her people, she knew that every thief in the city, from guild members to those that thought the guild was too soft to those that had stolen a sweet as a child, had been notified of her ascension.

"Well, that's fun," Resmine groaned as she pushed herself off the stone floor. Time to get somewhere safe.

11

~Khiri~

SUBMERGED IN NEARLY scalding water was Khiri's happy place. It was so different from the bucket-to-bucket bathing she'd grown up with. Despite having been away from home for months, there was still a novelty to soaking that Khiri found freeing. She didn't have to think about where she was going or where she had been. If she closed her eyes, Khiri could imagine she was floating in the night sky. Nothing but her and the stars.

Of course, that wasn't actually the case. Khiri was in a wide, stone-lined room with four other women. Where the majority of the room's floor should've been, there was a great big pool of steaming water. There was a walkway made of the same stone slabs as the walls surrounding the pool on all sides. Large sheets of linen were folded and stacked on the wooden benches that lined the wall furthest from the door. As Khiri understood it, Kal was currently in an identical room on the other side of one of her walls.

When Khiri had asked for a bath, she'd been told that The Copper Mug had a bath house behind the stables, open for public use. Khiri hadn't heard of a public bath house before, but she'd been shown the way by one of Gracelin's barmaids. The barmaid had shown Khiri where to undress and stow her possessions, and then she'd joined Khiri with the three guests already floating in the water.

Floating in a shared tub was a new experience. There seemed to be more than enough room for everyone to have a swim, but the other four women were content to stay close to the sides of the bath and chat. After the first few minutes of idle gossip, Khiri lost interest in their conversation. Soon she tired of pretending she was floating alone and grabbed a handful of soap out of the communal dish. As she was scrubbing, something caught her attention.

"... never forgotten my very first sweetheart, naturally. He was raised on Temple Row. Either orphaned or abandoned," the barmaid who'd escorted Khiri to the bath house said.

Was she talking about Estan? Khiri wondered. She had no idea how many orphans were raised on Temple Row. But if Khiri had learned to gage human ages correctly, the woman looked to have seen about as many summers as Khiri's two temple-raised friends. Assessing the woman with fresh eyes, Khiri saw she was very pretty. Freckles dusted her nose and ran along her pale-as-holly cheekbones. The woman had soft curves and smooth skin... Not a fighter's build or any scars to speak of. She had her curly brown hair pulled up out of the water with a hair pin, like she was afraid to get it wet. Like a few of the others, this stranger had neglected to pull off her jewelry. A copper medallion, no larger than a coin, hung by a thick cord just over her heart.

"Are you from Seirane then?" one of the other women asked.

"I lived there for a time," the barmaid said. "But I've been here for longer than I care to think about."

The woman she was talking to laughed. "Could always hire out with one of us. Be a merchant, see the world!"

"No, no," the barmaid chuckled. "I've not got the knack for trading! You have to know who to flatter and who to ignore, and recognize when someone means no or means they want to be convinced—no. I may travel someday, but not as a trader."

The answer seemed to satisfy the merchant woman, who moved on to other topics, but something about the conversation bothered Khiri. Something about the barmaid seemed off. After having been duped by a few too many false friends, Khiri wanted to figure out what it was the woman was hiding.

"Does it matter?" Micah asked. *"You're only going to be staying here overnight. You'll be gone in the morning, and she'll still be here. Let the woman keep her secrets."*

"And what if her secret is that she's a member of the Gray Army or an agent of the Venom Guild? What if she's just waiting for us to fall asleep tonight so she can set fire to the inn?"

Micah couldn't really huff as a bow, but Khiri felt it all the same. *"You've become paranoid, my dear sister."*

"But she mentioned Estan earlier. What if that was a hint?"

"She mentioned someone who might've been Estan during a conversation about her lovelife in a small town. Just because you find gossip dull doesn't mean the rest of us tune it out entirely."

Khiri sighed. Micah was probably right. The woman probably wasn't maliciously planning to burn The Copper Mug and everyone inside of it. But in Khiri's experience, probability didn't usually skew in her favor.

IT ONLY SEEMED PRUDENT to wait until after they were out of the tub and dressed before Khiri ambushed the barmaid on the way back into the tavern. Making sure to leave the bath house at the same time, Khiri started speaking when they were well out of earshot of the merchant women. "So I overheard something about your first sweetheart being raised on Temple Hill?"

"...Yes?" the barmaid said. Khiri could hear the quaver in the woman's voice. The barmaid was already nervous.

"Was his name Estan?" Khiri asked.

"How do you know Estan?" The woman's hazel-green eyes widened in surprise. "Are you from Seirane?"

"No," Khiri said. "I've never entered Seirane. I'm of the Life Tree clans."

"By Taymahr, thank all the gods! He made it that far at least! You have no idea... I've had no way to ask or send word or even talk about anything for so long!" The barmaid started crying. She bent down and put her hands on Khiri's shoulders as though she were fighting the urge to hug the elven woman. "I mean, Gracelin knows how I got here, but there's still so much I can't tell her. But wait... If you've come from the Life Trees, where is Estan?"

Whatever Khiri had been expecting, this deluge of emotions wasn't it. Maybe an attack or some sort of smug revelation of horrible intentions. Even the use of mind-altering runes like Fennick seemed more likely to her. Micah was right. Khiri was getting paranoid.

Not without good reason.

"Please, slow down," Khiri said. "How do you know Estan?"

As though the barmaid just realized how exposed they were, she whipped her head around to look for anyone that might be listening. *She's not trained for this*, Khiri thought, watching the woman. Micah, while alive, or Dewin would've checked discreetly. Estan or Ullen would've gone quiet to listen. Kal would've laid down a protective barrier. Khiri had already checked before beginning the conversation.

"Well... I don't know if I should really get into this out here."

"My friend and I have a room. What if you met us there later?" Khiri suggested. The cold was already seeping all the warmth of the bath out of her system and she was eager to get back inside with the comfortable fire. Now that it was obvious the barmaid had no intention of attacking anyone, Khiri was embarrassed for pressing the issue. Micah was going to start rubbing it in the moment they were alone again.

"Told you. I don't have to wait for you to be alone," he said.

"Weapons aren't supposed to be smug," Khiri sent back.

"What's your basis of comparison? Talked to many swords lately?"

Khiri responded by imagining a donkey. In a world full of demons and gods, her brother feared the weirdest things. She could practically feel the Lifewood bow shudder.

The barmaid was unaware of the mental exchange, but she still hadn't responded to Khiri's invitation. Chewing her thumb, she looked like she wasn't sure how much she could trust Khiri. "I don't know if I should."

"Look, if you do decide you want to come talk, we're in Room Ten," Khiri said. "My name is Khiriellen Fortiva and my friend is Kal. Just knock, okay?"

"Right," the barmaid said. "Khiriellen and Kal. Oh, I'm—" the woman cut herself off. Khiri watched as the barmaid swallowed back whatever she'd been about to say. Her name was part of the secret then? It was all Khiri could do not to ask. Her curious nature was at odds with her desire to let the matter go. "People call me Tiss."

The opening of one of the bath house doors alerted Khiri that their time alone had come to a close. If someone saw the two of them standing outdoors in this cold, they might start to wonder what was going on. Khiri had never been good at lying, so if they asked her any questions, they'd get even more suspicious.

"Alright... Tiss," Khiri said. "Maybe we'll talk later."

Leaving it at that, Khiri scurried into The Copper Mug as quickly as she could manage without running.

THERE WAS SOMETHING odd about staying at an inn. Khiri was more used to the idea of sleeping out of trees at this point in her travels, but renting a room for one night was such a bizarre concept. Who had first decided to build a bunch of rooms for travelers? Prior to inns, had people knocked on the doors of random strangers and asked to use their bed for money? Did more inns mean more travelers or did more travelers mean more inns?

Gracelin had led Khiri up to Room Ten, explaining that her companion was already inside. "Normally, I'd give you separate rooms, but we're solid booked tonight. No use worrying over what you two might be about anyhow. 'Where long roads lead,' and all," Gracelin chatted.

Caught up in examining the copper painted room numbers on the whitewashed doors, Khiri wasn't paying much attention to the innkeeper. The hallway was lined with horizontal wooden planks that reflected amber in the light of the lantern wall sconces. Here and there, copper, yellow, brown, or red decorations were carefully arranged. Even the rug running up the stairs was a soft, warm honey hue. It was like someone had tried to bring an autumnal forest indoors. "I guess the road led us here?"

"Well, this one's it, my dear. Good night, and should you need anything at all, our taproom's always open. I've got a bedroom right behind the bar. Just knock loud if you hear snores! Try not to be too loud. Plenty of others just here to sleep."

Khiri wasn't sure what that was supposed to mean, but Gracelin was already walking back toward the taproom. With a shrug, Khiri opened the door and slipped inside.

Stretched out face down across the bed, Kal barely moved when Khiri came into the room. His feet were sticking out over the end of the lumpy mattress. Khiri hoped the bed was softer than it looked. "Mmph," he grunted. "I suppose you'll want me to take the floor for propriety's sake."

"Do you know what the innkeeper meant about long roads?" Khiri asked. She walked over to a table set up in the far corner and propped Micah against the window. After so long on the road, it would feel good to sleep out of armor. Sitting down in one of the two ladder back chairs, Khiri began to strip off her bracers and loosen the bindings on her chest piece. While her gear was all masterwork and padded for comfort, it was still armor.

Kal laughed. "So much for propriety then. Seems our host isn't bothered about such things."

"What are you talking about?" Khiri asked, more puzzled than ever.

Folding his long legs up underneath himself, Kal pushed himself into a sitting position. "There's an old saying about travelers. 'Travelers lay where long roads lead.' It doesn't sound like much, but the context is that people who journey sleep in whatever beds they find open to them."

"I don't understand," Khiri frowned. "Why wouldn't they sleep in an open bed?"

Kal started laughing harder. Khiri attempted to wait for him to recover, but her patience was already at its limits for the day. "You'd best tell me now. We may have company soon."

Wiping his eyes, Kal shook his head. "Sorry, *laska*. It's just refreshing how pure you can be. Open beds means people willing to have sexual relations."

Khiri's blush started to rise. She'd basically told Gracelin she intended to sleep with Kal under this roof. There was no helping it, though. If she tried to go back and explain to the woman she hadn't meant it, that would only mean a whole taproom full of people would know what she'd accidentally conveyed. And she'd been casually stripping off her armor, so she'd be chasing the woman down in less clothes, which wouldn't help matters.

"Spirits!" Khiri swore.

"Now, what's this about company?" Kal asked, taking pity on her and letting the subject drop.

"The barmaid that showed me how the baths work knows Estan," Khiri said. "I tried to talk to her outside, but she seemed concerned that someone might overhear."

"Interesting..." Kal said. The light coming through the window was rosy and waning. He made a gesture and the four lanterns in the room all lit at once. "Who would our fearless knight know that would live way out here?"

"She said he was her first sweetheart," Khiri said.

There was a mischievous gleam in Kal's eyes at war with his spark of curiosity. "Really?"

"Kal..." Khiri's voice held a note of warning. As hesitant as Tiss was to meet with them in the first place, the last thing Khiri wanted was the mage's rivalry with Estan to scare the woman off entirely.

"I'll behave. I promise... Anything I intend will be saved for Estan himself," Kal said.

That shouldn't have made Khiri feel better, but it did.

An apprehensive knock sounded at the door. Khiri gave Kal one last meaningful look as she let Tiss into the room.

"I—" Tiss started but Khiri held a finger to her own lips, asking silently for Tiss to wait before whatever she was going to say. Kal obligingly cast his sparkling golden glitter walls around them to prevent anyone eavesdropping. It was almost like being back inside the palace overlooking Taman.

"Okay," Khiri said. "We're safe. So what were you going to tell us?"

Tiss took in the glistening walls like it was the most beautiful thing she'd ever seen. "Wow, real magic! I've never seen someone cast a spell before. Runethrowing, but not fresh spellwork, you know?"

"Estan?" Khiri prompted.

Coming back to herself, Tiss seemed a lot less jumpy. "Right, Estan. Where is he?"

Khiri was about to answer when Kal shook his head. "I'm sorry, but I'm a little behind on this story. Who are you and how do you know our associate?"

"Right, sorry. I'm Tiss and... Well, no, that won't do. You two aren't from Temple Hill, right? I'm not about to get taken back to Seirane for execution?"

In a shared look that didn't even require mental speech, Khiri and Kal processed the woman's fear of the temples Estan had also fled. Whether she knew it or not, this woman had confirmed her standing on their side of the current war.

When Khiri and Kal both reassured her they weren't there to find her and kill her or take her back to people who would, Tiss relaxed even further. She walked over to the empty chair and pulled it over to the spot she'd been standing. "I hope it's okay that I sit. It's a bit of a long story. See, my real name is Loni Ashfield, and Estan truly was my first love. But after I tell you everything... Can you help me find him? I just want to see him for myself."

The name meant nothing to Khiri. But then, she hadn't asked Estan much about his life prior to joining her on the road. "We're on our way back to the Life Trees, but we know where Estan was headed and it's on our way. If we like your tale, I don't see why you couldn't come with us."

Kal didn't argue, though Khiri could tell he was disappointed. Another tagalong. Khiri had to admit she had a knack for picking them up.

12

~Estan~

SETTING A SINGLE MOSSY green tea mug on the shelf of his new room, Estan felt worse than he had the day Ysinda died. Maybe the grief had finally caught up with him. Or maybe it was because when he'd imagined going through Ysinda's things to protect them from other eyes, he hadn't envisioned them getting destroyed. Perhaps it was because his new room had belonged to Evic, who was also gone.

Corianne didn't bother to knock as she leaned against the open door. "Settling your trinkets all cozy?"

"I—" Estan bit his tongue as he realized how callous it would be to complain about Ysinda or Evic to Corianne. Ysinda was Corianne's friend and boss for years before Estan had met either of them, and Evic was Corianne's brother, best friend, and roommate. Any loss Estan felt, Corianne's was greater.

"Don't go getting all kitten paws on me, love. I know you for a weeper and it's not gonna chop my onions any if you're needin' a sob."

Estan chuckled. The sadness was still there, but Corianne's patter eased the rough edges. The sound of her velvety voice had moved him the first time he'd ever heard it. Someone else always seemed to distract him before they had a chance to explore anything deeper than their friendship. Now that he was living in the same apartment, Estan wondered if that might change. They'd had several moments when he was still with Ysinda when things had gotten dangerously close to crossing that line. "I'm okay. Really.

Rushing out like that was just unexpected. Reminded me of the way she and I never really resolved things. I'm not sure how much longer we were going to last."

A wry smile hovered at the edge of Corianne's lips. Her deep brown eyes seemed to look straight through all of Estan's walls. "It was dreadful obvious from the outside, love. Could be someone were trying to help you notice it weren't all sweets and snowdrops."

Estan tried not to lose himself in thoughts about all the times he and Corianne had nearly gone down their own path of discovery. He continued finding homes for the rest of his possessions. Not that he carried much. Even raiding Ysinda's horde, he'd only acquired a few extra weapons and some armor he'd have to trade for pieces that fit.

"Honestly, Ysinda reminded me of someone," Estan said after a few moments of quiet. "My first love, Loni Ashfield. She was soft and sweet... As innocent as Ysinda looked. She was always surprising me with her inner strength. Loni's the one that got me out of Seirane. I would've been captured on day one of my adventures without her. I think Ysinda called to me as strongly as she did because I've never truly gotten over Loni. But I was told Temple Hill delivered Loni's ashes to her husband. I'd like to believe she managed to slip out, but she may very well be dead... Either way, I doubt I'll ever see her again."

When Corianne didn't respond, Estan turned back toward her. He wasn't sure if he'd hoped to have Corianne rush to reassure him or give him a comforting hug, or if he feared she'd find his talking about yet another woman enough reason to abandon him altogether. What he found instead was a look of utter triumph as Corianne stared hard at the dead end of the corridor outside his room.

"Sorry, Essie. Reminiscing on our former heart flames will have to wait. Long live the Queen, eh? And she'll live a lot longer if we don't stand about collecting dust here."

It only took Estan a moment to decipher that Resmine's crazy stunt had paid off. How Corianne had known, he'd ask later. If Resmine was in trouble, all of Arra could wait.

STREETS THAT HAD BEEN quiet for weeks as people avoided the shadows and alleys for fear of Flayers were suddenly a flurry of activity. Mortal shadows darted from corner to corner. City guards, whose rounds had been relatively relaxed with the lack of crowds, were suddenly on edge with every raised hood and bare weapon they spotted. A number of people were finding any excuse they could to poke their head out of their doors or windows and glance nervously in the same direction Corianne was leading Estan.

"This is eerie," Estan said, keeping his voice low as Corianne tugged him out of sight. Two more human shadows slunk right into a triad of guards. "Is this all directed at Resmine?"

"Whatever that arch what tests our lieges is, it sent a right loud call out to all us lunkers under her reign," Corianne said. "Odd that you're not hearing it, being in bed with our lot and all."

The shadows and the guards started to yell at each other. Corianne grabbed Estan by the wrist and rushed past the altercation before it could become a full brawl. She didn't let go until they'd reached the next side street and began to cut through a new neighborhood. There were less people actively looking in Resmine's direction in this part of the city.

"I'm not a thief," Estan shrugged. "I'm pretty fond of a lot of people who are, but I've never knowingly taken anything."

Corianne gave him a skeptical look and then shook it off. "Who am I to question a bunch of rocks what say you ain't a nipper? Fair odd for one named Friend o' the Court, sure. But you're a fair odd love."

As they ducked down another alley, Estan thought he glimpsed Dagan slipping out the other end. The knight had only met the male thief a handful of times, none of which had been very pleasant. Dagan was among the suitors Estan had disappointed when he was named Ysinda's consort. While the thief man's dusty brown hair and golden-flecked eyes weren't very memorable on their own, he had a malicious grin that brought out his apple cheeks in a predatory way. Dagan's tan, wiry frame held more muscle than one would expect. Corianne had needed Shiv to hold Dagan back from killing a prisoner once. And Shiv was enormous. Dagan was also as quick with his daggers as Corianne was with her runes. A deadly, vicious fighter.

Estan had a feeling Dagan wasn't on his way to help the new Queen of Thieves to her throne room.

"We'll never make it first if we keep to the ground. Thieves' highway's best left to dark, but needs must," Corianne grumbled. She launched herself off the ground and caught a peg meant for drying lines. Estan followed her lead, huffing his way up the well hidden path of hand and toe holds the thief woman uncovered for him. Corianne may as well have been climbing a ladder.

"Is this normal for a new leader of your guild?" Estan asked as he and Corianne heaved themselves onto the roofs of Jarelton. "This mad dash to their last known location?"

"That would be a right sight. All the thieves running about the city letting all the duffers know we're about. No, this ain't remotely normal, love. Nothing's been since you lot came into our city. This is a direct line of too many factions bein' at odds and right sudden finding a target. Which is why we need to stick to her like gravy on bread." Corianne didn't let talking slow her down. She maintained a brisk pace as they leapt from one building to another—shoulder rolling, running up walls, and jumping alleys as they went.

A lifetime of knightly endurance and agility training kept Corianne within Estan's line of sight but, while Corianne was gliding through the city, Estan could feel the stitch forming in his side. Even with his years of physical conditioning, he was scrambling. *Though*, Estan admitted to himself, *I have been gentle with my daily regimen since taking a knife to the chest. It might be time to take off the bindings.*

Estan was so distracted with his thoughts of keeping up that he nearly plowed into Corianne's back when the thief woman came to a halt. The knight's boots slid on the roof tiles, knocking loose a smattering of grit. Corianne grimaced at the sound. With a shake of her head, she brought a finger to her lips. With a sideways head tilt and flick of her eyes, she urged him to look at the street below.

The thieves of Jarelton hadn't been the only ones to hear whatever call the arch had released. Flayers were stacked three deep in a half circle around a sunken basement stairwell.

13

~Ullen~

"DRAW!"

A wave of arrows arced through the sky, shattering on shields, peppering the ground, and plunging into flesh. The line of carts pulling through the hastily erected fences surrounding a forest of tents struggled through the muddy patches created by snowmelt and bloody puddles.

"DRAW!"

Another round of shots loosed from bows. The pounding of dozens of boots and angry shouts echoes through the hills as the enemy soldiers charged toward the ridge the initial strike had come from.

Ullen could feel his heart hammering in his ears. It wasn't the largest battle of his life. It was a raid on a supply camp. But it was a supply camp Hon'idar had sent one of his favorite generals—Tericia Geryan, a woman with keen strategies and a sharp tongue—to inspect. Jathy Ettleway's spies had intercepted the news only a few days before and Jaspar had helped Ullen persuade his war room to let him take point. This was his first time in the position of command in over twenty years, but it was crucial to the overall war effort. If he succeeded here, it would go a long way toward proving Ullen's loyalty to those that still doubted him. And he'd have taken Hon'idar's best strategic mind out of the war.

"DRAW!"

The time for arrows was dwindling. Ullen gave the signal for the archers to pull back. This battle wasn't about holding a line, after all. It was about drawing the bees out of the nest. Even now, he could see smoke rising from the far end of the camp. His sappers had managed to light the outer walls. So far, so good.

But General Geryan's reputation wasn't built out of empty whispers. Even as the fires began, she redirected the camp's forces. Where the camp's captain would've sent the majority of his troops to deal with the archer threat, she pulled soldiers back to fortify their lines. She directed the rune throwers to douse the fire with their frost or ice enchantments, cloaking the camp in a layer of steamy mist. It would be unpleasantly warm down there but, unless one of General Geryan's rune throwers or Ullen's sappers was too close to the fire to start with, it wouldn't burn anyone.

The layer of mist did make it damnably hard to see what General Geryan intended to do next, though.

Ullen had told his sappers to fall back as soon as the fires started. He hoped they'd made it out. Things had gone wrong much too quickly for this attack to have caught their foe off guard. Everyone in the war room had been aware Ullen and his troops might be marching straight into a trap, but the odds were already against them. Even a small chance at victory was worth some risk. He had to make his next move and hope it didn't play into whatever General Geryan had planned.

"Rigger!" Ullen called.

The young dwarf ran to his general's side with an eagerness that Ullen associated with the bounciest of puppies. Black curls of fresh beard tufts tickled the edge of Rigger's sepia jawline, indicating the boy was finally approaching full adulthood. His brown eyes gleamed with excitement as he hopped from one foot to the other. "Barrel walkers?"

"Not yet, lad. You've got a way of thinking outside a problem. We can't see what they're up to right now, but we know it's nothing good. Our plan to draw 'em out has gone to the Stone and back. What would you do?"

Rigger opened his mouth, but seemed to change his mind before anything came out. Ullen waited, though every second felt heavier than the last. What if they took too long and lost the initiative? What if they'd already lost it? What was General Geryan planning? Rigger interrupted

Ullen's musings by taking off in the direction he'd come from. Calling back over his shoulder, the younger dwarf chittered, "I've got to grab something!"

"General Dormidiir!" One of the sentries called. "We've got movement to the north!"

Ullen spun around. A line of troops were cresting the horizon. Hon'idar's banner and the royal standard both hung loosely from their poles, fluttering against the pull of gravity rather than any rogue breeze.

Cursing under his breath, Ullen turned back to the misty camp. He needed a victory here. There were too many rumors about his loyalty to the cause. Ullen knew what some people were calling him. He'd even heard it whispered in the tents on this mission. The Traitor Prince. Retreat would be the safest option, but the whispers would grow into shouts and demands for abdication. Too often, following the safe route was seen as a weakness in the commander.

"Here it is!" Rigger said. "Now, it's a prototype, mind. There's still a lot of tweaks and problems that need fixing but isn't she beautiful?" Thrusting a case into Ullen's hands, Rigger's face scrunched up with pride.

Bemused, Ullen set the case on the ground and opened it. He wasn't entirely sure what he was looking at. A wooden handle, like that of a crossbow was affixed to the bowled end of a longish pipe. There were three different levers on various bits of the device. "What on Arra is this?"

"I'm calling it a hand-held rune cannon!" Rigger said, dropping to his knees in the squelchy soil to pull the object free. "See, rune throwers can only throw runes so far, so I was trying to figure out a better delivery method. It's too easy to throw off an arrow's weight, so this uses a lightning rune to convert thunder into thrust and propels the rune much farther than a person's arm might. The problem is—I should say, one of the problems—I've not entirely compensated for misfires. Sometimes the runes shatter. Also, sometimes the propelled rune doesn't leave the barrel. Their casings leave this sticky residue, and I'm not sure what causes that. I've had a few explosions."

"Wait, explos—" Ullen was about to demand further explanation, but he stopped himself. "Never mind, just tell me how the blasted thing works. I've got a plan, but we need to move fast. This thing, it fires all kinds of runes?"

Chattering happily about his creation, Rigger followed Ullen as they made a quick round to speak to all of the commanders. General Dormidiir was about to make his comeback.

THE FIRST THING THEY had to do was convince General Geryan that her ploy was working. It wasn't hard to look like they were panicked and desperate. Charging down the hill, roaring as they went, Ullen's forces looked more like a mob of civilians than a cohesive unit.

Arrows pierced through the misty veil hiding the supply camp and arced over the field. Despite rune throwers holding up their magical barriers and mundane soldiers holding wooden shields aloft, some of those arrows found purchase in Ullen's people. Ullen's heart twisted and wrenched with every pained cry that met his ears, but he couldn't stop now.

Later, he would revisit those screams in his head and wonder what he could've done differently. Later, the images of bodies and blood would haunt his sleep. Later, he could afford to war with his soul. This was the burden of leadership.

Rune throwers tossed fire, ice, water, anything they had at whatever was in front of them. Enchantments collided and tore through the logs of the supply camp's fence. A line of enemy soldiers met Ullen's forces as the barrier faltered. General Geryan had anticipated the bluff behind the panic. But that was okay. Ullen wanted her mental guard to slip. The more foolish his actions looked, the better the chances his plan might actually work. His people struggled and began to fall back into a small crowd, as though Geryan's troops were too much for them.

In all honesty, Ullen didn't think it was much of an act. The majority of those brought on this mission were green and unblooded. Real training in Eerilor meant spending time in the Royal Army, which was largely loyal to Hon'idar.

The front line threw down their weapons and held their arms up. It was a risky moment for those holding the enemy back. But General Geryan proved honorable and called for her people to halt.

"Ready to concede, Your Highness?" General Geryan asked, stepping forward.

Ullen took a deep breath and met the woman's eyes. Even with the distance and her helmet between them, he could see them sparkling like proud diamonds as the mists finally parted. He brought the hand-held rune cannon up and took aim, the world around him slowing into a single frozen heartbeat. As he pulled the trigger, Ullen silently begged Tharothet to let Rigger's contraption work.

The rune exploded from the barrel, spinning and flipping in the air. If General Geryan had been standing closer, the stone itself might have been lethal. But it smacked against her breastplate, found purchase against her neck and stayed there—probably thanks to the mysterious sticky residue. A moment of confusion, doubt, and then her sparkling eyes dulled.

"Yield," Ullen demanded.

"You're kidding," the captain of the camp started to laugh.

But his laughter cut short when his general walked forward and knelt in front of Ullen. The rest of the camp started to mutter. One or two of the more restless soldiers seemed about ready to impale Ullen's front line.

Heavy sounds, almost felt rather than heard, thrummed through the ground. Ullen and his troop recognized the sensation, having trained alongside the barrel walkers for a handful of weeks. That didn't make Arra shaking beneath them any less disconcerting. Their enemies were less prepared for the looming shadows of four barrel walkers to appear over the edges of their perimeter fence. What was left of the camp's mist veil had kept the barrel walkers hidden as they moved out of the covering copse of trees to flank Ullen's raiders, but nothing could disguise those footsteps.

Several of the enemy soldiers broke, dropping their weapons as they ran for cover.

"Stand fast!" the captain ordered, though his throat sounded half-choked with fear.

"Stand down. I have surrendered. No need to draw this out," General Geryan said. Her voice was much softer, her eyes still dulled by the effects of the mind control rune she'd been shot with. Such was her hold over the soldiers that even the bravest of them stepped back and lowered their weapons.

Ullen sent a quiet prayer of thanks to Tharothet, and a few to Taymahr and Locke for good measure, as he and his troops gathered those that could be gathered and fled the battlefield. They'd gotten what they'd come for and there was no telling how long the rune would continue to hold. If General Geryan had possessed even the slightest magical gift, Ullen doubted his ploy would've worked.

THE WELCOME AWAITING Ullen and his troop was less warm than he'd hoped. Despite the overall success of his operation, there were still mutters of disapproval. He'd lost soldiers and hadn't taken the whole camp. He'd returned with General Geryan alive. He'd revealed the existence of their barrel walkers to the enemy.

As disheartening as the whispers were, it hurt more that one of the voices—one that wasn't bothering to whisper—belonged to none other than Sir Quinton Ilyani.

Earl Tolen Terilles didn't keep a dungeon at his home estate, so their army had been forced to convert an old stone stable into holding cells. Vess Lorrei had overseen the refitting while Ullen had been in the field, ensuring that there were no darkened corners unprotected or loose, drafty stones to be tunneled through. It wasn't pretty, but it was functional. Each cell had a sturdy cot and a privacy curtain for the privy. The blankets provided were the same their soldiers used. Ullen was looking over the facility and checking that the prisoner was well kept when Quinton found him.

"You brought the enemy back to our stronghold?!"

"I brought the prisoner we all agreed we needed to take back to where we could keep her, aye," Ullen said, careful to keep his tone even.

General Tericia Geryan, seated on her cot, watched through the iron bars that had replaced the old stall panels. She looked smaller without her armor on, almost waifish. Her cool, sapphire-shadowed, tawny skin was drawn tight against her bones. Burning amber eyes, practically bulging from their sockets, didn't miss a single thread in the fiber of Quinton's cloak. The captive general wasn't even bothering to disguise her interest, despite the bowl of stew one of the soldiers on prison detail shoved through the slot at the foot of her door.

To be fair, the bowl wasn't steaming, so it wasn't as though hurrying would make a great deal of difference about how cold it was likely to be when she started eating.

"You should've killed her! You should've killed the whole camp of them!" Quinton fumed. His armor glinted in the torch light as his nostrils flared. Veins were popping out along his temples and his skin, normally ruddy, was practically purple with rage.

"Taking prisoners is harder than killin'," Ullen said. He hoped he could talk his old friend down from this sudden blood fury. "We showed more strength by stayin' our blades. None of us profit from needless slaughter. You know that. You're a Knight of the Protective Hand."

Quinton looked down at Ullen with a disdain that Ullen felt deep in his chest. It had been twenty years since they had fought together as both allies and avatars, enough time for some very fundamental changes in temperament. Whatever had happened in that time, Ullen realized the current Quinton Ilyari was a very different man than the one he'd considered his brother-at-arms. "Make no mistake, *your Highness*," Quinton sneered, "the only way to stamp the Gray Army out of someone is to make sure you take their breath, too. We've got to purge these snakes out of the very soil of Eerilor."

A fire Ullen hadn't known he possessed stoked in his gut. He wasn't responding to Quinton as Ullen, the runaway prince. He was Prince Ut'evullen Dormidiir, Scion of the Royal House of Eerilor and chosen heir of Queen Di'eli. "These are *my* people, General Ilyari. Until we know who's Gray Army and who's only guilty of being loyal to Eerilor, we aren't going to cull entire camps of soldiers."

"Just because Genovar left you in charge—"

"Aye, he did leave me in charge. What's more, we're in my kingdom. Which means you'd best watch your next words very carefully, General," Ullen said, his spine as immovable as the Stone. "You could find yourself spending the night in the cell next to our prisoner."

Whatever Quinton had been about to say, his mouth snapped shut with an audible click. The knight turned on his heel and nearly bowled over the soldier on guard duty. While it had been satisfying in the moment to pull rank, the protective layer of certainty melted almost as quickly as it had formed. Without Genovar to keep Quinton in check, the knight was like a flour keg in a fire. It was only a matter of time until something exploded.

"You stood up for me. For Eerilor."

Quinton had taken enough of Ullen's attention that the prince had nearly forgotten he had an audience. It took the last of his reserves to keep himself from jumping at the sound of General Geryan's voice. He looked at her, making sure she hadn't snuck up to the bars while he'd been distracted. The prisoner was still sitting on the edge of the cot, watching him with those keen, burning eyes.

"If that was an act to shift my loyalty, it was well performed. It certainly felt honest."

"Weren't no act," Ullen huffed. "And certainly weren't for your benefit."

Finally standing and walking the ten paces to pick up her stew, General Geryan nodded. "Maybe I'd prefer it were an act. If you leave me alone with that man or someone loyal to him, I'll be dead before dawn."

Enemy or not, General Geryan was right. Ullen knew better than to say so, though. Agreeing with the prisoner wasn't going to quell the rumors about him being a traitor. He patted the guard on the arm and a promise for extra hands before walking in the same direction Quinton had headed. The cold that enveloped Ullen the moment he exited the prison had little to do with the winter sun.

14

~Resmine~

INTERESTING...

Resmine watched the mob of Flayers bob and sway in their eerie silent rhythm. The hisses calling for her blood, flesh, bone and viscera were disconcerting, but they hadn't shifted since the initial wave of alertness when she'd opened the basement door. Either they were waiting for instructions, or they couldn't touch the stairs. If the Flayers were waiting for orders, Arad Rhidel or Irrellian Thornne had to be out there somewhere, watching.

And if the Flayers can't touch the stairs, what exactly does that mean?

The city was slowly enchanting certain streets with runes to keep Flayers out, but those didn't make the Flayers balk so much as seal off access. Resmine had witnessed a Flayer slam itself against those runes during an outing with Shiv. Blue light had flared up like a transparent wall, keeping the demon-bound creature at bay. It had been attempting to ambush them, apparently as unaware as they were about the runes guarding the street. Shiv had reached through the barrier with his massive hands and beaten the Flayer to death against the magical blockade. No, the steps weren't protected by the usual runes.

Which meant there was only other place Resmine recalled Flayers being unable to approach—the sanctified ground of Dothernam Square.

Dewin's ceremony had obliterated any Flayers caught within the newly consecrated temple, and the demon-bound kept a respectful distance from the holy space. They also seemed mesmerized by it. Flayers were thicker in the streets surrounding Dothernam Square than anywhere else in Jarelton.

The demon-bound loved the holy space as much as they loathed it. When Corianne had escorted Resmine this way, Flayers hadn't cared about this stairway. Dothernam Square was in a different part of the city. For these steps to be holy now—

There were some implications behind that thought that Resmine definitely wanted to explore later, when she wasn't trying to figure out how to escape the horde.

Other faces were starting to appear in the area surrounding her exit. She glimpsed Estan on the top of a nearby roof. Once she'd spotted him, it was easier to pick out Corianne's shadow next to him. Shiv's massive silhouette was hidden against an alleyway entry. A few less friendly figures were also paused in various recesses, waiting for a clear target. All of them, friendly or not, were paused outside of the ring of Flayers. All eyes were on the stairwell Resmine was currently trapped in.

All she needed was a shift in the Flayers' focus. If the Flayers started fighting anyone, she could get free in the ensuing chaos.

Shiv's blue eyes locked with Resmine's for a brief moment and an unspoken understanding passed between them. He charged into the Flayer nearest him, two short swords drawn. Shiv was large enough to make the blades look like daggers as he plunged and twirled into the demons with a roar. Estan took Shiv's attack as his own signal, launching himself off of the roof with his sword out. Resmine winced as her oldest friend fell into the massive crowd of mottled demon-bound.

"...wrench...tear... drip... feast..."

"...devour... rend... kill..."

"...eviscerate... blood... grind... perish..."

"...AAAAGH!"

The hisses blended with screams as—one by one—thieves, enemies, and allies started to pour into the fight. It had started with Resmine's friends, but the less friendly figures didn't want to miss their chance to take her out because they'd sat on the sidelines. Resmine drew her whip from her belt and waited for the nearest Flayer to turn toward one of the fighters. Fighting her way out was risky, but she didn't see another way to open a path.

There's always another way.

The thought came unbidden, but it wasn't Locke's voice. She whipped her head around, trying to identify the source. It had to have originated somewhere. Oddly, Resmine found herself staring back down the tunnel toward the arch that had tested her. Had it spoken to her just now?

There's always another way.

Chaos reigned in the courtyard outside her stairwell. Resmine needed to move, but the voice didn't want her to enter the field of battle. Watching the fighting with the same detachment she used to play Knives and Nobles, Resmine looked for the opening.

And there he was. Skirting his way through the field like there was nothing in the way, a small child carrying a tiny dog. Catapult's favorite disguise. He trotted right up to the stairwell and turned his back to the rail, as though this kid had nothing better to do than watch a bunch of demons fight a swarm of thieves.

"Hop on! They'll still see you in the doorway," Catapult told her.

Resmine didn't need a second invitation. The moment her hands touched the horse's flank, she saw the roan in his full glory. Fortunately, the illusion held for the rest of the courtyard as Resmine swung herself across her savior's back.

Corianne must've also seen the small child with the tiny dog because she'd stayed out of things until Resmine and Catapult were nearly free of the courtyard. Once they were clear, runes fell down into the mob, causing small explosions and blasting Flayers into sizzling fragments of bone and sinew. There were a few human cries mixed in with the demonic screams. Resmine spared a prayer to Locke that Corianne remembered not to blow up anyone on their side.

RESMINE DIRECTED CATAPULT toward The Dusk and Dawn. Her first objective was to claim the seat of power in The Pit. As the new Queen of Thieves, it was important to let those waiting to see where the dust settled that she meant business.

Catapult knew the back alley next to the tavern well. After all, Estan had been using the Guild's royal suite as a hiding place since the Solstice. Locating the secret plate that covered the rune lock, Resmine tapped in the combination she'd received upon passing her tests. The hidden door opened as silently as a thief could wish.

"Thank you, Catapult," Resmine said, hesitating in the doorway as a thought occurred to her. "How did you find me? That chamber sent out a signal to all those bound to the Thieves' Guild, but that's not it, is it?"

Catapult blinked big innocent eyes at her. "How do I ever find any of you? Letting a horse like me wander the streets on my own, it's downright shameful. What if someone were to steal me?"

"You're a sentient warhorse with illusion abilities. Of us all, you're probably the safest when on your own. But I take it that attempted deflection means you're not going to answer me."

With a whinny of amusement, Catapult trotted off. His preferred disguise of a small child holding a puppy was in place before he exited the alleyway. Resmine looked after the horse with a huff of exasperation. It was impossible to tell if Catapult was keeping secrets or if he was merely playing games. Catapult had always been a mischievous horse, but serving as avatar to Numyri—Goddess of Mirth and Mayhem—had pushed the roan's antics to new levels. The whole of Arra was lucky the gods had returned home, even setting aside the Flayers and wars. But whatever Catapult was up to, it could keep until later.

Stepping into the Thieves' Guild royal chambers, Resmine thought she knew what to expect. Estan was her oldest friend, her brother in everything but name. Even when he thought he was keeping things close to his chest, she'd gathered that Ysinda's living space wasn't as hard as the image the former queen had projected. Which, given that Ysinda seemingly died while protecting a child from Flayers, wasn't as shocking as Estan seemed to believe. It only took Resmine a few moments to realize she wasn't walking into the former queen's chambers, but her own.

She wasn't sure if she'd stepped into a dining room or a war room. A map of Jarelton showing every safe house, tunnel, and hidden passage was hung over a large table with plenty of chairs. A table meant for planning. One end had a Knives and Nobles board—a gorgeous set, crafted with copper and jet pieces. What passed for a kitchen was tucked into the corner. The utensils and service ware visible were all heavy, serviceable, and could probably be used as weaponry in a pinch—thick wood or chunky metal. Not without inherent beauty, but definitely not soft. The chamber's light seemed to come from the ceiling above through some interestingly designed skylights.

Resmine felt at home in this space. Like she belonged. It was a feeling that made her skin crawl. She never felt at home in a place before, only with people. Syara, Estan, Dewin, maybe even Khiri and Ullen a few times. Shaking herself free of the sensation, Resmine continued into the bedroom.

Leather mannequins were located on either side of a fairly simple, but elegantly dressed, bed. One of the mannequins was the right size and shape for Resmine's armor, while the other was made for Dewin's gear. Empty shelves were built into the walls, awaiting trophies, books, or even clothing. A portrait of Dewin and Resmine hung over the headboard. Resmine was certain she would've remembered posing for a portrait, especially one of this nature. It was provocative, though it didn't quite cross the border into obscene. Dewin wore a long, indigo robe which hung loose and open. Her face turned over her shoulder, but her body was in profile so only the outline of one breast was visible to the viewer. The painted priestess held one hand at her waist, tugging the robe tight against her backside, as though she were about to draw the garment closed. Her other hand rested on an empty doorframe, a simple golden band with a faceted onyx on one of her fingers. With a playful smile on her lips, her eyes were focused on the painted Resmine, who wore an equally long, diaphanous robe of the palest gold. Resmine's representation was reaching for Dewin's face with one arm and holding a white rose in the other. The golden robe was closed, but the outlines of her body were visible through the thin material.

This was not merely a bedroom. This was a wedding chamber.

A box Resmine hadn't noticed before rested on one of the shelves. It was small and fit easily into the palm of her hand. She didn't even bother opening the box to check its contents. Something told her it was a match to the ring Dewin wore in the portrait.

First Corianne was teasing her about making things official, and now a magic chamber under a tavern was giving her a push. There was a part of Resmine that balked at letting herself be goaded by her new dwelling, but she was smart enough to recognize the chamber was a reflection of her inner wishes. Being stubborn about it would benefit no one.

But proposals were for later. It was time for Resmine to take her throne.

15

~Arad~

AGAIN. FORTIVA'S BRAT and her friends had managed it again. Arad Rhidel realized his niece wasn't technically in the city, but that didn't make things any more palatable.

Ysinda had been a good leader for the Thieves' Guild, by Arad's reckoning. She'd been clever enough and skilled enough to take the position, but not clever enough or skilled enough to hold it for much longer than she'd managed. If Arad's Flayers hadn't finished her off during the Solstice massacre, her own people would've only taken a few more pushes. And Ysinda had known it too. The fear had been roiling off of her. Too many supposed allies had coveted her or her position or both. Her fear had made her malleable. It had been easy to convince her to consort with his niece's knight, a man Arad intended to kill even before he'd stuck his nose into Jarelton's politics. A crumbling brick to shore up a faltering house.

Only, even with the knight's death, and Ysinda's, nothing on the Solstice had gone to plan. What should have been his victory left Arad with a holy hole in the middle of the city, and Arad was still embroiled in the fight to control the rest. All thanks to that Fortiva brat's friends.

Irrellian wouldn't be happy if this business wasn't wrapped up soon, and the Flayer Mage wouldn't be easily subdued. More than half of Arad's Flayers were summons provided by Irrellian.

And that brought Arad to his current headache. One of his niece's allies, this *Resmine* woman, had not only stolen the leadership of the Thieves' Guild out of Arad's grasp, but she'd managed to weave her way through a number of his forces—and he couldn't figure out how she'd done it!

Arad had come to Jarelton under the guise of his birth name, Rothan Haud, hoping to draw out the creature that had seduced and stolen his sister all those years ago. It was the same reason he'd tagged along on that initial job last summer that had Fortiva's name attached to it. A chance at the revenge he'd long craved.

Growing up in the Haud household had been a nightmare. Most of their older siblings had been as prone to beating Elithania and him as their parents. There were frigid nights in the straw with the pigs he'd only survived because Elithania managed to keep them both warm. She was the lone beacon of light in his lonely existence. For years, Elithania had kept his spirits up with her stories of running away. She'd promised him that she'd find a way for the two of them to be free.

Memories of Elithania always led him to the same place. Before either of them had changed their names, shortly after Fortiva had shown up in their town, Rothan had done something bad. Rothan had seen maybe fifteen summers, and Elithania maybe eighteen. They may have been older or younger. Age was largely irrelevant to their survival. Their father had died earlier that season, but they were still stuck at the Haud house with their mother and older brothers. One of their brothers had come after Rothan with a switch, common enough though there was no reason for this beating beyond amusement. Then Rothan's vision went red. Next thing he recalled was standing over a still body while holding a knife. He was sticky and wet, and Elithania screamed. With perfect clarity, he recalled the look of horror on her face. His sister, his beacon of light, was staring at him—shaking her head and trembling in terror. Rothan found out later that she'd been looking for him.

But that night Elithania disappeared. She'd left him behind with their mother and remaining brothers. Rothan dealt with the rest of the family and then went looking for Elithania. Only when he found Elithania Haud, he found a red-headed elven woman. He dealt with her too. No one was allowed to use his sister's name except his sister.

Rothan discovered that a woman matching his sister's description was now accompanying Genovar Fortiva. But Rothan couldn't get to them. They were on the front lines of a war with the Flayer Mage. He lacked the skills to move through such a skirmish unnoticed. And Fortiva was a renowned fighter. Not like the bullies the Hauds had been, that only preyed on those weaker. No. Rothan had to find another way to reunite with Elithania.

It took him nearly two years to track down the Venom Guild and convince one of their assassins to recruit him. A lot of bloody, bloody work. He left the name Rothan Haud behind—the same way his sister had left her name with that elf woman—and took on the mantle of Arad Rhidel. When he finally caught up with his sister, he intended to let her know he'd made it without any reminders of the past. And he'd make sure she was as alone as she'd left him.

Of course, that meant killing off Genovar Fortiva. Arad's ill-gotten niece would be given to Irrellian Thorne. It wasn't the same as killing her himself, but in some ways it was even more delicious. Irrellian was only back because the girl had undone Fortiva's work to start with.

Arad didn't much care what Irrellian's plans were for the girl or Arra or any of it. So long as Fortiva fell into the trap being made for him here in Jarelton, and Arad was the one to tell his sister the good news, nothing else was of any real concern.

If his niece and her friends could stop screwing up Arad's plans, everything he'd worked for years to accomplish would finally be in his grasp. He just needed a little more time. After the Thieves' Guild was out of the way, either by union or force, the nobility would fall into line. Holt Treag would see to it. Once the nobility were in order, Jarelton's holy space would have zero defenders.

Irrellian could do whatever he liked with the city. The presence of the Flayer Mage would definitely draw Genovar into the trap Arad had designed.

Arad had gotten very good at designing traps during his climb up to the top of the Venom Guild. It was a position every bit as treacherous and difficult to hold as King or Queen of the Thieves' Guild, but Arad had managed to keep his guild in line for more than eight years.

How much trouble could this Resmine person really be?

16

~Khiri~

THE SPARSELY-FURNISHED rented room wasn't exactly made for intrigue. While the sturdy, timber bed was technically large enough for two friendly sleepers, it wasn't actually made for two people. Khiri perched on the edge of the bed's foot while Kal had propped his back against the headboard. There were only a handful of steps between the bed and the chair Loni had claimed. A small table, practically a sawed-off stump with varnish, sat against the wall near the door holding a single oil lantern to battle the darkness.

Few people expected Khiri to be as proficient a fighter as she was. If Loni tried anything, Khiri was confident she could hold the woman off until Kal fired off a spell. Kal's staff was hidden on the far side of the bed, within easy reach. His magic already saturated the room, between the wards for privacy and a few extra warning spells he'd discovered along the road, but Khiri's sensitivity no longer caused her any pain or irritation.

It had been a long time since the tell-tale ear twinge of enchantments had bothered her, now that she thought about it. Her body and mind were developing new ways to channel the energy which meant nearby magic no longer bit at her like persistent mosquitos. While it was much better for her in the long run, Khiri inwardly mourned her loss of such an alarm system. Not that it had ever saved her much trouble.

Telgan Korsborn, the name in her head agreed.

Loni, for her part, didn't seem concerned with attacking anyone though. She fidgeted nervously with her skirt a bit, seated on her chair. "So, my story begins with Estan fleeing Seirane. He came to me for aid after Temple Hill labeled him a blasphemer. I threw him in a vat of orange dye to evade the guards and then managed to smuggle him out one of the gates. If you know him, I'm sure he's told you this much," Loni said.

"He left out the vat of dye," Khiri said. Kal coughed into his hand, not covering his laugh at all well. "Honestly, he didn't mention many details about Seirane, other than he was raised by the Temple of Taymahr and it was overrun with agents of the Gray Army. Resmine talked about her first love being a knight also, and hiding as a stablehand."

"Resmine made it out, too?" Loni asked. "But I thought she suffered some sort of blow to the head? Why did she need to hide?"

Exchanging a glance with Kal, Khiri wondered if she'd already said too much. If Loni Ashfield was genuinely being hunted by the Gray Army, it wasn't a big deal if she found out Resmine wasn't the simple horsehand she'd pretended to be. But Khiri still worried that this woman was another spy.

"Of course. Syara. Syara would've reacted the exact same way Estan did, and he only survived because of a series of lucky choices. Poor Resmine. I never knew. But then, when you live in Seirane, you do learn to avert your eyes often. It's already a lesson I regret." Loni's eyes were distant, not seeming to see Khiri or Kal—or even the room the three of them sat in. "I didn't see my husband's allegiances until it was nearly too late."

Khiri's stomach flipped in sympathy as Loni continued her story.

"After I got Estan out of the city, I returned to my house. Estan told me to convince Jestin to pack up and go, and those were my intentions. I was already packing a bag when I heard him come in. I was still jumpy because of Estan's flight from the city, and something felt off about the way he'd opened the door. It was aggressive—angry. I'd never heard him raise his voice for less than an affront to my honor. I stuffed the half-packed bag under the bed and then shifted myself under, too. I stayed as quiet as I could, barely able to breathe. The Jestin I knew, the Jestin I loved, was a total stranger to me. He stomped through the house muttering under his breath about how much time he'd invested in stealing me from Estan to make 'that fucking knight easier to manage,' and how he hoped they'd let him 'do the deed' when it came time to make an example of me. We'd been together for years... So many seasons, so many celebrations, so many nights of love-making and plans for the future.

"My entire reality, nothing but ash in a single hour's time. Jestin left the house to check for me at my booth. It was only by Taymahr's grace that he didn't actually check my hiding spot. I managed not to cry out or sob until he was truly gone. I stuffed anything I could grab into packs and headed for a different gate than the one I'd smuggled Estan out of. I didn't stop to say goodbye or let anyone know where I was headed.

"After I'd been on the road for a day or two, I spotted a merchant caravan that I'd traded with in the past. I didn't dare let them see me, so I waited until the early morning hours when their guards looked the drowsiest to swipe a small bundle of dye-making herbs. It was enough to color my hair for a few weeks. Months if I was careful when I bathed. I ran as far from Seirane as I could without help, sleeping in barns when I was able, stealing food along the way. I wasn't proud of myself, but I survived. I borrowed the name Tiss from a history book I remembered Estan talking about many years ago, and settled on a stripped down version of my story—I was in a loveless marriage and my husband wanted me dead. Gracelin knows a bit more, of course. It wouldn't have been right to seek shelter here without her knowing the risks. She isn't a mage or a rune thrower, but she bought me a rune of obfuscation."

"What does that do?" Khiri asked, her curiosity finally overruling her good intentions.

Before Loni could answer, Kal let out a low whistle. "A rune of obfuscation makes it harder for someone to find a person or object they are actively searching for. It's a rarely crafted rune—hard to make correctly—which makes it very expensive. Our hostess must do very well with this place to give out such a piece."

With a shrug, Loni seemed to deflate. "There's always someone here. And there's the bath house. That draws travelers. If it weren't for Gracelin's generosity, I'm sure this was probably one of the dumbest places for a person on the run to come. And now I've gone and told two strangers all of my secrets because they knew names I was familiar with! Taymahr, I'm bad at this!" Tears streamed down the barmaid's face and sobs wracked her shoulders. "I just want to go home!"

And something in Khiri broke. She understood. The desire to go home when home was no longer a location, but a time. A time before her world had turned topsy-turvy, when things made sense, and everything was stable. There were problems during the before times, but they didn't exist on the same scale. Before Irrellian Thorne, before meeting her friends, before the Name Breathing and everything that followed... She missed that feeling of safety and understanding. Khiri's world had shattered so many times, she understood better than most how truly lost Loni was.

Khiri had Loni wrapped in a hug before she'd consciously made the decision to cross the floor. Though Loni was practically a stranger, she hugged back without restraint. Sobs shook both of their bodies, and Khiri realized Loni wasn't the only one crying. Uncertain of how long they cried against each other, neither loosened their grip until they were both once more under control.

Clearing his throat and looking pointedly away, Kal reminded Khiri nonverbally of his continued presence in the room. "I take it we're all moving on together, then?"

AFTER SEVERAL DAYS on the road, Jarelton's shadow loomed on the horizon like a heavy cloud of stone.

Gracelin had assured Loni she would always be welcome to return to The Copper Mug and reassured the woman she could keep the rune pendant. Then the woman had turned to Khiri and Kal with her hands on her hips and fixed them with a motherly glare Khiri wouldn't soon forget. Should anything happen to Loni on the road, Khiri was certain Gracelin would take on Irrellian himself—but only after taking a chunk out of Loni's new traveling companions.

The road dipped into a small valley, dividing them from the next hill with a copse of trees. Khiri attempted to keep her eyes focused on the present—the road, the wind, the hint of a storm hanging in the air, Jarelton in the distance.

"Come to me... Meet your Destiny," Irrellian's dream voice taunted Khiri's waking thoughts. The vision was starting to intrude into her daydreams and meditations. If there was a quiet moment when her mind wasn't focused, Khiri found herself walking through the curling mists without her brother and her knife hanging uselessly against her hip—unable to stop her progress toward Irrellian Thornne.

"Are you okay?" Loni's voice cut through the fog of Khiri's thoughts.

Loni wasn't much of a traveler, needing to stop frequently for rest and refreshment. She didn't have any interest in learning to fight, wincing at every blow on the occasions Khiri and Kal sparred, and had been astonished that Khiri knew nothing about domestic life skills. It only took one insistence on getting Khiri to help with dinner for Loni to promise never to bring it up again.

Khiri debated waving the woman off and keeping her mouth shut.

But Loni was also sweet, and genuinely seemed to care about her traveling companions. She'd salved and wrapped an injury Khiri acquired while hunting. She'd mended Kal's cloak when he'd ripped it on a fallen branch.

As Khiri was opening her mouth to tell Loni about the dream and how much it plagued her, Kal interrupted them. "I think we may be in for some trouble."

They were approaching the grove at the bottom of the hill. Even before Khiri reached out with her magical senses, she could tell Kal was right. Something about this place seemed off.

"Are there bandits?" Loni asked, her voice barely even audible. "Is it the Gray Army? Should we go back?" Khiri thanked the forest spirits that their newest companion at least had some sense when it came to avoiding danger. When Rigger had traveled with her and Kal, she was certain he would've marched right into the woods to study a tree up close.

"You see trees?" Micah asked. *"All I'm getting is shadows. It's like the road vanishes into a mass of fog, or void, or something and then comes back on the next hill."*

Glancing at Loni, Khiri relayed Micah's message. They'd never really gotten around to telling Estan's friend about Khiri's weapon being her brother. If Kal and Micah had to talk, and Kal's ability to mindspeak wasn't working, they waited until Loni slept for Khiri to act as her brother's translator. This was too important to keep until Loni was out of earshot.

Whatever the former barmaid's thoughts were regarding a mysterious missing person within their party, she kept them to herself. The only noise she emitted was a tiny whimper of fear. The unnatural aura of this place seemed to increase ever so slightly.

It wasn't a conscious decision on Khiri's part, but an instinct. Before she realized she was doing it, Micah was in her hand, an arrow nocked. She aimed for the largest trunk she could see, one that a novice would find hard to miss, and released. The arrow vanished as soon as it hit the treeline. Shadows danced in the corners of her vision, but nothing else seemed to change.

"Should we go back? Swing around?" Kal asked, echoing Loni's earlier question.

Khiri considered it. From the top of the hill, this wood looked to stretch for miles in both directions. Not vast enough to be a forest, but too long to avoid unless they traveled all the way back to Illesdale and took the route she'd followed with Fennick, Micah, and most of her friends all those months ago. She wasn't sure she could retread those steps. Too much had changed. The Flayer Mage was loose in the world again because of her. And his eyes were on her.

This was a challenge.

Irrellian Thornne wanted to delay her. She could feel it as surely as if he was standing next to her, whispering into her ear. But, why? Why would he care if she made it back to Jarelton today or tomorrow or even weeks from now? In every interaction and encounter, Khiri had been unable to stop things Irrellian had set in motion. Her friends in Jarelton and her father were responsible for any victories scored against the demon-bound mage.

Telgan Korsborn, the name in her head agreed. Her soulbound mate, and somehow also the Flayer Mage.

"We can't afford to go back," Khiri sighed. "I think we've got to go forward."

"*Laska*, you know I will follow you through the hells themselves, but that might literally be where we'd be going in this situation," Kal said. "Any other options might be worth pursuing."

Loni let out another frightened squeak. "Through the hells? No... No-no-no-no-no... Please, let me just go back! I'll hide with Gracelin in The Copper Mug for the rest of my life. By Taymahr, please, don't make me go through the hells!"

Giving Loni a reassuring shoulder pat, Khiri turned her gaze toward the trees-that-weren't. "Forward doesn't necessarily mean through. Kal, you and Rigger went over a lot of his ideas concerning flying contraptions, right?"

Kal's eyes, already abnormally large, widened as far as they could go.

COMPARED WITH THE WEEKS of back travel, constructing their crude little glider took much less time. With Loni's experience working in the Weavers' District, she took on the task of knitting together blankets and branches into something that looked vaguely like a skeletal egg with wings. Now that it didn't look like they were going to wander into the hell trees on purpose, she seemed as eager to move on as either of her new acquaintances. Kal spent hours infusing the creation with fire runes, protection spells, and other magics far beyond Khiri's current level. He tried to instruct Khiri on the crafting of runes, but her abilities weren't honed enough yet. The stone he'd given her to practice on was still as smooth as the day she'd received it. For her part, Khiri acquired hides and tanned them, giving Loni every scrap of fabric she could.

Nothing went to waste. Khiri only skinned what she was already hunting for food. Kal tended their meals absently while concentrating on his spells, and still managed not to cook as poorly as Khiri.

Maybe I've been cursed, Khiri thought.

"It is astonishing how someone that enjoys food as much as you has less than zero aptitude for its creation," Micah said.

Khiri tormented the bow by imagining a single, rather obstinate looking donkey.

"Now you're just being mean," Micah grumped. It seemed he was getting over that particular method of payback. She would have to find another way to poke him.

There was access to a stream on the other side of the hill from the hell trees where the trio worked. Khiri had found a spot hidden from view of the road, though it didn't seem anyone was traveling this way. After a few days of not seeing anyone approach from the Jarelton side either, Khiri expressed a growing concern to Kal as they sat in the warmth of the evening campfire. Loni was busy cooking Khiri's latest kill, giving her companions a moment of brief privacy.

"Are we really seeing the other side of the trees? What if whatever has rent the face of Arra is distorting our view? Just showing us what we want to see?"

"This contraption is your plan, *laska*. If you want to abandon it and go around, that's still an option. But I doubt that even in Irrellian Thornne's wildest dreams, he ever anticipated we would try something like hopping over this barrier. There's probably a much easier explanation for no one approaching from either side," Kal said. He took one of Khiri's hands and wrapped his long fingers around it.

The warmth of his grip made Khiri's thoughts go fuzzy for a moment. She regathered herself and asked, "Such as?"

Kal shrugged. "They know it's there."

Khiri wasn't sure she believed it, but she allowed herself to be comforted.

"*Laska*... Khiri..."

Blinking in surprise, Khiri's shoulders straightened as she turned her full attention to her lanky friend. She couldn't remember if he'd ever called her by name before. "Kal?"

He released her hand and picked up his staff. The runes carved into its surface glowed orange, and then blue, and then a green she'd never seen Kal's magic use before. Like the sun through a thin layer of leaves. "I think... I may have figured something out. Something important. It will help us beat back Irrellian Thornne. I'm not sure, and I'm afraid to test it before we're ready. If I'm right, it will definitely draw his attention. But—*laska*, should anything happen to me—take the staff. You have the same potential and it will show you what to do."

Khiri studied Kal's gold eyes in the dimming light of the sun, glinting as the fire danced. "Don't ever make me take that thing, Kal. If I have that, it means I lost someone else. I don't think I can stand to lose another person."

"I'll do my best. But, should it happen—"

Shaking her head, Khiri stood up and went to refill the water bucket. It was still full, but she needed space to shrug off a growing sense of unease.

It took them nine days to complete the flying thing. It still looked a bit like a skeletal egg with false wings, but the basket at the bottom seemed solid enough not to drop them. Kal, Khiri, and Loni dragged it up to the top of the hill and sat down in the center of the egg.

"This being based on a Rigger design, we really might want to do a test run of some sort," Kal began to protest. "Maybe you'd like to..."

Mist began to swirl in her vision even as Kal urged caution. She couldn't wait for the vision to play out again. Something was coming, and Khiri needed to be there. Whether she was going to stop it or start it was anybody's guess.

Activating the runes only took the pull of a lever. "We go now!"

Every rune woven into the fabric of the contraption glowed to life. Through the protection spells, Khiri could feel the way power cascaded from one row to the next, causing thrust. They were lifting off the ground, climbing into the sky.

Kal's shielding spell wrapped around the craft, putting a thin blue glow between them and the sky, but it flickered away almost instantly. "I don't think I can hold that the whole trip," Kal said. "Not after a week of enchanting."

It was only then that Khiri really saw how exhausted her friend looked. He'd been careful not to show it when they camped each night, not telling her or letting her see just how much the creation of so many runes had drained him. And even now, he was trying to hide it from her.

Because she needed to get to Jarelton the fastest way possible.

When they got back on the ground, Khiri made a mental note to have a talk with Kal about honesty. If he'd talked to her about how drained he was, she'd have given the egg plan another day or two so Kal could recover. Or maybe even chosen to go the long way. Despite her visions, she didn't want to drive her friends to their breaking points. Kal especially. She still wasn't sure what they were—while he'd made his feelings clear about what he wanted them to become, Khiri wasn't there yet. She felt more than friendship but, every time she thought about relationships in more solid terms, she still slammed against the wall that was *Telgan Korsborn*.

Maybe there was even more to that wall. She'd made the decision before not to be held back by the Flayer Mage, but... Despite some very intense feelings when they kissed, she still didn't know that Kal was her soulmate. Not the way he seemed to feel it.

Maybe she didn't belong with anyone that way.

The thought caught her by surprise. She tucked it into the recesses of her mind for further perusal at a less tenuous time.

"Blessed Taymahr and her divine grip!" Loni hissed. "I didn't think it would actually work!" The former weaver and barmaid grasped the sides of the basket and scrunched her eyes shut as tightly as she could. "I think I might be sick."

"Please, don't," Kal pleaded. He was using his staff to guide the egg's flight since they hadn't created any sort of steering mechanism. Every few feet, the mage sent a blast of fire in the opposite direction of where he wished to go.

The basket bobbed and shuddered as it ascended into the cloudy sky. As they rose higher, the ground beneath them looked like an odd patchwork of farms, fields, thickets, and places snow still clung. Despite growing up in the Life Trees, Khiri's stomach lurched in protest as the winged egg bounced against the wind. Perhaps this hadn't been her best idea.

"*Khiri*—" Micah started, but whatever he'd been about to say was lost as a scream tore through Khiri's entire being. It was so loud, she thought it might have been own bones rebelling at this unnatural method of flight.

But then she heard it again.

Something horrible shot out of the hell trees—straight for their creation—rending reality with its unworldly screeches as it came.

17

~Estan~

IT HAD BEEN ROUGHLY a fortnight since Resmine took possession of the Thieves' Guild and Jarelton was starting to feel the difference.

Only hours after the Flayer brawl in that weird little back alley with the stairwell, there was a ceremony where Resmine officially took her seat as the Queen of Thieves. Estan protested that his status as Friend of the Court was unconfirmed and he was still in hiding from the Venom Guild, but Corianne dragged him along anyway. With his cowl up and Catapult keeping a disguise over Estan's face, he became one of the many that came to witness the new leader.

And Estan was glad Corianne made him come. He'd never been prouder of Resmine.

Resmine didn't hide her ascension down in The Pit. While the owner of The Dusk and Dawn was not technically a guild member and ran the tavern as a legitimate business, he apparently raised no objections about Resmine claiming her residence in the main taproom. She'd gotten someone, mostly likely Shiv, to move the throne from the hidden, cramped basement receiving room to the upper tavern.

Her speech was delivered in The Dusk and Dawn's common room. So many people showed up for a glimpse of the new queen, they nearly didn't fit in the tavern. Normal citizens outnumbered the guild members. Estan even caught a glimpse of Ren and Adela, the owners of the Talon Acre Inn. They'd always made it a point to stay out of Thieves' Guild business. A flush of guilt panged Estan's chest at the sight of them. As far as they knew, Estan was dead. They cheered as hard as anyone when Resmine made her appearance.

With Shiv on one side and Dewin on the other, Resmine held her hands up for quiet. The crowd stilled. Estan scanned his area for any threats to his oldest friend's safety. She seemed so exposed here in a common taproom, but her attitude was one of ease. Like she'd been addressing audiences for years.

Like a noble.

Estan swallowed back that secret as he spotted Tak standing in the crowd. He'd agreed to Tak's terms. He couldn't tell Resmine about her mother. Not yet.

Not even if he wanted to.

The magic that sealed their bargain tightened Estan's jaw closed at the very thought of telling his oldest friend about Araylia Treag. If he could go back in time and unmake that deal, he would. Estan would rather have remained ignorant than be bound like this.

"I haven't lived in Jarelton my whole life, as many of you here have, but I've lived here long enough to know what this place is. It's my home. This is *our* home! It's a place of learning and shaping, trade and commerce, safety and survival! Jarelton is more than the stones of its foundation. It is a city of *people*. And the Venom Guild would have us forget that we are the ones that make this place what it is! *They* would have every person here cower at the sight of them. *They* would see us flee and start over somewhere else so they could take our home from us. *They* would bleed everyone here to feed their damn demons. The Venom Guild took our leaders on the Solstice and mocked Jarelton for being weak. But we're still fucking here, aren't we?!"

A cheer from the crowd filled the building, nearly loud enough to make the rafters tremble.

"Yeah... Yeah, we're still here. If they want us to flee, we'll stand together. The Venom Guild wants us to cower, so I say we fight! I say we drive those Flayers out of our walls!"

"And how are you gonna do that?" The question was practically a jeer. Estan thought he recognized Dagan's voice as the speaker. "Thieves aren't known for their armies."

"I have been tapped to run a guild of thieves, yes. But thieves are exactly what Jarelton needs right now. We know the shadows of Jarelton better than anyone. We know how to lure a mark. We know that sometimes, you have to cheat to win. The Venom Guild isn't weak, but the Thieves' Guild knows how to cut down an opponent. It's time to send a message—this is our damn city. And it's about fucking time we take it back!"

Another cheer erupted—a wall of sound that buffeted Estan's body from all sides. If he didn't still have Taymahr's gift of healing, his ears would've taken days to recover.

"This is our damn city! We're taking it back!" was soon scrawled on every flat surface Jarelton had to offer—walls, doors, even the side of the City Guards' barracks. Citizens that hadn't even heard the speech were starting to say it over their evening pints. News quickly spread around the city that one elderly grandmother had been so inspired that she was actively hunting Flayers in Jarelton's alleys with an iron frying pan and a bag of fire runes.

It was really only a matter of time before the Venom Guild pushed back. Each day that passed without an incident made Estan's battle-forged instincts draw tighter. He felt like an overwound coil, ready to snap at the slightest pressure.

Corianne shooed him out of the apartment one morning. "Don't be comin' back til you're a right love and not this wild dog what paces every heartbeat. It's more than I can bear to see ya bottled up and like," she said, closing the door behind him.

It was a mild winter day—still cold enough that his breath puffed in the air, but the sun was doing its best to warm the cobbles between cheery, white clouds. There was the promise of something heavier brewing in the air but, whether rain, snow, or hellfire, nothing seemed imminent. Estan drew his cloak over his head, since there was no Catapult present to disguise him, and ventured out to find something to take the edge off his nerves.

He ran into Dewin on her way to Dothernam Square. The two of them hadn't gotten to talk much since she'd taken on the mantle of High Priestess. Not really since he'd been made Ysinda's consort. Actually, thinking back, they hadn't been alone together since Tak joined them on the road and the information merchant had taken the former thief on as an apprentice. Dewin and Estan were both fully armed, weapons drawn, but there was a familiar ease he had missed.

"How're things with you and Res? Have you moved into the Pit yet?"

Dewin shocked him with the shake of her head. "Naw, love. We're still more bedded down at The Talon Acre. She says she has something of a surprise for me before the official Consort Consummating and doesn't want to rush out on Adela and Ren."

"They didn't ask the two of you to leave?"

"Resmine ain't holding her court there, which is really all they objected to with Ysinda. They don't want to play host to the guild, but they're good people that recognize a love. Course, they were a bit blind to all Ysinda was. Don't suppose you'd relate to that none," Dewin said, a soft grin stealing the bite out of her words.

"Yeah, not at all." A pang of sadness and guilt followed his returned smile. Corianne had told him repeatedly that he wasn't seeing the whole Ysinda. He hadn't wanted to hear it then, but it was somehow easier to see now that she was gone. "We haven't really gotten to talk about Evic."

A ripple of grief seemed to pass through Dewin's frame and she let out a small sound, like a gasp or a sob. Perhaps even both. "Not sure what to say, love. He was the best brother I coulda had, and I miss him. Even when I'm doing a thing he woulda thought daft. Maybe especially when I'm doing what he woulda argued with me on. But he wouldn't want me and Corianne to fret about him forever, neither. So I remember him. Cry when I can. Smile when I can't. I let myself miss him, and I keep going. We've got a war to win."

Estan opened his mouth to respond, but he was distracted as an unexpected shadow snuffed out the sun's reflection on his sword. He hadn't been paying attention to the sky as they walked. Dewin's focus had probably been compromised when he'd started chatting to catch up—like they were safely tucked into a tavern, sharing a pint. A ceiling of darkness obscured the rich azure he'd witnessed earlier.

There wasn't even time to warn Dewin to be on her guard. Once the sun was gone, the smell of sulfur was accompanied by the hissing sing-song of Flayers melting out of the surrounding gloom. Estan lunged forward with his blade extended, determined to make the Flayers work for their prey. He gutted one and slashed the throat of another. But he knew, deep down, it was useless. The demon-bounds' numbers were stacked against them. This was like the trap he'd wandered into with Tak and Catapult, but things were different without the war horse. Estan's arm was wrenched behind him as one of the stronger Flayers caught him from the side. His sword was clawed out of his grip. Blood oozed across his empty palm, but not one of the monsters bent to lap at the liquid.

An avalanche of the demonic creatures swarmed out of the shadows. Dewin chopped another of her attackers down, three bodies sizzling at her feet, but new Flayers immediately took the vacant spots. She was grabbed from behind and disarmed, as gently as Flayers were able.

He was wrong. This wasn't like the trap he'd wandered into before. It was much worse.

The previous trap hadn't been designed with one of Estan's group in mind. He'd merely interrupted a hunting party. These Flayers were going out of their way to subdue and restrain. Which could only mean capture. Death would likely be welcome compared to the fate awaiting them. Estan could only imagine one reason they would be held—

They were going to be leverage used against Resmine.

Arad Rhidel pushed his way in through the ring of demons. The leader of the Venom Guild smiled at Dewin like she was the first pastry he'd seen after a year of fasting. "Excellent! I thought you'd manage to squirm through my fingers once more. You and your precious Resmine have spoiled enough of my plans for one lifetime. I'll dangle you like bait, and she'll come running."

Dewin shrank away from Arad's outstretched fingers, pressing into the Flayer behind her. It spoke to the depths of madness in his eyes that she preferred the demon-bound's touch to that of the Venom Guild leader.

Before the unwanted hand made contact with his friend, Estan spat at the wiry, bald man that still haunted his dreams. Even now, he could see the moonlit dagger hanging over him just before Arad plunged it into his heart. The muscles in Estan's chest tensed around the remembered pain, but he was a Knight of the Protective Hand. Even if drawing Arad's attention meant more injury, or death, Estan couldn't hold himself back.

It took every ounce of his courage not to flinch when Arad turned those intense, blood-shot eyes toward him. Surprise rippled across the assassin's features, melting into anger almost as quickly.

"*You*," Arad hissed. "How are you still alive?"

"What's the matter, Rhidel? Losing your touch? Afraid a stab to the chest just isn't what it used to be?" Estan said, unable to keep the sneer off his face.

Despite the hellish smell of rotting flesh emanating from the Flayers around them, Estan momentarily caught a whiff of dread coming off the Head Assassin. That jab had struck something within Arad. How unexpected. Estan had merely been aiming to sound brave. Unfortunately, he didn't really know how to follow up on Arad's lapse and the opportunity passed.

"The next time I kill you, I'll make sure it sticks."

Bracing as well as he could in the restraining arms of the horde of demon-bound, Estan readied himself for a blow that never came. Arad turned on his heel and waded out of the circle of Flayers. "Take them to the chamber I've prepared and make sure they're secure. We wouldn't want anything untoward happening to our guests beforehand."

"Estan," Dewin said. Her expression was one of regret and self-recrimination. "I'm sorry. I can't do it for more than just me anymore, and I can't hold it as long as I used to, love. If he'd moved a right bit quicker, I maybe could've found where he's taking you. Just hold on. Me and Resmine, we'll come for you."

And she popped, vanishing into mist.

The Flayers holding her rummaged around in the spot Dewin's copy had been, as though she'd merely shrunk or become invisible to them. Estan started laughing deep in his chest. He'd sparred her often enough on the road to remember the avatar gift she'd been given. Dewin could make duplicates of herself that were indistinguishable from the real thing. Unlike Catapult's illusions, they were solid and could hold their own in a fight. She knew what they knew and they knew what she knew. There was no way for him to know when she'd splintered off. Nor did he care. What mattered to Estan was Dewin's safety. The Venom Guild only had one prisoner in their trap, and it was the man they'd already tried to kill once.

Taymahr, hear me. I entrust myself to your hands, Estan prayed. It was all he was able to do before the Flayers carried him through a shadow and into the realms of hell.

18

~Ullen~

AT SOME POINT, THE evening had slipped away from Ullen. Despite not having a window in his makeshift office, he could practically feel the stars staring at him through the ceiling of the Terilles estate as he huddled over his desk. It was a room normally used to store ball decorations, but those had been moved elsewhere when the ballroom was shifted into the war room. There was enough space for a campaign desk, a few chairs, and a rune lamp on a hook. Rubbing his brow with the back of his hand, Ullen's vision blurred as he stared at the reports in front of him. More soldiers lost—both to battles and desertion. More ground lost. At least the capture of General Geryan had made a difference. His people were losing less quickly.

But they were still losing.

It wasn't hard to understand why, either. Quinton continued to divide their leadership. Fights had broken out over General Tericia Geryan's continued existence in the ad hoc barracks. More soldiers had been put on guard duty, but there was always the risk one of them would be loyal to Quinton and try to kill the prisoner. The allegences of every soldier Ullen could field were tested on a near daily basis while Quinton was in residence, but Ullen couldn't risk sending his old comrade into the field either. A seasoned veteran with a good tactical mind, Quinton brought home victories. Bloody victories. Victories with no quarter given to enemies, whether they surrendered or not. Ullen couldn't bring himself to call those battles won.

Ullen was fighting too many wars. One was the civil war with Hon'idar for control of Eerilor, another was the second rise of the Gray Army, and a third—this war for authority against his former friend. It was exhausting. If there was any chance of winning the first two wars, the third couldn't be allowed to continue. This constant contradiction had to stop.

He had to make it stop.

The reports in front of him blurred into another massive blob. Sleep clawed at Ullen, dragging him toward the desk. A yawn forced its way through his clenched jaw muscles. He barely noticed the shadow passing between himself and the rune lamp glowing in the corner. But suddenly there was a steaming mug hanging in front of his face.

"You look like you've been dragged through the outer edges of the hells," Jaspar said.

"Feels that way, too."

Ullen reached for the mug handle, then hesitated. He'd not followed up on her invitation to reconnect. Not in the way she clearly intended. It wasn't from a lack of interest. Looking into Jaspar's violet eyes, Ullen could have lost himself to the Stone smiling and never even notice. She was still the most beautiful person he'd ever met—not to mention brave, dependable, fierce, insightful, and a million other qualities he was too tired to list.

No. Interest was not his issue.

She'd been yanked away from him once and he'd left home for fifty years to heal. If Jaspar was taken from him for a second time, with Eerilor in the state it was, Ullen was afraid of what would happen if he ran again.

"Just take it, before it gets cold," Jaspar sighed. "I'm not some virginal maid that will go all soft if our hands brush."

"You're not," Ullen agreed. "But I might be."

"I'm not entirely sure if that was meant to be glib."

"It wasn't." The admission escaped from him, his exhaustion freeing his tongue in a way not even alcohol could. He clenched his teeth and took the mug, but it was too late to take back his words.

"You're no virgin, Ullen. The two of us made sure of that in the past—well before I was nearly traded off in two different betrothals, neither of which were your equal. And I know neither of us waited in abstinence for the other to reappear, so would you mind explaining?"

Knocking back a swig from the steaming mug like it was a beer pint, Ullen attempted to draw up what mental reserves he still possessed. Mulled cider shot through him, either the heat or the sweetness giving his over-tired senses a slight kick. He didn't want to have this conversation right now. If an entire army of Flayers erupted from the floor, he might even welcome the distraction. But Jaspar would be right back in this office waiting for him after the battle. And it wouldn't be any easier to speak then.

"Alright, Lady Terilles. As you wish."

Jaspar pulled one of the empty chairs close enough that when she sat, their knees were touching. It seemed she wasn't about to let this be any easier. "Don't go formal on me, Ullen."

Ullen gulped down another shot of liquid courage before setting the mug on his desk. He loved it when Jaspar called him Ullen. She'd been the first person outside of his family to ever dare give him a nickname. Royal names were always needlessly complicated and Ut'evullen was worse than most. If they somehow succeeded, Ullen thought he may officially change it.

Focus, he told himself.

"As you... Alright, Jaspar. The plain truth of it is... I love you. Like a thrice-cursed fool, I ache for you the same way I did when we were youths, barely old enough to dance at court functions. You are burned into my heart and I weep for all the years lost to us. But I cannot be with you. Not yet. Not until things are settled between Hon'idar and me. Not until Eerilor is whole again. I cannot split my allegiances between my country and my affection. It's hard enough to keep them separate now. If I were to relax, if I were to let this happen, and something should separate us again, I don't know that I'd be strong enough to make my decisions as a king and not as a lover."

Once he'd started talking, it was remarkable how easily everything he'd been trying not to say came tumbling out of his mouth. He found it harder and harder to keep his gaze on those cat-like eyes, and by the end of his explanation, Ullen was staring at their touching knees. It was quiet now that he was done talking. His chest was looser. Not entirely unburdened, but one worry lighter.

"And what happens if I get taken away after we win this war, Ullen? What if we win, you are crowned, and something happens to me then? I fall ill or there's an accident. Another war breaks out and I'm among the first casualties," Jaspar asked. "Is your crown going to keep you from running just because you're wearing it? Will losing me later be any easier than losing me now? Because if you think it will be, I'll walk out the door now and save us both a lot of heartache further down the road."

Ullen's chest immediately constricted again. He had to be sure he understood. As tired as he was, the urge to jump to conclusions was high, but to lose Jaspar over a misunderstanding would haunt him for centuries, should he live to see them. "Are you saying it's now or never?"

Jaspar shook her head. "No, Ullen. If you need to wait until the war is over, I understand that. I don't mean that we need to rip each other's clothes off this minute so you can prove how much I matter to you. But there's a difference between waiting for the Ullen I love and waiting for the Ullen that's going to run when things get hard. I've already seen you choose Eerilor over Khiri, and you love that girl like a daughter."

"Someone's got to," Ullen muttered, then immediately regretted it. It wasn't fair to Genovar, and it certainly wasn't fair to Leyani. Genovar had loved Khiri the best way he knew how, training her to survive. Of course, Ullen also knew a lot of that was as much done out of guilt as love. Still, Genovar wasn't the worst father in the world.

The mulled cider boost was starting to ebb. If Ullen didn't get to his bed soon, he might pass out on the floor. It wouldn't be very commanderly of him to be found in one of the hallways, slumbering like a drunk outside a tavern.

"Come, your majesty. Let's make sure you get to your quarters. There's not a status meeting until tomorrow afternoon and I'll see to your schedules. I'm as aware of who's loyal as you are. I can keep your captive safe for you," Jaspar said. She stood and pulled Ullen to his feet. Their knees had still been touching, so they were close enough to share breath when he rose. For several tense moments, they stood locked in position—not quite embracing, not quite kissing, but connected in a much more intimate manner than they'd been in decades.

Ullen swallowed, wishing he could lean those few inches forward. But that would start something he couldn't afford to finish. Not yet.

Jaspar stepped back and the moment passed. She walked with him through the hallways, holding him steady when he stumbled and shut his door behind him. He trusted that she would see to the schedules he'd not finished. It was hardly the first time he'd asked her to perform such a task. Ullen wasn't sure what god he'd pleased to earn the love of a woman like Jaspar Tirelles, but he slept soundly knowing she was on his side.

IT WAS NEARLY MIDDAY when Ullen finally woke up. He eased himself off his bed and shook the last of his dream's cobwebs loose from his mind. Tharothet was speaking to him about the war... Something important had happened. Or was it about to happen? Ullen couldn't remember the details. Unlike his dreams of the god when he'd been an avatar, this was fuzzier. He couldn't even be sure it was really prophetic or if it was a dream of missing his friend.

While not a true worshiper of the human gods, Ullen had carried Tharothet with him twice now. If that didn't count as friendship with a god, he wasn't sure what would.

As he dressed, it occurred to him that he'd been left to sleep later than anticipated. Even with the afternoon meeting, Ullen was usually required to oversee something or make an unanticipated decision. Something seemed different. Off.

"General Dormidiir, Your Highness, um... Sir!" Rigger burst through the door, only knocking after he'd already entered the room. Normally, Ullen would've been amused at the younger dwarf's lack of decorum. Tutelage under Vess Lorrei, a woman with a limited tolerance for social niceties she deemed irrelevant, had done little to temper the lad's enthusiasm. But Rigger's expression cut away any levity Ullen may have experienced. "I'm sorry! I didn't know... Not the issue, right. We need you! Right away. Lady Tirelles, General Ilyani caught her trying to free the prisoner! He's dragged both of them out to the square!"

Ullen shoved his foot into his boot with enough force that he jarred his ankle. This was bad. He was certain Jaspar had her reasons. Whatever they were, they wouldn't be enough to assuage Quinton or those loyal to the knight. Cursing himself for a fool, Ullen wished he'd dealt with the division in his camp weeks ago instead of letting things go this far in the name of friendship.

The Quinton Ilyani that had faced down the Gray Army next to Ut'evullen Dormidiir in the last war had been more compassionate. Over the twenty years they'd been apart, he'd hardened and Ullen had been reluctant to push.

But his reluctance now threatened Jaspar.

Ullen wasn't sure if this could be resolved without bloodshed.

19

~Resmine~

READING THE PARCHMENT for the third time, Resmine wished she had more to go on.

If you want your friend to live, come find me in the place it all started.
You have three days.
Come alone.

Where did Arad Rhidel think it had all started? And all what, exactly? His war against Khiri seemed unlikely. Leaving Jarelton to meet somewhere near the Life Trees, where Resmine and Estan had encountered their first team of assassins wouldn't make much sense. Idly, she wondered if that contract on Estan was still valid. There was little doubt in her mind that Rhidel meant to kill both of them as soon as he could, regardless of what the note said. While Dewin had said the man looked unhinged, he'd proven too clever in the past to let a little madness dull his reason entirely. No, if anything, Arad thrived with his mania. Which made it unlikely he'd want to leave Jarelton, even if it meant getting her to follow him.

Resmine absently brushed Dewin's knuckles with her thumb as the two of them sat at a balcony table at The Dusk and Dawn, sipping at mugs of some very bitter ale. Corianne had gifted these particular mugs to the couple after Resmine's ascension to Queen of Thieves. They were enchanted with runes that purified lethal poisons. Alcohol could slip by undeterred, as could any number of potions or poisons with minor effects or brews that just tasted foul. But the mugs did take the edge off of one concern Resmine now had to deal with.

They didn't help at all with Estan's abduction.

"I should've waited longer. If I'd just stayed long enough, maybe..."

Resmine shook her head. It wasn't the first time Dewin had started to blame herself for Estan's current predicament, but Resmine didn't believe there was anything her lover could've done differently. "If you'd waited longer, I'd be trying to figure out how to save both of you. It would've split my focus. Getting out of there was the best thing you could've done. Corianne would tell you the same thing."

"Aye, that's a right statement sure enough," Corianne said, gliding up the stairs as though she'd been summoned. "Estan's a plonker, always slipping into the skinny of it. Only a matter of time 'fore he got himself nicked. But he's our plonker and we'll nick him back, sure as buttered apples."

Normally, it was easy enough to let Corianne's odd turns of phrase slip past, but Resmine couldn't stop herself. "Buttered apples?"

"Festival staple here in Jarelton during the harvest, love," Dewin supplied. "They core them, stuff them with honey, butter, cinnamon, maybe some lavender, and then roast them soft. One of Corianne's favorites."

"Are they?" Resmine turned an assessing eye toward Dewin's older sister. She hadn't been paying too much attention to Estan's romantic exploits since he was declared Ysinda's consort. When they'd met Khiri, it was easy to rib him about his hopeless crush on his hero's daughter—but Resmine didn't want details about the bedroom habits of a man that was effectively her brother. But, if she had to guess based on Corianne's guarded body language, Estan was probably in the dark about the rune thrower's feelings. "Well, good thing he's one of my favorites too."

She went back to pondering the meaning of the note. The place it all started... But not outside of Jarelton. Dewin withdrew her hand from Resmine's grip to walk downstairs and request food. Now absent her lover's knuckles to caress, Resmine found herself patting the pocket with the hidden ring box.

The place it all started.

Dewin had been the original target.

And Resmine's first brush with the Thieves' Guild...

Rhidel was waiting for her at The Two Beams.

Well, there were more secrets to the Thieves' Guild than how to get into the backrooms of the Pit. Now that Resmine knew where to find Rhidel, she could start planning.

"Corianne, I need you to find Shiv. And see if you can't track down Tak while you're at it."

"Tak?" Corianne frowned. "He's not rightly governed by our sort for all he's sworn. Should I tell him business or give him business?"

While the information trader was good friends with their group, Resmine had no illusions he would give her what she was after for free. Even if it was probably going to save Estan's life.

And Resmine wasn't about to give away the one thing that made her unique to any other member of the Thieves' Guild. The reason she'd moved out of the Pit with no fear of Jarelton's guards was because she wasn't a thief. She'd been chosen by the magical arch under the city, but Resmine had yet to break any of Jarelton's laws. Her guild existed under treaties with Jarelton's nobles, treaties long neglected but still valid. As long as she kept her hands clean, she could march into any guard house in the city and demand release of someone in her guild.

Which was why she needed to talk to Tak.

"Tell him I'd like to make a deal."

"THAT WAS WEIRD, RIGHT?" Shiv asked. "We've watched him make deals before, and it doesn't usually go like that."

"Fair lost his bob, that love has," Corianne agreed. "Never been another like that, sure."

Resmine stood in the Pit in the space her throne once stood with her lieutenants in their old seats on either side of her. The room looked larger without the massive chair, but it was still confined. Not enough space for the guild Resmine envisioned. With Tak gone, she felt more free to pace from the dais to the stairs and back. She could still feel the empty benches against the walls watching her, weighing her actions, judging. The meeting hadn't gone the way she'd anticipated. Yes, she'd gotten the information she wanted, but when it came to negotiating price—it seemed too cheap.

All Tak had said was, "Tell Estan I release him. Then our bargain will be complete."

It was a demon's bargain. But Resmine had made it. She knew Estan would do the same for her.

"So who is this Wenrir Esserton person we just bargained for?" Shiv folded his massive arms and leaned back, his blonde eyebrows drawing together in puzzlement.

"A man that tried very hard to become forgotten after surviving a deathblow from his protege," Resmine answered. "He was the King of Thieves once and, more importantly for our purposes, he built The Two Beams."

20

~Irrellian~

TRAVIN ESK, FORMER right hand to Irrellian's great dream, twitched in his sleep. Keeping the man confined to his dreams was barely worth the magic expended, but Irrellian wasn't ready to reveal himself to his wayward commander yet. Instead, he bent down and whispered in Travin's ear, "Remember me. Remember our vision. *Fear my coming.*"

A whimper escaped Travin's lips as the large man pulled his covers up like a child hiding from the creatures in the dark. Irrellian grinned. Soon. The walls of confidence Travin had erected in the twenty years of the Flayer Mage's absence were cracking under the pressure of constant surveillance and selective pruning of the man's underlings.

Every night, while Travin slept, Irrellian sent a Flayer or two to stand in Travin's office. Nothing was moved or shifted. But mortals always reacted to the presence of the demon-bound.

They had a bone-deep awareness that a predator was nearby.

And it was working.

Irrellian smiled as he stepped through the shadows and into the mountains below. The expression faded as he walked the shadow paths to his next destination.

It was imperative to increase his efforts in Gyth, Firinia, Verem, and Ethica. Those loyal to him in those countries were still building armies, but not all of the Eerilorian nobles he'd allowed to escape had joined in on the civil war. They'd sought shelter with neighbors, and if Irrellian neglected those countries entirely, his people might not build the kind of belief reserves he needed.

But first, he had an appointment to check on Hon'idar and the progress in Eerilor. Their rivals on that front were doing better than expected, capturing one of the prince's best tactical generals with only a handful of troops. Ut'evullen Dormidiir was regaining his confidence in the field. Sowing discord was all well and good, but Irrellian's plans worked better with an Eerilorian victory. Hon'idar had to win so he could die in front of his people when he refused to bend a knee. Ut'evullen wouldn't bow either, but the High Ones still had an eye on the younger prince. Irrellian couldn't touch him until the scales tipped further. That was the problem with *all* of these former avatars. Irrellian could still feel the presence of something holy within them. It wasn't enough for all of his divine enemies to still be within the mortal realm, but neither did he know who remained.

Fortiva might know.

Irrellian's hands twitched involuntarily. He didn't know where the elf was currently and that bothered him almost as much as the mystery of which High One he was playing Knives and Nobles against. Taunting Fortiva with the bond between Irrellian's demon half and Fortiva's daughter was entertaining, but the young woman wasn't his decades long rival. No one knew him as well as his enemy, and in a way, that made Fortiva the closest thing Irrellian had to a friend.

No one was ever closer to his thoughts than Fortiva, and no one's death would be sweeter when Arra finally burned.

STEPPING FROM THE SHADOW realms into the warmth of the Eerillorian palace, Irrellian took a moment to center himself. Even with as much power as Irrellian wielded, this palace was a lot to take in. Visually, the place was stunning—an orb of glittering midnight rock, surrounded by four towers of equally semi-precious materials. Every inch of the interior corridors was lit in such a way that those witnessing their surroundings were walking through galaxies rather than being made to feel they were underground or encased by rock. Accents of yellow goldstone only heightened the effect.

But there was more to it than visual appeal.

There were still traces of Arra's will bound into the stone, both here and in Taman—Eerilor's capital city—proper. Even though no dwarf had returned to the Stone in Irrellian's lifetime, Telgan Korsborn had witnessed many years of Taman's growth. The demon could even recognize certain voices within the spirits watching. Living Stone had no love for Flayers. They wanted to bar his entry, but they'd lost too much of themselves over the decades. It took a concentrated effort for the spirits to keep out the weakest of the demon-bound.

Irrellian was far too powerful for the guardian spirits.

He'd stepped out into an empty room to give himself time to adjust to the discomfort of a thousand whispers telling him to leave. Now it was time to find his princely playing piece.

Wrapping invisibility around himself like a mantle, Irrellian made his way through the halls, checking every one of Hon'idar's usual haunts. Despite the crown prince craving his mother's throne for so many years, he rarely sat in it. Generally, when Irrellian came to look in on the prince's efforts, Hon'idar was in the war room, his private combat room working on weapon forms, or the palace library.

Irrellian was mildly surprised to find Hon'idar and his personal guards standing over the spot where Captain Aldash had died during the Solstice. The prince's sandy brown mane was slightly unkempt, but more the neglect of a morning than several days, and his beard was similarly scruffy. His piercing eyes were focused on something Irrellian couldn't see.

Discarding the spell that hid him from view, Irrellian dropped both guards into a deep sleep. They would only rouse when and if he allowed it. Simply stepping from the shadows wasn't enough to intimidate some people, and though the Hon'idar of Winter's Solstice had been broken by fresh betrayal, Irrellian knew better than underestimate the prince and his people. Hon'idar had managed to curtail stories of Irrellian's arrival. The fresh waves of belief in the Flayer Mage were a trickle of what they ought to have been.

Solstice should've added so much more to his scales than it had.

"Master Thornne." The vaguest hint of surprise played over the prince's features as Hon'idar gave a bow only a noble trained from birth could. It was barely deferential, conveying that he was showing courtesy while also managing to deliver a hint of mockery. Not quite enough to demand correction, but Irrellian caught it. More accurately, Telgan caught it.

The demon was not in a mood to be trifled with. "*To all the hells with your schemes. Let us feast on his soul and drench the walls with his pulp. They'll believe in us well enough then.*"

"*Patience,*" Irrellian told his counterpart. "*This will all be worth it when we step into the heavens and return to your rightful seat.*"

Telgan wasn't appeased, but he stilled within Irrellian's soul. It was enough, for now. They shared a purpose. Sometimes that was all it took. Because Irrellian had taken the time to learn who the demon was and what he wanted.

But Hon'idar was not playing by the rules. He'd wanted a chance to claim power. Irrellian had given the prince his chance. Hon'idar requested troops. His ranks were swollen with Gray Army soldiers. The only thing Irrellian asked in return was to spread belief in the Flayer Mage. Fear, love, hatred, envy... The method didn't matter. As long as people were thinking about him.

"You've lost an important asset in your war," Irrellian said out loud. "Should I be concerned?"

"You killed a bigger asset. Why be concerned now?"

Irrellian considered the best way to answer Hon'idar. There was a flatness to the prince's tone, but also a touch of scorn.

It was time to remedy some misunderstandings the Crown Prince of Eerilor was struggling with.

The wall between Irrellian and Telgan was thin. Sometimes in order to maintain balance, Irrellian had to skew toward Telgan. Never enough to let the demon take over entirely, but this meeting merited a show of force.

"*Let us educate the prince on what it means to cross us.*"

He'd been looking forward to this.

Quicker than a firebolt, Irrellian had his long fingers wrapped around Hon'idar's thick throat and the warrior prince was pinned to the floor. Hon'idar squirmed and kicked impotently at Irrellian's chest, but he couldn't make contact with the Flayer Mage's body. The prince pulled a dagger out from a hidden sheath, but it was a sad sliver of unruned metal. Telgan liquified it with an unspoken spell, protecting his vessel. Molten steel splattered across the stone floor.

The demon was bleeding through and Irrellian drank in the power offered. It was like touching his home waters after decades on land.

"Don't think I can't succeed without you, princeling. You live because you're useful. I suffer your arrogance only so far, and my patience wears *thin*." Letting a flash of Telgan's rage sweep over his features, Irrellian kept his voice level until the very last word. He could almost taste the dwarf's blood on his tongue. "Unless you wish to be the example I make to your people, I would begin upholding the bargain we made."

Hon'idar struggled to speak, even within the iron vise of Irrellian's enhanced grip. "If you could do... without... me... I'd have died on... on the Solstice!"

Picking the prince up and slamming him down on the floor again, Irrellian wasn't at all careful or gentle. The Flayer Mage was not one to make idle threats. He would use the prince as an example to the rest of Eerilor now if Hon'idar didn't crack before his skull did.

"I can make your country the foundation on which my new world is built, or I can erase it as though it never was. Your petty squabble with your brother, the death of your mother, your family name, none of it matters," Irrellian said. Another slam and Hon'idar's head bounced. Blood matted the prince's regal locks, but he was still struggling against Irrellian's grip. One more bash against the stone and Hon'idar's struggles ceased, though the dwarf was still alive. He glared as Irrellian lowered his voice to little more than a whisper, "I will not give you this option again—fall into line or fall into ash. I can use you either way."

Releasing his grip on Hon'idar's neck, Irrellian waited for a response. A torque of bruises around the prince's throat made it hard for him to speak immediately. Between coughs and sputters, the reply was as deferential as Irrellian could've wished.

"What would you have me do, Master Thornne?"

Finally. It was time to make some progress.

21

~Genovar~

KHIRI SHOULD'VE ARRIVED in Jarelton by now, Genovar sighed, even though he knew in his heart it was a false thought. She would arrive too late. Too late for him, anyway. If he could just talk to her, explain that he hadn't wanted to disown her...

But why should she believe him? His motivations were driven by the future. A future no one else could see. Leyani loved him—trusted him—in a way that no one else ever had, but even she had been angry when he told her their daughter would ultimately pay for their happiness. Eventually, his lovely wife had forgiven him, something Genovar wasn't able to do. How could he? He still climbed through visions of what was coming, what Khiri was in the middle of... What he had done to her.

There were branches, always branches. If he moved here, maybe he could still change what he'd seen there. But no. There was only ever one path up. Ever since the Solstice, ever since he'd had to choose between the most people saved and his daughter's heart. He could no longer see past the next twig. And he knew what that meant.

With his hood up, Genovar moved through the shadows like a whisper. He'd seen Estan, the knight that had sought his help all those months ago, taken by a pack of Flayers. The young priestess—a daughter of a lost friend—had gotten away. This was all as it was supposed to be. A glimmer of recognition played at the edges of Genovar's memories when he'd seen the man directing the demon-bound. Something resonated there beyond the usual vision memories, but he couldn't place it.

Tracking Estan in ways only a seer could, Genovar had followed the Flayers here. Outside of a place called The Two Beams. This was where his branch of the future led. The only way through was forward.

Ullen would've told him to stop, that things weren't bound by the visions. But Genovar knew this was inevitable. This was the best thing for Arra. It's where that path had led him. Not that knowing made it any easier.

One deep breath.

And release.

Picking up a bucket filled with exhausted rune stones from a nearby porch, Genovar spun on his heel until he gained enough momentum and then released, launching the bucket through the largest tavern window. Steadying himself for only a second, Genovar leapt into the tavern with his knife drawn. Assassins and Flayers all seemed struck dumb at the sight of him, though the demons recovered in an instant. Ducking under one arm, dodging a claw, sinking his knife into unholy flesh, Genovar fought to take down as many as he could. It was a pointless battle. But Genovar refused to go down easily.

He was the General Fortiva and that position demanded respect.

Gutting a Flayer so its sizzling flesh scalded one of the assassins, Genovar leapt off the wall as an arrow passed through the space he'd occupied. His silver hair pulled free from his braid as he tore himself loose from another assassin's grasp. Landing a kick in a mottled face, Genovar catapulted off one Flayer and barrelled into another, knife first. No less than fifteen bodies, some already ash, littered the floor by the time the Venom Guild managed to subdue him.

He hoped his sacrifice was worth it.

22

~Khiri~

WHATEVER THE THING flying out the trees was, it shot past their contraption and repositioned itself higher in the sky. That brief fly-by settled Khiri's stomach like nothing else could've. The call to battle coursed through her veins. Even a beast from the hell realms wouldn't intimidate her into submission.

It was one of the ugliest things Khiri had ever seen. A bulbous head, like the cap of a mushroom, was balanced on the body of a horse. Thick, translucent skin barely kept the creature's insides, a bloody reddish black mess, hidden. Bats wings, impossibly long and fragile, erupted out of the creature's shoulders. The number of eyes varied, but all of them were a sickly glowing green. What should've been the mouth, the source of the shrieks, didn't seem to exist like a normal mouth. There were no lips and no tongue. Just teeth. Rows and rows of teeth. When the creature closed its maw, those teeth were still visible through the jelly skin, as were thin trails of red—as though it injured itself when it wasn't eating.

Before she had time to second-guess herself, Khiri was perched on the side of the basket with Micah in her grip. She locked one leg around one of the egg's support structures and hoped it was firm enough to take her weight. They'd been riding in the thing, but that was much different than hanging off on a single support branch. If it couldn't hold her, she'd find out in a hurry. She nocked two arrows at once and loosed them toward the on-coming abomination.

One bounced off the creature's thick, translucent hide. The other found purchase in the thinner wing membrane.

Another Arra-rending shriek pierced the sky, the egg itself shuddering as though hit. Khiri nearly lost balance.

Kal shot a bolt of flames at the thing, causing the egg to move back toward the wrong side of the trees. The creature didn't even dodge. It inhaled the fire as though feeding off of the magic. What flames it didn't suck in through its teeth washed over it, causing sickly green swirls to pulse through its body.

"I don't think that helped!" Khiri yelled.

"*Aim for the maw,*" Micah said. It seemed odd that he wasn't yelling, but Khiri shrugged it off. Mind-speak had never followed the same rules as normal speech. She wasn't sure why it should stand out now. Rather than argue, Khiri loosed another shot. Her aim was off though. The arrow bounced around on the thing's teeth before being crunched into nothing.

"If I'm going to get a clear shot, I'd need to be staring straight down its mouth," she said.

"You want to do what?!" Loni's eyes bulged as she whipped her gaze between the creature and Khiri. "Please! Let's just land! Maybe it'll leave us alone if we're on the ground!"

Kal shot several plumes of fire in a row, attempting to get the egg back on course for the road to Jarelton. Between the creature's wings interrupting the air flow and shrieks of the beast beating against them, they'd managed to start drifting sideways over the strange trees. The last thing any of them wanted was to draw out a second beast.

Jelly wraith, Khiri decided. It was as good a name as any. They didn't need to bring out any more jelly wraiths.

Khiri ignored Loni's pleas to get back in the center of the basket. Swinging Micah around her shoulder, Khiri tested the branch she'd wound her leg around. It would hold. She met Kal's eyes. There were plenty of words they both wanted to say—spirits willing, they'd get the chance—but all they had time for was a grim nod and a wry smile. Kal didn't approve. That was clear. But this wasn't about approval, it was about survival.

Hoisting herself up the support, Khiri climbed to the top of the egg and balanced on the wings. *Just like climbing a tree*, she told herself. Her stomach flipped a couple of times in disagreement, but she ignored it. Micah was in her hands again between one breath and the next, an arrow settled against the string.

The jelly wraith pivoted in the sky, Many glowing green eyes blazed with interest as it seemingly recognized an easy target. It bellowed one of its forceful, ear-shattering cries. A thin bubble of blue energy appeared around Khiri, dulling the attack before popping back out of existence.

Kal had just saved her life. Again.

Not wasting the opportunity the mage had given her, Khiri pulled Micah's string to her cheek and looked straight through the concentric circles of teeth. For a single moment, everything seemed to hang frozen in time—the beast, the floating egg, the bowstring taught against her fingers, the air in her lungs, the wind whipping through her hair, the hug of her armor, the awful brimstone odor wafting off the jelly wraith. Every smell and sensation was open to her and embedded itself in her mind. Later, Khiri would have time to unwrap this new sensation and what it meant.

She released her shot.

Then time tried to catch up with itself. Khiri's arrow found its mark in the back of the jelly wraith's throat just as Kal released another plume of fire to direct the egg. Reeling in pain, the jelly wraith jerked in the air and rolled, one of its massive wings and part of its back colliding with the bottom basket. Crunching branches and cracking bone carried over the roaring in Khiri's ears as she lost her footing. She fell off the crafted wings and for several terrible steps was running along the back of the jelly wraith. Leaping back toward the egg, Khiri barely managed to catch the bottom of the mostly broken basket.

She watched as the beast continued to wheel and tumble its way out of the sky. It fell back into the trees. The collision had spun what was left of the basket toward Jarelton. One solitary bit of good news. Loni was sobbing somewhere above Khiri, but there was an ominous silence where Kal should've been. A thickness in Khiri's throat made it all but impossible to speak, but she had to say something. She had to know for sure. "Kal?"

Loni's face appeared over the edge. "Khiri? You're alive?"

"Kal?" Khiri called again.

Khiri... If she hadn't seen it spelled out on Loni's face, Micah's tone told her everything. *I'm sorry. He... Kal didn't make it.*

IT HAD TAKEN AGES TO climb up into the wrecked basket with Loni. Kal's limp form was still there, impaled on the splintered branch Khiri had used during the battle with the jelly wraith. His staff—inherited from Maleck Dorell, a mage friend of Khiri's father that she'd initially sought to help her bring her magic under control—was stabbed through the opposite side of the egg, inert. When Micah had told her of Kal's death, she hadn't believed him. Not really.

She hadn't wanted to.

Seeing Kal's body, it still didn't seem real. This couldn't be happening. If she just tried hard enough, she would wake up and he'd be watching her with those golden owl eyes. He'd smile and call her *laska*. When she got some stupid, outlandish idea, he'd be there to help her make it work. It *always* worked! Because he was there. Kal was always there.

Outside of Micah, she'd rarely trusted someone so implicitly. Even when he'd been a captured assassin, Khiri had been more comfortable around him than Estan.

Warmth radiated off of Micah's bow. It almost felt like her brother was there, physically hugging her. *"I didn't know you could do that."*

"Neither did I. But I told you when I chose this form that you'd never be alone," Micah said.

Loni was still sniffling, though it was obvious she was trying her hardest not to interrupt Khiri's grief. It was Loni's presence more than anything that informed Khiri this moment was real. If this had been a dream, Khiri would've had the basket to herself, or Ullen may have mysteriously appeared and told her where to go next. Or a talking squirrel may have grown out of her foot and thrown raisins that became boulders as they fell. But Loni was too much a stranger to feature in Khiri's dreams very often and too much a companion to be truly unusual.

As awful and selfish as it was, Khiri couldn't help wishing the roles had been reversed. Guilt washed over her for just thinking such a thing. It was undeserved. Loni had been a decent traveling companion and taken her turns at the cook fire without complaint. She'd been friendly and conversational, but not intrusive. While the woman wasn't much of a fighter, she'd even volunteered to take watches before Kal demonstrated his wards.

Memories of Kal's protective spells and warming domes released a whole slew of emotions Khiri wasn't prepared for. She was bawling by the time the basket touched down on the surface of Arra once more. Even then, she didn't stir. Leaving the egg meant leaving Kal behind. It was too much. Too soon. How was she supposed to face a world where her best friend was only in her memories? She'd gone through it once before, when Micah died, and it had nearly broken her. But he'd become Lifewood. Even if, initially, they hadn't been able to speak, Khiri knew he was still there, guiding her shots and watching over her in the way of their people.

A gentle hand placed on her shoulder brought Khiri out of her own head.

"Do you know how he'd have wanted to be laid to rest?" Loni asked. "We should see to him before nightfall."

"We never really got around to talking about that," Khiri admitted. "His father was Odlesk, but I don't know if his people return to the water the way my kind return to the wood. I guess if they did, he'd have done it by now..."

Standing, Khiri took in their surroundings. The basket had landed well away from the actual road in a field that was still dusted with snow. There was an old sentinel oak looking over the grassy field like a grumpy elder that couldn't be bothered with the young orchard that grew on the far edge of the clearing. These were nothing like the unworldly trees they'd flown over, still looming in their valley, but the flying contraption had carried Khiri and Loni over half the remaining distance toward the vast walls of Jarelton. Although battling the jelly wraith and losing Kal had taken hours and days of mental and emotional fatigue, according to the sun, it was barely even midday.

It took a strength Khiri didn't know she possessed to walk up to Kal's lanky form and press a hand against his chest. Pulling him off the basket seemed impossible and she really didn't want to do it, but neither did she want to leave him untended and forgotten like someone's refuse on the side of the road. She held her breath, waiting for some response to her touch. Some twitch or gasp. A silvery hand on her hand. Anything. But there were flecks of dried blood on his lips and his eyes didn't blink to sudden awareness.

Kal really was gone.

She already knew that, of course. But each step of the way, it was like she learned it all over again.

"We might be able to use the flying basket as kindling," Loni suggested. "For his fire?"

Khiri took hold of Kal's arms and jerked several times before the mage came off of the broken support. She dodged as he fell unceremoniously onto the floor of the egg. Memories of helping him out of Rigger's barrel walker when they'd broken out of an Eerilorian jail intruded on her present. Later, when she tried to sleep, she could let all the memories play out. Before that, she needed to focus. It was up to her to get Loni and herself to Jarelton where there were friends and safety. Then she needed to get herself back to the Life Trees. More than ever, all Khiri wanted was to talk to her mother.

Loni worked the staff out of its hole in the side of the egg. She handed it to Khiri. As soon as the wood touched her skin, Khiri saw more branches and paths in her magic than ever before. Arcane words and pieces of spells she'd never even imagined tried to ram themselves into her mind. It was a barrage of nonsense and smoke. If she had more training, perhaps it would translate into power that she could wield. But she wasn't Kal. Her friend had been teaching her small ways to manage her gift. This staff was too much.

"We may not want to be in here when I try this," Khiri said. She waited for Loni to exit the remains of the egg and then knelt to kiss Kal's forehead. Then she straightened and followed the former barmaid. Drawing up the single fire spell she knew, Khiri channeled it through the staff. Flames erupted from a point beyond the staff's end, so blue it was almost black.

But it caught hold of the basket and its occupant, becoming the orange cheery hue that Khiri had grown used to during their innumerable campfires. Sparks of pink, green, and purple popped where the growing flames consumed the runes that contained all of the magic Kal had fed into the craft over the previous days. Khiri stopped feeding the fire with more power and rested the staff on the ground as she watched the egg collapse.

The conversation by the fire returned to her. Kal had wanted her to take it. Did he know this was going to happen? He'd been avatar to Shydan. Anger surged through Khiri. She couldn't stand the thought of moving forward with this staff, even if Kal had practically begged her to take it. She hated the very sight of the thing.

After a moment's hesitation, she tossed the staff on the pyre as well. It wasn't hers. It was his. "Spirits guide your dreams, Kal."

An explosion of magic and color forced the two women to jump even farther away from the pyre as the staff caught. A part of Khiri wished to rush forward and rescue it from the fire she'd plunged it into, but it was already too late. There was no way to undo what she'd already done.

Without asking if Khiri wanted or needed it, Loni opened her arms in invitation for a hug. Khiri nodded and buried her face in Loni's collarbone, letting herself pretend that Loni's arms were actually those of Leyani Fortiva. Then she pulled free and watched as the fire took her friend.

Eventually the blazing heat ebbed into a pile of smoking coals. Micah sent another wave of his own hug-warmth through Khiri's body. She reached back and squeezed his grip. It was time to continue toward the city.

23

~Estan~

WITH HIS WRISTS BOUND to his ankles and positioned so he was kneeling in a barred cage, Estan was well and truly trapped. Despite his time spent with the Thieves' Guild, he hadn't taken to keeping a hidden set of knives or lockpicks somewhere on his person. He didn't have any stashed runes or clever tricks. All he had was an endless supply of faith in his friends. Dewin, Resmine, Tak, and Catapult would find a way to free him. And Corianne... Corianne would make sure they never took him again. While Resmine was the new head of the guild, his bond-sister wasn't as ruthless as Corianne could be.

Estan had seen it in Corianne, in a way he'd never let himself recognize in Ysinda. But he'd been using Ysinda as a stand-in for his lost Loni. He'd wanted Ysinda to be gentle and sweet, because Loni had been gentle and sweet. Corianne had only ever been Corianne to him. And he loved her for it. No. That wasn't quite right... He loved her.

All those times he'd promised himself to think about it later, later had finally caught up with him. Estan loved the way Corianne called him out, the way she flicked her wrist and grinned when she was about to blow something up, the manic gleam in her eye when she was about to do something dangerous, her stern face when things were about to get serious. The heat between them during the raid on the kidnapping warehouse hadn't been a fluke. It had been simmering under the surface the first time he saw her. Back then, he'd still been too stuck on the rights and wrongs of the world to let himself admit his attraction to the morally gray thief who'd told him she had been planning to rob him during their first encounter. Even if she'd ended up guarding his kit instead.

Things had changed.

He had changed.

Estan still saw himself as a devout follower of Taymahr and was as much Her knight as ever, but he no longer thought of himself as a step above the common masses. He'd adopted too strongly the teachings of a corrupt temple. It had taken more time than he cared to admit to shake it off. Traveling across Mytana three times, being taken in by thieves when no one else would have him, and even dying once. He'd lived more during this year, seen more combat than even the front lines had shown him, and learned so much. If he managed to see the outside of this prison, Estan promised himself he'd actually tell Corianne about his feelings.

Whether she'd have him or not was another matter.

Remembering the kiss he'd forced on Khiri, Estan's ears burned with shame. She'd told him repeatedly about her soulmate situation and he hadn't wanted to hear it. Hadn't even attempted to understand.

How could she not want a Knight of the Protective Hand? Didn't she know he deserved her affection? Those old thoughts haunted him now.

Love wasn't a thing he could earn or deserve. No one could plan it. It happened occasionally. And if two people were fortunate enough to feel it together, that was such a beautiful thing. Watching Resmine and Dewin had taught Estan a lot about how precious and rare those feelings were. Tak, when he thought no one was watching, would pull out a small portrait of his husband and a soft smile would cross the trader's otherwise inscrutable face. Even the softer, paternal bond between Khiri and Ullen, or his own brotherly feelings toward Resmine and—more recently—Dewin. Love was such a tender, gradual thing, it was shocking how sharply and deeply it could cut.

Shaking his head, Estan tried to pull back his wandering thoughts. He should be coming up with a plan. If he could get himself free, no one else would have to risk themselves on his account.

Despite having already scoured his cage for some sign of a serrated edge he could use to saw his ropes, Estan turned his gaze to the rest of the room.

The secondary cage still puzzled him. Arad Rhidel hadn't seemed to anticipate capturing two people, so why were two cages prepared in this room? Perhaps the Venom Guild kept a few rooms with cages and Estan was reading too much into being placed next to an extra one. Or maybe it was meant for Resmine. But if Arad's end goal was to see Resmine dead and take over the Thieves' Guild, why capture her? Something was off, but Estan pushed the quandary aside and continued taking an inventory of his cell.

Nothing really leapt out though. Bare, gray stone walls met the bare, gray stone, scuffed-up floor. Wooden panels made up the ceiling. A window was cut into the wall behind him, but it was boarded up from the outside. An iron, oil lamp chandelier anchored to the ceiling was his only source of light. Why bother to provide light for their prisoner? It seemed a needless expense. It did nothing to help him tell time either. Estan guessed he'd been in this cage for hours, but there was no real way to measure.

While Estan was trying to puzzle it out, he heard steps approaching the door to his cell. Perhaps Arad had finally come to interview his prisoner. Estan was waiting for the assassin leader to come and question him—if not about Resmine's guild, then surely the man had questions about how Estan had survived his assassination. Not many people could come back from being stabbed through the heart. The footsteps got louder as they approached. Estan threw out the notion it would be Arad at all. No one in charge of a guild of hired killers would tromp that loudly.

Before Estan could entertain thoughts of rescue, the door to his cell swung out and a man nearly the size of Shiv thudded his way over to the other cage. Estan began to take a warrior's measure of this newcomer, but all thoughts of build, stance, or features immediately fled his mind when Estan caught sight of the large man's prisoner.

Genovar Fortiva was bound and unconscious. Blood seeped from several wounds, and heavy bruising was visible around his tattooed eye. Estan jerked against his ropes as Genovar was unceremoniously dropped into the empty cage like a sack of potatoes. Every corner of Estan's being screamed to help the Hero of the Burning Valley.

The big man, still just a walking pile of burlap in Estan's mind, chuckled grimly at the futile gesture. "Don't like the way I'm treating the meat?"

Estan didn't bother to respond. He hoped the Venom Guild had no idea who Genovar was. They had to be ignorant. Otherwise trying to hold the greatest general in Arra was pure folly.

What was Genovar even doing here? Had he come for Estan?

It made no sense.

But then, Estan wasn't the best at seeing bigger picture strategies or tactics. There were so many factors he couldn't keep in order. The Flayers had sunk through the shadows with him in a street and Jarelton. It was possible that, despite the stonework of the cell, he wasn't in Jarelton. Or Genovar had been captured elsewhere and brought here. Perhaps Genovar hadn't been captured alone, and there were others somewhere. Perhaps Genovar had been the only survivor.

Burlap locked the cage and lumbered back out, slamming the door behind him. Estan tried to pry his eyes away from the roughly breathing lump that was Irrellian Thornne's greatest enemy. A glimpse at what lay beyond the door could be helpful later. But it was fruitless. Much like Burlap, Estan's eyes refused to grasp any details beyond the injured Genovar. It was like what he saw there was so unreal and unnatural that reality twisted around him.

Blessed Taymahr, what am I supposed to do?

While Estan had been alone, he was happy to wait for rescue. His divine healing was still functioning, wicking the pain of his bonds and kneeling position away before he could feel them. Maybe another stab to the chest would prove too much, but he stood a better chance than anyone else of surviving incarceration by the Venom Guild.

But now that there was someone in here with him—Estan's childhood hero and Khiri's father no less—the equation changed. Somehow, he had to find a way out.

Arra needed Genovar. There had to be a way out.

HOURS PASSED. FOOD was brought in by a smallish figure in a voluminous hooded robe. Estan tried to make up for his lack of vigilance with Burlap, but it was useless. Aside from the impression of someone short and waifish, even their hands were hidden with woven wool gloves—the kind available at any farmer's stall in or out of the city. When Estan escaped, he wouldn't be bringing a lot of information about their adversaries back with him.

Listening to Genovar's unsteady breath was a new and unpleasant way to mark the time. Someone or something had definitely damaged the general's chest. A broken or bruised rib, or perhaps an injured collarbone. Estan didn't think a lung had been punctured. Aside from being too horrible to contemplate, Genovar's breathing didn't sound wet or rattling. Merely unsteady. Painful, but not enough to kill him.

The petite hooded figure brought food again, this time also carrying a water bucket. Estan hadn't eaten his previous hunk of bread. A dipper of water was waved at his face. Begrudgingly, Estan drank.

"I could manage much better if I wasn't trussed up like a hog," he grumbled.

A shrug and then the figure bent to wave the dipper at Genovar. The elf let out a shuddering cough, then opened his eyes. "Please," he said. "I can't at this angle."

Tilting their hood one way and then the other, the figure hesitated before drawing the dipper back and moving to the far side of the bars. Estan couldn't see what they did, but Genovar was upright only a few moments later and receiving a fresh dipper of water. Genovar thanked the figure for their help. They shrugged again and left the cell, barely cracking the door enough to take the bucket out.

Estan tried to think of something witty to break the silence that fell between him and the visibly uncomfortable Genovar, but everything felt trite and inconsequential given the enormity of what lay before them. Ullen or Dewin would've known what to say, but Estan only had himself. "I promise, I'll do everything in my power to get you out of here."

He wasn't expecting the rough chuckle Genovar gave him. "I wouldn't count on it. My fate was set long, long before we arrived here."

Countless protests threatened to overwhelm Estan's tongue. What about Genovar's duty? What about his position? What about the people counting on him? What about his daughter? How could this legendary person be sitting next to Estan in a ramshackle cell—not even a proper prison—and sound so defeated? Legends didn't give up. It didn't make sense.

Genovar's hands were bound behind him in the same fashion as Estan's. Despite the difficulty and discomfort of his injuries, the elf bent himself to nibble at the bread left in the corner of his cage. Estan wished he could free himself. Even a few moments to ease Genovar's struggles by lifting the bread to the general's mouth.

"...*What would you give?*"

That voice had been directly in Estan's head, and it definitely hadn't belonged to Taymahr. Genovar was still eating, oblivious to the alarm ringing through Estan.

"*You have a wish, yes? I can grant a wish...*"

As the voice spoke, Estan saw a ring of glyphs glow red around the base of the cell's chandelier. What he'd originally taken for an ordinary circle of iron seemed to be engraved with sigils of the hells. While it was possible to make a deal with a demon anywhere in Arra if the will was strong enough, someone had created a weakness in between the realms in this room. Any wish might reach the other side.

Estan finally saw the trap he'd been set in. A few days without decent meals, a lack of freedom, watching someone else suffer... How many could resist the lure of having their wishes granted in a room like this?

"They mean to make us into Flayers," Estan said.

Genovar sat back, giving up on what was left of his meager dinner. He heaved a sigh holding so many emotions, it took Estan some time to separate and recognize them.

Concern. Surrender. Longing. Fatigue. Regret.

Hate.

Love.

Fear.

"I know."

24

~Ullen~

"WHAT IS THE MEANING of this?!" Ullen demanded. He was more careful with his cadence and pronunciation than he'd been in fifty years. It was more important for him to sound regal now than it ever had been before. Lives hung in the balance.

Jaspar's life hung in the balance.

Nearly half of the troops still in residence were gathered around what had come to be something of a village square or common yard between the manor and the army encampment. Dirty snow melted into what small clumps of grass remained after so many feet had scuffled and stomped through on a thousand different errands.

It was an inauspicious stage for this drama.

In the center of the mud and grass, the two women were being restrained by four guards. These guards were not people loyal to Ullen. His heart hammered at the sight of Jaspar's curls lowered over her face. Even through the curtain of tresses, it was obvious she was bleeding from the forehead. Her face was rigid with barely contained fury. General Tericia Geryan's eyes were closed and her lips compressed, as though she was tired of all the pageantry and wished for things to be over with. Neither of them answered Ullen's query, but it seemed likely they'd been threatened by their captors.

Sir Quinton Ilyani loomed forth, stalking to the center of the square as though Ullen's shout had been an introduction to his part in this macabre play. Not all the regal tone in Arra had the weight to dampen the gleam in Sir Ilyani's eyes. The Knight of the Protective Hand wasn't actually holding the two women down himself, but he had the look of someone eager to see an execution, and the guards he'd tasked with holding his prisoners seemed equally pleased with the idea. If Ullen had any doubts his old friend was gone, the bloodlust emanating from Quinton was enough to douse them.

"I caught a traitor trying to return our prisoner to the horde!" Quinton's ruddy complexion was nearly purple against his washed out hair. He was fully armored and, though sheathed, his sword was in his hands rather than belted at his waist. The winter sun gleamed off Taymahr's shining plate in a thousand flashes. Quinton appeared as a holy knight returning from a victorious crusade. Drawing his sword out and flinging the sheath to the ground, Quinton started toward Jaspar rather than the captured general. "And I'm about to make an example!"

"HOLD!"

Ullen put all the force behind the word he could. There was no chance of putting himself between Quinton's blade and its intended mark, so he had to trust in Quinton's adherence to the chain of command, as rusty and weak as those links were between them.

And it worked.

The knight was practically vibrating with tension, but he stopped. His sword was still raised and hovering over Jaspar in a way that made Ullen's toes curl in dread, but there was a chance here to solve more than one problem. A slim, frail, whisper of a chance. But it was more than Ullen had possessed when he'd arrived.

"Since when do we execute our own people without so much as a trial?" Ullen asked.

Hushed voices echoed Ullen's words. Some were grumbling but a good portion of those gathered agreed with the prince. *If I can win the crowd...*

"Why is a traitor caught in the act worth listening to?" Quinton demanded. "We caught her freeing your pet general. Has love made your heart soft? Some of us remember this woman was betrothed to your brother not a full season gone."

Small smatterings of anger seethed through the crowd, but there were less than Ullen feared. Convincing Quinton might be beyond his skill, but swaying a crowd—there was an art to that.

"The first time you said, 'I caught her,' but now it's 'we' is it? This is a war for Eerilor's very soul, Sir Ilyani. I'd like it not to begin by needlessly slaughtering the daughter of our host." Ullen's time as a bard allowed him to sound as though he was speaking softly, but project enough that everyone gathered could hear. Murmurs of agreement and realization tumbled from dozens of lips.

Quinton had erred. He'd forgotten Jaspar wasn't only important to Ullen.

Earl Tolen Terilles seemingly materialized in the front row of those gathered. "Please, Sir Ilyani... Do explain to me how a ranked noblewoman of Eerilor and my own daughter deserves less than a fair hearing." The ice in Earl Terilles's tone rivaled the winter breeze for dominance, dropping the temperature of the war camp below what fur-lined cloaks and boots could keep at bay. Irrellian Thornne and the High Gods all might've balked at crossing the earl had he turned his current expression on them.

Slowly, Quinton lowered his blade to his side and straightened his spine. If he hadn't flung his sheath down, he could've hidden his sword from the sun's judgment, but it stayed naked in the knight's hand. "I concede that a trial may shed new light on the situation. I may have erred in my haste to see justice done to one that has betrayed our righteous cause. Let us perform the trial as soon as possible, though. I hate to leave a snake alive this close to a chicken coop."

The way Quinton eyed Ullen, there were no doubts whom the knight thought was at the most risk. Not for the first time, Ullen mourned for the friend he'd known twenty years ago. This version of Quinton was so quick to violence and anger, it was almost as though an entirely different man wore his skin.

As Jaspar and General Geryan were escorted to the cells to await trial later that evening, a sigh escaped Ullen's lips. It was less than the whole mess deserved, but it was all Ullen could allow himself. There were soldiers watching. Wherever their current loyalties, none of them would respect a prince who broke into tears over a possible traitor.

Ullen hadn't missed this aspect of being royal during his time away. His foundations could be shaken, his world ripped asunder, and his heart incinerated to a lump of ash—but he couldn't let it show. There was no telling how those emotions could be weaponized.

Quinton's expression from across the courtyard underscored the importance of an emotional mask. Sir Ilyani would doubtless attempt to skew the facts, to push Ullen into making any mistake he could. The knight was out to rip control of this army away from Eerilor and put it firmly in his own unyielding hands. If Ullen allowed that to happen, his people would suffer.

Khiri, Kal... I could really use your help now, my friends...

It did no good to stand around wishing for people that were elsewhere in Arra. More recently, Jaspar would've been the person Ullen turned to for counsel about this mess. That also wasn't something he could risk right now.

Oddly, the question that ran through his mind was not what Genovar would do, but what would Estan do? Who would the younger Knight of the Protective Hand turn to if this happened to him? But, it had happened to Estan... Those he'd trusted had turned out to be untrustworthy and Estan had put his faith in a hero from a war he was too young to recall.

Estan hadn't known where to turn, but he'd turned anyway.

He'd *trusted* anyway.

Maybe it was time for Ullen to start trusting.

"I HOPE YOU KNOW WHAT you're doing, sire." Earl Terilles kept his voice low as nobles, soldiers, and those servants and civilians that could be spared from their duties filtered into the seating now arranged in the square.

Ullen had left the staging arrangements in the hands of the earl's steward. Large, unadorned rugs kept the worst of the mud off the benches—some of which were richly varnished as ballroom seating and some were the unfinished mess tent furnishings that would later be returned for the army's use. They all faced the center of the square where a small, portable stage—likely used for summer plays—had been placed. It was barely four steps high, but it was tall enough to ensure all those gathered could see and wide enough to accommodate maybe twenty people. A podium was set on one side with a stool behind it, waiting for its judge.

"That makes two of us, my lord," Ullen said. Though his voice was grave, he kept his face as neutral as he could. Standing on this stage, overlooking his people, Ullen's shoulders strained against the weight of the morning. It had taken all of the hours up to this trial to hammer things out with individual parties and everything still depended on how this trial went.

If Jaspar really had been guilty of trying to desert with General Geryan in tow, all of Ullen's efforts would not only have been in vain, but his bid for the throne would become that much harder. His allies wouldn't endorse a fool.

And he had been foolish. In an effort to keep himself safe, to appear princely, and to ease into his role as eventual king, Ullen had been keeping himself apart from his advisors. It wasn't until Jaspar was taken from his side that Ullen realized how little he'd allowed those fighting for him to support him. They'd backed him until now as the lesser of two evils. Better the runaway prince than a prince supported by the Gray Army. Better still would be a ruler that listened to those they led.

Ullen was listening now. He'd spent the last several hours proving it.

Quinton had spent those hours sequestered in his quarters with a handful of his most trusted officials. Even if this trial went well for Ullen, he had a feeling Quinton and his allies were going to make as much trouble as they could in the aftermath. Undoubtedly, the knight would make trouble during the trial itself. But Ullen and his allies were as prepared for trouble as they could be.

General Geryan and Jaspar were brought into the square. They were being handled more gently this time, both cuffed with their arms in front of their bodies. Someone had bandaged Jaspar's cut forehead. Ullen wished he'd been able to see to it himself, but the circumstances of her arrest still kept him from closing the distance between them.

He saw the understanding in Jaspar's violet eyes. A bit of pride, even. She'd wanted him to take up this mantle. He begged Tharothet this wouldn't be the last time he saw her. Looking over the crowd, Ullen caught sight of Rigger and Vess working their way toward the dais. Vess's rank, along with most recognizing Rigger as the Barrel Walker's inventor, ensured them easy passage through the rows.

"So, Prince Dormidiir," Quinton's voice rang through the courtyard as the knight emerged from the rows of tents. "Are you prepared to see this farce of a trial through?"

"Farce, Sir Ilyani? This trial is a matter of justice. The farce was your earlier performance."

"How is watching you pass no judgment on your pet and your future princess any different?" Quinton leveled a vicious smile at Ullen, as though he'd already struck a blow to the proceedings.

"I agree. That would've appeared less than just. Which is why I've asked one of our other generals to oversee this trial. Master Lorrei, if you'd be so kind—" Ullen offered a hand to Vess as she approached the stairs.

"She's as suspect as you are!" Quinton protested. "She... She's..."

Vess didn't bother to take Ullen's hand or look at the knight as she walked up the steps of the platform and over to the podium. "What am I, Quinton? Aside from someone who fought side-by-side with both of you against Irrellian Thornne the first time and was deemed worthy enough to serve as avatar for Shydan for a time. I've stayed well out of your feud thus far and my first allegiance is always going to be to the High Ones. If you'd like my attention to swing from my creations and onto dealing with whatever wrongs you feel I've committed, tell me what they are. Otherwise, allow me to hear both sides of this mess and get back to more important matters."

The look on Quinton's face was far from defeated, but he gestured toward the podium as though to say—*By all means, proceed.*

The master engineer hadn't broken her stride. Settling her ever-present apron over her brown trouser legs like a skirt, Vess appeared more like she was about to conduct a class than oversee a trial. None present doubted her authority to do either, which was the important part.

"I request the guards that captured my daughter be held within the house until the prisoners' statements are heard," Earl Terilles said. "I'd rather they not be allowed to tailor their stories to match whatever might be said here."

"It is a reasonable request," Vess said. "Those of you that were involved in the incident, please recuse yourselves. Anyone that intends to witness against the prisoners and remains, your voice will not be heard. Maleck?"

Maleck Dorell, seated in the front row on the opposite side of the stage from Quinton, nodded. The mage raised his staff and a tracing of indigo encircled the platform. "None shall be heard that aren't playing by the rules," Maleck said.

Ullen had considered asking Maleck to oversee the trial, as he was also someone who'd been present in the first battle against the Flayer Mage. His hybrid nature would've prevented most small-minded arguments about his loyalties being biased toward dwarves or humans; however, Maleck hadn't been an avatar and Quinton didn't hold the mage in the same esteem as the others. As powerful as Maleck's magic was—strong enough to match Irrellian Thornne—the mage was no leader. He was Genovar's shadow, an affable friend of the group, or missing entirely. Even now, with the seriousness of the proceedings and Quinton's dangerous scowl on him, Maleck grinned as though he were watching a play in which he'd been asked to participate. Ullen knew better than to believe Maleck was as simple as he sometimes pretended, but the mage's unknown agenda made counting on him as an ally unreliable. Genovar usually had the best luck wrangling the mage.

And if Genovar were here, Quinton wouldn't be as dangerous as he's become.

"First, I will hear Lady Jaspar Terilles. Allow her to step up and tell her tale," Vess commanded.

One the guards on Jaspar escorted her up the stairs and stood at a respectful distance as she made her way to the center of the dais. Despite the bindings, Jaspar held herself with all the dignity of her station. Her armor had been stripped and her clothing was smeared with dirt and blood, but she couldn't have been more poised in a ballgown and jewels.

Heart in his throat, Ullen waited for an explanation. What could've possibly led from their conversation about the future to her releasing a hostage and getting imprisoned?

"Prince Ut'evullen Dormidiir has charged me with the guard rotations concerning our prisoner," Jaspar said. "It's a responsibility I've taken great care with as certain parties have made it clear they'd rather we never took prisoners. I was checking the rotations this morning when I discovered that one of my soldiers was in the infirmary rather than at his station. He told me he'd reported to the lieutenant on duty. Despite the directives set in place regarding the prisoner, the lieutenant's captain either hadn't heard anything about it or hadn't seen fit to report it to me personally. I ran to check on the prisoner because something was definitely amiss with this morning's schedule. As soon as I entered, I discovered the remaining guard actually on the schedule had allowed two unsanctioned soldiers into the cell. They were jeering at the prisoner, but it didn't seem any violence had yet occurred. I asked them what they thought they were doing. I got no answer. They turned and called me the Prince's Lapdog among other names that I don't care to repeat. I reminded them of my rank and theirs and told them to step out of the cell. I thought they would comply, but three more uncleared soldiers appeared with weapons drawn. I recognized the situation as untenable. My first duty was to make sure the prisoner was safe, so I withdrew a confusion rune that I keep stashed on my person at all times and activated it. The soldiers all captured each other, convinced they were either laying hands on me or the prisoner. I did remove General Geryan from her cell at this point. I was escorting her to a holding room within my father's house where she would be safe until the prison was once more under our control."

With a theatrical scoff, Quinton stood from his bench. "You would have us believe that six soldiers of our army would be so derelict of duty that they'd openly mock a superior officer?"

Jaspar didn't bother to respond to Quinton's outburst. She examined the knight's smug features with all the interest of someone contemplating whether it was worth it to step on a stink bug.

"Enough, Quinton," Vess said. "You've agreed to this trial. You've acquiesced to my authority to judge. If you can't contain yourself and refrain from these outbursts, I'll have Maleck extend the silence to the whole courtyard. The guards in question will have their own turn."

Sneering, Quinton turned from the stage. While Ullen couldn't see what the knight did, if he gestured or signaled, there was some activity in the back of the crowd. Movement as people shifted and whispered amongst themselves. Grim faces. Not everyone was pleased with the story thus far. Not a surprise, but worth noting.

"While I had the general in my custody, more guards in the company of Sir Ilyani happened upon us. Rather than requesting an explanation or pursuing any rational discourse, he immediately told his escort to seize me and the prisoner under my care. We were both beaten and cuffed and dragged toward the courtyard where Sir Ilyani assured me we would be executed for our alleged crimes."

"Alleg—" Quinton began to roar when Vess nodded to Maleck. The indigo ring expanded over the entire courtyard. Sir Ilyani's ruddy face went violently puce as turned to face Jaspar and then Vess. He was not at all happy about being silenced, even though he'd been warned about his interjections. It was clear he'd considered himself above the authority of the convened court. He'd likely only agreed to the trial because he'd imagined inciting a mob against Ullen.

The realization snapped something inside of Ullen's chest—a frayed thread of trust and friendship he'd thought still bound him to the knight. He thought there was nothing left between them after that morning. Something had remained though, hidden under a blanket of fond memories. Everything from their first meeting to their last shared pint in Illesdale. Those memories were now burning, leaving the taste of ash in Ullen's throat.

General Geryan took the stage next. Her story matched up with Jaspar's accounting. The original guard showed up alone and she'd recognized something was amiss. When the next group arrived and were allowed into her cell, she'd given herself up as lost. Jaspar's arrival hadn't phased the gathering hostility in the least. "It had all the appearances of an ambush," the general said. "The way their attention shifted when she entered, it appeared they'd been waiting for her. I was an afterthought."

After Jaspar and the general had gotten their say, the guards that had chosen to wait in the house were escorted back to the stage one at a time. Jaspar's infirmary guard told the crowd how he'd felt fine until he and his counterpart grabbed food before their shift. He had gotten up at one point, leaving his meal unattended and it had tasted a bit off on his return, though he'd believed it nothing worse than a bad potato at the time. The remaining guard scheduled for the shift said the others had just shown up and the cell had remained closed until Jaspar knocked them all out. The next two agreed with the guard that had been assigned to the prison: they had just come in to check on things after hearing their fellow soldier had taken ill.

But when the first of the three to come in after Jaspar's arrival took to the stage, it was different. This soldier was younger than the others and flinched when they saw Quinton in the crowd. "Please, I'd rather not testify. I didn't want to be there in the first place."

"It's alright," Vess said. "We won't let any harm come to you from this. We just need to know what happened."

"I didn't know it was gonna be Lady Jaspar, I swear I didn't. We were just supposed to put the fear of the High Ones in someone Sir Ilyani said was overstepping. He wanted her scared, he said. We were supposed to lock whoever it was in with the prisoner. No one was supposed to die. I didn't sign up to get anyone killed! Not in our own camp! And certainly not Lady Jaspar! She's one of the better ones—always making sure we've got enough blankets, or the lye's softened, or water's warmed for the bath house. I've seen her making the rounds. She ain't one to overstep anything!"

Quicker than a flash of lightning, Quinton lunged onto the stage with his weapon drawn. The young guard shrieked and scrambled back. Ullen tried to rush up the steps but Quinton's guards that had given their stories already blocked his approach. The knight's mouth moved silently as he tried to spit condemnations at the focus of his current ire. Lifting his sword above his head, he brought it down.

Instead of blood splattering the platform, sparks flashed as Quinton's sword bounced off the reinforced chains of General Geryan's cuffs. Before he could recover for a second swing, Jaspar jumped forward and landed both feet in the center of the big man's chest. Already off-balance, the knight fell backwards, rolling off the stage entirely.

Soldiers loyal to Ullen swarmed toward the stage and seized the guards that stood between the prince and the conflict. With a nod from Vess, Maleck released the silencing spell and bound Quinton within an orange cage of fire. "You can't do this to me! I'm no Eerilorian, bound to obey that weak-willed excuse for a prince!"

It cut to the quick, hearing his former friend slavering and foaming for his blood. "Aye, you aren't Eerilorian. You care nothing for my people, nor anything past killing those that could potentially be aligned with the Flayer Mage."

"Your people chose to follow Irrellian's agent. They deserve death," Quinton spat. "And so do you, you half-hearted git. A true believer would raze the entire country and start over! Better to burn the innocent than leave the rats in the barn."

If Ullen had any remaining qualms about what had to be done, they were lost in the storm of emotion that followed his former-friend's speech. "Razing everything to start over is what we fight against. You were not Eerilorian, but you were oath-bound to our cause. I declare you an oath-breaker, with all the penalties that implies. Those loyal to you will be banished from the borders of Eerilor. They will be made to leave camp at dawn. You, Sir Ilyani, are to be executed."

"And how long will it take for you to find someone with the stones to execute a Knight of the Protective Hand and former avatar of Taymahr herself?"

"How easily you've pushed aside the memory that I have carried Tharothet, and been found worthy not once but twice." Ullen allowed himself a sigh, but kept his shoulders from slumping. This wasn't the verdict he'd been hoping for, though it had seemed inevitable since the day Genovar departed.

IT WAS TOO DANGEROUS to delay the execution of Sir Quinton Ilyani. There were still those that felt he was the better leader, the one Genovar should've left in charge, and would start to question whether charging the stage hadn't been an act of leadership rather than crazed sedition.

As promised, Ullen hefted the ax himself. It was as quick and clean a cut as he could make it. He was stalwart on the stage, saving his emotions for when he was alone in his chambers.

Jaspar had been freed, cleared of all charges. Her father had requested a private evening with her, after the ordeal of her trial. Ullen granted the request. It seemed too small a gesture for everything Ullen had inadvertently put her through. If he'd been better at taking the reins when Genovar left, perhaps the last few days would've been different.

He questioned what to do about General Geryan. She'd been returned to her cell, only slightly worse for the eventful day of near executions and trial plots. But she'd put herself between Sir Ilyani and the guard he'd attempted to silence while she was unarmed and bound. It was an act of selflessness and bravery. One that Ullen wouldn't have hesitated to award under different circumstances. It was a matter to discuss with his newly formed council.

Following the execution, Jathy Ettleway led a whole troop of soldiers loyal to Sir Ilyani away from the camp. The glint in her eye promised more trouble down the road. Despite the risk that the former Scout Captain had left behind spies, Ullen would focus on rebuilding the trust between him and those he led.

25

~Resmine~

WENRIR ESSERTON HAD changed his name after losing his title as the King of Thieves. It was necessary. After all, if any of the new monarch's henchmen had believed he was still alive, they would've been driven by loyalty or greed to finish the job. Ysinda's predecessor didn't leave much of a legacy. Resmine could tell much of that had been due to Ysinda's efforts to scrub the slate clean, but what fingerprints the previous king had left didn't impress the current queen. The fact that Wenrir hadn't even felt the need to leave Jarelton after changing his name made it icicle clear how lax things had been.

With Dewin on her left, Shiv on her right, and Corianne guarding her back, Resmine approached the house of the only living retiree of the Thieves' Guild Throne. Like most of Jarelton, this neighborhood was largely made up of gray stone buildings with a scattering of soot-stained timber accents. A single pub sign swung tiredly farther down the street and the scent of metal and forges clung to the stone despite the chill breeze. An easily forgettable corner of the city to house a man that dearly wished to be forgotten.

Resmine would've liked to turn around and leave him his peace. But if anyone knew the ins and outs of The Two Beams, it would be the man that built her from the ground up. Logic followed that if there was someone who would create a hidden bolt hole in a tavern, it would be a man presumed dead by a guild of thieves.

His house was unassuming. The stoop had rune-work carved in. Protection from Flayers. Protection from fire. Just enough protection to appear cautious, but not enough to stand out. If one knew where to look though, there were trap triggers hidden inside the front window frames and camouflaged into the wood stain. This place was a fortress painted in townhouse colors. Impressive.

"I don't want to spook him into hiding," Resmine said. "Shiv, Corianne, could you two wait out here?" Her lieutenants exchanged skeptic looks. "Just until I smooth the way."

Dewin grasped her by the hand. "I want to be with you, love. I still can't believe I up and left him the way I did. I couldn't figure out how to duck us both and I..."

Giving her love a reassuring squeeze, Resmine understood. This wasn't her first time hearing Dewin's recriminations about her part in Estan's capture, and it likely wouldn't be the last. She wasn't sure if having Dewin at her side would help or hinder this meeting, but like Wenrir, Dewin had survived retiring from the guild. Perhaps her pressence would work as a show of good faith. As the current guild leader, Resmine wasn't trying to clean house and rid herself of guild ghosts. She needed every ally she could get in a city under siege.

With the greatest reluctance, Corianne and Shiv slid away, taking positions not visible from the townhouse windows. There were still risks. If Wenrir killed his visitors before they could cry out, there wasn't much the two waiting bodyguards could do. Neither Dewin nor Resmine were useless in a fight. It was unlikely someone would get much of a drop on the two of them, former King of Thieves or not.

Resmine recognized she was stalling. She'd hidden herself for years and pushing someone else out of hiding didn't sit well. But this was for Estan. She needed to get him out of the Venom Guild's grasp—any delay could put him at greater risk. With one last squeeze of Dewin's hand, Resmine straightened her shoulders and tossed the cobwebs from her mind with a shake. Stepping up to the door, she gave an authoritative knock.

"Yes, what do you want?" called a voice from inside. "I'm not expecting visitors."

"Wenrir? Wenrir Esserton?"

There were tromping steps and a scuffling sound at the door's locks. A small hatch slid to the side and a pair of eyes peered down at Resmine from behind an iron mesh. A voice like smoke personified seeped out through the opening. "If you know that name, then you'd best have a very good reason to be disturbing me in my home."

"A very good reason, indeed. And unless you want your business to spread all over the street, I'd suggest you let us in where we can keep this conversation private."

The eyes on the other side of the mesh darted from Resmine to Dewin and back. "Just the two of you, or your other companions as well?"

"My associates will wait out here, unless you wish all of us to enter," Resmine said. As she'd feared, Wenrir was still in good form despite his long absence from the guild. Whatever traps he had waiting, she'd have to be on her toes.

Despite her assurances, Wenrir glared out the mesh at the two women for a few moments longer before more scrabbling sounds emitted from inside the house. The door swung open and a weathered hand beckoned them to enter.

"For Estan," Dewin sighed, barely audible even though Resmine was standing right next to her.

"For Estan," Resmine echoed. She tried to smile reassuringly, even though she was every bit as nervous.

Upon entering, there was no immediate sign of a threat. Wenrir didn't jump out from behind the door to hold a knife to either of their throats or emerge from the shadows holding a crossbow. It was almost a disappointment when he shuffled away from the door and into a comfortably furnished sitting room. "Shut the door and mind your fingers. The locks are Eerilorian runeworks. Self-binding."

Dewin still jumped when the locks sealed behind them, but Resmine was too busy studying the man in front of her. It took a certain kind of bravado to be this at ease with strangers in one's home. Especially strangers that made their way in by asking for a man that was supposed to be long dead. Wenrir walked with a slight hunch, though he didn't look as old as she'd expected. His hair, while silvering, still held enough color to tell it had once been a rich chestnut brown. The man's blue eyes were like crystals, glinting as they reflected the house's candlelight. A sharp nose pointed toward a scar that ran across his full lips. It looked like he'd kissed a dagger. His skin had an aged-leather texture, as though he'd once spent a lot of time outdoors and the tan hadn't fully left him. One of his arms was missing from the elbow down, his sleeve torn off to reveal a mechanical claw replacement. Averting her eyes, Resmine wondered briefly if he'd been born without the hand or if it had been lost to wound or accident. Neither answer would change their current circumstances.

"Have a seat, both of you." Wenrir indicated two wooden chairs on the door-side of a small table. He propped himself into a well-worn spot on the plush couch opposite. On high alert for some sort of trap or runic circle or anything to alert her to what the former Thief King was planning, Resmine still couldn't spot the danger. This sort of man wasn't careless, and he had money. That was obvious with his Eerilorian locks and his mechanical arm. Most people with prosthetics settled for a hook or a simple wooden hand. Resmine had seen plenty of people that went without prosthetics entirely during her time as a temple foundling. Either Wenrir had squirreled away a good deal of coin during his days as a thief or his current business enterprises had been very lucrative. With enough money, he could afford something very well hidden or intricate.

There was nothing for it. Asking for his help meant putting herself at this man's mercy. Resmine sat in the indicated seat and beckoned for Dewin to follow her.

Once his guests were settled, Wenrir leaned forward and propped his elbows on his knees, steepling his fingers against the metal digits of his prosthetic. Silence danced between the three of them as he studied his visitors.

"You're the new leader of the Thieves' Guild," Wenrir said. It wasn't a question.

"Yes." Resmine didn't see the sense in trying to deny her position. "And you're one of my predecessors."

"Are you here to kill me? To threaten me away from your seat? Are you trying to ferret out any secret ambitions I harbor? Because if that's why you're bothering an old man, I can tell you straight away—you're wasting time."

"I'm here to ask about the Two Beams, actually."

"My old tavern?" It was the first look of genuine surprise Wenrir had given since they crossed his threshold. "Why would you need to see me about that place? I sold it off years ago and haven't gone back since the guild made it into a regular haunt. Too dangerous. Though with you here now, not sure I should've bothered."

"Other leaders would've been a danger to you," Resmine said. "I have no interest in old grudges."

"And I'm to take your word on that?"

Meeting Wenrir's piercing gaze, Resmine waited. Nothing she could say would alleviate his fears. The only possible way he would trust her intentions was if she kept moving forward. Once he saw that she was focused on other goals, maybe he'd realize she wasn't interested in him as anything other than a keeper of information.

But the dance of stature between two guild leaders, former and current, was taking too long. Dewin broke through the tension with a rushed interjection of her own. "Sorry, love. I know this ain't the way you're wanting to handle this and Master Esserton, I'm sure us bursting in here with a name you thought long buried isn't the best start to your day, but we have a friend what's been taken by the Venom Guild and they are holed up in the Two Beams, and we were hoping you made yourself a bolt hole or something equally useful, so we could maybe spring him out or surprise attack the bastards what's currently in residence of the place you built."

"I'm sorry. Who are you?" Wenrir glanced from Resmine to Dewin and back, raising one peppered eyebrow as though questioning Resmine's judgment in bringing this particular friend along.

"Dewin, High Priestess to Adari," Dewin answered. She cocked her head to one side as though she were listening to someone nearby whisper and then smirked. "Hello, love. Our Goddess thanks you for your devotion even after losing the throne to your usurper."

Blinking rapidly, Wenrir jumped out of his chair. He began pacing in an agitated manner. "You serve our Lady? High Priestess? Since when does the Goddess of Guile and Greed need a High Priestess in Jarelton? Are you truly bound to Adari? Prove it!"

Cocking her head once more, Dewin's smirk became a proper grin. "You've not been following the local politics much recently, but I trust you're at least passingly familiar with the events of the Winter Solstice, yes? The attempted coup by the Venom Guild, the deaths of the new Lord Ilamar and the first Queen of Thieves, and the consecrating of Adari's Temple? You do not recognize me as the former thief Dewin, sister of Corianne and Evic, that was evicted from the city during the rule of Ysinda? Then by your leave, I will prove it as only one who has an ear to hear our Lady can. You've a mechanism within your prosthetic arm that allows you to trigger a series of darts, each tipped with enough tranquilizing powder to take down a large war horse, to shoot into these two seats you save for unwanted guests. Go ahead and try it, love. You tested the trigger, what? Two days ago? Should work just fine. No love or duster has had an opportunity to tamper with the device. Not a soul should even know it exists."

With a fierce expression, Wenrir raised the false arm and there was a metallic click within. Nothing seemed to happen.

Biting his lip, Wenrir's arm clicked again.

Still nothing.

Click.

Click.

Click.

Resmine leaned back and picked at her nails as though she were bored. Whatever was happening with his device and Adari was really none of Resmine's business, despite her position. She would always belong to Locke, God of Beauty and Battle despite her current vocation. The stalemate between the former King of Thieves and Dewin was fairly entertaining, but it was hardly going any more quickly than the staring contest had been.

For a moment, Resmine entertained the notion her lover was the one avatar still among them—but if that had been true, Dewin would've been able to get them both out of the Flayer trap. Having been raised in the temples, the way Dewin was cocking her head and squinting slightly reminded Resmine more of when the priestesses would pretend Locke was speaking. Dewin was not pretending, though—which became more obvious with every insistent trigger.

"Are you satisfied that Dewin is the High Priestess of your Lady, or are we going to continue to listen to your arm misfire all day? We do have a friend to rescue."

One last click, and then Wenrir sat down again. "Very well. Whether you did somehow deactivate my mechanism or are Adari's messenger, I've no idea, but that's between you and her—"

A dart shot out of some hidden tube and planted itself dead center in the sitting room's table, interrupting whatever point the man had been making. Dewin didn't seem at all surprised, though Wenrir's eyes were as wide as midday daisies. "They ain't calibrated to land there," he said, answering a question no one had asked. "You're genuine."

"Real as steal," Dewin said. "Don't worry none. Our Lady delights in questioning falsehoods. She's a Lady of Guile after all."

Wenrir shook his head and sighed. "I think the three of us should start afresh. Welcome to my home. Can I get you some tea or refreshment? You had questions about the Two Beams was it? I'll tell you all I can, right enough. And then, as it is clear I'm well out of hiding, I think we should probably set up some sort of treaty or guidelines as to where this sort of visit falls in and what I am to my former guild."

Nodding, Resmine assented. "That's more than fair. Our guild does need a much better retirement plan than it's currently got in place. I'd like to think our former members would have a lot to offer. Dewin being a prime example."

WENRIR WALKED DEWIN and Resmine to the door. "I'm not sure if I would call this a pleasure. But it's a relief to get it out in the open. At least I don't feel like the guild is going to be constantly looming over my shoulder anymore."

"I will hold my people to the agreements made here today. We appreciate the maps and not being poisoned," Resmine said, a half-smile tugged across her cheek to show she was attempting a joke.

The response was something between a snort and a huff. She was willing to take it.

Something else flitted through her mind as she saw the reverent spark in Wenrir's eyes while he held the door open for Dewin. Resmine wasn't sure why the question popped into her head, but if she didn't ask now, she may not get another chance. Especially with the new treaties still drying on Wenrir's sitting room table. Just dropping in to have a chat and a cup of tea wasn't something either of them had been comfortable with the other doing. "One last thing I would like to ask—not a favor or anything," Resmine amended hastily as the former king's brow tightened. "I was just curious if you were familiar with the underground archway that granted me the leadership of the Thieves' Guild. It's much too powerful for that to have been its original purpose."

For a long moment, it seemed like Wenrir might not say anything. He pursed his lips in thought and worked over her question. Resmine could practically see the threads of his mind weaving back and forth. Finally, when Resmine was about to tell him not to worry about it and bid him farewell, he spoke. "I can't rightly say. I'm familiar with it, of course. It's been a secret passed within our guild for generations. There's a good few that I entrusted with its location myself, so I know it ain't the most guarded knowledge out there. But the place is older than most of upper Jarelton. Mayhaps even older than the gods themselves. What its original purpose was," Wenrir shrugged, "not sure even the gods remember."

Thanking him for his time, Resmine ducked out the door and let Wenrir seal it behind her. His comment about the arch being older than the gods danced in her head. When she had time, Resmine wanted to spend some real time ruminating on the arch beneath Jarelton.

It was a silent trek back to The Dusk and Dawn. As much as Resmine wanted to get Estan back, it didn't make sense to plan where they might be overheard. With her freshly made agreement to keep Wenrir out of guild business except for emergencies, she didn't want to immediately invade his sitting room for a planning session, either. There was very little to prevent him from betraying her to the Venom Guild, should he feel the new Queen of Thieves was overstepping.

He wasn't an idiot, so she doubted he'd put himself in Arad Rhidel's power just to spite her—but smart people did dumb things on occasion. Better safe than sorry.

Studying the map Wenrir had drawn of what had once been his tavern, it was easy to see the bolt hole she'd been hoping for did exist. But it wasn't as helpful as she'd hoped. During her one night liaison with Dewin, Resmine had seen very little of the interior, and less of layout. Dewin, Corianne, and Shiv had already been able to describe the taproom and main hallway with a few overnight rooms. There was an upstairs portion of the hallway, and then a basement area that Wenrir said mostly housed casks and barrels of mead, ale, and other spirits. The most likely rooms for holding a prisoner were upstairs according to Dewin, but Wenrir's bolt hole was behind the bar in the tap room, closer to the basement than the hallway. It would make almost as much sense to enter through the front door.

"Really, the only thing the bolt hole entry has going for it is the element of surprise," Resmine said. "Not without merit, but it will hardly let us sneak in and out quietly like I wanted."

"Nothing for it, then. We ruckus up the hive, get them swarming, and pluck him out like a rotten tooth," Corianne agreed.

It wouldn't be pretty, but with luck and a good diversion, maybe they could get everyone in and out of the enemy stronghold in one piece.

RESMINE COULD FEEL her erratic heartbeat from her fingertips to her toes. She was practically vibrating by the time they made it across the street from The Two Beams.

Come on, Res, shake it off. Estan's fine. He's got that whole healing gift thing from our time as avatars. He's Taymahr's favorite little follower. He's fine. This is all gonna be okay. Just breathe.

Her internal monologue wasn't helping but, if she stopped the thoughts, worse images would invade her mind. Memories of Syara were hovering on the edges of her awareness. And the image of Estan with the gaping dagger wound in his chest still haunted her dreams.

She wasn't going to lose Estan. He was her brother. They were kin. Arad Rhidel would *not* be permitted to finish what he started.

Hushed footsteps seemed to echo through the empty streets. The sun shining down on them from above seemed out of place for the covert mission, but it was the best time of day to fight against Flayers. Demon-bound bodies were weaker in bright light and the Thieves' Guild needed every advantage.

They slipped past the Venom Guild guards. Two humans sat on stools on either side of a barrel. They looked to be incredibly bored as they glanced disinterested down the lanes and played a dice game that involved money changing hands. If they'd been Resmine's underlings, they would've risked a solid reprimand. If things went to plan, she doubted the two of them would see the next sunrise. The current Queen of Thieves was much kinder than their head assassin.

Finding the false wall without Wenrir's description would've been impossible. The wall appeared seamless except for a slight notch about the width of a knife blade at roughly her chest height. A very specific knife blade, at that. Resmine pulled out the knife Wenrir had given her and stuck it into the wall. There was a click not unlike those Wenrir's false arm had produced earlier that day. Corianne was the first in, followed by Dewin, and then Shiv. They'd been unable to find Tak before leaving The Dusk and Dawn. Catapult had also been absent.

Wherever they were, Resmine hoped they were both safe. She didn't want to get Estan out of Venom Guild hands only to have to go rescue the warhorse.

Slipping into the wall behind Shiv, Resmine wrenched the knife free and let the outer wall shut. Now to navigate their way to the exit behind the bar, and from there, find wherever Estan was being kept. Possibly fighting a few dozen assassins and Flayers on the way.

Nothing to worry about.

26

~Khiri~

EVEN THOUGH KHIRI HAD been to Jarelton before, she didn't remember it being that difficult to navigate the various roads and districts of the stone city. Or the pervasive smell of filth. She'd also forgotten how incredibly dismal the place seemed. The stone surrounding her was as gray as her mood.

Getting past the town guard at the gate had been much harder than when Fennick had been her guide. She hadn't realized he'd been bribing their way through. Or maybe he'd been using his mind-altering runestone.

"It's unlikely he used the stone," Micah said. *"We were naive, but we weren't blind."*

"If we were naive enough not to notice him bribing people, there's no reason we would've been keen enough to see the vacant expressions on the guards."

Loni seemed unperturbed by the guards asking so many questions of people entering the city. She also was staying remarkably quiet as Khiri led the way down yet another street, indecipherable from the last three.

"She's giving you space. She didn't know Kal as well, but she's sad too. She doesn't want to intrude on your grief."

Khiri wasn't sure how to feel about Loni's grief or silence. She guessed she appreciated Loni's quiet. The last time Khiri felt this kind of pain, Micah's Lifewood was still with her, even if she couldn't hear him at the time. Best to keep her mind on deciphering Jarelton's maze.

Kal probably would've known the way, Khiri sighed. Tears threatened to break through her wall of irritation. Being angry was so much easier than being hurt, but she couldn't yell at anyone or shoot at anything right now. She remembered getting jumped in an alley during her last visit to the city and considered walking down the least inviting street she could find. Maybe a fight would do her good.

Recognizing the idea as grief-induced self-destruction, Khiri brushed the thought away. She'd promised Loni to get her to Estan and she was going to do just that. If she kept turning corners and walking forward, surely she would recognize something somewhere eventually. Or the Thieves' Guild would find her again. Evic, Corianne, or maybe even Dewin would find her.

It would be nice to see Dewin. Khiri hoped Dewin and Resmine had managed to make up. She hadn't really thought about the two of them in what felt like ages. She'd been in a constant state of movement since—well, since she'd left the Life Trees really.

"Khiri..." Loni's voice was small and breathy, as though she were fighting to get the name out of her throat. "What—What are those?"

Brimstone hung in the air, thick enough Khiri could taste it. She'd mistaken it for the smell of Jarelton before, but now she recognized what she'd been sensing in the alleys. Once she had regained her focus, it was hard to mistake the aroma. Looking in the direction her companion was pointing, Khiri's battle instincts flared to life. She didn't know what Flayers were doing in Jarelton, but she knew it was nothing good.

Screams erupted around them as the Flayers bled out of the shadows nearby, hissing the usual unsettling demands.

"... *Blood... Bone... Viscera... Meat...*"

There were too many people to let arrows fly through the streets. Palming her dagger, the now-familiar ripple of power coursed up Khiri's arm and through the tips of her ears. The dagger housed a million secrets, but her father had assured her it would never break. She wasn't sure why she still trusted him about that when it seemed like he'd been lying to her about a thousand other things.

None of it mattered at the moment. All that mattered right now was her weapon holding together long enough to dispatch a few more demons.

Racing headfirst to meet the leading Flayer, Khiri skidded under the creature's long arms and came up behind it. This Flayer was relatively fresh, still retaining much of what had been young and pale freckled skin under the mottled bruising. Older Flayers tended to gray, gaining the appearance of a walking corpse. He may have been a man only twenty summers old. About the same age as Khiri. She wondered briefly why he'd made a bargain with a demon.

"Everyone has a wish," Fennick had once told her. She hadn't really understood back then. It was a conversation she'd had before she knew what it truly was to lose someone.

Had this Flayer been the product of loss? Had this man been trying to regain what the world had taken?

It was remarkable how much time slowed in the middle of a fight when someone was familiar with the steps. Khiri plunged her dagger into the creature's back twice for good measure and darted away as the body began to purge itself of demonic blood.

Dodge. Dodge. Stab. Retreat. Block. Stab. Slice.

Thoughts melted away as Khiri battled, leaving her with a blessed moment of silence. It was almost pleasant. Then she heard Loni scream.

She'd only killed three of the creatures on one street, but there were more seeping out of the alleyways. Not all of them were chanting for blood anymore either. Some of them were hissing the name *Fortiva*. They were here for her.

Of all the unlikely rescuers she'd considered coming to her aid, Khiri had never heard a sweeter voice than the neigh that met her ears. "Catapult!"

The blue roan kicked his way through a Flayer's chest and leapt over the downed body. He clopped over the paved streets and took up Khiri's flank. Khiri was flattered the roan remembered her that well. They'd been apart for months. Granted, she didn't know what a horse's memory was like. Even a horse that had carried a god. For that matter, Khiri didn't know if she or Catapult or someone else amongst their party was still an avatar.

It certainly hadn't been Kal.

No room for sadness right now.

Even with the warhorse at her side, the chanting of, "... *Fortiva... Fortiva... Fortiva...*" from the growing number of Flayers was growing more intense.

"Loni, get on the horse!" Khiri said. She recalled that Loni had given her false name at the gate, but it was unlikely anyone could hear them over the tide of demon-bound chanting.

"What about you?" Loni hesitated.

"I'll be fine! Just get on Catapult!"

Loni's mouth worked, but no words tumbled from her throat. Concern was etched across the woman's face as she grabbed hold of Catapult's empty saddle and hoisted herself onto the huge horse's back. It was a marvel she kept her balance as the roan stomped and kicked at the Flayers approaching his other side. Khiri kept the Flayers back with a few broad slashes. "Catapult, get her to safety!"

The warhorse's skin twitched as though he was about to protest. "This woman is a friend of Estan's and I promised to get her to him. Please, go! I'll be right behind you!"

"Khiri! You shouldn't do this!"

Making a split-second decision, Khiri also handed Micah over to Loni. "If they aren't sure whether to trust you, just show them Micah and tell them I gave him over freely."

"Khiri! No! Bad idea! I'm supposed to go with you!"

"I need you to be safe right now. If this goes wrong, and you get splintered, I cannot handle that right now. I will not *lose someone else!"*

Loni looped Micah over her shoulder and anchored herself as well as she could to the warhorse's back. Catapult flicked his tail and reared, nearly spilling Loni from his saddle, and landed squarely on one of the largest Flayers in the gathering swarm. If Khiri were to follow him, it seemed he was going to make as big a gap as possible.

Finally, the roan took off with a jolt. Loni's startled scream hung in the air for a moment before evaporating into the sea of Flayer noise. Khiri made a dash for the opening left by Catapult, but it was closing faster than she could run. At least with the Flayers chanting her name, she thought it was unlikely they meant to kill her. Whether they were minions of Irrellian

Thornne or members of the Venom Guild, she was less certain. In the end, it probably didn't make much difference. The two enemies appeared to be working together.

Even when they were taking a captive, Flayers were far from gentle. Khiri got knocked to one side and grabbed by one of the creatures. Pain lanced through her arm as claws sank through her padded armor. She kicked one of the beasts in its shins and tried to squirm away from the demon gripping her. Another arm roped around her waist while more hands caught her legs and pinned her arms down.

One of the Flayers tried to take her dagger only to have the weapon flash and spark, shocking the creature's fingers. It snarled, objecting to this new torment. Its clawed fingers grabbed hold of Khiri's entire hand as though it thought to disarm her by tearing the objectionable limb off. Lightning sizzled through the knife's runes, dropping the creature where it stood. Some of the electricity jolted through Khiri as well, tearing a cry of agony from her throat. The momentary shock was enough to interrupt whatever fight Khiri had left.

It was over.

Flayers had her.

She struggled, but there was no way to break the grip of so many hands. Darkness grew around her, despite the strength of the sun overhead. Khiri tried to call for help, even though she knew in her gut there wasn't anyone to save her from the deepening shadows.

KHIRI EMERGED FROM the dark in the middle of a tavern.

If not for the crowd of Flayers and people in Venom Guild attire, the tavern interior looked rather cozy. There was a bar along one wall of the taproom, an open balcony with a number of doors, plenty of tables and chairs that were all a warm honey-oak in the firelight. The front window was boarded up and the presence of glass shards on the floor spoke to a recent break, but the building itself was inviting. It might have even been a nice place before the people inside had taken over.

"Well, well, well," a familiar voice said. "If it isn't the spawn of Fortiva. Isn't this convenient?"

Still in the bonds of several dozen demon-bound hands, Khiri couldn't jerk away from Arad Rhidel's grasp. The Flayers parted to let him inspect her as though she was a prize trout pulled from a stream. He placed his hand under chin and tried to lift her eyes to his. With what mobility was left to her, Khiri recoiled and snarled at the Venom Guild leader. She had no idea what he meant by convenient and she didn't want to give him the satisfaction of asking. "Let me go!"

Arad laughed. "Not yet, I think. I have a much better idea. Why don't the three of us have a little family reunion?"

Khiri couldn't help it. Her curiosity broke out of her grip. "The three of us?"

"There's someone here I believe you know rather well."

"Who?"

"Not yet. You'll see soon enough."

As Arad spoke, some of his human minions were shoving their way through the Flayers to bind Khiri in manacles rather than claws. The ease that the assassins had in the presence of the demons was uncanny. They acted like being this close to the mottled, inhuman creatures was no different than saddling a horse. Khiri wanted to get as far away as she could from the stench of the hells.

Either the Flayers had warned the guild humans not to touch Khiri's dagger, or there was some other sort of magic at work, because the weapon was left in her grip. If the Flayers grasp loosened or the other assassins gave her an opening, Khiri would have a choice to make. Arad was acting as though he was keeping someone precious to her captive, and she needed to find out where he had them. After losing Kal to her own recklessness, she couldn't rush things here. Not if it might cost her someone else she cared about. But was finding out where someone else was kept worth her own freedom? If she allowed herself to be caged, how would that help free anyone?

One problem at a time. First she would find out who was here, keeping the dagger palmed, and then she'd get out when she could.

None of the Flayers followed as two of the human guards took hold of her bonds and dragged her out of the taproom in Arad's wake. They climbed a set of stairs and carried her to one of the guest room doors.

Khiri wasn't ready for the view that met her within.

Genovar and Estan were both listless inside separate cages that barely fit within the room. Despite the cages, both men had their arms restrained. The mess buckets in the corners were practically a taunt with the way the prisoners were trussed. What was once a window had been boarded up as tightly as the one in the taproom. A sullen blue ring of runes glowing beneath the candles of the room's simple iron chandelier turned Khiri's stomach as soon as she spotted the arcane light. She didn't recognize the magic at work in this room, but she could tell it wasn't benign.

"Father! Estan!" Khiri cried. Despite her manacles, she attempted to rush forward only to stumble as her guards held her back. She squirmed to get out of their reach, but their grip didn't falter.

"Khiri!" Estan echoed her surprise. "What are you doing here? How did they find you?"

"She was always going to come here." Genovar's voice was hushed. Resigned. "She was always going to end up in the hands of her uncle, just as I was meant to free her." He turned to Estan and said, "Recall your promise from the last time we met."

Estan's face went completely rigid, but he nodded. As odd as that interaction was, Khiri's mind was still fixed on the first tidbit.

"Uncle?" Khiri was shocked enough to cease fighting her captors. "My uncle? But that would mean... You're Elithania Haud's brother?"

"Rothan Haud was the name he was going by when he entered Jarelton," Estan said. "Who is Elithania?"

"It was my mother's name, before she became Leyani," Khiri said.

"Before she was corrupted by your father's magic and kidnapped from her rightful family!" Arad snapped. He yanked Khiri away from her guards and dragged her over to her father's cage, shaking her in front of Genovar like she was a dead game bird. "Just so you could fill my sister with your seed and make this! This worthless piece of refuse that brought the world the birth of a new war! Are you proud of her? Are you proud of yourself? You ripped my family apart at the seams and ruined all of Arra with it."

Dropping Khiri entirely, Arad turned. For a moment it looked as though he was going to walk away and leave the three of them alone in the room. Khiri was ready to pass her dagger through the bars the moment the door closed, but Arad suddenly lunged back with his own wicked knife drawn. It was inches from Khiri's throat when time seemingly froze.

A gurgling, boiling sound erupted from behind her and the putrid scent of brimstone and rot filled the entire chamber. Estan let out a hiss. "No—"

Metal shredded behind her and a claw, mottled but familiar, intercepted the attack. "I will protect my daughter," Genovar said, his voice more gruff and harsh than Khiri had ever heard.

It wasn't real.

This wasn't really happening.

Her brain tried to erase the bruising, the fierce claws, and the acrid smell from reality. Her father had been the one to warn her about the dangers of demon wishes. This creature couldn't be Genovar, the war hero that defied the Flayer Mage. Her father couldn't—wouldn't—make a wish at the cost of his soul!

While Khiri was trying to deny what all of her senses were reporting, Arad began to laugh maniacally. "Yes! Finally! Let all of Arra see you for the monster you truly are! I always knew you were no hero! Just a miserable wretch like the rest of us! As willing to kill as I was!" The Venom Guild leader took a fighting stance, his knife in one hand and a rune in the other. "Fight me, and I'll let your miserable spawn lead me to my sister before I kill them both!"

"I will protect my daughter," Genovar repeated. Khiri's stomach roiled hard and she tumbled over, barely in time to aim most of her bile into what was left of her father's cage. Her dagger seemed to throb in her hand.

"Khiri, you have a weapon?" Estan hissed. "Get over here! You can slice my ropes and maybe we can escape!"

Her head felt like it was stuffed with wool. Looking at the door where her guards had been standing, Khiri saw an empty exit. Had they bolted when the new Flayer entered? Had her father scared them off?

It was like two different pictures of what had happened were trying to form in her memory at the same time, but there was only room for one.

With a shaky breath, Khiri shoved herself away from the broken cage and over to Estan.

Estan was the only thing in this room that still made sense. He was a knight and fellow avatar. He was her friend and he needed help. They had to face in opposite directions for her to cut through his bonds, since their arms were tied behind their backs. He grunted once or twice when she misjudged where his hands were in relation to her blade, but he didn't complain. Once Estan was free, he turned around and studied her manacles. "I'm not sure how to get these off you. I'm not any good at picking locks."

"Just try to pry one of the links open with my knife," Khiri said. She wasn't sure how feasible that would be, but she needed to get free to help her father.

The fight between Arad Rhidel and the Genovar Flayer was hard to follow. Both of them were moving faster than Khiri's addled brain could keep up with. In the midst of the action, Arad smashed a rune against her father's shoulder causing Genovar to snarl and whine. Ice crystals formed over the mottled skin and Genovar clubbed the rune out of the assassin's grip. It bounced over to where Khiri and Estan sat watching. Estan bent and grabbed hold of the partially spent rune and tapped it against the manacles. "This might hurt a little, so try to breathe through your teeth."

Khiri's dagger didn't shock Estan when he took it from her grip. She felt the impact of something hard slamming against the frozen metal. There was some pain involved, but Khiri barely noticed. Another impact and she did hiss a breath through her clenched teeth as the metal tore skin. But she was free, which meant the minor discomfort was wholly worth it. Estan did the same freeze trick with the lock on his cage and handed the dagger back to Khiri.

They were trying to edge past the two combatants when Arad turned and hurled a fresh rune at them. "Don't you two even think of leaving! This dance is just getting started!"

Estan threw himself between Khiri and the projectile, and Khiri let out a startled yelp as flame engulfed the big knight.

"I will protect my daughter!" Genovar's altered voice screamed. Arad was thrown out the door as the Flayer charged toward Estan. Khiri reacted on instinct and hip-checked Estan out of the path of Genovar's descending claw. She met the talons with the flat of her knife. Blue sparks sizzled through the air at the impact. The knife itself seemed to shriek. Falling back toward the cages, Khiri and Estan managed to avoid Arad Rhidel's next volley of thrown rune stones.

Rushing back into the room with his own knife in front of him, Arad slashed repeatedly at the demon wearing Genovar's face. As the Flayer performed a series of dodges, Khiri recognized the movements of her father. He'd done many of those same steps during his years of training her how to fight, how to hunt, how to survive. But then, as he began to attack, all familiarity bled away as the vestiges of her father melted into the flailing of a ravenous monster.

Pulling her away from the spectacle, Estan once more tried to guide Khiri out of the room so they could escape. She resisted him, wanting to spend as long as she could in this room where she'd last seen her father as her father. There was a thought, buried deep within her, that if she could just stay in this spot, maybe Genovar would return to his old self if she waited long enough.

"Would you like to make a wish?"

Khiri shook her head, her eyes drifting up to the chandelier. It flared a brighter blue for a moment there. When the voice had asked her about a wish. Her ears burned with the foreign blaze of magic. She couldn't articulate the discovery, but she understood. This room was a trap. That's what her father had meant when he said she'd always been meant to come here. He'd seen this room in a vision, he'd known what would happen, and he'd come anyway.

More stupidity born of his choices and secrets. Rage burst to life within her. Rage at her father and his secrets. It warred against the grief already gathered in her heart.

It was all too much.

She launched herself into the fight. She jump-kicked into Arad's side as he was dodging a series of attacks from what had been her father. Khiri followed up with a series of slashes at her surprised uncle.

Despite attacking the man who had chased her all the way to Eerilor, Khiri's verbal assault was reserved for her father. "Why couldn't you just tell me why I had to leave the trees! Why did you disown me rather than ask for my side of the story! Why does everything have to be one of your stupid spirits-forsaken secrets! Did you ever trust me?! Did you ever even really love me?! I'm your fucking daughter! And I didn't even know my mother was human! I didn't know where I came from! I thought I had done something wrong for months! Months! Only to find out that it wasn't me—it was all your doing! You and my mother, before I was even conceived! Do you have any gods-bent idea what I've been through! And now, now... You're a Flayer! A spirits-forsaken Flayer!"

Even as he dodged and deflected her attacks, Arad started laughing again. "How delicious! This is the first time I've really considered the benefits of having a niece. Too bad our course is already set, otherwise, I'd be tempted to take you under my wing and maybe teach you my trade. You've got a healthy dose of anger and killing for hire is an excellent way to burn through that."

Genovar plunged a full hand into Arad's side. The assassin cried out in anguish as Genovar pulled his claws free to begin licking the blood off. "I will protect my daughter," he said. Arad shuffled weakly away from the Flayer.

Khiri's rage chilled inside of her as she witnessed the attack. As angry as she was, she was still an elf of the Life Tree Clans. They didn't kill needlessly, and the sight of blood was too much.

Estan took advantage of the assassin's surprise and sucker-punched the man. Once more grabbing hold of Khiri to drag her toward the doorway, the knight was flung away from her by Genovar. "I will protect my daughter."

"Father, you have to let me leave! This is Estan! Estan! The knight you sent to guard me after I left home!" Khiri couldn't help remembering Liren, the assassin that had turned Flayer after Khiri had killed her brother—a man who'd been made a Flayer before Khiri had ever met the siblings.

Why had Liren seemed so much more cognizant? She'd recognized Khiri out of a group and even talked with her, if only to taunt her.

Something cleared in Genovar's eyes, like a cloud lifting. "Khiri?"

For one glorious second, Khiri had her father back. Then a flash of black metal hurled past her face and sank into Genovar's stomach. He roared in pain and flung her away, crashing toward Arad Rhidel before falling to the floor. Arad's expression gleamed in triumph, though it was short-lived. Khiri shoved her dagger at Estan. Without hesitating, Estan took the enchanted blade in his hand and closed the distance between himself and the Venom Guild leader.

Khiri didn't bother to watch the knight face off against the assassin. Instead she rushed to her father's side and rolled him so he was facing the ceiling. His eyes were still those she'd known as a child, though she could see yellow attempting to push its way into the deep blue irises. "Khiri," Genovar said, and it was only his voice. Not the discordant echo or hiss of a Flayer. It was gruff though. Like he was trying to talk around a lump in his throat. "Khiri, my brave girl, you've been through so much. All of it—" a cough interrupted him, followed by a groan of discomfort. "—all of it, my fault."

"Father, please. Why?" Khiri couldn't vocalize more than that. Tears threatened to choke her voice out entirely. She wanted to hold him, to hug him close, but the evil was growing within him and she couldn't stand the oily slick presence coating the warmth that had been so dear to her. It was vile. Even so, this was probably the last time she would ever get to talk to her father. There was no returning to the Life Trees for one that became a Flayer. He would be lost to her and her mother forever. With effort, she swallowed back the grief and managed another, "Why?"

She saw the struggle it was for him to speak, and so leaned in. Despite the awfulness coating his soul, she cradled his head in one arm. Her tears were falling into his face, but either he couldn't feel them or didn't mind.

"It seems I miscalculated. I thought wishing to protect you would leave me a larger window, but I've been resigned to this fate for too long. I've little will left to fight back what's coming."

"No..."

"My daughter," he said. "Your mother and I did you a great disservice. We brought you into the world knowing the path we'd created for you would be all but impossible. Leyani didn't know as much as I did. The price we paid to be together, I knew our debt would fall on our child. But I loved your mother, and I couldn't bear the idea that she and I wouldn't be together. I was selfish. Selfish enough to tear the very fabric of reality. It's all come full cycle now. My actions caused the weaknesses that Irrellian Thornne exploited to become what he is. If I'd known everything that would befall Arra—I'd still do it all again. I'm so sorry, Khiriellen. This... This life is far from what you deserved. Just know that I do love you. I am proud. So much prouder of you than I am of myself."

"Father..." Khiri's heart threatened to rip itself from her chest. It was breaking. She'd thought it was already beyond repair when she'd entered Jarelton only that morning. "I can't keep doing this. Why?"

"I'm sorry," Genovar said again. "But I must ask something even worse of you. Even now, I'm losing the battle to the demon I bargained with. Khiri, you have to kill me."

"What?!" Khiri dropped her father's head which thumped roughly against the floor as she jumped away from his body. His blood was leaking from the dagger wound in his gut, but she could see the wound was less than fatal. "No... But, I can't..."

Estan returned at that moment and handed Khiri her knife. "I got a good hit in on Arad, but he might survive it. He disappeared into the chaos downstairs."

There was no room for curiosity. For once in her life, Khiri didn't feel inclined to ask for clarification about anything Estan said. Her fingers closed around the hilt of her masterwork blade automatically, as though it was a favorite toy a child might clutch for security. She looked down at the rune-etched blade and the hunting bird hilt. This was the gift her father had bequeathed her on the day before her Name Breathing. This and the ring, long since returned to its owner, had started her on this path. "Estan, please... I can't... My father doesn't want to become a Flayer. Help me!" she pleaded.

Her friend looked like he'd received a punch to the stomach and had the wind knocked out of him. He wrapped one of his big hands around her fingers clutching the dagger. "I can't. I'm sorry, Khiri. But your father made me promise. I can't break my vow."

"No! No, you're my friend! *My* friend! How can you ask this of me! How can he! After everything—How can this be my path!"

Khiri was distantly aware that she saw other faces in the hallway. Some of them even looked familiar, but it was hard to make them out through the veil of tears coating the world. She sank down to the floor over top of the being that was her father. Had been her father. Even as she wept, she could feel Genovar slipping away. The rest of Arra considered him to be a great hero, the elf who defeated the Flayer Mage during the War of the Burning Valley. Khiri, looking at the broken figure of her father, was the only one that knew his entire sorted history. Once, he had declared that she was no longer a Fortiva and had ejected her from his house. Had that been an attempt to protect her from this moment? Changing names had changed the entire face of Arra once, and that had also been his doing.

It didn't matter.

Whatever his intentions had been, Khiri was facing the impossible choice of killing him while something of her father remained, or letting the demon he'd bargained with have him. Her arms shook as she raised the knife. She was counting on the magic within the blade to do most of the work, because it was all she could do to keep hold of the weapon. Jamming it down into her father's chest, Khiri cried out as though she were the one receiving the blow.

A thunderclap surged through the point of the knife and echoed through the stones of the tavern. Khiri came away from the corpse which was sizzling away its demon-blood. The unbreakable dagger that had been with her since the start of her journey was now missing its blade, leaving her holding an empty hilt.

Tossing it away, Khiri collapsed into a heap and let herself sob.

27

~Estan~

AS ESTAN LOOKED AT the deteriorating corpse of his childhood hero, there was a hollowness growing within him.

Arad had escaped.

Genovar was dead.

And Estan hadn't been able to do anything to stop either event. He hadn't heard the whole conversation between Khiri and Genovar before the dagger came down. It had taken every ounce of internal strength he'd possessed not to give in when Khiri asked for his help. Back when he'd made his promise to her father, not to help when she asked him, there was no way Estan could've seen this moment coming. How could he have known?

Why had he agreed to such an outlandish request?

Yet, remembering that day, Estan recalled how easily he'd acquiesced. At the time, Estan believed he was in love with Khiri, and Genovar hadn't questioned any further. Estan had imagined, somewhere in the back of his head, Khiri's request would involve returning to the Life Trees with her or asking him to team up with Kal for some reason. It would've been hard to deny traveling with her back then, but turning down Kal would've even brought him a bit of vindictive satisfaction. If his love had been true, Estan wouldn't have agreed so blindly.

Even with Genovar asking, he wouldn't have promised not to help Loni— Taymahr keep her—or Corianne. And Khiri would definitely never see the man that made her kill her own father in a romantic light, even if Estan had still believed himself in love. Kal had won their ridiculous competition now, certainly. Estan wondered briefly where the former assassin was. Had he remained with Ullen, wherever the dwarven prince was? Why was Khiri here?

Why was she alone?

"Estan!" A relieved voice said from behind him. All of the sudden, Estan was tangled in a sea of arms as Resmine, Dewin, and Corianne all enveloped him. Corianne and Dewin were both laughing with relief even as tears rolled down their cheeks. Resmine was the one speaking. "You're alright! You're really, truly okay!"

Hugging each of them back in turn, Estan wrapped their warmth close, like a balm against the events of the last few days. "I'm so glad to see you! All of you! But..." His words failed him as he gestured toward the sobbing heap that was Khiri.

"Khiri!" Dewin's eyes widened. "But, how? When? What happened, love?"

Even the voices of her friends weren't enough to bring Khiri out of her puddle of grief. Estan wasn't sure what to do, but Corianne was already on her way over to the elf. She nudged a bit of the ash with her boot and sighed, squatted next to Khiri, and put a gloved hand on the woman's shuddering shoulder. "Was your da, that was," Corianne said. "Don't have to tell me what it looks like to be a bird without a nest. Evic's gone to join our Mam and Pap Pap sure enough, and ain't a right lick what makes it ache less. But we're here, love. And we've gotta make away right quick. More beasties coming, what?"

Swallowing back several more gulps, Khiri seemed to surface a bit. "Corianne?" The elven woman blinked her large, hazel eyes and seemed to notice the others for the first time since they entered the room. "Resmine? Dewin?"

She reached up, asking silently for her own round of hugs from the women.

It wasn't until Khiri was swept up by the hug pile that Estan caught sight of Shiv lingering outside the door. As touching as this reunion was, and as much as Estan's own heart still ached, it was past time to get everyone out of this tavern and somewhere safe. He wasn't sure why, but he bent to scoop up the hilt Khiri had flung away. Tucking it into his own belt, Estan strode forward and laid his own hand on Khiri's shoulder. "We should go."

Her gaze swung back to the pile of ash that had been her father. "Go with the gods, or whoever you belonged to in the end. I can't—I can't..."

Estan could hear the sobs beginning to catch in her throat again. Rather than waiting to see if she'd be able to move on her own or collapse into a heap again, Estan scooped her up and held her against his chest. "Feel free to cry into my shirt. It needs replacing anyway."

There had been a time when Estan would have relished the chance to carry Khiri out of a building like this. He would've imagined himself cutting a dashing, heroic figure in her mind as he nobly escorted her to safety. Things had changed in the months they'd spent apart though. He found himself locking eyes with Corianne and trying to tell her without words all that he'd found swimming within his heart during his brief captivity. This wasn't the time or place for confessions, with another woman in his arms, and possibly more enemies on the way. But Estan still hoped some of what he felt was visible to her.

Following Resmine down the stairs and through the taproom, the sounds of fighting reverberated from outside. Ash piles and bodies littered the floor and slumped over tables. Far more bodies than Estan would've expected. Later, when they were all safe, he would ask for the details of what seemed a truly epic battle.

Resmine did a hand signal for quiet, even though no one within their group was talking. She led them to the bar and through what appeared to be a broom closet with a false back. A small maze of shelves and store rooms exited into an alleyway. Taking off as quickly as they could through the sunshine, they left the sounds of fighting in their wake. Whatever was going on, the Venom Guild seemed to have bigger problems than a handful of escapees to worry about.

THEY WERE NEARLY BACK to The Dusk and Dawn by the time Khiri had recovered enough to walk on her own. Estan set her down gently and offered her his arm to steady herself, should she need it. Waving him off, she fell into step in between Dewin and Resmine. She hadn't told anyone how she'd come to be in The Two Beams that morning. She hadn't said much of anything, really. Her friends respected her need for silence, though that didn't stop the questions from forming in Estan's mind.

Where was Micah? Estan couldn't imagine Khiri giving up her brother, the bow. She seemed even more distraught now than she had during those days between Micah's death-transformation and when her avatar gift had allowed her to hear him again. Did the Venom Guild break Micah? Would they even know he was more than a regular bow? Had she been traveling alone? Where were the rest of their companions?

Before Estan's curiosity could overtake his empathy, the sound of hoofbeats over Jarelton's pavestones heralded the return of Estan's wayward warhorse. Despite the sorrow of losing Genovar, Estan felt his spirits lift as his steed approached. It floated through his head that it was unusual for the horse not to adopt a disguise of some kind as he wandered through the streets. Even more odd, it seemed there was someone riding Catapult. Estan anticipated Tak—the trader was the only absent human Estan knew Catapult would permit the liberty—but as the roan neared it was increasingly obvious his mysterious rider was a woman.

"Estan!"

His jaw dropped as though it no longer had muscles. "Loni?!"

"Oh! Thank Taymahr! And Khiri's with you!" Loni scooted herself off of Catapult's saddle. She nearly kissed the road as she fumbled the landing.

Estan was closing the distance between himself and Loni as though there was no one else in Arra. Was it really her? Were his eyes playing tricks on him? A part of him feared he was still caged with Genovar, and everything he'd experienced from the moment of Khiri's arrival onward was some sort of cruel dream. Perhaps this was a demon's trick to entice him to wish for the impossible.

"I thought for sure you were dead," Estan said. "I'd heard—"

They were embracing before he was ready for it. Loni's arms squeezed him almost as tightly as Shiv's could. He returned the hug for all he was worth before pushing back so he could reassure himself he was really seeing her. His eyes drank her in. The shape of her nose, the dusting of freckles, those big doe eyes, the way her mouth curved. Loni's hair was the wrong color, dyed a mousy brown instead of her usual halo of golden curls, but there was no mistaking her for anyone else in the world. Estan wasn't sure whether to cry, kiss her, or collapse from relief.

Rather than let him continue to stare at her as though she were a ghost, Loni ducked around him and handed Micah over to Khiri. When she saw the state Khiri was in, she gathered the elf into a hug too. "What happened?"

Khiri just shook her head, and clutched Micah as though he were the only thing keeping her sane.

"I imagine we've all got a fair bit to tell each other," Resmine said. "Once we're safely back inside a warded tavern with a good fire and food, we can talk 'til tomorrow morning should the mood strike."

Catapult trotted over to Khiri and nuzzled her with his large velvety nose, giving her his horsy version of a hug. Khiri nodded as though he'd asked her something, and proceeded to climb up on the charger's saddle. Estan wondered if Catapult had used his illusory voice in a manner that only Khiri could hear or if the elf and horse merely understood each other that well.

Despite the joy singing in his heart at finding Loni alive and somehow here in Jarelton, Estan hadn't forgotten the grief left behind at the Two Beams Tavern. The entire group fell into another uneasy quiet as they plodded on toward Resmine's Court at The Dusk and Dawn.

CHUGGING BACK ALMOST an entire pint, Estan tried to make sense of his thoughts. Everyone else had tankards of ale, lager, or mead at various levels of empty. Khiri nursed a much smaller mug of something pale, bubbly, and sweet that the bartender had told her he made with a bean of some sort and cream.

Loni was here. *Loni.* Estan still couldn't believe it. He had feared the worst for nearly a full year, only for her to be here in front of him. Her soft, sweet smile. Her gentle eyes and steady nature. She was everything he remembered and so much more. She'd survived a nightmare much like his own. It was all Estan could do to focus on the words as she told her story.

"—and it was like I'd never known him. This man I'd been married to for years was out for my blood. I couldn't stay in Seirane. Estan was the only person I knew I could trust, and I didn't even know if he was still alive."

Fresh on the heels of Estan's revelations during his capture, his heart swelled with the knowledge that Loni still thought about him the way he'd always thought about her. She trusted him. If he was interpreting her warm glances correctly, she might still love him. She was the one who had left him, the one he'd never gotten over. His feelings for Ysinda had been a mere echo of those unresolved longings he'd harbored for someone he thought forever beyond his reach. And now she was here. *Within touching distance.* And no longer bound to a husband. Estan could hardly believe it.

And yet...

The bubble of golden light that filled his thoughts about Loni's return hadn't completely blinded him to the other revelations he'd had during his time in that cell.

Corianne was also right here, right in front of him. Her gaze darted back and forth between the knight and the newly-arrived Loni. Estan was sure she was observing far more than he wanted her to see. How to tell her what she meant to him? Did he want to tell her? Or did he want to pursue Loni now that they were both alive and free? He knew better than to talk about his feelings with either woman until he'd figured them out himself.

Khiri, whom he'd professed to once, was the only of the three he was certain about. They were good friends, and always would be. But she was mourning the losses of her father and Kal, and his imagined feelings had run their course. While Estan and Khiri had never seen eye to eye where the former assassin was concerned, Kal had been a fellow avatar to the High Ones and very important to Khiri. Estan would've been glad to see the lanky mage if only because he would've brought Khiri some comfort after what had occurred in the Two Beams.

Ullen would've known what to say. He probably would've had some advice for Estan's current situation as well. It was a shame the dwarf was stuck in Eerilor, and probably would be for the rest of his life given what Khiri had managed to share of her story.

Dewin hadn't left Khiri's side since the elf had opened up about her adventures. The news about Evic's loss had caused Khiri to cry even harder. No one had known she'd felt that strongly about the thief trio's brother, but he'd apparently been very kind during her first visit to Jarelton. Given Estan's own memories of Evic, it wasn't surprising the man had left a mark during their brief connection.

As Loni's story came to a close, there was a shared silence as those within The Dusk and Dawn taproom absorbed the monumental sense of shared loss. No one had managed to reach this place untouched. Even Loni, who should've been the safest of them, had seen too much on the edges of this twisted battlefield. Estan wondered if the first war against the Flayer Mage had been this confusing. Had every household held a potential Gray Army agent, just waiting for orders? Or was the turmoil a result of how the last war had ended? Was this hotbed of corrosion only possible because the High Ones went missing for twenty years while the Gray Army wormed their way into all available shadows?

Again, Ullen probably would've had some valuable insight. The moment it was safe to do so, Estan intended to write the former bard a letter.

"Well, I think between whatever caused the Flayers to revolt against the Venom Guild and the loss of their prisoners, we may have earned a brief respite. Khiri, Loni, I've guest suites down in the Pit, if you care to stay here. We have other friends in the city if you'd rather be in a tavern not affiliated with the Thieves' Guild. Completely up to you both. I know how fond Khiri is of a bath, so no matter where you stay, I'll ensure the largest tub Jarelton can offer," Resmine said, rising from the throne she'd won. "As befits guests of royalty, you'll not want for anything within these walls. Nothing I can provide, anyway."

Khiri gave Resmine a soft, wet smile. There was no joy in the elf's large eyes, but there was gratitude. That was something. It was heart-wrenching to see how defeated she looked. She was a far cry from the Khiri Estan had originally met, leading an entire circle of strangers without even trying. "Wherever is easiest for you, Resmine. I'm not going to be here long. I—I still need to get to the Life Trees. More than ever, I just want to go home."

No one objected out loud, but Estan found himself in a lengthy conversation of significant glances and facial expressions. Given what Khiri had already been through, they weren't going to stop her from leaving, but it seemed wrong for no one to escort her.

It was Resmine's emphatic shake of the head that ended the unspoken argument. No one was to interfere with Khiri's rest tonight. Further discussion could be initiated after a bit of recovery and solace.

Entrusting Shiv with seeing her guests down to the Pit's rooms—actual guest rooms and not torture chambers, Corianne assured Estan—Resmine pulled Estan aside and began pacing. She was more agitated than Estan remembered seeing her. Granted, they'd spent many years apart after Syara's passing, so he only had their travels to and from the Life Trees to pull from. But he still didn't remember her pacing to get through a conversation before.

"What's on your mind, Res?" Estan asked.

"You! You big ox!" Resmine punched Estan's arm as she passed. It was hard enough to sting, but not so hard as to invoke retaliation. Especially since she wasn't done. "You get yourself captured by the same idiots that stabbed you and I don't see you for close to two days! We didn't do any bonding ceremony or anything like Khiri and Micah, but you're the closest thing to family I have! You're my brother in all but name! Do you have any idea how worried I've been! I made a devil's bargain with Tak just to come rescue you!"

Estan's stomach sank through the floor. "What do you mean?"

Resmine proceeded to tell her proclaimed brother about the adventures leading her and her lieutenants into the heart of the Venom Guild's claimed Jarelton base. The former King of Thieves was much less interesting than what Tak charged her for the man's location. Estan almost didn't hear the rest of her story through the roar of blood through his ears. He'd known this secret would come due eventually, but he hadn't been prepared for it.

The newest head of the Thieves' Guild had known Estan too long to continue talking when he wasn't listening. "Out with it, Estan. What did Tak mean by 'he released you,'?"

"I made a deal with him to learn a secret. I should've left it alone when he asked me if I wanted to strike a bargain, but I was curious. Too curious to be smart about it. All he charged me was keeping quiet until he told me I could speak."

"Estan..."

With a deep breath, Estan summoned his courage. This conversation was harder than any battle he'd ever fought. He had no idea how Resmine would take his knowing something so huge without telling her for this long. Would she be furious enough to break ties? Would she be hurt? Estan couldn't imagine her crying over something like this, but he wasn't sure it was outside the realm of possibilities. Would a secret this large ruin their friendship? Looking into Resmine's concerned-yet-miffed eyes, Estan would've given just about anything to go back and stop himself from making the deal with Tak. But his time in the room with the Flayer-binding chandelier was a recent reminder on how dangerous those kinds of wishes could be.

"Res—" Estan's voice stuck in his throat. He threw back his head and sent a silent plea to Taymahr to give him strength. "Res, I know who your mother is."

For a moment, time seemed to stop around them. The whole of Arra slid away as an avalanche of emotions crashed over Resmine's face: confusion, joy, betrayal, rage, wonder, and bemusement. One emotion would dominate the others for the space of a heartbeat before being overwhelmed by the others. Estan wanted to reach out and hug his oldest friend, but he wasn't at all sure how such an action would be received. Even though it was killing him to be patient, he forced himself to wait. He couldn't rush her through this.

After what seemed like both eons and only seconds, Resmine's expression stilled into something like a true neutral. "Who?"

"Lady Araylia Treag," Estan said. Without realizing it, Estan found himself telling Resmine the entire story Tak had shared about the noble woman's search and Resmine's father's treachery. How Resmine's appearance at the Temple of Locke had been shortly after the entire fiasco and how Tak had pieced things together were a bit blurrier, but Estan told her what he could of that as well.

As he spoke, something flashed across Resmine's face that Estan didn't understand. Recognition, or maybe comprehension? Given how surprised Estan had been to find out his friend was technically nobility, it seemed odd that she wasn't entirely shocked. Or, more accurately, that she was over the shock so quickly. "So that's why one of my scenarios was about being a lady. Interesting..."

"One of your scenarios?"

His question popped Resmine out of whatever revelation she'd been in the middle of. "It's something from my Queen of Thieves test. Let's just leave it at: I've some confirmation for Tak's theory."

"Between that and the family resemblance," Estan muttered. It still struck him as odd when he remembered how long he'd been staring at the young Araylia Treag's likeness that he hadn't been able to piece it together until Tak said something. But the knight was self-aware enough to know he wasn't the best when it came to working out puzzles. He hadn't really thought about Resmine having family outside the temples because he didn't think about any of the orphans taken in by the temples having families. They were raised to belong to whatever temple took them in. Whatever their past had been, they were all sons and daughters of the High Ones. Given how Sir Jersal and High Priestess Shalora had turned on Estan after he discovered their true affiliations, perhaps it was worth looking into his own blood relations at some point. Right now, his main concern was with his avowed sister. "You aren't angry with me for not telling you sooner?"

Rolling her eyes, Resmine treated Estan to another arm punch. "Irritated at you for making a bargain like that, yes. Mad at you for adhering to it? Estan, you couldn't go back on your word to a fly you'd promised not to swat, let alone break a deal with Tak. If I'm angry with anyone, it's our information-selling friend. Why not just offer me this deal? Why'd he have to drag you into it? Tak's something of a spider with a great many webs. He's a good friend when he's on your side, but I think this is a good lesson to us. We're not always going to agree with his boundaries of friendship versus business."

Estan couldn't argue with that. He wasn't sure he wanted to.

Resmine punched his arm again. "Idiot."

Finally, Estan was secure enough to give Resmine the hug he'd been holding back.

Dewin and Corianne were conversing quietly in a different corner of the taproom. It was obvious they'd been giving Estan and Resmine space when they both jumped off their stools and hurried over while Estan had his arms wrapped around Resmine. Res hugged him back for all she was worth, cracking Estan's back with her grip. Even with his Taymahr-gifted healing, the pop released something and he immediately tingled all over from the rush of relief.

"So what's next, loves? The Venom Guild may have their poison sacs good and milked, but it ain't as though they're without fangs entire," Corianne said.

Breaking away from Estan's hug, Resmine's expression was immediately more calculating and pensive than Estan had ever seen it. When Shiv had suggested Resmine take the Thieves' Guild position, it had shocked Estan to learn how crafty his proclaimed sister really was. Having been at the heart of a few of her schemes, he thought he had a better idea of how intelligent she'd always been. Whatever she was ruminating on, it promised to be ambitious beyond his current conceptions.

"Jarelton needs to consolidate some power, and I've been made aware of a very intriguing connection. I think it's high time I met my mother."

28

~Ullen~

BATTLE TRUMPETS SOUNDED in the east with the rising of the sun. Enemy soldiers were pouring into Earl Terilles's estate and the adjoined battle camp from all sides. Ullen thanked Tharothet, the Stone, and any other deities listening that he hadn't still been in bed when the alarm rang out. There hadn't been any time to spare. If not for the barrel-walkers, his people would've already been overwhelmed.

"Drive them back! Back!"

"Hold that line!"

"Get those fires out! Move it! Double-time!"

A thousand other commands seemed to fill the air as Ullen's commanders attempted to make a dent in Hon'idar's forces. Archers hurried to create formations, shooting into the field of enemies still approaching. Rune throwers created walls of fire to try and funnel the sudden sea of bodies at their door. Ullen wasn't sure how his brother had managed to get this large an army so close without his people noticing, but he was certain it had something to do with the head of his scouts choosing exile after Quinton's execution.

It was a relief to see Jaspar's figure cutting through the crowd toward him, even though the lines of concern etched across her features promised nothing good was coming in her report. "Our southernmost tower has fallen entirely. Those walls are breached and short of driving the enemy all the way back to the palace, I don't see us getting it repaired."

"Casualties?" Ullen asked.

Jaspar tightened her lips and gave him a shake of her head. He'd known better than to ask, but there was still a sliver of hope residing in his chest. Ullen would almost prefer not to nurse hope at this point. It hurt all the more when his hope was dashed. "Jas, what am I gonna do? I canna very well slam my troops against the rocks until there's no one left, but Hon'idar's not giving us much of a choice. We ain't been sent terms or anything. He's here to wipe us out, plain and simple."

As the Prince of Eerilor, Ullen couldn't indulge in the battlefield embrace he felt in that moment. A final goodbye to the woman he loved would be an admission of defeat—and they weren't dead yet. But things were bleak and everyone in his camp knew it. The smell of overwhelming odds stank up the air worse than a vat of soldier socks.

"We're gonna fight until we are able to stop. Last breath or you're firmly on the throne," Jaspar said. Even though her words were brave, Ullen could see her sense of longing matched his. In a perfect world, they would have married decades ago and any embrace would've brought the luck of a queen to the battlefield. As it was, Jaspar snuck in a quick squeeze of Ullen's wrist while they made their way from one wall to another, speaking with troop captains and commanders as they went. Shifting this squad and filling this gap with that group would only take them so far, and they were running out of people to shift.

"Fire! FIRE!"

This voice wasn't an order, it was a call for aid. The new halls of the earl's manor, built with all that expensive wood, were starting to blaze. "My father's house!" Jaspar gasped. She rushed away from Ullen's side and grabbed one of the buckets being offered. Screams from inside the manor made it obvious—there were people trapped inside the building inferno. Ullen didn't even pause to think about how daft he was being, he plunged into the fiery great house and began hunting for the sources of the yelling. A servant had her skirts pinned under a shaft, but no physical damage. Ullen ripped the fabric with his bare hands and ushered the woman out of the building before turning back to find the next victim. Not all of the bodies he came across were as fortunate as a woman with the shredded skirt. Some were beyond saving. Someone in servant's garb was still breathing, but unable to walk. Carrying the servant out the door across his shoulders, Ullen could tell he was running out of time.

Smoke was choking the air, and the heat was bearing down on him. He could only go back for one or two at most.

As smoke strained his eyes, Ullen spotted one or two souls braving the fire as he was. One was a rune thrower that had thought to frost their armor before wading in. That thrower would get a promotion as soon as Ullen could push through the papers, assuming any of them came out of this alive.

Despite the despair threatening to eat his steps, Ullen pressed forward. There was someone calling ahead. Someone whose voice was starting to fade. Whether it was because their throat was burned past use or they were about to lose consciousness, Ullen could only guess. But he was determined to save this one last person. If he could save them, maybe he could find a way out of this hell-trap of a battle. The two things didn't equate, and he knew that, logically.

Logic didn't matter though.

All of his thoughts were about pushing through the oven of a house and finding one more lost soul.

He could save them.

He could.

He had to.

One step at a time. Breathe. Push through the heat. Push through the pain. Another wispy plea for help. The person calling was about to give themselves up for lost. If they stopped calling, Ullen wasn't sure he would find them.

No.

He would find them.

He would save them!

It was getting harder to think. His lungs threatened to erupt from his chest as a coughing fit took him. Everything from his nose to the deepest parts of his torso burned with every breath. A thread of doubt attempted to worm its way into his thoughts. *Even if you make it to this person, what makes you think you can make it out again?*

I'll make it out because I'm the Stone's own fucking son! I am Ut'evullen Dormidiir, the next fucking King of Eerilor, and no demon-sput fire is gonna stop me from taking what's mine! The person crying in the dark is mine. *Every thrice-cursed citizen of Eerilor is* mine! *I ain't letting anything kill me 'afore I deal with Hon'idar.*

The silent tirade pulled Ullen through the last leg of his journey.

He was pleased to find his quarry was still alive. He was less pleased to find it was Earl Tolen Terilles. More than the earl's voice was fading fast. Ullen hefted the older dwarf up on his shoulders. It was going to take all the strength he had left to stumble his way through the dark, smoke-choked halls. Turning back the way he'd come, Ullen narrowly avoided being pinned by another collapse. He couldn't retrace his steps and everything seemed foreign and changed. This was not the same manor he'd come to know during the last few months.

Beyond the way the smoke ravaged his breathing and the heat robbing him of strength, Ullen was fighting against the house itself for every step. The floor seemed to buckle and turn against his feet. No matter where he looked, there was no clear exit. Earl Terilles's coughing was enough to throw off the rhythm of Ullen's steps. Why was everything so dark when fire was used for light?

Ullen plowed forward, despite the roaring and creaking around him. If he allowed himself to stop, death wouldn't hesitate to collect the would-be king. Finally, he saw the outline of a window against a field of blackness.

Freedom. Relief. Safety.

One step.

Two.

They would make it. They were almost there.

Just a few more feet.

Shattered glass barely clung to the outer frame. Someone had already used this exit, which was all the better because Ullen doubted he had the strength to do more than shove the earl through the opening before he collapsed. The rush of fresh air moving through the frame was feeding the nearby flames, but it was a welcome respite from the soot-saturated stuff he'd been breathing. Ullen tried to navigate the best way to deposit

Earl Terilles through the broken window, but the wall itself had weakened enough that a lucky stumble broke them both through and into a courtyard of waiting soldiers.

Ullen had only enough time to recognize the sound of cheering and his own colors on the uniforms surrounding him before darkness filled his vision.

AS ULLEN REGAINED CONSCIOUSNESS, a thousand pains seemed to awaken with him. He groaned and attempted to sit up.

"None of that, now," Jaspar's voice said from behind him. Her touch was as gentle as it could be, but still caused a ripple of fresh needles to course through him. "You're supposed to rest for a few days still."

"...your father?" Ullen asked. The question was enough to throw him into a coughing fit, which hurt enough Ullen almost wished he'd never made it free of the fire.

"Also recovering, thanks to your stubbornness."

"...the battle?"

"Here, suck on this." Jaspar came to sit on a stool within Ullen's line of sight. Her soft, dark curls bounced around her ears as she pressed a wet cloth against Ullen's lips and waited for him to follow her directions before answering his questions.

With as close as he'd come to death, Ullen allowed himself to bask in her presence. If they had an audience, he didn't even care how much he was revealing in this stolen moment. He'd nearly lost her twice now, and there was still no certain future for the two of them. The moment he won his crown, Ullen would propose. Whether her father approved or not, Ullen wanted to spend his life with Jaspar and was tired of fighting the urge to tell her. Still, duty bound him to win this damn war first.

"We managed to drive them back, as unlikely as it seems. Vess freed General Geryan after you went into the fire. That first maid you rescued from the manor came out gushing about how our Warrior Prince, framed in a halo of light, had lifted a burning beam off of her and it galvanized the troops. Between Geryan's leadership, the boost to morale, and Rigger's newest weapon, we managed to pull out an unlikely win! Well, that and reinforcements from Gyth arriving shortly after you waded into the manor."

Ullen understood why Jaspar had made him begin sucking on a cloth. If his lips had been free, he'd have continued asking a thousand questions, coughing fits or no. While he'd been at odds on what to do with General Tericia Geryan since the trial, he doubted asking her to step into a leadership role in his own army was something he would've trusted her enough to attempt. Rigger having developed another new weapon was also intriguing, and Gyth sending unexpected reinforcements was a gods-send. Eerilor's neighbors had been pretty clear about not wanting to get caught up in Eerilor's civil war. He couldn't imagine what had changed minds in Gyth.

"I know you well enough to start with the last thing first," Jaspar said. "We have several companies of Gythian soldiers and one of their mounted cavalry units, and we're to send word if that's not enough. They had to beat back a smaller arm of the Gray Army that reared up on their own soil, which was enough for them to reconsider our request."

With a grunt, Ullen fought back the urge to cry. Something had finally gone right.

It would've been nice to cry for a good reason after the last few days. His tear ducts seemed empty after the fire, but that didn't stop the clutching within Ullen's chest or the way his throat muscles tried to close up. He'd felt the passing of Kal, and then Genovar's death nearly on the mage's heels. There hadn't been much opportunity to mourn his friends. Ullen wasn't even sure how to explain knowing about their deaths.

What my lass must be going through...

He wished with all his heart he could've gone with Khiri. He hoped she wasn't alone out there. It was dangerous enough, sending a message to Leyani with his condolences. *Tharothet watch over my messenger.*

Though the gods probably had enough on their plates without trying to watch over every messenger in a war zone, Tharothet and the other High Ones did owe him something for all his service. And this was a special case.

Jaspar leaned in and straightened the blankets around his neck. Ullen waited for the scent of her to wash through him, but he couldn't smell much of anything. *I must've burned out my sense of smell with all that smoke.*

Removing his cloth and rewetting it, Jaspar gave Ullen a small gap in which to speak. He tried to take full advantage. "Vess..."

Once more, the coughs rolled through him like a quake. It took forever for them to quiet down. Jaspar's dark brows were drawn together in concern as she resettled his blankets and gave him a freshly moistened cloth. "You really are the most pigheaded dwarf I've ever met. I'll tell you everything I can. Just rest. The better you rest, the faster you'll be up and about."

Grimacing, Ullen rolled his eyes and tried to focus on something other than the urge to get up and do something. He'd never been the best patient. Why wasn't he covered with healing runes? *Because we had a massive battle and anyone that can be saved must be saved.* Ullen didn't actually need the mental reminder to know he wasn't the worst off in their camp. Speaking of their camp, Ullen wondered briefly where they were at this point. He was very obviously housed in a tent, but he didn't know if the burning of Earl Terilles's manor meant they'd pulled up and relocated or if the manor was a smoldering ruin in the center of a broken series of walls.

"When General Geryan stood in between Sir Ilyani and the guard that spoke against him, Vess had an inkling that our prisoner was more than slightly sympathetic to our cause. She came to me, since I'd been imprisoned with the woman, to ask me my impressions. Tericia and I did get to discuss quite a bit during our shared incarceration. You've impressed her, you know? First, you managed her capture with limited casualties. That's not something many generals are so careful about on either side, but you pulled it off with a small force and limited resources. Second, when you managed to keep her alive in this camp for so long. Thirdly, you impressed her again with how you didn't play into Sir Ilyani's hands during the trial. Granted we didn't get to talk about that one until after the execution. But she's been a loyal member of Eerilor's forces for long enough to recognize Hon'idar's claims and the way he leads don't add up. Someone as concerned with limited casualties as you wouldn't kill his own mother for a crown he avoided for many years. The way she explains it, she's not even shifting loyalties. Her first pledge as a member of the Eerilorian army is to defend the country. The crown comes second. And even then, she'd be adhering to your mother's professed wishes as anyone other than Hon'idar last knew them."

Letting that sink in, Ullen found he couldn't argue. Had he not been in the middle of a blazing building, he might've even taken the chance himself. It would've come with a lot more repercussions given the amount of speculation still surrounding him. Even after the execution and dismissal of those loyal to Quinton, the rumors and mistrust were still strong. It was much easier for Ullen to approve someone else's actions after they'd occurred than to risk appearing disloyal to his people.

Easier for his people to swallow his approval after a miraculous win, too. "How long..."

A quirk of Jaspar's shapely lips told him she'd understood the half-formed question. "You've been under for almost a full day. You missed the end of the battle, and slept through the night. My father woke up roughly an hour ago. He doesn't remember much of his rescue. Just that he'd all but given up hope when you arrived—" for the first time since she'd started talking, Jaspar's throat caught on the words. She swallowed and breathed deeply, working her way through something that seemed to be part sob and part sigh. She leaned forward and rested her forehead lightly against Ullen's hand, one of the only places on his body that didn't feel too terrible. "Thank you... Ullen, I can't even... I can't imagine what it would've been like to lose him. We don't always agree or get along, but he's my father. I—Thank you."

"Jas..." Pouring as much of what he felt into one syllable, Ullen moved his pointer finger against Jaspar's smooth skin. Equal parts comfort and caress, this stolen moment was precious to him. He'd run into a thousand more burning buildings if it meant getting more moments like it.

It was over before he was ready for it to end. "I've got to meet with Vess, Tericia, and the rest of the commanders. They'll want to know you're awake and recovering. I'll speak with your healers and make sure you're kept to your bed until they release you, your Highness." With a teasing smile, Jaspar gave him a slightly wet wink and made her way out of the tent.

Left on his own in his convalescing tent, Ullen continued to suck on the damp cloth pressed against his mouth in frustration as much as to soothe his thirst. He still wanted to know about Rigger's latest weapon.

29

~Irrellian~

SHATTERING AN ICE SHARD the size of a raccoon into the craggy wall of rock next to Arad's head did nothing to alleviate Irrellian's fury. "YOU STOLE MY RIVAL! I WASN'T READY FOR HIM TO DIE YET!"

Unflinching, the leader of the Venom Guild didn't seem to gather he was no longer on the sunny face of Arra. Irrellian had deposited the assassin on one of his favorite dormant calderas of the shadowy hell realms. Despite the frigid wind whipping against Arad's thin coat and the bleeding wounds steaming in the cold, the assassin leaned forward on his feet with his arms open—almost as though he wanted to give Irrellian a hug. Arad grinned. A frantic, twisted giggle started in the back of the man's throat and erupted out like a cough, and his eyes were shining with a madness he'd long kept hidden from the Flayer Mage. "He was my rival first! I finally saw him get what was coming to him. I still mean to slaughter his spawn in front of my wayward sister before I slice her up good!"

Irrellian was more than a little tired of people not fearing him, but madness wasn't something he could scare out of a person. It wasn't even something he could work with. Arad's giggle was still growing into a laugh. The man had started digging around in the rune bag he wore on his belt with one hand. Watching him search for whatever he thought would change their positions was almost sad. While Arad was certainly not of sound mind, Irrellian could admire the dedication to revenge. Somehow,

Arad had clung to his schemes for two decades without binding himself to a demon for help. There were plenty of sane men that wouldn't have made it this far.

He also took down Genovar Fortiva, Irrellian admitted to himself. *Probably saved me a lot of future trouble.*

But, Genovar had been a seer. There was no telling what paths the elf had closed with his sacrifice. Seeing had also always been Genovar's weakness. Irrellian knew from experience that if he was creative enough, whatever future Genovar had seen didn't have to be the future that came to pass. Hadn't the elf once told Irrellian he'd only win once he accepted that he'd already lost? Something that still made no sense, and here they were—Irrellian tiredly watching the man who had orchestrated Genovar's fall.

Khiriellen Fortiva would be made to pay for her own hand in her father's demise. She'd denied Irrellian the lesser pleasure of having his rival's demon-bound husk as a puppet for however long the Flayer Mage chose to indulge in playing with the thing. It wouldn't have been nearly as satisfying as any of the plans Irrellian had toyed with during his extended crystalline sleep, but it would've been better than this feeling of impotency.

Arad finally found whatever he'd been searching for. Dashing along the wall he'd been leaning away from, the assassin planted a boot against a rock and launched himself into the air, hurling his chosen rune at Irrellian's face.

After two decades spent leeching the magic out of seven divine beings, Irrellian barely noticed the miniscule refreshment to his mana pool as he drained the projectile. He caught the inert stone with a bare hand and tossed it to the ground. "Are you nearly finished?"

Landing with a roll, the assassin continued to throw his runes at the mage, despite the way they all fizzled out before making contact. He ran this way and that, trying to obfuscate his position with runes meant to smoke or blind—but Irrellian drank the magic from those as well. It wasn't until the bag was visibly starting to empty that Arad started to lose his madness-induced confidence.

"Perhaps now you understand what it is you're seeking to undermine," Irrellian said. He felt it the moment his eyes switched from Odlesk reflectiveness to burning with a demon-lit fire. "I gave you the resources to rule a city for me. I allowed you power beyond any of my generals, control of the Flayers second only to my own, and the liberty to do with them as you would. As repayment, you took the person I declared off limits—whom I'd dreamed about revenging myself on for twenty years—and ripped him from my grasp forever! DOES THAT SEEM LIKE A FAIR TRADE?"

Arad cowered against the side of the caldera and turned his useless sack of rocks over, letting them tumble into a pile at his feet. "No, no, *no*! This isn't right! I was winning! I was *winning*!"

As last words went, Irrellian had heard worse. It was time to end the madman's suffering.

30

~Jathy~

FUMING AT THE FIRE, Jathy Ettleway watched her people set up camp on the edges of the Eissessi Mountains. Spring was in the air, but that didn't mean warmth this far into the mountain range. Her old scouting coat was layered with a thick cloak and her thickest shirt. It still made her shiver when the wind picked up. She studied the troops she still possessed and tried to figure out their next move. She was the highest ranked of the entire group and everyone kept looking to her for leadership.

What food they still had was rationed, supplemented by what game they could find and keep safe from the gnorels. Ugly creatures. Some described gnorels as hooved dogs or carnivorous mountain goats. Jathy thought of them primarily as a nuisance. The local pack had taken to raiding her camp's supplies, shredding anything they could get their teeth on, and occasionally even attacking her people. The creatures didn't bother larger settlements, like the war camp now occupied by the traitor prince and his supporters. Her stomach gurgled at the thought of proper bread.

This wasn't right. None of it made sense.

Sir Ilyani should be here!

How had everything gone so sideways? That traitor prince should've been the body rotting in a ditch, not her knight commander—he'd only wanted to protect Arra from the demon-spit roaming freely through Eerilor.

Jathy knew the horror of Flayers better than anyone. Under her armor, she had the scars to prove it. When she only had twelve or thirteen summers under her belt, her older brother and his friends had decided it would be funny to abandon Jathy in the woods. Her wood craft had been better than Hessit's, as young as she'd been. She'd confronted the older boys, tears in her eyes, as the Flayer fog had crept up on all of them. Sometimes at night, Jathy still woke in a panic—she could still hear the echoes of laughter melting into screams, could still feel the burn of demon teeth tearing chunks out of her back, could still see life draining from her brother's eyes as he distracted the monsters. Hessit had chosen to protect her in the end. They'd been foolish, unthinking children. She never wanted anyone to experience anything like that night ever again.

Fighting against those things, beating back the Gray Army—people who wanted to coat the whole world in fiends—and killing those that sympathized with the Flayer Mage; Sir Ilyani had promised Jathy that was what she was signing on for. But Prince Ut'evullen Dormidiir was as weak as Sir Ilyani had said. Unwilling to kill the nest for fear of harming a fly in the midst of hornets.

"General Ettleway!"

Inwardly wincing at the battleground promotion ahead of her name, Jathy turned to face one of her most trusted scouts. Mereth Otanell had been in the field during the initial exile, and Jathy had been more than happy to welcome her into the fold when she returned. She was one of the only scouts Jathy had that could move back and forth over the Mytana border without trouble. "Scout Otanell, you have something?"

"Confirmation by way of letter. The traitor prince attempted to send a note of condolence to a Widow Fortiva. The messenger was waylaid before I arrived, the note still unread. I memorized and burned it along with the bodies of the ambush. Looked like bandits."

Bandits were a common problem out here in the hills. They were getting worse, as the civil war progressed. People that didn't want to take sides, opportunists, displaced city thieves and beggars, farmers with plundered fields—they all gathered to pluck what they could off anyone wandering too close. The bandits weren't important. It was easier to contemplate bandits than the news Jathy's scout had just reported though.

"Fortiva is dead," Jathy repeated. Saying it out loud didn't make it any better.

Scout Otanell didn't say anything. Her face was a mask of grim lines. After Sir Ilyani's execution at the hands of those that feared *real* leadership, this was the worst blow her people could've had. General Fortiva had been the last hope against the Flayer Mage and his army. What was Jathy going to do against an entire world?

But there was something she could do!

The realization struck her with almost physical force. Sir Ilyani had been pushing for this before General Fortiva had even left camp, and Fortiva himself had denied the request.

But that was before. Before they'd both died and left everything in her hands. Jathy would carry on with their mission, to free Arra from the hands of the Gray Army. And they knew where there was one hell of a hornet nest.

"People! We move at dawn! We're going to need as much black powder, flour, or fine dust as we can barrel, and as many fire runes as we can get! It's time we take the fight to Seirane!"

31

~Resmine~

DESPITE TAK'S ADVICE to wear a dress for her first meeting with her birth mother, Resmine couldn't stand the thought of being in anything other than her armor. It was comfortable. It was practical. It told the world who she was, and who she was willing to be. If none of that fit with Lady Araylia Treag's expectations, it was best to get the disappointment out of the way now.

The waiting chamber with the painting Estan had described was cozy enough, easily seating Resmine's small party. Tak had made the arrangements, so he was there, both in his merchant capacity and as a friend. Dewin was next to Resmine, frowning at the painting and looking back at Resmine. "Love, I don't even understand how Estan could've been thick enough to miss it. You two are near enough to be sisters if'n she were closer your age!"

Resmine nodded. "As much as I love the lunk, he can be a bit thick."

"Just remember to let me introduce you," Tak cautioned. "I only told Lady Treag that I thought the two of you should meet. I didn't tell her why."

It was all Resmine could do not to start pacing. "Lovely. I'm sure I'll be a wonderful surprise then! Is that why you wanted me to dress up? To emphasize... Well, that!" She gestured to the painting where her mother gazed back at them all, a proper and prim lady, full of noble fire. Looking at the thing was starting to make Resmine feel confined. Or maybe her nerves were on edge because Tak was about to fling her at a blood-relative stranger without warning the woman first.

While Resmine had never considered herself ambitious, it was like chasing the position of Queen of Thieves had awakened something in her. For so much of her life, Resmine had hidden in the shadows. Syara had been a shining beacon, easily overshadowing anything Resmine had to offer. After Syara's death, hiding had been a matter of survival. Following Khiri had been easy enough. Khiri possessed a natural presence and really, Resmine was used to following. She'd more or less been there to make sure Estan didn't get himself killed. One of the first times Resmine actually took hold of her own destiny was when she'd admitted to herself her relationship with Dewin was more than a salve against the pain of losing Syara.

Taking the Thieves' Guild Crown, though. That had been...

Transcendent.

Squeezing Dewin's hand, Resmine grinned at her love. "Thank you for doing this with me. It means a lot that you came here instead of going to your temple today."

"Sure enough, love. Gods or no, you're the most important thing I've got," Dewin said. Her elusive dimple was showing as she smiled back.

Reaching out, Resmine brushed the dimple with her thumb and brought Dewin's face close enough they could bump foreheads. She didn't dare go in for a kiss in Lady Treag's parlor, not because of decorum, but because if she did she wouldn't want to stop. That ring was still burning a hole in her pocket.

Well, why not? This seems like as good a moment as any.

"Dewin... I'm not sure how much longer she's going to make us wait, and there's a question I've been meaning to ask—" Pulling the box out of her pocket, Resmine's eyes were locked on Dewin's sweet expression of befuddled curiosity. "Would you consent to be my wife?"

With a squeal of joy, Dewin launched herself at Resmine and began laughing. "Of course! Of course! Of course! Sweet Adari, I thought you'd never ask!"

As Resmine had suspected, the ring box she'd been carrying around since first entering her quarters off of the Pit held a simple golden band with a faceted onyx gem. It slipped onto Dewin's finger as though it had been made for her. Dewin showered Resmine's face in a thousand kisses.

The sun itself couldn't have filled the parlor with more light than what was currently bursting out of Resmine's heart. Her nerves couldn't withstand the might of her current happiness.

"Congratulations!" Tak said from his chair on the other side of the room.

Resmine's mood shifted as she recalled she was actually here for other reasons. Though the joy beaming at her through Dewin's gaze was no less intense, the priestess did attempt to school her expression to one of more serious and somber matters. They couldn't hold hands without Resmine's fingers brushing against the ring though. This was a road Resmine hadn't known she'd ever willingly go down, but Dewin was special. Resmine had been entranced by the priestess from their first meeting, and while Syara would always hold a special place in Resmine's heart, it was Dewin that Resmine wanted to spend her eternity with. It had taken a while to make peace with her memories—to let go.

If Syara was looking on from the other side, Resmine was sure her first love approved. This was right. This was her truth.

It was almost disappointing when the servant came and announced Lady Araylia Treag was ready to see them.

"IS THIS GOING TO BE another meeting to encourage my bid for the Ilamar title, Master Tak? Because, I do have actual—" Resmine found herself facing an older, taller, broader version of herself. Lady Araylia Treag was nearly as still as her portrait in the parlor they'd been escorted out of as she drank in Resmine's hair, eyes, lips, nose, and everything else that made Resmine who she was.

"Lady Treag, allow me to introduce Resmine, Queen of the Thieves' Guild," Tak said.

Whether the Lady Treag heard him or not was anybody's guess. The woman popped straight out of her chair and stumbled around her desk as though she were walking in a dark room. Her servant tried to rush past the strangers in his way to help his lady, but she waved him off without seeming to see him. Resmine watched everything like she was swimming through soup herself. The air seemed thick and eternal. There were no words to express the confusion of emotions and time that swirled around her.

This is my mother. My mother!

While Resmine knew she was going to meet her mother on an intellectual level, and had thought herself prepared for it... She was wrong. So many emotions stormed around and through her, she couldn't isolate one. They stormed around and through each other as well. There was no such thing as color anymore. The vortex ate it out of the world. Along with language. Scent. Memories.

Resmine was a blank on the face of Arra.

And then those arms, stronger than they looked, were embracing her.

"Oh, my sweet, sweet girl! I knew you were alive! I knew it! All this time, I never lost hope! Nothing as precious and as strong as my baby could've died without my knowing! And you're here! You're whole and perfect and here!"

Tears began streaming unbidden down Resmine's cheeks and her arms seemed to wrap around Lady Treag of their own accord. They sank into a weepy mess together, Resmine's leather catching against the lady's fine dress and likely pulling several threads out of place. All of the questions Resmine had about why this woman had left her alone, in the hands of the temples, were pushed back for later. Estan and Tak had told her a story about how Lady Araylia Treag had tried her best to find her missing child, but it wasn't until the grief-stricken euphoria of Lady Treag's outburst that any part of Resmine had allowed herself to believe there was really someone who had wanted her as a child. Just as she hadn't really believed someone wanted her as an adult, until Dewin.

The thought of Dewin brought Resmine to herself enough that she gestured for Dewin to come forward. "This is my betrothed, Dewin. We're going to marry soon."

Lady Treag didn't hesitate to draw Dewin into the hug she was sharing with her long lost child. "All this time I waited for one daughter to come home only to find I have two!"

Tak and the servant seemed to have vanished by the time Resmine, Dewin, and the Lady Treag untangled themselves from their knot on the floor. "I'm sure Caspen took Master Tak somewhere for refreshments. He's been with me long enough not to say anything to the rest of the staff about our momentary lack of decorum. Of course, Tak will be back to negotiate a price. But that's all for later. You're here now, and this is your Dewin, but tell me more about you! What's your life been like? How did you come to be Queen of Thieves here in Jarelton, right under my nose? I thought the thieves were run by some blonde cutthroat? Did you fight her?"

As Resmine told her story, the three women gravitated toward a formal sitting area on the far side of the office, tastefully arranged with a couch and a few puffy chairs. They were watched by a painting of a silky black and white dog with umber undertones to the white fur. The artist had arranged the background to look vaguely like a forest, but having herself tromped through what felt like every forest on the face of Arra, Resmine doubted the artist or dog had either spent much time in woods. Still, it was a pleasant enough painting to focus on when her mother's scrutiny threatened to overwhelm her. She'd never had someone so invested in listening to her talk before. Even Dewin, always willing to lend an ear, hadn't looked at her with such intensity. Lady Treag wouldn't look away, as though she were afraid that Resmine might suddenly evaporate given the chance. It took an hour to get all the way through her childhood, and a second to reach her escape from Seirane with Estan and their journey to the Life Trees. At this point, Lady Treag interrupted and rang a bell, summoning back her servant to bring refreshments and to return Tak to the room.

Knocking back an entire cup of tea, Resmine slowed herself drinking the second. She hadn't been raised as a noble, but she did know how to sip. It was just hard to remember her manners when she was talking so much. An entire assortment of small sandwiches, pastries, fruits, cheeses, and other dainties were arranged on a silver platter.

Khiri would love this, Resmine thought. Assuming she didn't manage to alienate the Lady Treag somehow in the next few hours, she would try to take a few particularly sweet cheese pastries back to the elf woman. Maybe it would cheer her up? Resmine's conscience flared, reprimanding her for being so happy in the wake of Khiri's heartache. Shaking the feeling away was relatively easy though. There were enough other emotions wading through the Queen of Thieves for unrequested guilt to get swallowed by the malaise.

It wasn't long after refreshments were served that Resmine came to the end of her story. Which naturally led to the real reason she'd come to find her mother in the first place. Facing Lady Treag, Resmine understood the scope of her audacity. To stroll into a noble's house and demand backing for claim to a city would've been a lot to ask from someone she'd known her whole life, but Resmine had only known this woman—her birth mother, yes, but still a stranger—for the space of an afternoon. *And I give Estan grief for rushing into things!*

Still, the threat to Jarelton wasn't over. Despite the quiet of the last few days, Resmine didn't think the true threat would be gone until Irrellian Thornne was dealt with. Arad Rhidel and the Venom Guild were only symptoms of a much larger, much deadlier, disease.

"—and so that's what brings me here," Resmine said. "I want to be the next Lady Ilamar."

Lady Treag set her teacup on its saucer, the ceramic clack muffled by her pinky discreetly cushioning the bottom. A mark of Lady Treag's upbringing. One of those earmarks of nobility Resmine didn't have. "I see... So your intentions weren't solely to be reunited with your lost mother, which—" Lady Treag met Tak's gaze and gave him a nod, "—I'm sure you were more ready for than I was. I've dealt with the nobility my entire life. I can tell when someone's hoping to catch me flat-footed. I've always been good at regaining my balance."

Resmine opened her mouth to protest that she'd no intention of using her mother's emotions against her, but she stopped herself. It wouldn't do any good to say her intentions had been honorable from the start, because they hadn't. She was the Queen of Thieves for a reason, and honor wasn't it. Even if she was running the guild from the unique position of not having robbed anyone, that didn't mean she *wouldn't*, just that she *hadn't*.

And am I not trying to steal the throne of Ilamar right out from under the nose of the whole city?

"Rather than tell you 'no' out of hand, I would like to know why? Why should I back your claim to Ilamar rather than pursue my own claim or choosing to back Holt? Because this isn't a small request. Even if neither Holt nor I step in, there's still the matter of our younger cousin, who might challenge your legitimacy. The entire council will try to argue against your sudden appearance. Mother and I did create your records and I've maintained them, but there will be those that balk at the convenience of a new heir popping out of the shadows in the middle of our current troubles. Holt might even be among them. He's good at feigning indifference, but—" Araylia ended the query with a small shrug.

A fair question, and one Resmine had anticipated the moment she'd concocted this ridiculous plan. But as hard as she'd tried, she hadn't been able to come up with an explanation she found satisfactory.

Be with me, Locke. Guide me through this.

"I was there when my uncle died. Lord Orin Treag— Lord Ilamar for all of a heartbeat. I know what it's like to watch hope fail. I know what it's like to watch the world burn. Jarelton needs someone who can see through the blood and ash and still cling to a brighter future. I knew about my uncle's plans to join the darkness of this city with the light and create a place where we could all function and thrive together. This city needs me... Not because I've got noble blood, or because I was chosen by the gods to free Jarelton from the Venom Guild—but because I can see the jewel that shines beneath the stone."

Round beads of water clung to Lady Treag's eyes like earrings on earlobes, catching the light and appearing almost decorative. "He would've liked you, I think. Orin. Well, never mind that. If I can't talk you out of this, I'll begin making arrangements. It will take time to get the council to convene, and likely bribery and favors to get them to agree. Then, I'll have to deal with Holt—"

It sounded like a dismissal and Resmine had a thousand other things she intended to get done before she had to convince even more nobles to let her be in charge of Jarelton. She got to her feet and waited for Tak and Dewin to join her. When it came to saying her farewells though, the words wouldn't come. Was she supposed to call this woman Mother or Lady Treag? Araylia?

Were they supposed to hug? Bow? Shake hands?

Lady Treag stood and drew Resmine up for another fierce hug. "Whatever brought you here, I'm very glad you came."

Allowing herself to hug back, Resmine said, "Me too."

32

~Khiri~

"KHIRI, COME ON... YOU'VE got to leave this room. Estan's outside," Micah coaxed.

"I definitely don't want to see Estan right now," Khiri sighed. "I don't want to see anyone. I just want to cry for a few days and leave before anyone notices."

She wasn't fond of what her friends referred to as The Pit in the bottom of The Dusk and Dawn. There weren't any windows—there were small skylights which were little more than holes—and it was hard to tell what time of day it was. Jarelton already tried its best to suffocate her with its buildings and streets of endless dull stone. But the self-recriminating part of her thought it was no less than she deserved. She'd killed her own father. She didn't deserve the Life Trees, the forest, or even a sliver of unfiltered sunlight. No, The Pit was perfect for someone as stained and filthy as she felt.

"You are neither stained nor filthy. You've taken enough baths your skin is starting to squeak when you scrub."

Wrinkling her nose and sticking out her tongue, Khiri made a rude noise at her brother. If he wasn't going to let her mope in peace, perhaps it would be better to face Estan and get it over with.

"Yes! Exactly! Go!"

Hugging her pillow to her face, Khiri let out a sound somewhere between a scream and a sob before giving in. She didn't want to leave the physical darkness. The world outside kept moving, not caring how broken Khiri's private world was. People laughed. People played. People loved. Everything people did reminded her how alone she felt.

TELGAN KORSBORN, the heavy name rang through her like a great iron bell. Even it seemed to protest her attempts to draw into herself. Oddly, there was a sense of kinship she'd never experienced with the name before. A mutual resonance of great loss.

"I told you before—you'll never be alone. Especially when you actually take me with you instead of handing me off to your latest stray."

"Loni isn't a stray. She wanted to find Estan," Khiri argued.

"Uh huh," Micah said.

He was still irritated about Khiri's decision to keep him safe when she got captured by the Venom Guild. Not that Khiri could blame him. She'd made a split-second call in the moment without even asking what he would've preferred. Knowing he would've chosen differently, had he been able to choose. It hadn't been fair, but Khiri couldn't bring herself to be sorry. If she'd lost Micah again, along with everyone else, she wasn't sure she could take it.

Also, he was goading her. Making it harder to mope.

"Damn right I am. Let's get out of this stupid room and let the knight buy you some food."

Before Khiri could think of a new way to put off leaving, her stomach agreed with Micah. As miserable as she was, Khiri still had a weakness when it came to the offer of a decent meal. She slid off the bed, shifted into her armor, grabbed Micah, and opened the door.

Estan really was waiting outside. He'd towed a stool down from the taproom and stationed himself across the hall. The immediacy with which he jumped to his feet concerned Khiri. They'd danced around an attraction, stronger for him than for her, and Khiri really didn't want to deal with a lovesick friend on top of everything else. But that ember of interest Estan's eyes once possessed didn't ignite. Khiri allowed herself a sigh of relief. "Micah said you were waiting for me. I thought you'd still be catching up with Loni. She came a long way to find you."

There, a spark of that longing flared briefly before Estan managed to smother it. *Good*, Khiri thought. *I think they would suit each other well. Or someone else maybe. As long as it's not me.*

"I... I have a lot to figure out before I talk to Loni," Estan said. "But I wanted you to know that I'm sorry. I'm sorry I couldn't save you from what happened with Fennick, that I forced my attention on you when you'd been pretty clear you weren't available, and I'm sorry I couldn't take the knife from you when you asked. None of that adds up to what I feel a friend should be, and I would still like us to be friends. If that's okay?"

Khiri looked at Estan's outstretched hand, waiting for her to shake it or smack it away. She was so tired of talking about everything. Apologies, guilt, accusations, questions—all of it. She needed to do something impulsive and physical. Something fun that didn't require thought. "Estan, you want to be my friend right now? Find me something to eat, and then find me something to fight."

The knight let out a small chuckle and then nodded. "I can do that. It's been a bit since we've had a proper sparring match."

WITH STEW AND BREAD calming their bellies, along with a healthy amount of cheese, Estan led Khiri to a well-kept stable yard. Catapult and two other horses were occupying stalls, but the stable was large enough to shelter five times as many. The dirt in the fenced exercise paddock was free of horse dung and puddles, which made Khiri breathe a sigh of relief. As much as she wanted to fight out her feelings, she preferred not to do so in a pile of excrement. It was also nice to see a patch of ground in Jarelton left unpaved.

Catapult bobbed his head and a voice came from the horse's direction. "Hi, Estan! Khiri! Are we going to tell each other secrets? I do like a good secret!"

As hard as she tried, Khiri couldn't see the person addressing them. Were they behind Catapult? Why hadn't Micah warned her there was a stranger? But... No, it couldn't be a stranger. They had called her by her nickname, not Khiriellen or Fortiva. She was about to demand that whoever was watching them show themselves when Estan walked over to his steed and said, "Not here for secrets, but I did bring you a carrot."

"Excellent," the voice said. "I don't suppose you might have brought an apple as well?"

"No, just the carrot, you ungrateful beast," Estan laughed.

While Catapult munched happily at the vegetable, Khiri mentally addressed Micah. *"Did you know he could do that?"*

"Talk to the horse? Or you mean the illusion trick Catapult's using?"

"Illusion trick?"

"His gifts from Numyri allow him to cast very strong illusions, and he's learned how to modulate speech with it. We spent some time talking while I was being carted around by Loni. Turns out Catapult can hear me as well as you or Kal ever could."

It surprised Khiri less that Catapult and Micah could communicate than that the horse could talk. But as weird as it was, Khiri let it go with a shrug. She wasn't ready to trade secrets with Catapult any more than she was wanting to absolve Estan of his guilt. It was time to work off some of her pent-up emotions and do something that made sense. Placing her brother on a tidy workbench, Khiri spared a thought of appreciation for the assortment of tools hung on pegs and nails. Even if Arra were to shake the entire city, it seemed unlikely Micah would be in danger of taking a tool shower.

Khiri began to warm up her stiff limbs and did a few stances. It felt good to go through her training steps without the fear of having a Flayer bite into her. It probably said something unpleasant about her life that she couldn't remember many fights she'd been in which *hadn't* involved one of the demon-bound. If she'd been looking for a sign another Flayer war had started, she'd found it.

No, Khiri. No grimness. No darkness. This is about getting all of that out of your system.

While she was prepping, she had another shadow grip her when she reached for her knife. The bird-of-prey knuckle guard mocked her with its stagnant presence, silently reminding her there was no blade, no enchanted runic vines, nothing to send the familiar jolt of magic through her ear tips. "I can't spar armed with arrows," Khiri said.

Estan stopped his own exercises when he heard her. "Do you want a new knife? We could probably go find a weaponsmith or a shop. Though I don't have the kind of money required to get anything close to your old piece, we may be able to find something workable."

The thought of strapping a new blade to her belt opened an emptiness in Khiri's gut no food could fill. She wasn't ready to switch weapons yet. "Are you okay to go unarmed?"

Showing more wisdom than he normally did, the knight didn't press the issue. He nodded and released his sheath clip, placing his sword next to Micah where it was safely away from horse hooves and hay. The rest of his armor remained in place as Estan readied himself and signaled his challenge.

On the road out to Harish, Khiri and Estan had fought against each other a few times, but Khiri had thought she'd taken his measure on the journey. Something had changed though, and she found herself glad the two of them weren't using blades. Openings they both would've let slip in the past were met with hard jabs and solid blows. They were both less timid about initiating contact. Where once their sparring was more like a handshake, now it was more like seasoned warriors testing their mettle.

Because we are.

The words floated through Khiri's head as she ducked under a fierce punch Estan's whole weight carried. She threw her own knuckles into his empty armpit, causing the knight to grunt with appreciation and pain. There wasn't enough time to gloat about the strike because he was already coming in with a backfist. Deflecting most of the force with a guiding hand, Khiri twirled away from the larger man's reach and ran straight up the wall. Estan swore as he cleared out of the way, narrowly avoiding the heel she'd flipped to aim at his shoulder.

Arm bars, choke holds, throws, punches above and below the belt—nothing was off limits and both of them gave it everything they had. There was only one unspoken guideline they both silently agreed to: No lethal blows.

Khiri lost track of time. Sweat drenched her hair and her clothes despite the coolness of the early spring day. And while she was drenched, Estan was revealing his secret ambition to create a river. The knight was breathing through his nose and panting out of his mouth in an effort to keep his breathing steady, but he was still starting to flag.

"Do you— You think— we should—stop?" Estan asked.

"I think—when—neither of us can—finish a sentence," Khiri wheezed, "it's probably time."

Sinking down onto his knees in an exhausted squat, Estan nodded. "Good! Because I'm spent."

Khiri was tempted to fall down on the dirt, but she knew better than to skip the necessary cool down after such an intense match. She wanted nothing more than to stumble back into her bed in the dark. Instead, she started walking in laps around the yard.

Catapult trotted over to Estan and started nuzzling the knight's face. Estan reached up to pat his roan's nose when Catapult reached down far enough to push against Estan's chest, knocking the knight over with his massive horse head. "I win!" the horse laughed, both in his project voice and snickering whinny, trotting back over the food trough.

Sputtering and cursing, Estan scrambled back to his feet. "That's not how you win at sparring!"

"It's how you win at tag." There was a friendly challenge in the horse's voice, and he flicked his tail as though he were inviting them to come chase him.

Estan grumbled as he stumbled his way over to the workbench where he pulled off his chest plate and pauldrons. "Alright, horse. You want to play tag... We'll play tag."

A laugh jumped out of Khiri's mouth as she watched the exhausted Estan chase after Catapult. The war horse was careful not to wind his tired friend further. It was as much a cool down exercise as Khiri's own laps, but it was vastly more entertaining to see Catapult dash and strut as Estan failed to lay a hand on the silvery fur. A memory of Kal being strapped to Catapult's back in the early days of his capture flashed through her mind.

The darkness of her grief threatened to overwhelm her again, but Catapult bumped her with his velvety nose. "Come play," the roan said, dancing away from Khiri before she could argue.

Catapult led the two on a merry chase before declaring it was time for them to go inside because they were stinking up his pen. Taking the sword and armor off the work bench, Estan was careful not to touch Micah. Retrieving the bow, Khiri was almost happy to have Micah grumble at her about how she should've been more careful during the sparring match.

Estan arranged for a bath to be brought down to Khiri's quarters for her, and a scrub bucket for himself in what had been the Throne Room before Resmine's take over. "I would go to the local bath house, but there are still people in this city that think I'm dead. Finding me alive in a bath house isn't the way I want to break the news to them."

"People think you're dead?" Khiri repeated. "And Resmine is the Queen of Thieves. It sounds like Jarelton has been very busy the last few months. Also, Dewin mentioned something about showing me the Temple of Adari before I leave for the Life Trees. I know a lot of these stories were probably shared after... When we got here, but I— I could use a refresher. Once we're both less pungent."

"Of course. Maybe Res and Dewin will be back by then and we can hear how their meeting with Lady Treag went, too."

The hole in Khiri's heart wasn't anywhere close to healed, but she felt less alone. It helped to have stories to look forward to and people to share time with. No longer was she planning to sneak out in the middle of the night without a word to anyone. At the very least, she owed her friends an explanation and a goodbye. She'd only been planning on a brief visit before things had turned sideways, and she still had to talk to her mother. But one more night with people she cared about and that cared about her would be better than setting out toward the Life Trees in a fog of self pity and grief.

One more night with a proper bath and tavern food—yes. She could stay one more night.

TELGAN KORSBORN.

The name echoed through her, filled with more rage than she ever remembered pointed in her direction. She hadn't yet come to meet him in the mists, and somehow she knew that was still to come. She would come to him in the place of cobblestones, as she'd dreamed countless times before. This was a new dream, and it was one of fire. Black fires, like the ones she'd witness destroying the armies of the past. They were coming.

She had tried to ignite the darkness and soon, fire would burn without light.

Soon.

Soon.

Khiri was halfway out of bed when she woke up, already sliding toward Micah and her armor.

Her night of friendship had been everything she wanted. She'd played Knives and Nobles with Resmine, she'd thrown hatchets with Dewin, and she'd placed a friendly wager with Loni over Corianne and Estan's drinking competition. She'd won, betting on Corianne. Khiri didn't actually know the thief woman that well, but she did recall a story about Ullen pursuing her at one time. Khiri couldn't imagine Ullen being romantically impressed by a woman that couldn't hold her pints. Tak, a friend of the group Khiri hadn't met before, had been introduced. He'd told her he would respect her privacy and treat her as a friend and not a client. Khiri hadn't known what he meant, and asking had led to a long, confusing explanation from a drunk Estan about information trading. They'd all toasted and congratulated Resmine and Dewin on their engagement, and Estan had gotten even drunker. It was fun. As fun as anything could be with all the sorrow still clouding her heart.

But the dream about the coming fire... She couldn't be in Jarelton when it found her. It was time to go.

Resmine, Dewin, and Loni had all been sober enough to understand when Khiri told them she was leaving in the morning. Hopefully they would be able to stop Estan from following her. Whatever she was heading toward, she planned to face alone.

33

~Estan~

THE ONLY REASON ESTAN'S head wasn't splitting in two was surely his Taymahr-given gift of healing. He seemed to recall imbibing a full barrel of ale all on his own the night before.

It definitely wasn't like him to drink that much, but—with Res and Dewin's news, Loni's return from the dead, Genovar's demise, and his own rescue still all being fresh—allowing himself a night of abandoned dignity hadn't seemed out of line. This morning, he regretted abandoning dignity that hard. His head pounded with every heartbeat and the light beyond his eyelids was sending daggers through his skull. If his imbibing was meant to be a celebration of life, why did the morning after feel like death warmed over? Why hadn't his healing gift cleared away most of his hangover?

Probably because it was still working on the beating given by Khiri when we sparred, the logical—and unwelcome—inner voice of reasonability supplied. While accurate, he still growled at his inner voice to shut up.

Keeping his eyes closed, Estan tried to gauge his location and level of dress. Bare skin against sheets. Concerning. He hoped his drunken-self hadn't gotten ahead of his conscious-self as far as making a decision between Loni and Corianne. It would be awkward enough figuring things out without jumping into bed with either of them. He loved both women and neither one seemed like the willing-to-share type. It had taken a long time for Estan to get to the point where he stopped to think about the consequences before jumping headfirst into the easiest option. One drunken night may have taken his hard-won caution and dumped it out the window.

Worse still, what if he'd ended up in a stranger's bed?

Reaching slowly with his arms to either side of him, Estan begged Taymahr to let him find himself alone. He had a bad moment when he felt something smooth and soft, but it turned out to be a glove. Bringing it to his face and peaking through his eyelashes, he examined it. One of Evic's gloves. Not something a lover would leave behind as a token. With a sigh of relief, Estan flopped the glove back down on the bed. He wasn't sure why it was next to him and didn't want to think about it. Best to just dispose of the thing entirely.

But knowing it was Evic's glove meant Estan had made it back to the apartment he was currently sharing with Corianne. Had he made it back alone? Had he undressed himself or had Corianne helped?

It's not like she hasn't helped undress you before. Remember the time you got poisoned?

The memory wasn't at all helpful for calming himself down. Heat flowered across his cheeks and up his ears. No matter how many romances he had, something in Estan was determined to be eternally bashful.

Finally, the worst of the headache started to ebb. The knight rolled off his bed and located his clothes, thrown in a haphazard pile on the floor. Not in the manner of someone stripping for sex, in a hurry to bring nakedness to nakedness in order to slake a rising lust. More like a dog shaking off water, everything was left wherever it had fallen. After an experimental sniff or two of his breeches and socks, Estan decided to dump the previous day's castoffs in a basket and pull out fresh garments. When he had time, a wash day was overdue.

Corianne didn't seem to be in the apartment anywhere. It wasn't unusual for her to leave before him, so he didn't question her absence. More likely than not, he would find her already at The Dusk and Dawn. Having Khiri and Loni in residence under the same roof where Corianne and Resmine dealt with guild business made Estan's decisions for the day much easier. There was a strong possibility of finding Dewin and Catapult, as well. Ducking out the door and locking it behind him, Estan started for the tavern with a slight spring in his step. He couldn't say why he was so light-hearted today.

But his headache was improving.

Genovar's loss was still a stone in his gut. Arad Rhidel had gotten away—a failure on Estan's part that ate at him like a thorn in his boot. Despite the quiet of the last few days, the Venom Guild was still at large. The war with Irrellian Thornne was far from over. But for the space of a single day, there hadn't been any major catastrophes. Breathing in a chest full of Jarelton's spring air was still foul, but in a way Estan found comforting. It was almost like he'd found a place here. Yes, he still kept an eye on the shadows, and yes, he still held on to his hilt while walking the streets. He no longer got lost in Jarelton's maze, though. The dangers he faced were familiar dangers. For the first time since his escape from Seirane, Estan was wrapped in a sense of belonging.

Home.

While he wasn't sure it would last, it was welcome.

During his light-hearted stroll of discovery, Estan was surprised to spot Catapult's man-shaped disguise walking down the street toward him. "Estan! Good, I found you!"

"What's wrong?" Estan asked. Immediately all of the ease and comfort hissed out of Estan's pores. He half-expected the sizzle of demon blood escaping a Flayer corpse.

"Khiri's gone. She left for the Life Trees this morning before the sun was really up. I waited as long as I could before I came to find you. You should know I'm going after her."

Something about Khiri and the Life Trees seemed familiar, if foggy. Most likely she'd attempted to tell people of her plans during Estan's drinking the night before. He hadn't anticipated her leaving at dawn, though. He doubted anyone had anticipated such an early departure. "She's already gone? Does she need help? Should I get my things?"

Catapult shook his head. "I'll go faster without you. Micah thinks Khiri needs some time to herself, but it's not a good idea to travel alone currently. I can follow without her noticing and keep all of us safe."

"But you can't climb the Life Trees," Estan protested.

It was a weak argument, and Catapult rolled his illusory eyes and stamped a foot. Some things just translated better in horse. "If I don't go now, I might not catch up before nightfall. You are my friend and my knight. If you tell me I need to stay as your steed, I will. But Khiri is also our friend and I agree with Micah. She needs someone watching her back."

"Okay. Alright. Yes, go! But, Catapult—be careful out there."

Estan reached out, wanting to pat his horse's nose but it was too awkward with the visage of a man in front of him. He changed to an open arm stance, waiting for a hug. Closing his eyes, Estan waited for the weight of a horse to press against him. He got a velvety lip nuzzle against the side of his face. "Keep yourself out of trouble, friend."

With a much heavier heart, Estan continued toward The Dusk and Dawn.

THINGS WERE BUSTLING at The Dusk and Dawn when Estan walked in. Several people he recognized from the Thieves' Guild were dicing and playing cards in the corner tables, while more guild members were singing rowdily at the bar. Spotting Corianne and Loni laughing together at a booth slightly removed from the crowd, he practically had to yell to be heard. "What's going on?"

"Big raid on them what's standin' in the old warehouses! Splitting them Venom lovers good and true out of our nests!" Corianne leaned against the wall rather than her backrest and had her feet up across the bench, preventing Estan from sliding in next to her.

"I don't really understand why it's good, but everyone seems very excited!" Loni said, beaming. She was taking up the middle of her spacious seat, though if Estan asked her, she'd probably make room. "Also, the mead here is absolutely wonderful!"

Reassessing Loni's condition, she did seem a little deep in her cups. Not that Estan would judge her for such a thing after his break with sobriety the night before, but it was rather early. "You're keeping an eye on her, right?" he asked Corianne.

"Aye, love. No harm will come to your love-friend. We've got her on apron strings, we do!"

Estan wanted to object to the way Corianne labeled Loni as his 'love-friend,' but he wasn't entirely sure what it was supposed to mean. He sighed inwardly and hoped Corianne didn't have the wrong idea. Or the right idea? He still wasn't sure of where either of them stood in his own estimation. "Did you know Khiri was gone?"

"She told us yesterday she weren't staying. Can't say as I'm surprised she nicked off in the night to scurry back to what family she's got. Need to see them that's breathing, what?"

"Catapult went after her!"

"Your horse went without you?" Loni's expression was an exaggerated mask of wonder and confusion. "How's he know where she's going?"

"He's a right magic horse, love!" Corianne patted Loni's hand. Loni's lips made an 'oh' and her eyes went as wide as bucklers before she set her chin on the lip of her mug and slipped into a contented smile. Shaking her head, Corianne bounced with an amused snort Estan couldn't hear against the din. "If you can manage to plow your way through this lot, Resmine wanted to throw words with ya. About what, she's being a might mysterious, but we've all got our mysteries, aye?"

Giving a salute in thanks, Estan made his way through the crowd. Even being a reinstituted Friend of the Court, with this many rowdy thieves, Estan kept one hand on his coin purse the entire way up the stairs to where Resmine had one leg hooked over one armrest of her throne and her back against the other. She was gazing up at the ceiling and only half-listening to the man attempting to talk to her from the other side of Shiv. "...which is why I feel I would be your best option for second-in-command!"

It wasn't until Estan closed the gap between himself and Shiv that he recognized the thief wanting to be named Resmine's second. Dagan, with his boyish face and predatory grin, was trying to convince a woman he'd hunted during her ascension that he was the best candidate for someone to guard her back? Estan almost had to applaud the man's brass.

Imagining Ysinda's response to something so audacious gave the knight a momentary pang of both grief and regret. So many things he would've done differently, had he the foresight to know Ysinda would die so suddenly and Loni would return. Or if he'd recognized his mounting attraction to Corianne for what it was rather than thinking it was something he could ignore. But all of those memories and regrets were in the past. He couldn't change anything.

This mood is because I want to rush after Catapult and not stay put and deal with my current problems, Estan scowled inwardly. *Focus on Dagan. He might be about to try to poison Resmine or something.*

Not that Shiv didn't have the smaller man well in hand. Shiv was keeping his massive body between Dagan's wiry frame and Resmine with small steps. He didn't move more than he had to, keeping his center of balance low. Trying to move Shiv out of the way was like trying to shove a mountain. There wasn't enough room for Dagan to use his speed to dash around the large bodyguard.

"I'll consider your application," Resmine said. Her tone was sopping with sarcasm. "I'll keep it in the same place as your offer to be my consort."

A laugh escaped from the back of Estan's throat. Due to a trick of acoustics, the balcony was quiet enough Dagan heard it. The mousy-haired thief spun to face the knight, a deep frown contorting his smarmy features. "*You...*"

Estan held his hands up in a pacifying gesture. "I'm not here to start a fight. The Queen asked for me."

"You won't steal my position again!" Dagan snarled.

"Queens choose their own consorts, Dagan. And you won't get far with my sister for a multitude of reasons, but none of them start or end with me."

Dagan's expression shifted into one of calculation. "What do you mean, sister?"

"I believe you and my brother met under my predecessor's reign," Resmine said. "Now, if you don't mind, Dags, we do have some family business to see to."

With a quick look between Resmine and the sizable knight she'd referred to as family, Dagan let out a string of curses as he exited the throne area. As though Dagan's exit had been a signal, several more petitioners and a few dozen onlookers also headed for the stairs. It was unclear if they were getting out of the Queen's hair so she could conduct her "family business" or if they'd been there to support the lanky thief in his bid for power.

"Dagan's definitely up to something more than aiming for your bed," Shiv muttered. His sunlight blonde hair bobbed in a breeze Estan couldn't feel. "That one has more ambitions than a merchant in a field of money."

"Up to something, alright. I've already announced my engagement to Dewin to half the city. We need to have him followed. I want to know if he's working alone or if he's part of someone else's plan. I don't have enough information to decipher his actual goals," Resmine sighed and turned in her seat to face Estan. "None of that is why I asked to see you, though."

"So what do you need?"

Resmine looked up at Shiv and gave him an over-there-please head tilt. With the grace of a giant, Shiv picked his way through the chairs and tables and settled himself as a door at the head of the stairs. As soon as it was clear Shiv was out of earshot, Resmine beckoned Estan to come sit at one of the nearby tables, removing her own butt from the throne and sitting across from the proffered seat. Recognizing that Resmine was taking pains to treat him as an equal, Estan hurried over. He had no idea what was on her mind, but it seemed pretty serious.

"You recall the cellar steps you and Corianne came to save me from, yes? The ones surrounded by Flayers and thieves that weren't necessarily there to congratulate me?"

Estan nodded. He remembered every detail of looking down at his friend stuck in a stairwell. The trip there was something of a blur, as was the fight to cover her escape. But the stairs were clear in his mind. "I remember the race over the roofs of Jarelton and the crowd of Flayers. I would probably recognize the stairs if I saw them again. Do you need me to go find them?"

"Corianne knows where they are. What I need you to do is far more complicated—I need you to go there with her and go through the archway at the bottom."

His mouth dropped open in shock. Working his jaw, Estan still couldn't get the words out for several long moments. "You want me to take over the Thieves' Guild? Res—that's not something I can do! Even if it didn't mean displacing you, how could I—I couldn't! It's not even remotely something I'm made for!"

"Exactly, Es. You are not looking to become part of this guild and you never were. I need someone to go down there that *isn't* looking to join the guild or become a noble or anything of that nature. That place wasn't built by the Thieves' Guild, we just use it. I want to know what its original purpose was. And the only way to find out is to go inside. But I've already been there. It took all of my personal ambitions and tested me with them. Your only ambition has ever been to serve Taymahr, which you already do. Admirably. I'm hoping that if I send you down there, you can bring me answers."

It was a long shot. Resmine was fully admitting her ignorance in this matter, but Estan had to admit he was intrigued. He'd assumed the archway she'd mentioned was a remnant of the Thieves' Guild from however far back. But Estan had studied Arra's histories for years before being knighted and, as far as he knew, Jarelton had always been there. Something buried beneath the city might be older than the city itself. As old as the Thieves' guild might be, there was no way it predated Jarelton's foundation.

"I have to warn you, before you go down there... You might not come back," Resmine said. He could see the worry in her eyes, the tears that threatened to break past her mask of leadership. "If whatever is down there finds you wanting, for whatever reason, it can and will swallow you. It only let me go after I passed its tests."

Rather than scaring him away, something about the idea of being tested appealed to Estan. He didn't think he had a death wish, but he liked the idea of being weighed by his merit. Whether it was a measure of his faith or fighting prowess, he was flattered that Resmine believed he could do this. He was eager to get started. One concern stopped Estan before he volunteered. "What about Dewin? She's also achieved her life ambitions, hasn't she?"

Her face contorting as though she'd bitten into a raw onion, Resmine shook her head. "I may not have told her I'm talking to you about this."

"Res..."

"I know! Okay! I know this is something she'd be interested in pursuing, and I know she's going to be mad I came to you first! But, Es, c'mon! We just got engaged and I can't risk losing her to whatever's down there! Asking you is hard enough, and I—"

Syara's name hung over both of them like a shadow. Resmine didn't want to lose the second love of her life, especially when—if Estan was any judge—what she shared with Dewin was even deeper than her first romance.

"Promise me—if I don't come out of there and you still need answers—you'll talk to her."

"But you're coming back," Resmine said. Her eyes were hard even though her raw-onion expression hadn't quite faded.

"You're the one that warned me this might be a one way trip," Estan reminded her. "I need your word on this. Don't mess up what you've got with Dewin because you're too afraid of losing her."

With a wince, Resmine clicked her tongue against her teeth and sighed. "I'm doing it again, aren't I? Staying in the cave when I should be running after her... Alright. You're right. I won't wait until it looks like you're not coming back, but I will wait until you've left. She's currently at the temple, so I couldn't tell her immediately anyway."

"Fair enough," Estan said. He hadn't gotten her to promise, but the concession was as much as he was going to get with Res. Pressing any harder would endanger their friendship and his opportunity to investigate whatever waited for him on the other side of the arch.

RESMINE'S WARNING THAT he might be on a one way journey made Estan's stomach tighten. He would've thought the idea of mortal peril would narrow his feelings about Corianne and Loni, but he still couldn't say which way he leaned. There wasn't time to narrow it down with a succession of outings and courting conversations before he left, so he was going to take his own advice. Estan was going to talk to them.

Both of them.

Descending from the upstairs throne room, Estan found Loni and Corianne still occupied their booth. While Corianne was in the same pose she'd been prior to his talk with Resmine, relaxed with the feet crossed and her back to the wall, he was surprised to see a much more sober Loni nursing a mug of tea next to an empty bowl of mashed potatoes. She was focusing on a glowing yellow rune in the center of one of her palms.

Grabbing a nearby chair and pulling it to the end of the booth's table, Estan caught Corianne's gaze and raised a curious eyebrow.

"Had a bit of a tick you might be wantin' a word with this one before the two of us go about our business, what? Our lady Queen needed to ask me along to guide you on her little experiment, and as I understand, you two have a history, no?" Corianne said, watching as the knight took his seat. Estan wasn't sure if he really saw a sadness lurking behind Corianne's features, or if it was his imagination.

If it was his imagination, this conversation would be even more embarrassing. "Actually, I'd like to talk to both of you."

Corianne's eyebrows shot up almost to her hairline. "A might ambitious for the blushing love."

As soon as she said it, Estan's cheeks started to burn. Unquestionably embarrassing. Loni gave him a sweet, still-slightly-inebriated, smile. "It's okay, Estan. I knew it was unlikely you would still be single after all this time. After all, I was married for most of our time apart."

He put one of his large hands out on the table, flexing his fingers as he tried to find the words he wished to convey. "I am still single. Or rather, single again. During this last year, I propositioned Khiri. She rejected me before I came to Jarelton. And then, despite some very wise counsel, I immediately fell into a relationship with Resmine's predecessor, Ysinda. While I've been pursuing these romances, I've come to understand a lot about myself. Loni, I never really got over you. Ysinda made me recognize that. She appeared to have your gentle nature, but she was also dangerous in a way I never really came to terms with. Corianne, I've also discovered feelings for you. Deep feelings. I don't know if anyone has ever understood me as deeply as the two of you, and I'm not at all sure which of you I hold in higher esteem. Resmine has asked me to do something for her, and it might be something I don't come back from. Maybe it's selfish for me to say anything when my own desires are still so nebulous and there's no guarantee I have a future to offer—but if I come back, I would love for the three of us to work this out, together."

"Estan, love... I weren't serious about the two loves bit," Corianne said, her face solemn. "I ain't never been one to compete for attention, let alone twice. You barely noticed me when I were near Ysinda and now you want me and Loni to both wait you out? It's a big ask, ain't it? Wanting me to wait for another scarred heart?"

Loni reached out and put her hand on Estan's. "I don't mind waiting for you, Estan. I already came this far figuring we would only be friends. And don't take this answer as an expectation of choice. Winning by default isn't winning in matters of the heart. I'll just be here to help you figure yourself out."

This talk had gone both better and worse than he'd hoped. No one had slapped him and stormed off, but he'd hurt Corianne's feelings. Hopefully they could patch things up on the walk to the archway.

GIVEN THAT THEY WEREN'T racing across the city to try and save Resmine from certain doom this time, Estan had expected to run across fewer rooftops. While it wasn't the mad dash it had been before, Corianne did keep them on the Thieves' Highway. Not hard to figure out why either when Estan could hear the Flayers hissing in the alleyways below.

"Their numbers seem to be building again," he observed.

Corianne was being unnaturally quiet, only speaking to guide Estan down one road or another or calling quick corrections when he went the wrong direction.

"Aye, and there's little wonder. More miraculous they sifted out for long as they did after an enemy's death. Unless o'course you got a better chunk out of Arad Rhidel than we thought. But if that's being the case, would've thought we'd run into his second by now."

"Assuming he had a second," Estan said, eager to keep the conversation flowing. The pace Corianne was setting was much easier than the sprint they'd used on the previous trip. He wasn't having to gasp words out between panting breaths or getting a stitch in his side. He actually had time to enjoy the fresher breeze up above the streets and the colors of awnings and laundry swinging in the sunshine. It wasn't like a stroll in the park, but he had a hard time imagining Corianne taking a stroll in the park. "It could be like when Ysinda died and didn't leave a clear successor."

"Hard to say," Corianne shrugged. They had to pause speaking long enough to make a particularly large jump between buildings."I never been on the Venom roster. What they do and don't wasn't none of mine until they made it mine."

Estan wasn't sure what to say after that. Despite his desire to keep her talking, Corianne's mouth was a tight line. The last thing Estan wanted was to part ways before he went through the arch with Corianne angry. What if he didn't come back and she ended up with guilt sitting on her shoulders? What if he did come back and she'd left, cutting him off entirely? It was her choice to make, but Estan hated the tension tethered between them. He had to make one more attempt. Not to convince her of anything, but to talk. "Cor—"

"No, love. I—No," Corianne sighed. "I know you don't mean to kick over the anthills next to every apple cart, but you do, love. You said yourself, you went for Khiri first. When she sent you on, you jumped at the next woman to look at you sideways. Now it's me and Loni what tickle you blushin'. I ain't denying we've got a spark o' something, you and I. It were there before you even called quits with my former queen. But I ain't one to be dancing on strings, waiting until you're ready to do something proper. That's your problem, and the one Ullen had before you. I don't need anyone bad enough to chance a shallow pool hides an ocean. I want the ocean, love. I deserve it. And I deserve to see it when I wade in."

Coming to a stop, Estan couldn't rip his eyes away from Corianne's profile. Sunlight caught her eyes like amber gemstones. The onyx waves of her hair made the blacks of her armor and sleeves seem dull by comparison. Her strong nose and the curve of her lips were the stuff of a sculptor's dreams.

It had taken him so long to see her.

Estan hated that it had taken him so long to say something—to recognize his own feelings. A thousand times, he recalled a voice in the back of his mind saying it wasn't time. It wasn't time. It was never the right time. He wasn't there yet. But now he was—and she was telling him he'd missed his window.

No, not that he'd missed it. It wasn't open wide enough. She couldn't see how much more she meant to him than Khiri or Ysinda. Because she was still sharing his heart with Loni. How was he supposed to show her the ocean when he was still torn between the two women?

I can't. Not without making a decision. Trying to convince her otherwise would be supremely selfish on my part. Estan sighed. There was still a little boy inside of his heart crying about not getting his way, but he'd grown up a lot over the past year. As much as he hated to admit it, Kal had been right about Estan. His infatuation with Khiri had always been more about winning than it had been about her. The rivalry between Estan and Kal had likely been as much because the mage had seen through the knight's motives as it was about Estan not forgiving the former-assassin for his background. Estan hadn't respected Khiri's choices, for all his pomp about following her lead.

He couldn't make the same mistakes with Corianne. Pushing her now wasn't his place. Whether or not there was ever a chance for them to be together in the future... It was entirely Corianne's decision. And she was giving him clear terms.

No. Not unless she could have all of him. And she wasn't going to wait for him to get over Loni.

Loni didn't want to be his choice by default.

Either way, Estan was going to have to figure out who he really wanted to be with, even if it meant his decision came too late.

Corianne swung over the ledge and began to scale down the side of the building. There was a ring of Flayers swaying outside of the stairwell again, though not near as many as the day Resmine had emerged and the place had been pulsing with whatever power had drawn the thieves to her. With a few well tossed ice runes, Corianne had a path made for them to dart through the demon-bound.

Estan wanted to draw his sword and wade through the creatures, but he was on a mission. If he got himself captured again—or killed—Resmine would have to send Dewin to investigate. His bond-sister had all but pleaded with him not to make her do that. So Estan's sword stayed sheathed and he followed Corianne's swift feet across the gap and onto the protected steps.

It was time to put away all his thoughts of romance and what waited for him in the future. He was here as a Knight of the Protective Hand. There was no one more devoted to serving the gods, especially Taymahr. Even though High Priestess Shalora had raised Estan to be devout as something of a sham—telling him only priestesses could talk to the gods, and feeding him other misinformation—it had worked. He'd been selected as Taymahr's avatar, to do her bidding on the face of Arra.

There was no way Estan was going to let his Goddess down.

34

~Ullen~

ULLEN SLEPT FITFULLY through the night. Dreams of hot coals and falling timbers hounded his rest. It was nearly a relief to wake up and find General Geryan watching him from a stool near his feet. While meeting with the austere and composed general while he was dressed in little more than bandages and a bed sheet was awkward enough, Ullen searched the tent for signs of other occupants. He didn't relish the idea of a full crowd watching him sleep. Finding no one, he sighed and decided it was time to break the silence.

"General," he coughed by way of greeting. "What brings you to my convalescing quarters?"

"It only seemed right that I come by and offer a formal declaration." The gruff woman stood and came to the side of his bed where she sank to one knee. "Were we not on a battlefield and were you seated more nobly, I'd be forced to do this with a lot more pomp. My apologies, Prince Ut'evullen Dormidiir for thinking you were not the chosen of your mother, and also for suspecting you of murder and treason. My actions endangered Eerilor and her people. Whatever punishment you see fit, I will abide by the will of the Crown. I only ask that should you wish to end my life, you stay your hand until I have made amends through use of my skills. I do understand if you cannot find the will to trust me. You have my fealty, for however long you deem me worthy of serving."

The headache Ullen hoped to sleep off returned in full force. "Given that I woke to find you in my tent without a guard, I reckon you're here with Jaspar's blessing."

"Lady Terilles did advise me to wait until after dawn, but yes, she was the one to approve my visit."

It would be a brilliant move, Ullen considered, to earn their trust and be allowed back into a position guiding their armies only to double-cross them later. He noted that during her fealty swearing Geryan hadn't said she would be loyal for the rest of her life. However long he deemed her worthy of serving. Did he get to decide on how long that would be, or would her loyalty end the moment a trap was sprung? While the woman seemed trustworthy and stolid, she possessed one of the most devious minds Ullen had encountered when it came to battle strategies and tactics.

"Do me a favor, lass," Ullen said. "Call out there for someone to bring Maleck over. Iffen you wouldn't mind, I'd like to have you swear again in a truth ring."

Without hesitating, Geryan opened the tent flap and called out to whatever guard or hangers-about were nearby for someone to fetch the mage. She returned to the stool and sat, studying him with those molten amber eyes. "It's a good call. I would've asked for verification too, in your position. You've little reason to trust me, or my motives. Lady Terilles is a good woman, and I appreciate her confidence more than I can say. But I was starting to question her sense, allowing me to come in alone while you slept."

Jaspar was raised in the courts of Eerilor and all her neighboring countries. If Ullen couldn't trust Jaspar's judgment of a person's character, he had faith in her to have some sort of plan in motion. While Jaspar didn't have the title of general, she had the mind of one. The troops believed in her, too. Ullen would have to see about getting Lady Jaspar Terilles her own ranking. Earl Terilles had blocked her from joining the legion in any formal manner thus far, concerned with his succession. He might be more amenable now that Ullen had pulled the earl's ass out of a burning building.

Refocusing his thoughts on the general in front of him, Ullen decided to make the most of their time. "While we wait, tell me your impressions of our Gyth allies."

"The cavalry unit is excellent. It's a crew hand-picked by their leader, Captain R. T. Honeyhill. He's native to Firinia and still has the accent. Not sure how he earned his spot in the Gyth legions, but he's a clever man with good horse-sense and better people skills. Everyone in his unit is loyal until death, possibly beyond. The foot companies are led by a Major Courla Vauntara. I'm less impressed there. She's green and she's got something to prove. Captain Honeyhill is not under her command despite her higher rank due to the way Gyth runs their militaries. Cavalry and foot are different divisions, run by different people. She keeps trying to force Honeyhill to listen to her orders, while he has requested to be camped as far from Major Vauntara's foot soldiers as possible to keep his people from getting hassled by her and some of the younger foot leaders. There's a few more seasoned officers and sergeants trying to see things done and keep the foot in line, but Major Vauntara could be a major headache."

Without ceremony, Maleck Dorell pushed aside the tent flaps and ducked his mane of blonde hair through the opening. His round cheeks pulled into a wide, fuzzy grin. "You called for me, Ullen?"

It was something of a relief to have Maleck around. The whole of Arra had begun treating Ullen as something different. Something royal. Someone else. Maleck never cared. He wasn't impressed by titles, riches, or pomp. As the most decorated mage since Irrellian Thornne—and in fact, the only mage known to be able to match the Flayer Mage for power—Maleck could demand a position with any court he wished. He'd joined Genovar's efforts against the Gray Army for unknown reasons. He'd always claimed it was to prevent Irrellian Thornne from wiping out his favorite tavern.

Which might even have been true.

"Yes, Maleck. If you could cast a truth circle for us, General Geryan wanted to pledge fealty."

"Not a problem. Hello, Tericia!"

Geryan gave Maleck a deep nod in greeting, her mouth twisted in bemusement. Despite this being a largely informal meeting, the general was still a creature of pomp and ceremony.

Silver glitter flowed out from the mage's feet, crawling along the floor of Ullen's tent, and springing up the walls to coat every visible surface with shimmering stars. The stars were smudged across cheeks and sparkled on noses, adding a bit of luster to everyone's hair.

"There we are! Give it a go!" Maleck said.

"I am Ut'evullen Dormidiir. I—" Ullen's tongue halted. He was attempting to say: *I am the Flayer Mage.* Straining against the lock on his tongue resulted in his teeth clenching. He diverted to a truth, and experienced immediate relief. "I was attempting to lie."

"My name is Tericia and I—" the general's teeth snapped shut with an audible click. "I was trying to tell an untruth."

With both parties satisfied, Ullen nodded his satisfaction. "Now, then, General Geryan... If you wouldn't mind going over what you said before."

Geryan knelt again. "I, General Tericia Geryan formerly of Prince Hon'idar's Royal Troops, hereby swear to serve Prince Ut'evullen Dormidiir as I once served his brother. I will be loyal unto my own death, or the fall of Eerilor."

"I accept your fealty, Tericia Geryan, and reconfirm your title as a general of Eerilor. Until this war is over, you'll have a place among my troops."

"Anything else you need, Ullen?" Maleck asked, dismissing the shimmering dome by clapping his hands once. Maleck usually carried his staff, but it was as much for show as an actual aide. This sort of thing Maleck considered a cantrip, but Ullen had known enough mages to recognize a spell from third year students of the Mage's Tower. If Maleck were ever to change sides and become Irrellian's creature, Arra was doomed.

"Not at the moment, but I look forward to seeing you later for a game of Knives and Nobles."

Maleck came over and gave Ullen a hug before ambling back out of the tent with a smile and a wave.

Shifting in his cot, Ullen nodded. "Well enough, general. I understand you guided us through the ambush, along with a surprise regiment from Gyth. My thanks for picking up the slack while I was dealing with a tiny crisis."

She snorted. "Diving into a burning building while the sky falls down around us is a tiny crisis?"

"Aye," Ullen grinned. "Short of Irrellian Thornne himself barging into my tent and casting each of us into the hells individually, I only have time to deal with the small ones. So everything from Hon'idar to fire has got to be a wee problem. That's just logic."

They shared a laugh between field commanders. Ullen could tell Geryan wasn't taking his claim seriously, which was good. He'd been concerned they wouldn't be able to work together with her seemingly dour moods. But he'd never seen her off a battlefield when she wasn't a prisoner. This was like a first meeting in a lot of ways. In others, they understood each other as only former enemies could.

ULLEN WAS BACK ON HIS feet before his healer thought it wise, but much later than he'd wished. He convalesced in his tent for a day and a half, waiting to see if the damage was more severe than the first wave. Drinking more water and eating more fruit than he had since he'd been too young for ale, Ullen did what he could to help the healer's task along, but he needed to be out among his troops. He needed to see the additions to his forces first hand. His people needed to see him as much as he needed to be seen. If stories of his diving face-first into a burning building had improved morale enough to turn the tide of battle, witnessing the Prince of Eerilor walking through the camp only a day or two later looking little worse for the wear should turn the tide of the war.

Exiting his tent for the first time since the fire, Ullen could see the entire camp had been relocated. While the charred remains of the Terilles Estate were still smoking visibly on the edge of the horizon, the tents now hugged the western walls of the Earl's land. Ullen's healer must have been making liberal use of sleeping spells, or even getting Maleck's help, because the camp was already surrounded by sharpened log fences on the other three sides. Even as injured as he'd been, Ullen found it unlikely he would've slept through so much construction. The spring sun in its happy sky was such a startling contrast to the war-torn landscape, it made Ullen's heart hurt.

Soon, I hope this is all done and my people can get back to their lives. When did Hon'idar begin caring less about the people of Eerilor and more about the power?

The first stop Ullen made was the bedside of Earl Tolen Terilles. While Ullen's lungs were less raspy and recovering, the healers feared the earl's might never fully recover. Even now, there was a rattle in the rise and fall of his chest. They didn't think it was life-threatening, but it was unlikely Earl Terilles would be as active as he'd once been. Whether Jaspar's father actually slept through the whole of Ullen's visit or was merely pretending didn't matter. Ullen doubted he'd wish to see anyone either with such a prognosis. Not until it was a certainty and not until he accepted it.

From Earl Terilles, it was a short venture into the other healing tents. Ullen smiled and thanked those that were injured in his service. He mourned those that were dead or dying. Convalescing tents were the worst part of any war, and it was his duty to remember them and visit them. Now that he'd accepted his role as the next ruler of Eerilor—and was not just *the best bad option*—Ullen vowed to himself and Tharothet that he'd make these visits more frequently.

Next, Ullen walked the tents of his troops and checked in with his generals. Jaspar fell in next to him, acting as his aide and his right hand. It was so effortless, talking with his leaders with Jaspar by his side. He almost forgot how little recovered he truly was. But he pressed on, determined to meet the allies that had saved them from his brother's surprise attack.

The cavalry was stationed closer to the healing tents which made it the easier place to stop first, but Ullen also remembered Geryan's warning about Major Courla Vauntara and her prickly nature. Was it wiser to bend a little first with a minor effort here or would letting her win a small victory by first visitation result in a lost battle later? Would Captain R. T. Honeyhill be offended at the obvious ploy to sooth feathers in the other direction? Ullen was internally debating whether to return to his tent and summon the two leaders to him, when he found the matter taken out of his hands.

"It looks like our Gyth allies grew impatient," Jaspar commented.

A petite woman with stormy features, angry as well as umber, ate the distance between herself and Ullen with fierce strides. Her charcoal hair, done in thick twists, swayed over her gleaming silver mail and blended into her blackened pauldrons and chest plate. Gyth's colors were echoed on the lighter leather riding armor of the ghostly pale man strolling along beside her, seeming completely at his ease. Freckles dusted his cheeks like autumn leaves over a forest floor, his shockingly orange hair was pulled into a horse tail, and his limbs looked like they'd been stretched through a wire extruder. Even with his longer strides, the man was in danger of being outpaced.

"Are you Prince Ut'evullen Dormidiir?" the woman, presumably Major Vauntara, demanded. "The one in charge of this enterprise?"

Even with all his time spent away from court, Ullen's hackles rose at the lack of decorum. Or perhaps it wasn't so much decorum as courtesy. His time as a bard had given him plenty of experience with hecklers, and this introduction was much more akin to being heckled than a meeting between allies. "I might be, depending on what it is you're after," Ullen said. "Is this how one addresses royalty in Gyth?"

While the major attempted to curb her ire, the man next to her bowed. Geryan's forewarning about the Firinian accent was appreciated, since Ullen's most recent experiences with any Firinian were with Fennick the Betrayer. "Allow me to introduce us, your Highness. I am Captain Ruthorford Tev Honeyhill, R. T. to my friends, and this is my esteemed colleague, Major Courla Vauntara."

Ullen nodded, barely dipping his head. Then he waited for the major to remember her own bow. She visibly fought the urge to roll her eyes as she performed the duty. *How did she ever make it to the rank of major?*

"Excuse my rudeness, your Highness. I am Major Courla Vauntara, Countess of the Everglen, twenty-seventh in line for the Gythian throne. I desire only to speak with you about the position of my troops and why they've been divided across your camp. Surely everyone under my command should be within one area."

Ah. It suddenly made sense as to how someone with that much ego could rise so high in the Gythian military. Going back to his royal training with books and books of how this noble family fit into that monarchy, this empress was related to that duchess from two disparate parts of the world, and these other countries handled their own deportment, Ullen recalled the House of Everglen. They were an old house, descended from the original royal line of Gyth. They'd allied with and married into new lines, maintaining their place in the succession by sheer determination. Major Vauntara was probably *very* used to getting her way.

It took every scrap of willpower Ullen possessed not to exchange an amused glance with Jaspar. They'd definitely encountered plenty of Countess Vauntara's ilk while growing up in Eerilor's court.

"As Major Vauntara is well aware," Captain Honeyhill interjected, "the cavalry are under my direct leadership, not hers. And we've been situated where she can't try and rope my people into her service. We're elite riders, not messengers and servants for them what need a faster pair of legs. Or just want to play at being Queen."

"How dare you!" Major Vauntara's nostrils flared and her eyes blazed with hatred. "I outrank you in every way that matters! Firinia doesn't even have royalty!"

"Because we don't need 'em! Our Diet functions just fine and everyone gets a say. Makes all of us equal to any of you royals, but at least I know when to bow to a prince in his own country."

At this juncture, Ullen cleared his throat to remind them both he was still there. They both shut their mouths and turned to face him. Captain Honeyhill had the grace to look abashed, but Major Vauntara only fumed harder. "As I understand it, it is the decree of Gyth's monarch separating the cavalry from the foot in all aspects of warfare, not merely Captain Honeyhill's troops from yours, Major Vauntara. In matters of rank, I believe even if your family is older, your liege—King Tomique of Silverhorn—has that authority. And if not, I and my family certainly do, as House Dormidiir is older than Everglen by several centuries and we've ruled Eerilor longer than Gyth or Firinia have existed."

His reprimand seemed in danger of sliding off the major's shoulders for a breath. But by the second intake of air, she'd stilled her rage. It was like watching someone hood a lantern while expecting those burnt to believe the fire was truly out. Giving Ullen a new bow, one with much more deference, Vauntara said, "It is as you say, your Highness. Forgive my eagerness. This is my first true command and my father taught me that every battle begins before steel is drawn. I wished to impress with my leadership and have only shown my inexperience. I will endeavor to comport myself better in our future encounters."

She turned to Honeyhill next and gave a less deep bow, but one more akin to that shared between equals in Gyth's hierarchy. "Captain Honeyhill, I've seen myself to be in error and offer my apologies. Should you wish to dine with the officers at my fire tonight, I will make a place for you, but not as one of my subordinates. I mean this to be a bridge for us to make amends."

Captain Honeyhill's jaw was at his chest. If the man didn't speak soon, it was possible the birds looking to roost would mistake it as a place to build their nests. After several moments, he shook himself and matched her bow. "Thank you for the invitation, Your Ladyship."

"Major," she corrected. "Until I am back at court, I will try to leave my titles at home."

"Major Vauntara," Captain Honeyhill said.

There was a shared quiet between Ullen, Jaspar, and Honeyhill until Vauntara was safely out of earshot. "Your Highness, it may not be my place to say this, but I never have seen that woman turn over that fast for anyone before, and I can't say as I set much trust in it."

"Do you really think it was that easy?" Jaspar asked.

Jaspar's silence during the entire exchange likely meant she'd been able to observe much more than the participants. Ullen wanted to dissect the encounter with her later, but not next to Honeyhill. And despite Major Vauntara's abrupt arrival and departure, there were troops to be assessed. Unfortunately, one green noble in a prominent position was only one of a long list of things he needed to focus on.

"When is anything ever that easy?" Ullen asked ruefully. "Now, then. Captain Honeyhill, if you'd escort us to your section of camp? I've heard good things about your riders and I'd like to meet your horses."

Honeyhill nearly tripped over his own boots. "Your Highness would like... to meet my horses? I—Your Highness is full of surprises. Only ever have I heard other cavalry talk about horses like people."

"A good friend of mine was born and bred as a war horse," Ullen said. "He'd give me a good kick if I neglected to look in on his kin."

35

~Dewin~

OF COURSE Dewin could tell Resmine wasn't telling her something. There was always something Resmine wasn't telling her. It was part of who Res was. Dewin was well aware that being with Resmine would always and forever mean secrets. No one could go through all the things her love had and not out the other side with trust issues.

It was about finding the faith Res put in Dewin, and letting Resmine know Dewin returned it and then some.

Pacing the length of Dothernam Square, Dewin traced the holy sigils carved into the cobbles with her eyes. It seemed like several years had passed rather than the trickle of months since she, Tak, Resmine, and Estan had chiseled the pattern into the stone during the dead of night. She still wasn't technically supposed to be within the Square, but Jarelton's guards hadn't bothered to patrol this area since the Winter Solstice massacre and the death of Lord Orin Treag, the latest-late Illamar. It was easier to get past the Flayers gathering around the temple in the light of day when the creatures were weakest—but even as the Priestess of Adari, Dewin wasn't sure how much longer she'd be able to make it through without a full party backing her.

It was troubling. Almost as troubling as the thought of marrying someone who constantly kept secrets.

No. That's not troubling. I love Res, and I know she'd never lie to me about something that actually *matters.*

All the same, this was one of those occasions that Dewin found it harder to be patient. Estan was her friend too, and they'd only recently saved him from a trap meant for her. No one had told Dewin that Resmine was sending Estan somewhere today, but Corianne had that *glow* about her this morning. Which meant Res was asking Corianne to do something with the knight. Because Estan was dumb when it came to women and would never do something easy like ask Corianne out for ice cream or a pint. Dewin didn't remember anyone ever igniting her sister like Estan did, and while she was smart enough to stay out of Corianne's affairs, she did wish the two of them would figure things out already. Which would be much harder with Resmine sending Estan off to do whatever she had planned.

At least, whatever Resmine was asking him to do would keep their knight out of Khiri's hair. As much as Dewin missed her brother, she couldn't imagine losing her father as well as her best friend so close together. Not that Dewin hadn't lost her father. But she'd been much younger and hadn't been holding the knife that killed him.

Shaking the links of such a chain of thought loose, Dewin sighed. If she let herself, she'd get immersed in a sad sack of sorrows and regrets. No one had time to mourn all that was. Growing up in a family of thieves had taught her a specific way to deal with sadness: cry fast, cry hard, don't dwell.

We're all still at war, Dewin reminded herself. *The Venom Guild, the Flayer Mage, the Gray Army... We're in a lull is all.*

Don't dwell.

Dewin wasn't entirely sure why she felt the need to come to Dothernam Square every day. This was holy ground and it would continue to be holy whether she kept her vigil on top of the circle or from Resmine's side. But Dewin missed Adari. Maybe that was why she came seeking the presence of her goddess every day, through increasingly dangerous territory. Maybe that's why she still felt guilty about Estan getting snatched.

Dewin could still hear Adari's voice from time to time, like with the former King of Thieves and his house of traps. But it wasn't remotely the same as when she'd been an avatar. There was an emptiness she couldn't quite shake.

None of them talked about their time as avatars out loud. It seemed dangerous. Adari had told Dewin when she left that one of the gods was staying behind to keep an eye on things in Arra. The High Ones were returning to their own war in the heavens though. Would they still be the High Ones much longer? What would that mean for Dewin and her friends on Arra's surface?

Despite her wandering thoughts, Dewin thought she caught a glimpse of a tall, dark figure she'd only seen once before. Unless her eyes were playing tricks on her, he'd been standing on the tiled roof of the walls surrounding the cobbled courtyard.

Her heart hammered against her ribs. A thin coat of chilled sweat immediately enveloped her, as though she'd plunged into a stream.

It had to be her imagination.

Just a trick of the light and a wandering shadow. Right?

But Dewin knew. She *knew*.

How long he'd been there or what he intended to accomplish on the edges of her temple, Dewin couldn't even begin to guess. Whatever the Flayer Mage's intentions, the brief glimpse no doubt meant trouble was on the horizon.

36

~Resmine~

THERE WAS NO TIME TO wonder how far Estan had made it, if he was in the archway yet, or what he would find on the other side. Resmine had a morning full of guild and noble duties. First and foremost was the problem of Dagan. She'd set a watch on him, but he'd shaken them less than a block out. At least no one was hurt, and it was in the nature of her people to be secretive so she'd not thought much about it.

But the man was making himself a nuisance.

Yet another demand this morning to be seen as a candidate for her bed was only the tip of the arrowhead. He'd attempted to become Ysinda's consort before Estan's arrival had interrupted those schemes. While Ysinda had rebuffed Dagan's upward progression in that respect, Resmine's predecessor hadn't been as vigilant in other arenas. Ysinda had left openings in the guild's protections and Dagan was slippery enough to take full advantage.

His most recent visit seemed more a matter of obfuscation than pursuit. As ambitious as he was, Resmine didn't think he was completely fueled by a burning desire to sleep with a woman that didn't find him attractive. And he did seem to be hiding something.

She perched on a bench and swiveled so she could take in the celebrations occurring below her new throne room and Shiv in front of the stairs. Once she managed to convince the Jarelton nobility to swear her in as Lady Ilamar, Resmine wanted to keep her day office here. It was close to the pulse of her people. Even with it being a known haunt of the Thieves' Guild, it was very popular with the locals. Perhaps because the Guild was more careful about robbing those considered friends, or perhaps because the locals didn't care for the city guard. Maybe this was a new development since the beginning of the war with the Venom Guild, bolstered by Resmine's moving the Thieves' Guild above ground. Whatever the reason, Resmine knew her continued connection with all walks of life in her city was extremely important. She didn't want to get swept into the trap of forgetting about her citizens because they lacked access to her.

As the Queen of Thieves, Resmine couldn't afford to lose track of her guild. How she planned to balance the two jobs... Well, that would be the trick, wouldn't it? She was still working on that part, but there was a lot to tackle before she had to deal with those issues.

Dagan. What is your actual game?

"Shiv, I need our best tracker."

RESMINE HAD PUT IN a full day of checking in with her district leaders, visiting those injured during Flayer encounters, and looking over new recruits to her guild. Not everyone applying to the Thieves' Guild wanted to be a thief, but they did all want to join the fight to free the city. Some of the youngest volunteers hadn't even seen their fifteenth summer. Resmine turned those she considered too young down, but not away. If they had nowhere else to go, no family to take them in, and no options, she sent them to one of her safe houses.

There were plenty of older volunteers looking for a way to help. She would do some research, or have Corianne and Shiv delegate, and get some actual orphanages set up. Orphanages under her protection. Venom Guild violence and Flayer killings had created too many wayward kids in her city and she wasn't going to leave them out in the cold.

Not when she had the resources to do something.

Estan would be the first to tell me it's the right thing to do, Resmine sighed inwardly. As hard as she was trying to ignore the absence of her leap-first-think-later brother and best friend, she kept remembering he was gone—doing a dumb thing merely because she had asked it of him. Yes, she did want him to do it, but would it have killed him to argue with her about it? Make it seem like he wasn't blindly jumping into danger on a whim?

It probably would kill him. Not doing something he thought was helpful wasn't how Estan functioned. He *had* to run in and save the day—whether it was the most idiotic course of action or not.

Shiv pulled Resmine back into The Dusk and Dawn for a meal and some rest when she would've started on another round through the city streets. "I know you're worried about your friends, but Jarelton doesn't need to see the closest thing they have to a leader right now pacing aimlessly and fretting like someone with a child on the way."

While Resmine made a face at her second, she privately admitted he was right. She would undo all the good she'd already done today if she gave the citizens more to worry about. Eating on the lower level of the tap room, Resmine managed to smile, chat, and pretend her mind wasn't following Estan through the mysterious archway under the city.

It was late in the evening when Resmine's second slipped away and came back with a message in hand—late enough that she'd nearly forgotten about the request to have Dagan followed. When Shiv met her gaze with grim eyes, her first fear was Estan's body had been ejected from the arch. Resmine managed to keep the tremor out of her hands as she accepted the sheet of parchment.

Reading the words written there took several tries. Even Dagan hadn't struck her as this stupid. She'd known he was ambitious from their first meeting, but he hadn't struck her as entirely foolhardy. "He's meeting with Lord Holt Treag at the Two Beams?"

Even with the vicious fighting between the Flayers and the Venom Guild which had occurred during the rescue of Estan and Khiri, The Two Beams continued to be the main gathering point for the Venom Guild. Resmine wasn't sure how many of the people hiding there were Venom Guild and how many were Gray Army, or if there was really a difference at this point.

What was her uncle doing meeting with her enemies?

Actually, it wasn't much of a question. She had a pretty good guess.

Dagan's presence in their enemy's stronghold wasn't something she could overlook, even if she had been inclined to forgive his ridiculous pushing to be named her consort—which she wasn't. He'd been in Ysinda's inner circle before the former queen had tired of his pushiness. Dagan knew almost as much about the Thieves' Guild as Corianne or Shiv. He knew where the weakest safe houses were, the runic entry codes to most of the secret doors, and all of the Thieves' Highway routes through the city. There was no way of knowing how much he'd disclosed with the Venom Guild—or Resmine's uncle—and how much he was keeping to himself as bargaining tokens.

Whatever had or hadn't been said, Resmine knew one thing for certain: Dagan had signed his own death notice.

Even if he came to her right this minute with the most brilliant excuse in the world, she couldn't be seen as lenient toward traitors. Not informing his queen of an intended mission of this nature—even if he actually was working to be a double-agent—would be bad enough, but he hadn't brought them any information at all. Merely mind games and harassment.

Resmine sighed. She didn't like asking for blood, but she nodded at Shiv. He knew as well as she did what this report meant.

They had to take out one of their own, and they had to do it fast.

And then they had to undo whatever damage Dagan had caused.

37

~Irrellian~

IT WAS CARELESS OF him to let a puppet of the High Ones see him, but Irrellian couldn't bring himself to worry about the gods. Not when he was so close to the fruition of all his schemes.

The High Ones had other things to worry about anyway. Twenty years away with dozens if not hundreds of minor gods looking to undermine them meant the heavens were every bit as volatile as the mortal plains. Irrellian had access to Telgan Korsborn's memories, which meant he'd seen plenty of High Ones ascend and fall over the centuries. Their strength was only as great as the following they cultivated. While twenty years wasn't enough to cast them off, they would be vulnerable. None of the minor gods were in the same position as Irrellian though, with full access to the mortal realm and the ability to shape belief in a matter of seconds.

Irrellian intended to keep the door open once he was through it. None of the nonsense about being bound to visits only when the veil thinned on certain holidays and only speaking to a select few. The heavens abutted the hells as well as the mortal face of Arra, and he already knew how to traverse the hell planes. If he could somehow be demon and god all at once, nothing would hold him back.

He was getting closer. His hand had passed through the barrier up to the wrist without burning.

Only one or two big events and he would have access to the Hallowed circle and from there, it should be an easy matter to climb into the heavens. It shouldn't be difficult to line things up in a way that would benefit him as much as it would hurt his enemies. He still owed Khiriellen Fortiva comeuppance for her father's demise, and he'd been watching the group Ut'evullen banished for some time as they gathered resources.

A nudge here, a word or two there...

Falling through the shadows of Arra into the hells beneath, Irrellian decided to check the progress of what had been Quinton Ilyani's people. It was a shame that Ut'evullen had finally cut that thread. Ilyani's zealousness had been more beneficial to Irrellian's cause than any of Hon'idar's machinations. He'd divided the dissenters most effectively. Had Hon'idar attacked even a week or two earlier, Eerilor's war would've been over and Irrellian could've walked into Taman and laid claim to the entire country. Which would make convincing the neighboring countries to join against him infinitely easier. Eerilor would likely be obliterated in the process, but Irrellian's ultimate aim was to wipe the slate of Arra clean. Eerilor and Mytana were merely kindling for the coming fire.

Gyth would be next. They'd already irked him more than he cared to admit.

BARRELS OF FLOUR, MINING powder, inactive incendiary runes, and oil were packed onto two wagons and a small cart. Irrellian was actually impressed with the amount of material the small group had accumulated.

There wasn't nearly enough fire power here to take out their targets. At best, they might collapse a few support buildings. But gods were meant to give blessings every now and then, and these people were doing works in Irrellian's name. Well, technically *against* Irrellian's name, but they believed in him more than most of his devotees.

No one commits themselves to evil quite so thoroughly as those that think their cause righteous, Irrellian grinned inwardly. He was more than willing to take advantage of an opportunity like this.

It would take him a few days to weave his chosen enhancements into the existing runes. Imbuing the various powders with more raw power was relatively easy in comparison. Creating a third wagon and filling it with even more supplies would be taxing, but he could manage that as well.

Staying out of sight would be both the easiest and hardest part. This group seemed to believe he was around every corner, out to prevent them from achieving their goals. He knew the type. They would double and triple-check shadows, stabbing at nothing with unfounded—or perhaps extremely founded—fervor. Irrellian's protections weren't threatened by the weapons these people wielded, but it wouldn't do to let them know he approved of their goals or was actively enabling them.

By his estimations, it would be roughly a week before they made it to Seirane. Between his other projects, he could work in all of his planned blessings. His final gift to the group was an enchantment to make it into the city unmolested. Travin had been slowly withdrawing his influence into the city like a turtle hiding in its shell. As though walls were any sort of barrier to Irrellian Thornne. It almost made Irrellian laugh aloud.

Not that he needed this group, but aiding them would take much less from his power pool than creating a calamity from thin air. He was conserving his energy for his next interaction with the Fortiva girl.

But first, it was time for Travin to prove himself useful.

38

~Holt~

CURSING UNDER HIS BREATH, Holt Treag paced the length of his study. He'd given Haud and the Viper League—or whatever it was they called themselves—free reign of Jarelton, with the understanding that Haud's assassins would rid Holt of his nuisance of a little brother, Orin. As long as the assassins cleared out when Holt pretended to make his stand, the city would see him as a hero. Araylia hadn't been a true threat since he'd blackmailed some servant into seducing her and stealing the baby more than twenty years ago.

But somehow—*somehow*—all of his machinations had gone terribly, terribly wrong.

Again.

The old rage threatened to crawl up his throat. He'd been in the prime of his life, drinking and whoring *as was his right*. As the next heir of the Ilamar seat, there was nothing to prevent him from sleeping with every woman in the city if he wished. Originally, he'd believed that as the heir of the city and the rightful ruler, the brothels had known better than to charge him admission. It wasn't until the nobles started to blather about his habits that he'd learned Mother had been paying his tabs. Brothels were discreet by nature, which meant Mother was the one letting his habits become public knowledge, most likely in an effort to shame him.

After Mother made her duplicity known, Holt noticed his sister's eyes lingering on one of the staff more than once. He'd formed a plan. If Mother was out to shame him for seeding a few possible brats, how much worse would it be for his sister to get with child while half of Arra was courting her? Holt put a great deal of gold into the servant's pocket. When the idiot actually fell in love and was planning to back out of the deal, Holt showed him an assassination contract he had prepared in case of cold feet. Either the servant abducted the child and ran away, or Holt would have all three of them dealt with by professionals.

Killing a single man and a small baby outside the protections of the Ilamar estate shouldn't have proven difficult either; and yet, the child had lived. She'd returned and she was popular with the whole of Jarelton, occupying the hero's place Holt meant to claim.

When his position had been threatened before, he'd always managed to undermine or eliminate the competition. And yet, somehow, he was still not Lord Ilamar. He'd gone to meet with Haud to demand answers only to find the motley assassins in new hands. They had hidden themselves in a cloak and introduced a thief named Dagan who'd promised to deliver the Thieves' Guild to the assassins in exchange for a position of power.

Holt couldn't help replaying the meeting in his head.

He didn't care about excuses. He told the cloaked figure and Dagan to give him results or join the previous guild leaders in whatever ditches they'd died in.

Those gold-flecked eyes stared at him from across the table as Dagan frowned. "You claim responsibility for the war between the Venom Guild and the Thieves' Guild?"

"Who else possibly could?" Holt demanded.

"Irrellian Thornne."

Even now, in the safety of his own house, a chill ran through Holt. Dagan hadn't said it to intimidate, which was all the worse. Ignoring the increased number of Flayers within the city walls had been impossible, even staying within the more sheltered parts of town. People had to die. The more, the better for Holt's goals. But the idea that they were sacrifices to someone else's cause—no. Some*thing* else's cause...

Holt shuddered and pushed the thought away. It was nonsense. Even if the Flayer Mage was back, he'd recognize Holt's talents. Surely someone with as much power as Irrellian Thornne would appreciate the planning and ambition Holt displayed in claiming a throne which never should've been denied him.

The most important thing was to make sure—whether it was Haud, Haud's replacement, Dagan, or the Flayer Mage himself—someone took out Holt's mistake of a niece.

39

~Travin~

CITIZENS OF SEIRANE fled the streets as more soldiers marched up Temple Hill. Travin watched from his office window forcing himself to smile with what he hoped could be interpreted as savage satisfaction rather than a grimace of discomfort. He pushed against the inner voice telling him that Irrellian would come for him soon.

Irrellian was nothing.

A ghost.

Just a memory.

Please just be a memory.

All pretense was gone now, within the walls of his city. He'd dealt with the royal family almost a full week ago. He and his people had layered dozens of sleep runes over the palace and had slit the throats of everyone in residence. Most of Mytana didn't even know they'd been without a monarch for days. No one was allowed in or out of Seirane without documents carrying Travin's personal seal. He'd thought of everything.

He was allowed to enjoy this.

He should revel in this.

Fear threatened to gag him.

No matter how Travin tried, he couldn't quell the tremble in his hands. The air in his office no longer seemed safe. Nor was it safe in his house. The odor of the hells seemed to haunt him every waking moment.

Reports of Gray Army activity in Eerilor had reached him, but Hon'idar was nothing to Travin's plans. The Flayer Mage's former second recognized the dressings of someone with similar ambitions. Hon'idar had no interest in letting Arra burn. He only wanted his brother's death and the power of a crown.

Travin had taken a crown already and hadn't needed to fight a war to do it.

And still, the Flayer Mage was not making himself known.

People claimed they'd seen Irrellian Thornne in Eerilor on the Solstice, and yet Hon'idar seemed no worse for his unmasked ambitions. If something untoward were to happen to Hon'idar, it would make more sense. Travin was careful. There was no way, if Irrellian were truly back, he'd suspect Travin of more treachery than the crown prince of Eerilor.

Would he?

Other chapters of the latent Gray Army were rising, but Travin told himself they were being opportunistic. He'd heard things had gone very badly for the remnants in Gyth. Hon'idar would soon have more on his plate than a handful of rebels. Which would definitely anger Master Thornne.

Had he returned.

Which was impossible.

Travin was shaking again. Maybe it was time to stoke the fire. But he knew his persistent chill had nothing to do with the cold. It was the damned eyes he felt boring into his soul with every decision. Every choice he made that didn't follow his master's—Irrellian, not his master, but Irrellian—wishes, Travin burned under the unseen gaze.

Perhaps I was seeing patterns in the mist, Travin thought. *Jumping at empty shadows.*

The thought was meant to sooth him, but Travin had fought beside Flayers. He'd seen what the shadows could hold between one moment and the next. Even when he could swear he was totally alone, like now, eyes bored into him from every angle.

"Travin Esk."

He knew that voice. More than that, he knew the *tone* of that voice. And despite the many reassurances he'd given himself, the rehearsed speeches he'd practiced in his head, and every plan he'd put into place, Travin knew—beyond all doubt—he was a dead man.

Slowly, he turned toward the shimmering entity he'd served so faithfully in his youth. Travin had forgotten how beautiful Irrellian Thorne was. His memories had shifted and warped the Flayer Mage into something less perfect.

More mortal.

More fallible.

But the creature in front of him...

Irrellian Thornne was a divinity.

This was why he'd believed in the cause. Tears began streaming down Travin's face. How could he have contemplated killing his master? How had he fallen so far from the path?

"Forgive me," he pleaded, dropping to his knees. Sobs wracked his body, driven up from the depths of his lungs until he was practically dry heaving. He couldn't stop himself. "Forgive me! Forgive me! F–forgive me!"

"You've betrayed me once. What's to prevent you from doing it again?"

Travin could barely breathe through his grief, let alone speak. The greedy voice that had guided him astray told him to pick himself up, to make up an excuse, to remember that the Flayer Mage had abandoned him for two decades. Shaking his head in defiance, Travin wished the voice would shut up and leave him alone. *You told yourself you were smarter and stronger than any of the weak-willed fledglings below you in the Gray Army's ranks, but here you are, pissing yourself in the dirt like a worm*, the voice persisted. *Some leader. Some self-proclaimed king of Mytana. You're pathetic.*

"I am—I am pathetic," Travin gasped.

Irrellian looked on. The Flayer Mage's bemused expression betrayed nothing of his thoughts as he watched Travin's shameful display. "Hardly an answer to my question, Travin. This is your last chance, and I'm only extending it because you served me so well in the past."

Gulping down air, Travin fought his way back up to his knees. He was being hysterical and he knew it. It took everything in him not to immediately prostrate himself again. That treacherous voice wouldn't stop feeding him all the disgusting plans he'd made. Ruling Mytana, drenching himself in its riches, using his army—no, Irrellian's own Gray Army—as his personal plaything. Travin had become one of the people he'd sought to purge from the face of Arra. And it had only taken him twenty years to get there.

He knew the price of clemency.

"I can offer you no assurances, my lord. You should rightly dispose of me. I am a traitor and I deserve death. Just, please, grant me that my failure will further your goals."

Irrellian smiled. It was malevolent and wondrous. Travin reveled in that smile as he found peace.

Thus it was something of a shock when he opened his eyes again to find himself, not only alive, but standing on a frigid mountain with no visible sky—as dark as midnight, but rather than the normal infinite bowl, this sky was a finite void. Despite the snows whipping around him and the crunch of ice beneath his feet, Travin was as warm and comfortable as he'd been inside of his office. The Flayer Mage still stood over him and was still smiling. "My lord?"

"You have been remarkably useful, whether intentional or not, so I am granting you a task. In a week's time, I want you to ferret out every true believer of the High Gods left in Seirane and I want you to pack them into the temples. Conduct true services every night if it brings the herds to the pews. Chain them if need be. But I want those seats filled."

"Where are we, my lord?"

"This is where I'll leave you, should you fail me," Irrellian said. His mirrored eyes danced with a wicked glee as he gestured toward the mountain side.

Peering through the snow, which seemed to be the actual source of light in this damned place, Travin could make out shapes crawling over the stone and scree—demonic creatures which were mashed up versions of other beasts, things with too many eyes and too many mouths, some with keratinous and scabby shells. The horde surrounding the mountain made the drekers he'd loaned Arad Rhidel look like house pets. Travin backed away, squeezing his eyes shut. His heart screamed for release from his chest. A quick death would've been a blessing. Instead, he had one week to try and persuade those who still believed in the gods he'd spent twenty years undermining to come pack the temples he'd driven them away from, or face the unthinkable.

All the faith he'd lost in Irrellian Thornne over the years had thundered back into place a thousand fold. He would not fail again.

40

~Khiri~

WITH THE LIFE TREES towering over the landscape, Khiri should've felt like she was coming home. Instead, there was something almost oppressive about entering the forests of her youth. Not that she was unhappy to see the familiar behemothian limbs and leaves eating up the sky, but they stared at her from across the distance, reminding her of her failure to bring her father with her. His essence was spent, forever apart from his ancestors and their people.

Khiri shoved back at the grief. She wasn't responsible for the choices her father made. It had been his path, his decisions, his burden. She'd borne the weight of her father's past for her entire life without knowledge or consent. There was no reason to carry it any further.

Except—

She still needed answers.

Would her people allow her to return?

Telgan Korsborn was still lodged in her head. Technically, while he wasn't with her, she had found him. The terms of her banishment, almost a full year ago, had merely told her she needed to locate her soul mate. No one should bar Khiri's entry into the Life Trees. Besides, she didn't intend to stay. She would tell her mother about Genovar's fate, maybe stay for the mourning period, and then return to Jarelton.

Hiding in the Life Trees forever while her friends battled against her Destined wasn't an option.

Sunlight was fleeing across the sky, running away from the darkening edge of night. Khiri would make it beneath the trees before darkness made her stop walking, but Khiri hesitated before plunging into the tree line. Sleeping in the forest was natural to her, but she'd spent a long time on the road with people who camped in large clearings. All she really needed was a tree with a comfy crook she could settle into for several hours. Maybe with enough room for a fire nearby for a warm breakfast, if she wanted to attempt her own cooking.

Generally, she settled for cold rations. Khiri was still an abysmal cook, though her latest attempt at cooking an egg had been surprisingly edible.

It was strange being alone on the road. Except for Micah, strung and ready in her grip, there was no one out here with her. She'd expected Kal's absence to eat at her with every step, but his loss was more like a hollow place in her chest, slowly filling with an ooze of sadness. Her father's death—she wasn't even sure how to process that pain. Her knife hilt was still strapped to her side, like it was more than just a pretty handle. Micah was now her only companion and her only weapon. Without him, who was she?

The question was an odd echo to the thoughts Khiri had pondered once before, when she was leaving the Life Trees. She'd believed herself exiled and alone. In mourning for a life she'd never truly wanted. Not even a full year had passed, but it weighed like decades across her shoulders. How long was a year supposed to take?

"Hey, I'm right here. You're still not alone," Micah reassured her.

Something like the golden warmth she used to derive from Micah's name echoed through her from his grip. Khiri no longer mistook it for romantic love, but it did send fortifying waves of comfort and companionship through her.

With every step taken closer to the Life Trees, Khiri thought she sensed more of her brother's essence in the Life Wood bow. While the weapon had always been him and was imbued with his spirit, it was like he was getting stronger. Or he'd been dulled by his time away.

"I chose to come with you. Don't start searching for more reasons to be sad. You have enough."

Khiri scowled and closed her thoughts to her brother.

Kal would've been proud of her for practicing the exercises he'd given her. When he'd been alive, he reminded her daily to exercise her extra senses, to extend her mental sight, to shield herself, to erect mental barriers between her private thoughts and mental speech. More or less alone on the road, with no one to spar or walk with and fewer distractions, she didn't need the reminders.

He would've been proud, she told herself again. This time Micah didn't respond. Tears started to well up, though Khiri wasn't entirely sure if she was happy-crying or sad-crying. Probably both.

"Khiri, listen."

Micah wasn't trying to initiate more conversation. She heard it, too. Or rather, she *didn't* hear anything. All of the normal chirps, clicks, and buzzing of a lively and thriving forest had gone silent. Khiri closed her eyes and reached out with her mind the way Kal had shown her, but even reaching as far out as she was able, nothing pinged as unnatural. No Flayers, nothing like the creature from the hellrift... Nothing.

She reached out farther still. Pushing this hard was a strain and Khiri wasn't sure how long she could hold her concentration with such a distance under her magical sight. There was a bit of a blip behind her, just out of range of her usual practicing circle. While odd, it didn't seem like a hostile presence. If anything, there was something very familiar about it.

"Who's out there?" Khiri demanded. "Show yourself!"

Maybe her uncle had tracked her down? It had been almost a week since the fight that took her father, and Estan had said Arad Rhidel managed to slip away. She wasn't sure Arad had the kind of magic necessary to hide from her searches, but anything was possible. Kal might have been able to tell her what she was looking for, or suggest a new course of action.

It took a surge of emotional energy to stop the on-coming wave of grief, but now wasn't the time to get bogged down.

Instead, Khiri nocked an arrow. "I won't ask again!"

Stillness.

The silence crawled over Khiri's skin like ants on an apple. Bit by bit, it was eating away at her strained composure. Concentrating on her breath, the way Genovar had taught her when she was still his apprentice hunter, Khiri steadied herself. If she couldn't sense what was coming, it was up to her training.

And Genovar had trained his daughter well.

Pivoting on her heel, Khiri searched the deepening shadows of the forest. A branch cracking echoed through the hushed trees, as loud in the unnatural quiet as a thunderclap. While her curiosity urged her to investigate, Khiri waited. While the sound had come from her right, her instincts were telling her to move forward, closer to the canopy created by the limbs of the Life Trees.

One cautious step at a time, Khiri crept farther into the darkness. That moment of hesitation at the tree line came back to her, and she wondered if she hadn't actually sensed something then. Had it been a blip of precognition? Was her gift growing?

Irrelevant. It was too late to change what had happened then. She had to focus on now.

"Khiri... Stop."

"Why?" she responded mentally.

"It's like the hell vent on the other side of Jarelton. It looks like trees, but it's not."

A hell vent. In her own forest. Disguised behind the trees she'd known all her life, and dividing her from the Life Trees on the other side. The last time she'd encountered this, she'd had help. The last time had cost the life of her best friend. *"Any idea how far it stretches?"*

"It's not as long as the last one... Maybe just an extra day to go around it?"

Scorching tears burned across her eyes, coming on as suddenly as the silence had earlier. She wanted to fight something. To lose herself to the do-or-die adrenaline of a hunt. To breath without the pain of loss for five miserable minutes while she dealt with the next problem.

Instead, it was a spirit-forsaken hole in the fabric of Arra.

Now that Micah had alerted her to it, Khiri saw the familiar tell-tale shimmer, as fragile and delicate as spider silk, ripple through the air in front of her. She hated it. She hated all of it. The Flayers, the hell vents, the weird tingle she got in the tips of her ears when she experienced new magics, the constant travel, the uncertainty she had whenever she met another stranger.

All of it.

Pacing in front of the hell vent, Khiri glared down at her feet. Periodically, she would pause and look back up at the vent, before resuming the frenetic march. There was no way to tell what was in there, possibly watching her every movement. Another flying maw creature, maybe. Something worse? A dozen smaller things?

"Khiri, I can feel what you're considering. Please don't."

She didn't respond to her brother's plea. She didn't want to hear it. All she wanted was to get things over with, whether it was getting to the Life Trees or dying at the hands of something monstrous. Genovar was gone, Kal was gone, Micah was a bow, and all of Arra was sliding down a hellish pit anyway.

And it was her fault. Or it was her father's fault with a lot of help from her. Either way, it all led back to her blood.

Taking a deep breath, Khiri made sure Micah was tight in her grip and made to plunge forward into the unknown hellscape.

An unexpected grip on the back of her belt pulled her backwards and she landed hard on her rump. Catapult's massive nose came down on her chest and nipped at her breast plate. "What exactly was that?" the horse demanded.

For a moment, Khiri thought she was hallucinating, but then she recalled Catapult's taunts during the game of tag after she and Estan had sparred themselves ragged.

Catapult didn't move his nose as he continued to ply her with questions. "Why are you trying to run headfirst into something that smells like Flayer farts? Where do you think you're going?"

Trying to dislodge the horsehead pinning her to the ground and failing entirely, Khiri fell back onto the ground in surrender. "I don't know. I wanted to fight something to make myself feel better, and when that didn't work— I guess it got into my head that I could either go through hell or die trying."

Catapult didn't say anything for a long time, but he didn't let her off the ground either. His ears swiveled in all directions, listening for threats even as those big calm eyes regarded her. "And would that help?"

Breathing a deep sigh of both regret and relief, Khiri shook her head. Even with the hell vent only steps away, there was something soothing about laying in the dirt and mulch of the forest floor. As hot as her blood was running only moments before, the cool spring air was like an embrace from a forgotten friend. This forest had been her home once. She needed to stay alive to fix what she'd helped cause. Words she'd heard during a festival in autumn, from the mouth of a minor goddess came back to her, as they did whenever she was about to give up—*Only by igniting the darkness, will you find the light.*

Igniting the darkness to find the light...

She still wasn't done. Khiri had much left to do, and she'd nearly done something extremely stupid.

Hugging the velvety nose weighing her down, Khiri started crying. These tears were different from the angry ones she'd been blinded by earlier. Each tear seemed to cleanse something dark from her heart, something which had been building up and dwelling within the holes left by her loved ones. She hadn't noticed how much the darkness weighed until it started to leak out.

Catapult let her rise, drawing her into a horsey hug. She imagined being engulfed in a more humanoid hug as a tightness like arms squeezed around her. Maybe it was a daydream. Or maybe Catapult's illusions allowed for phantom sensations. Whatever the case, Khiri accepted the comfort of a friend who had been with her for as long as any of the others.

A few chuckles even squeezed out when she realized that along with Ullen, Catapult was one of the few friends she'd had that had never gotten romantic fantasies about her or pressed for a kiss. Before Micah had been her brother, they'd thought they were going to have a much different life.

Thoughts of her brother alerted her to the absence of Micah's bow in her hand. He was still on the ground, unhurt. He seemed to be giving her a moment with Catapult, but as soon as she picked him up, he sent his own glowing warmth through her in his own version of a hug.

"How did you find me in time?" Khiri asked, dusting herself off and walking away from the vent with the warhorse.

"I've been following you since you left Jarelton," Catapult said. "You seemed like you needed a horse."

THEY WERE NEARLY TO the roots of the Life Trees when the bottom of Khiri's stomach sank to her boots. She didn't need the name inside her to scream *TELGAN KORSBORN*, its iron aftertaste shuddering through her soul, in order to recognize the presence of the Flayer Mage.

Irrellian Thornne was here, even if she couldn't see him yet.

"Catapult—stay close, but hide if you're able."

The blue roan didn't argue. One moment, there was a large, silvery warhorse at her back, and then there wasn't. She knew he wasn't really gone, but there was a part of her that wished he was still visible to her at least. His presence was reassuring and solid—something she would greatly appreciate when dealing with the monster she'd awoken.

Steeling herself, Khiri emerged into the clearing created around the trunks of the Life Trees. Her childhood home towered above her, more massive and imposing than even the figure standing between her and the stairway entrance. Irrellian Thornne wasn't looking up, though. He was staring off into the distance, the path toward the other Life Trees. He didn't call her by name or acknowledge her presence.

Khiri wasn't sure whether to pretend she hadn't seen him or not. Flayers couldn't make their way up into the Life Trees so if she could somehow get around him without his stopping her, theoretically he couldn't touch her up there.

But Irrellian Thornne wasn't like the other Flayers. She didn't know if the same rules applied to him. What would he do to her mother and the rest of her people if the rules didn't matter and she rushed past him? Better to keep him down here, focused on her until she knew what he was after.

"I thought I was supposed to come to you," Khiri said. It was less difficult than she expected to keep her tone neutral. With all that had happened recently, the Flayer Mage didn't scare her as much as he once had. "What are you doing here?"

"Ah, Khiriellen, daughter of my late nemesis... I was waiting for you, naturally. Not that this is the moment you're referring to—in which we both know you will come to me of your own accord. That time is nearing. I know you can sense it. But that's not what brought me here. No. This is about your punishment."

"Punishment?" Khiri stepped back. She hadn't meant to give ground, but not being *as scared* didn't mean fearless.

Irrellian's eyes flashed with a mixture of danger and amusement. He drank in her discomfort like someone guzzling their favorite mead. Taking one deliberate step closer, the Flayer Mage grinned. "You didn't think I could let someone else kill my favorite foe without retribution, did you? Genovar Fortiva was meant for me and me alone. And yet..."

As though it were happening all over again, Khiri saw her father's form at her feet, struggling to keep back the demon in his blood. His midnight eyes pleaded with her to end his suffering. She swallowed back against the lumps forming in her throat as waves of fresh grief and denial bludgeoned her heart. She knelt next to the memory, knowing it was false, but wanting with everything in her to have one last moment with her father. *Why?* she demanded silently of the shade. *Why didn't you just stay with Ullen? Why come to Jarelton at all, knowing they meant to turn you? Knowing what you would ask of me? Haven't I done enough?* Khiri reached out a hand to touch the image of Genovar, only to have it melt away beneath her fingertips.

On her knees in the grass, Khiri let out a shuddering sob. Irrellian continued to watch her with his self-satisfied smile. "You've redoubled my pain. Is that what you came here for? To see me suffer? To torment me with images of my dead father? What do you want from me?"

With a shake of his head, Irrellian offered her a hand. Khiri grimaced at him, and pushed herself back to her feet. "Dear girl, that was just a reminder of what you took from me. I didn't get the pleasure of knifing him myself. You did the deed and made a sniveling, weepy mess of the task. Genovar was meant to endure agonies uncounted, not say goodbye to his beloved daughter. And since you took away my chance to ensure his torment and loneliness... I'm left with creating yours."

"What—"

Before the question fully formed, black flames began flowing out over the Flayer Mage's robes. Khiri had seen these fires once before—in someone else's past. They had eaten away soldiers and horses from opposing armies and laid absolute waste to what people now called the Burning Valley. Only these flames spilled off of Irrellian's form and snaked their way toward the base of the Oak Wood Clan's Life Tree.

Khiri fully expected the Flayer Mage's spell to bounce away from the Life Wood, as unwelcome as the demon-bound. She waited for the moment it was obvious that his efforts were futile, to laugh in his smug face as he failed to hurt her people. As unwise as provoking him would be, she would take satisfaction in this failure.

She waited.

And waited.

But the flames weren't rebounding. They were sinking into the wood and expanding. Growing into a raging fire that licked up into the sky like a night without stars.

No.

No!

Understanding was slow to take root, but once it did, Khiri rushed toward the burning tree. Irrellian caught her shoulder and she froze in place, unable to move as she watched the fire eat her childhood home. They were too far down from the top branches to hear the screams of her clan, the cries for help that were no doubt being shouted to the spirits of the forest. Black flames roared, covering any response those spirits made. Khiri couldn't even hear her own cries, though she could feel the pleas tumbling from her lips. She begged the Flayer Mage to stop, to show mercy to her people, to leave them out of whatever fight he insisted her father still owed him. To take her instead.

Black ash fell through billowing smoke. Khiri and Irrellian stood in an untouched circle of grass as the dust rose around them. Irrellian drew symbols in the air, enabling Khiri to see through the dark clouds. The ache in her chest had been so great she'd thought nothing else could touch her but, as Khiri watched the flames tear through the forest and toward the other Life Trees, loss consumed more of her inner core.

Fresh screams ripped from her throat and she fought against the stasis imposed by the Flayer Mage's grip. She couldn't move. There was no way to break his hold on her. All that was left to her was the ability to plead and cry. What was left of her defiance threatened to crumble.

Perhaps it was inevitable, as Irrellian had told her all those weeks ago. She was doomed to be his creature, tied to him by invisible bonds. How could she fight against someone who could burn through the Life Trees?

"Khiri, I'm still here. You're not alone," Micah's voice broke through the growing despair. Khiri clung to the thread of hope he dangled toward her with all she was worth. It was so small, so fragile.

But it was enough.

Enough to pull her through the torment of watching their world crumble into soot.

She couldn't give in to a monster who slaughtered an entire society because he didn't get to kill one person.

When Irrellian released her, she stumbled away from him and toward the mounds of ash. Like the wasteland that was the Burning Valley, there wasn't enough left to decipher what had been tree and what had been bone. It all sifted through Khiri's hands like glittering black sand.

"I trust you see now how futile this is. You will come to me," Irrellian said. Smiling cruelly as he scuffed a bit of the ash with his boot, he glanced around the surrounding forest and up into the sky. "A pity this will be little more than a wall of smoke from Jarelton, but it should be enough. There are plenty of veterans housed there that will recall the last one."

Khiri's voice cracked under the weight of her earlier screams, but she managed to croak out, "Enough for what?"

Those crystal blue eyes thinned as the Flayer Mage assessed her. Straightening her spine and lifting her chin as much as she was able, Khiri refused to be cowed. She'd come so close to breaking, but Micah had reminded her she wasn't alone. As long as she had someone to fight for, she had to stay strong. No matter how much it cost her.

"You will come to me," Irrellian said, though his tone was less certain than it had been a moment before. "And then, you will see."

He left then, between one breath and the next, fading into shadow and leaving Khiri standing the unnaturally cool mountains of soot. As soon as he was gone, Khiri sank to her knees and let her tears break free once again.

The weight of a warhorse settled in beside her as she mourned, but most of Arra faded against her inner turmoil. So many lost. All because of her family.

This was her fault.

How was she possibly supposed to make something like this right?

41

~Jathy~

EVERYTHING WAS GOING smoothly. Jathy knew they were marked by the High Ones' favor when her crew walked straight into Seirane while everyone else was being held at the gates. The Gray Army, disguised in their sullied robes of the gods, were parading through the streets without shame. Ranks of unholy knights were claiming to enforce order in a city gone mad.

Jathy saw no madness in the citizens, just complacency. These people had willingly allowed their places of worship to rot from the inside and no one had done anything to stop it. Anyone living here was as guilty as the temples themselves. Sir Quinton Ilyani would be proud if he could see her group now. They'd managed to set up barrels and arranged fuses without getting caught. Gathering even more materials from inside Seirane had been as easy as picking cherries in her grandfather's trees.

Before the orchards had been ravaged by Queen Dormidiir's armies during the recent and already forgotten war with Mytana's Temple Hill troops, Jathy had helped her Pappy harvest every summer. And the whole ash-marked war that had torn through her Pappy's home was nothing more than a skirmish staged to help hide the real enemy in both camps. The Gray Army had stolen her memories, her Pappy, and her Pappy's orchard.

Then the Traitor Prince had stolen the only man willing to make a difference.

They would all suffer soon enough—Jathy and her group would make sure of it.

Starting with Seirane.

They were bunkered down in a nearby inn's stableyard—abandoned with no sign of an owner, squatters, or even rats. It was just far enough away for the explosions to be visible, but her people would be safely out of range. Jathy wasn't sure why this place was empty, but both the stable and inn were a great base of operations for her small crew while they put everything together. Perhaps the innkeeper had been against the Gray Army and made to disappear. Jathy liked the musing. It made it feel like they were sheltering in the home of a friend. One they would soon avenge.

"The explosives are live, General. We're just waiting for your order."

"Wait!" A breathless messenger, a relative newcomer to her troops, came running from the direction of Temple Hill. "General! They're having a full mass! The whole of Temple Hill is abuzz with worshippers. We're talking about hundreds of people, maybe thousands! Perhaps we should wait!"

General Jathy Ettleway hesitated. As firmly as she believed they were all Gray Army sympathizers, numbers made a difference. There were a lot of lives sitting right in the palms of her hands. Prince Ut'evullen's pleas to not murder the innocent along with the guilty had never made sense to her before. She'd always felt it was a mark of his weakness, a desire not to make the hard decisions, to keep the blood off his own shoulders.

Faced with the same moral quandary, Jathy hadn't thought it would be this hard. She fortified her mental walls. Anyone working with the Gray Army, with or without knowledge of their actions, was tainted. That was all there was to it.

That IS all there is to it, her internal voice told her. It sounded like Sir Quinton Ilyani. He wouldn't have hesitated for a moment.

"Light them," Jathy said.

Only seconds after she'd given the order, a strange roar seemed to be building in volume from Temple Hill. Jathy had witnessed explosions before, but this didn't sound like a boom. It sounded like an avalanche straining against a net. An impact unlike anything she'd ever experienced slammed against her ribcage and threw her back. Her head bounced against something. Pain seared through her skull as her vision turned red.

Jathy Ettleway's last thoughts were a muddle of half-formed regrets.

42

~Estan~

TIME SEEMED MEANINGLESS on this side of the archway. Estan lost count of how many alternate lives he'd resisted. In one, he lived out his childhood with a family of siblings who'd all looked a lot like him. His parents had been supportive and loving people, though they hadn't approved of Estan's wish to join the Temple of Taymahr. His father hadn't even looked Estan in the eye as his son packed a bag to journey to the nearest city. The brothers and sisters of the vision had trailed along in his wake, asking how long he'd be away and if he would be back.

Estan remembered having those kinds of fantasies in his youth, when the meaner squires teased him about being an outcast orphan, but it had been many years since he'd worried about his roots. When he'd taken his oaths as a Knight of the Protective Hand, Estan had found his place. He belonged at Taymahr's side.

A vision of life with Loni, had the two of them never broken up, nearly led him astray. While in reality, she had broken it off and he'd never quite gotten over her, the vision showed him a time in which he'd been required to make the choice between his knighthood and being a proper husband and father. He'd rejected the altered reality when Loni told him he had to choose whether he loved her or his goddess more.

He'd been a thief with Corianne, choosing whether to rob or worship. That one hadn't even lasted through the first robbery. Estan wasn't made for stealing, and even the force driving the archway's tests seemed to give up on making the scenario believable.

Estan went through more lives, more visions—he was a king, he was a beggar, he was Resmine's brother by blood, he was Khiri's soulmate, he was the Flayer Mage's general, he was a cat, he was a sailor for a distant kingdom, he was a memory, he was immortal, he was dying.

Nothing stuck.

Nothing was real enough.

None of it was true.

Somewhere during the course of his visions, Estan learned to recognize the void he would float through between one vision and the next. It was a kind of limbo, but he was fully himself during these times. Whatever was testing him was leaving him in the liminal space longer between the scenarios. As though it was running out of ideas. He could sense a presence like someone next to him while walking through a dark room. So far, it had paid him little heed between scenarios.

This time was different. Estan could feel the presence watching him. Weighing him. He tried to find something to look at in the void, other than his own hands and feet. "Hello?" he called into the blankness.

"What is it you seek, mortal?"

Even with his experience as an avatar, Estan was still surprised by this voice. It didn't roar or rumble like thunder, but he still felt it course through him. It was familiar and ancient. Alien and fresh. He'd never heard it before but he'd known it all his life.

It was a struggle to remember the conversation that had brought him here. Resmine wanted him to do something—something about serving Taymahr? No. She sent him because that was what he did. Who he was. He'd been asked to come here. "What is this place? What is its purpose? Who made it?"

"A seeker of knowledge," the voice responded. "It's been centuries since someone sought wisdom here."

Estan was fairly certain he wasn't meant to respond, so he pressed his lips together. He didn't wish to antagonize the being, especially not when he'd finally passed through the gauntlet of alternate lives. The constant shifting of reality was exhausting. Even in the visions that had allowed him to eat, drink, sleep, and attend to other needs, nothing had sated or sustained him. Was that why so many people never returned? Did they waste away in the false dreams, imagining they were living?

"You have passed the tests, and so I will grant you the boon of knowledge. It may not answer what you asked, but it will be the knowledge you truly need."

"I don't understand," Estan said.

"You will."

WAKING WITH HIS FACE planted in the dirt and grass, the smell of green plants having been freshly cut strong in the air. At first, Estan thought he'd landed in another false life. He prepared to pop himself out again, and maybe he would yell at the voice for its broken promise. But something was different.

He couldn't say what made him sure this wasn't another game—he was certain, though.

This place was real.

It just wasn't *his* reality.

Pushing himself into a sitting position, Estan took in his surroundings. There were people working the field around him with hand sickles, cutting the stalks with quick, practiced motions. The Life Trees were barely visible on the horizon, though Estan wasn't sure how he'd been able to recognize them. They were so small. Not mountainous limbs with blanket-sized leaves, merely largish trees peeking over the lower canopy. Sheep bleated nearby, sounding as content as sheep could. Estan looked over his shoulder at the smallish copse of trees in the center of the field as something burst out of the branches.

A laughing child ran past Estan, not even seeing the knight. The child was between six and eight years of age, wearing a shirt as blue as the sky and tattered tan trousers. Tangled clumps of wavy hair had twigs and clumps of leaves stuck against the child's head. Estan was fairly certain the child was a boy.

"Momma, momma, momma!" Only, those sounds didn't match the shape of the child's mouth as he spoke.

Shifting to his feet, Estan watched as a woman scooped the boy up in a big hug. "What is it, Telgan?" Estan heard, though again the mouth didn't match the words.

Telgan?

Did he know a Telgan? The name seemed familiar but there was a haze overlapping the memory. Not obscured, just distant.

Something about his current location was buzzing at the back of his skull. It seemed wrong. Like something was missing, or—

Whipping his head around, Estan checked the position of the Life Trees again and tried to imagine how they would look if he were able to stand in the center of Jarelton. "This is where Jarelton should be," Estan said.

"Where it *will* be," the voice from the void corrected him. A figure, the twin of the woman holding the boy, suddenly stood next to Estan. The knight had seen so many oddities during his time on the inside of the archway, the sudden appearance of a new companion hardly phased him, though it was odd for *this* voice to come out of an apparent mortal. "This is before the city was built. Before it was even a dream in that boy's mind."

"Who is he?" Estan asked.

They watched the boy and his mother twirl before she set him back on the ground. Telgan was talking excitedly about his adventures in the copse of trees, which bugs he'd watched and how he'd narrowly escaped a fierce beast, which sounded remarkably like a squirrel. His mother laughed and tousled his hair, "My brave little warrior. Come, we have to prepare dinner."

Next to Estan, the mirror of the woman smiled without any warmth. "He is many things. You will see."

Though Estan and his companion didn't move, the sun plummeted over the horizon and popped up on the other side of Arra, racing across the sky again. It gained so much speed that its path became a line in Estan's vision. Clouds formed, rained, snowed, thundered, and vanished in the space of seconds. Seasons went by in a blur of sensations and colors. Then everything slowed back to the steady pace Estan was familiar with.

When Telgan appeared this time, Estan wasn't sure how he recognized him. The boy was tanner now, but would obviously never reach the same copper as Corianne or Dewin. His tangled wavy hair had lightened to an auburn, become tamed, and been pulled back into a tail. His mother was still present, and though her changes were less obvious, there were lines creasing her cheeks and forehead. Laugh lines, and worry lines. The fields were no longer filled with workers and looked to have recently been burned.

"We can't stay here, Mother. The rest of our people are already gone. War will starve us or the warriors will kill us. Staying will only bring death," Telgan said.

His mother crossed her arms, her lips making a thin, stubborn line. "This is my home, Telgan. I will stay. If death should find me, it should find me at home."

Letting out an exasperated sound, Telgan shook his head. "If we must stay here, then so be it. I will create a city with walls to protect us."

"Telgan..."

"No, Mother. I can do this. Let me do this for you."

Again, the sun began to create a line across the sky. This time, Estan saw the foundations of Jarelton being laid. It was only Telgan and his mother at first, but more people arrived, more buildings sprung up, and more stones were placed. Walls were growing but the city was nowhere close to the towering behemoth of Estan's time yet. Still, he recognized certain shapes forming. Dothernam Square was in the center of the growing city. Streets he had walked were starting to snake out to form larger neighborhoods. More people came, and the city continued to expand.

Telgan was everywhere. He helped others raise walls, placed paving stones, and held children while others worked. Warrior groups would come to raid and Telgan led his own people in defense of their growing city. Slowly, Estan noticed a new circlet across Telgan's brow. The circlet grew as the city did, until it was quite obviously a crown, set with cabochon rubies. Telgan was a king, with a king's bearing and rings on his knuckles to match his crown. But he continued to be among the people of his city, involved in every stone placed—even singing and dancing at most of the celebrations. He loved his people and he loved the city they were helping him make.

Telgan's mother was at his side for most of the celebrations. Telgan had a family of his own, and when his children started following him around the streets, his mother accompanied them with many fond smiles.

Time slowed again, and Estan found himself watching through a downpour. Despite the rain hammering into Arra, Estan and his companion were sheltered beneath an invisible dome. Telgan sat next to the still form of his mother, his children and wife at a respectful distance. The dappled skin of Telgan's mother was no longer lit with an inner glow. Estan felt himself responding to the grief radiating off of the once-boy, now-king, tears streaming down the knight's cheeks. "I promised you a city, Mother. It will be the greatest city on the face of Arra. You will be entombed here, and never forgotten."

Estan looked at his companion, and back at Telgan. "Are you really the spirit of his mother?" Estan asked.

"No. But as he promised, she has not been forgotten."

The king ordered a chamber to be constructed, deep beneath the city. "Mother was this city's heart, and she will continue to watch over us from below. Her tomb will be a great place of power for all future generations!"

A statue was erected, wearing the same face that still stood beside Estan, with a boy—recognizably Telgan—clinging to her skirts. Time sped up and Estan and his guide walked through buzzing city streets, watching as Jarelton continued to mold itself into a city to withstand the ages. More statues popped up in other parts of the city, all of Telgan. Citizens began leaving the statues offerings. Telgan himself stopped aging. If anything, Estan was fairly certain the king looked younger and healthier than he had when his mother passed. Power radiated off of the king as he walked through the streets. His smiles took on a sharpness. Telgan's family no longer followed him on his rounds of the city.

Less outside warriors tried to raid as the walls grew, but when Estan's guide slowed time again, there was an entire army waiting in the northern field. The being with the likeness of Telgan's mother brought Estan to the wall to witness the exchange. "Leave my city in peace, and you will live through this day!" Telgan called out. He stood in front of the main gate, the same gate Estan had used to enter Jarelton for the very first time.

A man in armor of an extremely odd design—Estan couldn't help thinking it looked as though a mattress had been bent around the fighter's torso and sewn in place—stood in his saddle and shouted back, "Are you going to fight us from there? You've got walls, sure, but where's your army? We're good and ready to starve you out!"

"I give you all until sundown to vacate this place! This is my city, the home of my mother, and these people are under my protection!"

The entire army began to jeer and scoff. Telgan didn't retreat into the gate or raise a blade. He did nothing more than point at one of the opposing army, a man with a particularly obnoxious laugh. In a matter of seconds, the man withered like a grape in the sun. The blood and muscle liquified, running off of his horse's saddle, turning to dust before it hit the ground. A skeleton in the odd padded armor still sat astride the animal, though without the weight of its rider, the horse snorted and took off for parts unknown.

Cries replaced the jeers, both angry and terrified. Even Estan swallowed back a tremor of fear. That wasn't the magic of a mortal mage. Having functioned as an avatar, Estan recognized the potency of an angry god.

"Sundown, or you will all join him." Lowering his arm, Telgan didn't even bother to raise his voice. He stood impassively as the mighty army milled about, suddenly less certain of who had the upper hand.

The world went black so quickly, Estan almost didn't realize he'd returned to the void. "So, once-avatar of Taymahr, are you satisfied? You know this place now."

The tomb of a god's mother, he realized.

He hadn't spoken aloud, but the voice answered his thought. "The tomb of the *first* god's mother. A place imbued with the knowledge of love of the city above it. A place that can sense what's best for the people it watches."

"Like the succession of the Thieves Guild?"

"Thieves are a part of my city. It is best they are led by those that want to do right by them, keep them safe, not encourage them toward violence. I cannot rid my city of thieves, so it is best I imbue those I like with authority."

"What happened to Telgan?"

"I can show you, if you wish. His course intersects with yours."

Estan wanted to get back to Resmine and report what he'd already learned, but the offer of knowledge about someone—a god—that had crossed his path wasn't something he could easily ignore.

Setting his jaw, Estan nodded, "Show me."

43

~Ullen~

BATTLE ROARED IN ALL directions. Ullen heaved his own weapon, a halberd, over his head and then down, through the clavicle of one of Hon'idar's people. On Ullen's left, General Geryan sliced her own way through soldiers that had been under her command not long ago. Jaspar and several of Ullen's most loyal people were at his back. Major Vauntara's troops were visible on the hill, waiting for the signal. Captain Honeyhill and his cavalry danced their way through the front lines, pushing back the advance of the larger force.

Ullen cleaved his way through another foe that had managed to slink this far past the leading edge of combat. While Ullen would've loved to lead the charge during this battle, his lungs weren't fully recovered. With any luck, after this fight, Hon'idar would concede. Not that Ullen was willing to wager his limited breath on it.

Especially since there was no sign of Hon'idar on the battlefield.

The barrel-walkers were wading through the enemy. Rigger had equipped the things with his rune shooters and they were leaving vast swathes of destruction in their wake. Ullen remembered the feeling of pulling the trigger of the first rune shooter, uncertain if his ploy would even work. Seeing these monsters blast entire regiments with fire, lightning, fog, and any other runes his people could get their hands on was surreal. Every fallen enemy crushed Ullen's heart a little more. Even if he won this war, how long would it take Eerilor to recover? If only there was a way to weed out those belonging to the Gray Army before the fighting started.

Despite the carnage and chaos surrounding them, Ullen's gaze slid over to Geryan. The seed of an idea was wriggling around in the back of his mind, but it would have to wait for a more peaceful moment to flourish into something useful.

He had no more time for distractions. Hon'idar's forces had been pushed into the proper position, and Ullen's team needed to signal Vautara's troops. He gave the order.

Flares burst out from the two hand-held rune shooters his team carried, marking a huge V made of fire across their section of the field. From the hills above, it should look as though someone had drawn a massive arrow at the enemy.

Vauntara's troops didn't move.

Ullen watched for a few more seconds, before enemy soldiers made a hole through the front line and his focus was pulled toward more immediate concerns.

Chop. Block. Stab. Strike. Breathe.

Watch over his team. Keep his people safe.

Flank. Cut. Thrust. Sweat.

Honeyhill's cavalry plugged the hole and Ullen had space to glare up at the ridge. It looked like Vauntara was yelling at some of her commanders. The troops were fidgeting, agitated with the dissention amongst their superior officers.

What was Vauntara playing at? There was no way on Arra she could've missed the signal.

"Load it and fire again!" Ullen shouted.

No one on his team argued. All of them were aware the call had gone ignored before. It wasn't too late to course-correct. Very few of the battles Ullen had ever been in allowed for rigid adherence to war table stratagems. It was costing them valuable time for this second shot, but Ullen was giving Vauntara one last opportunity to pull through and live up to her rank.

Turning to deal with a few more enemies breaking through the front edge, he silently pleaded with Vauntara to follow the plan. Ullen knew she'd given in too easily when he'd chastised her for her attempt to usurp Honeyhill's regiment. The meek response hadn't been a convincing mask, but Ullen had still trusted her to prove better than her ambitions.

A scuffle broke out on the top of the hill. Vauntara was wrested from her position, a small squad holding her by the arms and escorting her from the ridge. And then the rest of her troops came down the hill like an avalanche, slamming into Hon'idar's forces.

Something inside Ullen buckled. It was similar to being stabbed—only, instead of blood, Ullen's wound was gushing sorrow.

Another betrayal.

This was why he'd fought against his mother's wishes to crown him in the first place. He never wanted to be the person dealing with all of the backstabs and positioning. A sob broke out of his lips, thankfully unheard by his crew in the clamor surrounding them.

"A shame that."

The voice was impossibly close, but Ullen would recognize it anywhere. Hon'idar.

"She has real promise. Apparently someone reminded her Eerilor is one of the oldest royal houses on Arra, and it was enough for her to seek me out with a marriage contract. I told her my last engagement fell through, so if she could give me proof of loyalty—but it appears she's too incompetent for my taste."

Despite his brother's voice breathing directly into his ear, Ullen couldn't see any sign of the golden mane and beard gleaming on the battlefield. "Where are you, ya bastard?"

"We share the same ancestors." Hon'idar's tone immediately switched from mocking to frosty.

Swiping his halberd through an enemy's hamstrings, Ullen scoured the field for any sign of the man he'd grown up with. "Anyone willing to commit matricide doesn't truly belong to their ancestors."

More enemies rushed through the lines. Ullen fought the urge to whimper as his lungs screamed at him.

"You should know, brother. You're every bit as guilty as I am. If you'd just stayed gone, Mother would still be with us. There wouldn't have been a reason for her to die. Eerilor wouldn't be in the middle of this pointless war and nothing would've interrupted my ascension."

Block. Strike. Punch.

"But you couldn't leave well enough alone, could you? First, you lead your pet Fortiva to wake up an old threat so you could look like a hero arriving to warn us of danger, and then you pretend you have no interest in my crown."

Pant. Stab. Stumble.

"It's all about the greater good, isn't it? At least, that's what you pretend. But deep down, you're only out for yourself."

Pushing himself up with the halberd's staff, Ullen wheezed.

"Just—"

Was that...

"Like—"

...a glimpse of metal?

"Me!"

Ullen sensed the coming attack more than he saw it. Something about the air against his neck and the impression of a body in an unlikely amount of empty space alerted his instincts. Rolling forward, the sword cut through where Ullen's neck had been only seconds before.

Panting, Ullen watched his brother reposition. Hon'idar's invisibility, glamor, or whatever he'd been cloaked by, was obviously not enough to handle direct attention. But had the charm only broken for Ullen? If he was the only one currently watching Hon'idar, he was as good as dead. He'd never matched Hon for raw power and, with his breath already failing him, there was little chance of winning.

"I ain't like you, Hon'idar," Ullen gasped. "I never wanted what you did. The crown is about caring for Eerilor and her people. All I ever wanted was to be free. To marry whomever I wished and have no one to bark at me when I took a wrong step. I didn't care for the intrigues and the scheming. For a long time, I thought maybe that meant I weren't good enough."

"You aren't good enough!" Hon'idar hissed. He moved in to strike again.

Backpedaling for all he was worth, Ullen cried out in sheer agony as the sword came down on his left leg. He hadn't moved fast enough. There was a gap between his calf and his foot. Blood was pouring out of him like an activated water rune. Hon'idar laughed a harsh, uneven chuckle and reached down to pick up the severed bit of his brother.

What he planned to do with it would remain a mystery. As Hon'idar leaned over, someone else's weapon sliced through the would-be king's neck.

A horrible parody of the blow initially meant for Ullen.

"Hon'idar never did know how to watch his flank," Jaspar scoffed.

She was on the dirt, tearing bits of gauze out of a field pack to tourniquet Ullen's severed limb before he processed his rescue. Or Ullen had lost some time between the attack and her attentions. Between the blood loss and his ragged breathing, Ullen wasn't sure if she'd taken several seconds or several hours to see to his leg. Whether it was shock or his spirit fleeing his body, the pain seemed much farther away than before. Ullen couldn't stop staring at the limp foot no longer attached to him. He tried to lift it and earned an admonishment from Jaspar.

Geryan was bellowing a cease fire across the battlefield, carrying something golden in her out-stretched arm. It took a real effort for Ullen to recognize his brother's head. He should be the one holding it aloft and demanding the armies stand down. No one needed to fight any more. He was still alive and Hon'idar wasn't. The civil war should be at an end.

Arrows continued to bounce off the shield Maleck held over Ullen's forces. Between the arrow shield and protecting the entire battlefield from Flayers, Maleck was sweating visibly. How hard were the Flayers trying to break through with Hon'idar now dead?

Ullen blinked at his friend, anger welling up from nowhere—Maleck hadn't even tried to save him from the invisible Hon'idar.

It wasn't fair, and a part of Ullen recognized the thought as being ridiculous.

Even Maleck wouldn't be able to reattach a foot on a battlefield.

But anger was preferable to the floaty weightlessness of unfeeling. So Ullen held on to the anger. It was an anchor to his body, and he wasn't ready to die. If he died—

If he died, this would all have been for nothing.

The Gray Army still waited.

44

~Resmine~

JARELTON WASN'T IN the midst of a full panic, but it was teetering on the brink. With the twin pillars of smoke rising into the sky from the directions of Seirane and the Life Trees, things were bleak within the large city's walls. The hellish rent through the road to the north was creating supply issues, driving up prices and creating more fear.

Fear made the Flayers stronger.

Things had gone from under a semblance of control to unsteady in a hurry. Resmine could feel the eyes of her people watching her. They craved action.

And she was stuck in the middle of what amounted to noble family drama. Drama she was actively trying to increase, no less.

Her last visit with Tak, she'd bargained hard for the information trader to use his network—normally used to gather information—to distribute rumors about her uncle's involvement in everything from the kidnapped children before the Solstice Slaughter to the current state of the city. Tak was ready. But Resmine needed to make sure. Once the arrow was loosed, there was no returning it to the bow.

Waiting in her mother's office, Resmine gnawed at a hangnail. She had never managed to kick the habit. It was an obvious tell about her nerves, and she'd worked very hard to weed out all other such tells during her years as a stable-hand. Showing nerves was dangerous when people thought you were dull-witted. It wasn't true that dull-witted people were never nervous, but people believed they showed it less often because they worried less.

Worrying was a sign of foresight.

Foresight was generally associated with intelligence.

Resmine knew it wasn't a hard rule. People were peppered with nuances from a thousand different experiences and insights. It was why someone like her could be outplayed on a Knives and Nobles board by someone that didn't know the rules very well. She didn't always see what they saw.

Not knowing she'd even had an uncle for most of her life, Resmine certainly hadn't seen his betrayal coming. She wanted to know if her mother knew more, or was equally surprised. If Araylia didn't see Holt's betrayal coming, Resmine had to warn her.

But what if she doesn't believe me? She's known Holt for most of her life, and we've only just met. Sure, I'm her daughter, but the first time we ever laid eyes on each other I was already the Queen of Thieves and I asked her to help me take the seat of Ilamar. Why should she trust anything that comes out of my mouth?

For whatever reason, though, Resmine thought her mother would trust her. There hadn't really been any reason for Araylia to help her stranger of a daughter pursue the Ilamar title either, but Lady Treag had barely hesitated.

"Resmine?" Araylia entered the room, a scowl creasing her forehead even as she lifted her arms for a hug.

Unlike their first meeting, when Resmine had been overcome by some sort of gratitude for a motherly embrace, this hug was jilted and awkward—two grown women unaccustomed to casual displays of familial affection. *Maybe it was easier because Dewin was here. She grew up hugging people.*

"Why do I think this is still not a mere social call?" Araylia asked.

"Because it's not," Resmine sighed. "Lord Holt, my uncle—" Her throat caught on the words. The concept of having uncles was still so new, and yet, one had died before she'd met him and the other was conspiring with her enemies. True, she didn't have hard evidence, but—there wasn't time for this. Coughing slightly, Resmine forced the words out in a rush. "—he's been meeting with the Venom Guild and one of my rivals for Thieves' Guild leadership."

Araylia's scowl deepened. She stepped away from Resmine and turned to her desk. Her eyes seemed distant as she picked up a quill pen and began smoothing the feather. "Meeting with the Venom Guild? Holt? That doesn't— Holt is— He's not the kindest, but *assassins?*"

Resmine could tell this was not directed toward her, and she took a few steps back to give her mother space. She couldn't imagine how she'd deal with similar news about Estan. Well, no. That wasn't at all true. Resmine wouldn't believe it if someone told her Estan was meeting with the Venom Guild unless it was followed up with, "He waded into their stronghold with a single sword and no back-up to demand they surrender."

Estan would definitely do *that*. And then she'd have to find a way to save him before he got himself killed.

Because she always did.

Sparing a brief prayer to Locke that her blockhead bond-brother was still alive and unhurt within the archway, Resmine shook off thoughts of Estan. She couldn't split her focus right now. As difficult as it was, she had to trust him to keep himself safe for a change.

Lady Treag was still locked in some sort of internal struggle. "Who saw him? Where was he?"

"One of my people saw him enter the Two Beams Tavern. It's a known stronghold for the Venom Guild. They were holding Estan and Genovar Fortiva prisoner there recently."

"General Fortiva was here?"

"He was," Resmine said. She debated whether to continue, but this was hard enough without keeping secrets. "The General sacrificed himself to allow us to escape with his daughter. Khiriellen Fortiva was captured on her way through the city to return to the Life Trees. She's a friend of mine."

Araylia nodded absently. "Khiriellen has been through the gates a few times. My people are pretty good about telling me when we have notable visitors in the city and an elf that young stands out. It didn't take much digging to find the tavern she stayed in on her first visit—the veterans there were practically glowing with praise for General Fortiva's daughter. And apparently on her recent visit, she saved a woman while getting herself captured by demons in the streets. But I assume you know all this already."

"Parts of it. I didn't know you had people watching the gates. Or that you knew about Khiri," Resmine said. She'd conjectured her mother had spies in the city, but confirmation was nice.

"All part of growing up as a Treag. Forming a network was also necessary to find news of my missing daughter," Araylia shot Resmine a half-hearted attempt at a smile. "I haven't paid quite as much attention the last few years as I might have. When my mother started to deteriorate, I made some impulsive decisions toward taking her seat. It was more about my anger toward her than any real concern for Jarelton or the people living here. If I could undo those last days, I would. I didn't even stop to think how my sudden bid for Ilamar might have bothered Holt or Orin. I think, honestly, Holt and I forgot we had a younger brother most days. Orin was the type to let himself fade into the background. Never saw his bid coming."

"Estan—"

Araylia cut her daughter off with a nod. "Your friend can be persuasive. He came to see me not long before we met, trying to get me to start my campaign again. I'm fairly certain he talked to Holt as well. That's what strikes me as the oddest part of all of this. If Holt was after the seat, why's he only making his move now? And why not tell your friend his intentions?"

Resmine had wondered something similar. It would've been much easier for everyone if her uncle had mentioned wanting the title of Lord Ilamar before the Flayers and the Venom Guild dug their roots into Jarelton. If he'd worked with her group after Orin's untimely death—but, that was it, wasn't it? "He may have blamed us for Orin gaining power in the first place. If Holt wanted the title badly enough to deal with the Venom Guild, he could already have been in league with them. How else would they have gained access to the city? The walls were enough to keep Flayers out during the Great War. Why would they suddenly fail now and only after Lady Ilamar's passing?"

Looking at her mother, Resmine was afraid she'd overstepped in her conjectures, but Araylia appeared pensive more than offended. With a huff of relief, Resmine let her mind continue down the newly opened avenue of thought. "If his goals were to take over the city with the backing of the people, he'd definitely want a scapegoat. Preferably one he could control and turn back when he wanted them gone. The Thieves' Guild is the obvious choice, but Ysinda wasn't the type to bend over and take orders from a noble. She'd been willing to work with Orin, but Orin didn't ask for much. He wanted the Venom Guild gone as much as she did. Which means Holt's only option was inventing a threat."

Araylia began pacing the length of her plush sitting area carpet, her slippered feet barely obscuring her footprints as they pressed into the soft pile. She met Resmine's eyes, started to say something, and then turned again. It was a show of Lady Treag's nerves that her hands were clenching and flexing as she walked. Minutes passed while the noblewoman created a channel across her floor. "By the divines, I hate this."

Before Resmine could respond, her mother began ranting in a voice that kept raising to higher pitches with every sentence.

"I don't want it to be true, but I can't... I can't say I don't see him doing something like that. Holt's always been an entitled ass. When our mother demanded he stop visiting brothels, he as good as told her that every woman in the city was his property anyway. I'd half-buried the memory, wanting to believe he'd outgrown such things. But if you're right—if my daughter who returned to me by the will of the gods alone is right—Holt has let in the demons and allowed them to kill our people for sport. He is responsible for the death of our youngest brother. And he's quite likely planning something horrible for the two of us."

The door swung open with a thud.

Given the subject matter and Resmine's own way with luck, the Queen of Thieves half-expected to see her uncle striding in with Flayers on each side of him. Instead, she met the gray eyes of Caspen, her mother's butler.

"My lady, is all well within your office? Shall I fetch a calming tea perhaps? I thought I detected some... Agitation," Caspen's voice was as crisp and flat as the butler's uniform he wore.

"No, thank you, Caspen. We are well. Merely discussing some family issues," Araylia said. She was attempting to draw back on her mantle of unflappable nobility, but it wasn't fitting quite as well as Resmine had seen it in the past weeks.

Caspen didn't move from the open door. "What family issues might those be, my lady?"

Something about his stance was off. Resmine watched his peppery red mustache twitch ever so slightly. He was waiting for something. Did her mother have a trigger phrase to indicate she was in danger? Or to indicate the danger was passed? Was she so flustered by the implications against her older brother, she'd forgotten to reassure her butler he could stand down?

Or was this something else?

Resmine saw the dagger emerge from Caspen's sleeve faster than a spell. It sailed across the room toward her mother's chest.

With the reaction time of someone who'd feared for their safety every moment of every day for most of their life, Resmine's whip shot forward to meet the knife mid-flight. As quick as she'd been, it wasn't quite enough to knock the dagger completely off course.

Her mother cried out as the blade caught her in the muscle of her arm.

Before Caspen had his second blade in hand, Resmine had placed herself between Lady Treag and her trusted servant.

"Caspen?" Araylia's voice trembled, but all of the questions she had were contained within one frightened word.

Another mustache twitch, and something like regret seemed to flash over the man's features for an instant. "You mentioned family trouble, my lady. That can only really mean one thing, now that Lady Resmine has returned and the rest of the Treags have died. I've been in your brother's pocket for many years. I can't say I'm proud, but his coin kept my parents comfortable in their golden years. Saw my younger brother safely through the Mages' College. You offered security for me, but never looked beyond my personal needs. I'm sorry, my lady. But if you've discovered my benefactor's secrets, I am compelled to complete my contract."

"Not past me, you won't," Resmine hissed.

Lunging from the door, Caspen sank the full measure of his weight into his dagger point. While Resmine was his equal in height, he outweighed her by a surprising margin. She caught his attack against the handle of her whip, but the parry she'd intended became a weapon lock. She wouldn't win a match of brawn-versus-brawn.

"Do you think I can leave either of you alive, girl?" Caspen said, shoving the words out from between his clenched teeth. "It's only a matter of who I kill first."

Resmine wished she'd allowed Shiv to come with her, but she'd gotten complacent about her safety in her mother's house. It was a large house with trusted servants and plenty of runic protections against things like Flayers and fire. Nothing was ever fool-proof, but Resmine had thought of the place as being safe as she could be outside of the Pit. Of all the dumb miscalculations, Resmine feared this one might prove fatal.

But she wasn't ready to die yet.

"Resmine!" Araylia cried. "No!"

The warning came in time. A flash of metal thrust through the air where Resmine's head had been. She spun to the side, releasing the handle of her whip with one hand just enough for Caspen's locked dagger to skid off. He'd committed too much momentum to the second dagger to keep the pressure up anyway. He floundered at the unexpected miss, but not enough to lose his footing.

Altering her grip on the whip, Resmine grimaced. The handle would have to be patched and rewoven, if not replaced entirely. It was amazing she'd held on to this one for as long as she had, given all the Flayers and Gray Army minions she'd faced, but it still hurt to lose it. This whip had been with her through a lot in the last year.

Shake it off and concentrate, Resmine told herself. *This is no sparring match.*

Caspen didn't leave her to regroup for long. As soon as he had reoriented, he was hurling himself forward again. His daggers were stacked as though he planned to thrust in and rip her apart.

Whips were made for range, of which Resmine had increasingly little. She dodged under Caspen's arms and rolled to her feet behind him. Drawing her own dagger from her boot, she attempted to thrust it into the attacker's back.

Attempted, and failed.

Caspen shoved her away from him and Resmine bumped up against her mother's desk. She didn't have time to scramble away so she thrust at him again—practically sitting on the desk—hoping the attack would make him give ground.

The man was as quick as thought. He whipped around and met her blade with his left hand, whirling into her with his right elbow. If not for all the training Resmine had done with Khiri, he would've gotten the Queen of Thieves right there. But as fast as he was, Khiri was lightning personified. Resmine redirected the elbow from anything vital, though it would still leave one hell of a bruise.

Two daggers, more weight, more speed.

And the will to kill.

Nothing about this fight was skewing in Resmine's favor.

Except Resmine was a survivor. It was what she did. This was far from the first unfair fight she'd been in—and if Temple Hill hadn't managed to kill her, there was no way she was going to let a two-faced butler from the richest houses of Jarelton have the honor. If he wouldn't give her the space to get away, she'd just have to make it.

With her free hand, Resmine searched the desk behind her and grabbed hold of her mother's inkpot. Hurling that at the butler's face, she hoped to blind him. He dodged away, the ink splattering harmlessly across his shirt and staining the pristine rug and part of the couch behind it.

No matter. She'd succeeded in getting more space.

Caspen had paused to watch the ink sink into the carpet. "I'll need to fetch some lemon juice," he muttered, his voice barely audible. His sneer returned as he roared, "Do you know how hard it is to get ink out!"

Using her whip, Resmine lashed one of the lightest chairs in the room and yanked it in between her and Caspen. He snarled, not going around the chair, but attempting to bowl straight over it.

Sloppy.

It robbed him of his momentum and gave Resmine her first real opening.

From his precarious footing, the butler swiped at his opponent's head. Resmine grabbed one of the man's wrists as it came near her face and pulled it in. She bit down until she tasted blood.

With a high-pitched scream, Caspen dropped the dagger clutched in the savaged limb. He made a wild slash with the free arm that didn't come anywhere near her. "You utter lunatic! Who bites during a knife fight!"

Ducking around the distracted butler, Resmine kicked the back of his knee and swept up his discarded knife. With him on the ground, it was easy enough to dispatch him.

"A lunatic that wants to survive," she told the corpse.

Leaving Caspen to bleed out on the carpet didn't feel right. But Resmine didn't want to stick around and find out who else in her mother's house was really working for her uncle. Her mother had pulled the dagger out of her arm and was shaking as she tied a clean scarf around the wound. It wasn't the best bandage, though it would do until they got somewhere safe.

"Mother, I think it's time you come see where I work."

CORIANNE AND SHIV WERE both glaring at their queen as she accepted healing runes and gauze from them to clean her mother's arm. The wound wasn't grave, though it was deep. Lady Araylia Treag would be fine after the assassination attempt, medically speaking. The betrayal seemed to have hit her much harder.

"I can't believe it," Araylia murmured again. "I hired Caspen myself when I first set up my own residence. He's been my butler for decades. I just... I can't believe it."

"Much as I hate to be bringing the guard into anything, we may want to let them know Lady Treag is here and the dead butler tried to kill her first," Shiv offered, with as much delicacy as he could.

Resmine nodded. "Send for them. And make sure our messenger is someone with an impeccable record. We're still on relatively good terms at the moment, but the last thing I need is for them to start arresting my people because someone beat us to reporting a dead body."

"I thought I could trust Caspen with my life," Araylia told Corianne, though her eyes were distant. Resmine wasn't sure her mother's eyes were really focused on her surroundings. "I thought he'd be with me until he retired. I thought he'd maybe settle down in the city and I'd even visit him for tea on the odd afternoon. He wasn't much older than me. I thought there was a good chance, if he liked me well enough, I might not ever need another butler."

Corianne nodded with a sad smile. "We ain't none of us prepared for family what cut ties, and he weren't nothing to you. Hard when trust gets tossed like rubbish. We'll get you nice and smackered."

"Corianne!" Resmine protested. "You really want to get my mother drunk?"

"Of all of us, she deserves it the most, yeah?" Corianne said. Then she took a longer look at Resmine. "Though you might be wanting to swish sommat about your gums before the guard come and take you in for a rabid beast."

That explained why Resmine could still taste copper. She took a swish from a nearby jug of fresh water and spat it into the bowl holding the bloodied scarf Araylia had originally wrapped her arm in. She winced as the motion of spitting pulled at her battered muscles. The bruise Caspen had given her across her ribs was deeply purple and tugged whenever she moved her torso.

"Oy, ya can't be wincing like a battered lamb afore the guard. They'll think the lot of us mewling sheep for shearing, no matter what we done several good turns of late. Here, then." Corianne smacked another healing rune into Resmine's palm. "It's the last I got pouched, so you'll be owing me a full recharge and a fresh one for the bother."

"You got it," Resmine said, a rough chuckle jerking a fresh wave of pain and nausea through her before the healing rune took full effect.

Reporting to the guard was a good idea, but Resmine couldn't wait for the investigations to follow before she moved. By the time the city was ready to choose their next Ilamar—or the guard was ready to arrest a noble—it would be too late. She now had definite proof of Holt Treag's intentions toward her and her mother. Whether he really had let the Venom Guild into the city or not, any doubts she had of his alliance with assassins were assuaged. The Thieves' Guild needed to deal with Holt, their traitor, and the interloping guild.

Her mind already at work, Resmine started putting together orders for her people. She would have Tak start work with his rumor mill immediately, but more was needed.

Holt was a wealthy man; however, wealth was a poor weapon against an entire guild of thieves. With a little redistribution of assets, Resmine could protect her city from the Venom Guild and sink Lord Holt Treag for good.

45

~Dewin~

Watching the roofed rim of the courtyard-made-temple out of the corner of her eye, Dewin saw the Flayer Mage step out of seemingly nothing. The first time she'd seen him, she hadn't been sure. Maybe it had been a trick of the light, or her mind was giving shadows a form where they had none.

But then he came again.

And again.

And again.

Each time, he approached from a different place on the roof, as though he didn't want to be noticed. He would stick out a hand and ease it against some sort of barrier Dewin couldn't actually see. She could see a glow pressing against him, though. At first, she thought it was a spell he was casting. Some sort of light spell, or an enchantment to help him step on hallowed ground. The more Irrellian Thornne came, though, the more she recognized the glow for what it was. Holiness pushed against him, keeping his shadows at bay.

Dewin could see his progress, too. The first few times, Irrellian hadn't been able to do more than touch the outside of her holy fortress. Even that had been alarming compared to the Flayers waiting outside the square. They couldn't even approach to tap against the figurative glass. The Flayer Mage, over the course of the last several days, had gone from placing a hand against the glass to sliding through it—all the way up to his wrist.

Her protective glass was becoming more and more like water.

"Adari, shield me," Dewin breathed.

She sensed the prayer flicker out of her mouth as a small flame, shooting toward the heavens. A tiny trickle of power in the torrent welling up from Dothernam Square. It wasn't enough to shove the Flayer Mage back out of the temple grounds, but he wasn't making any more forward progress either.

Her presence as the priestess of this temple wasn't going to hold him off for much longer. Dewin found herself hoping Khiri returned from the Life Trees and whatever had happened there soon. If there was anything people believed in as much as the High Ones and the Flayer Mage, it was the name Fortiva.

Maybe it would be enough to turn the tide.

Because—given what Dewin could see from the floor of the last true temple in Mytana—the gods were losing.

46

~Khiri~

"*Khiri...*"

Ignoring the voice like it was willful gnat, Khiri sank further into her misery.

"*Khiri.*"

She was so deep in her agony, it almost felt good at this point. As though the pain itself was an impenetrable blanket, woven of sorrow and loss. What else could be ripped from her now? What could possibly still touch her? It hurt so much, the edges of rawness burned like comfort.

"*Khiri!*"

Even this far gone, she couldn't deafen herself entirely to Micah. He was her brother. She clung to the connection like she was the last green leaf in a winter wind.

"Micah, what have I done?" her voice hitched and cracked every other word. There were no tears. She wasn't sure there was enough water in her for the tears required by this kind of grief.

"*Khiri, you didn't do this. More importantly, they're not gone!*"

The spark of anger at being denied responsibility fizzled before it found kindling, replaced by a muddled mess of hope and confusion. "What do you mean?"

"*Our people, their spirits... All of those that slept within the Life Trees! The Life Trees burned but they're all still here!*"

Shaky thoughts jumbled together as Khiri reached out to Catapult for support, wobbling to her feet. She didn't recall kneeling in the blackened ashes, but it was more surprising she hadn't fallen face down and stopped moving altogether. Despite the mountain of despair, Khiri traced the large empty space with new eyes.

The spirits of her people hadn't perished.

They were here. She could sense them through her connection to Micah. Thousands of lives, formerly lending the Life Trees form and majesty, now drifting like eddies of snow. They hadn't evaporated into smoke.

But they still might. They needed somewhere to sleep, somewhere to dwell so that Arra would know not to swallow them. They needed—

"Life Wood."

Micah didn't respond. He knew the conclusion Khiri was only now coming to. She could feel it in his silence.

"By Arra!" Khiri's chest constricted and she nearly fell back into the ash.

"...*I made a promise...*" Micah started, but Khiri was already shaking her head.

This situation was much bigger than any promise between siblings. Even if she was selfish enough to deny her entire heritage and allow the Clans to fade into dust, she couldn't hold Micah against his will like that. His ancestors were here. He'd had friends here. He'd loved his fletching master like a second father. His parents were probably among the elven spirits swirling around her ankles. She couldn't ask him to give up everything to follow her into oblivion. And she couldn't leave her people to flounder and sputter out like an untended candle. With all she'd lost, it was time to reclaim *something*.

Even if it means letting go of the only person I've got left.

Where the tears hadn't come before, they teetered at the edges of her vision. The loss of the Life Trees had seemed too big to fathom, but this... Saying goodbye was becoming all too familiar. She didn't have time to cry, though. There was work to be done.

Digging through the ash in some places would've taken weeks or longer, but Khiri used the skills Kal had taught her to sense where the ashes were the most shallow and shifted them with her will as much as her muscle. Catapult watched solemnly, but didn't offer assistance. Unlike his rider, the roan seemed to understand Khiri's independent nature.

This was a task meant for her people, to be carried out by her alone.

And it was accomplished much too quickly.

"Micah—"

"You're my sister. That's a bond I never expected and will hold with me forever. When it is your time, we'll find each other again."

"You'll never be alone," Khiri promised, echoing Micah's words after he fell. And then she jabbed him into the exposed ground.

It wasn't like when she'd plucked him out of the soil in the mountains. The ground didn't gently give way like it was expecting him—it sucked him beneath the surface as though Arra meant to devour him. Khiri cried out in alarm. *Oh, spirits, what have I done? Please don't let me have given up my brother for nothing!*

Beneath her, tremors rocked the hidden surface of the world as a small branch pierced its way through the sky, growing in width as it flung branches and limbs out like a hand meant to swallow the sun. Along the path of ash, swirling clouds of blackened dust began to coalesce into the shapes of the lost Life Trees. But they couldn't take the old forms without the Life Wood to seed them. The shadows of the old trees waded over the distance, bending to embrace the still forming Life Tree above Khiri. Intense light began to pulse from within the heart of the seven embracing giants. It promised new life but also sent a deep stab of fear through the young elf.

Something told her that to be touched by this light would be to join the souls of those who slept.

Scrambling to her feet, Khiri ran to Catapult and jumped, trusting her companion to eat distance faster than she could. They raced across the ash as it rose and merged with the towering form. The trunk was expanding like a flooded river, and there was no telling what would happen if they were touched by the hungry magic as Khiri's people rejoined each other. What had been seven reversed mountains with days of travel between the trunks was merging into the largest megalithic structure Khiri had ever seen. Most likely the largest thing anyone across Arra had ever seen.

And it was still growing.

Catapult let out a determined snort and galloped faster than Khiri thought possible. They ducked into the untouched forest and cut through a clearing Khiri recognized from hunting with her father. Leaping across a stream, Catapult finally slowed. He turned and they watched as the new Life Tree's glow ebbed and faded into the healthy silver of Life Tree bark.

Khiri looked up into the branches. While the Life Trees had merged into one trunk, she didn't think the branches were actually all that much higher than they'd been before. As she watched, a staircase began to emerge along the shorter side of the grand trunk. Who were the ancestors making a path for, though? Surely they didn't expect Khiri to live in this massive Life Tree all on her own?

Dismounting, Khiri ventured back toward the trunk of the new Life Tree. It seemed dormant now, but she hadn't quite brought herself to touch it.

"Khiri!"

"Micah?"

It was harder to hear him, like he was shouting from across a waterfall. Khiri couldn't hear the waterfall, but there was a similar magnitude to the silent interference.

"Khiri! They're not here!"

"Who's not here?" Khiri pressed her hand against the freshly grown trunk and was hit by the vision of Micah standing in front of her, pressing his hand against hers from the other side. "What do you mean?"

"The Oak Wood Clan, River Willow, Storm Grove, Pleasant Birch, Sun Maple, Ash Shadow, Elm Thorn... I mean, the Elders are here, as well as a few holdouts that didn't want to leave, and a few your mom couldn't convince danger was coming—but mostly everyone that was still awake evacuated weeks ago. Our clans survived!"

"How—" But she already knew. Khiri knew as soon as Micah started explaining. It had to have been her father. Knowing Irrellian Thornne as well as he did, Genovar might not even have needed a vision to recognize the danger to their people. He'd arranged for the salvation of as many as he could.

Except for her.

His own daughter, he'd doomed with his actions, while mitigating the damage for strangers. Even against the grief of losing him, her anger surged. There was no way to yell at Genovar for his part in things. For the part she'd been forced to play in this whole mess.

"Hey," Micah said. "I can see it in your eyes. It's okay to be happy about them surviving, Khiri. I know there's a lot going on in your head right now, but take a moment to breathe it in. Irrellian's not infallible. He made a mistake here. A big one. And if he made one this big—"

"He'll make others," Khiri agreed. "Micah... What am I going to do without you?"

For a moment, Micah's form wavered on the other side of the bark. It was like he'd tried to hide something from her, but Khiri could still feel the remorse in their sibling bond. It wasn't as strong as when he'd been a bow on her back, and she knew the time when they'd been able to communicate over distances was gone. Micah wasn't at risk of falling with his sister in some forgotten forest, far away from his people anymore—Khiri tried to be satisfied with that. But she hadn't even left yet, and she already missed him. "You'll keep going. You always have."

A rough chuckle fought its way through the urge to cry. "That's me. Unstoppable."

"You are, you know," Micah said, his voice more serious than before. "You've always been stronger than you realized."

"I love you, Micah. Not in the way we were promised when we were kids, but you're my brother. Now and forever."

"Always, Khiri. I love you, too. And I'm going to talk sense into our people about the whole soulmate thing. If I became soulless when your name was stripped from me, what am I doing here now? Your father ripped through reality to find love with a human just to escape from his original Destined. It's time for some changes."

"Definitely." Khiri let herself laugh, even though it wasn't funny. Micah was trying to lighten her spirits as they parted. While they were parting on much better terms than the last time she'd left the Life Trees, he wouldn't be following her this time.

He'd never follow her on another adventure again.

"Goodbye, Micah," she whispered as they both pulled their hands away from opposite sides of the Life Tree's trunk.

"Arra's own luck, sister."

WITH THE NEW LIFE TREE having absorbed most of the ash from the ground, fresh grasses were already sprouting over the space beneath the massive limbs. Khiri and Catapult paced next to each other in quiet companionship while Khiri tried to figure out what to do next. She'd come back to the Trees in the first place to talk to her mother. Originally, she'd wanted a sense of clarity after Genovar had disowned her, and then she'd continued because she wanted to see her mother even more after Genovar's death. Even now, she wanted to talk to Leyani more than anything.

But Khiri didn't have the first clue where Leyani might be.

"Starling?"

This can't be a coincidence. Khiri tried to send the thought by reflex, but no one was there to receive it. Even the space Imyn once occupied seemed hollow. The only response she got was the thrum of the ever-present *Telgan Korsborn*.

"Mother? What are you doing here?"

Leyani emerged from a dense cluster of trees, shaking a snagged boot free of a bramble. Seeing her mother with fresh eyes, Khiri couldn't believe it had taken her so long to recognize her mother wasn't an elf. All those years of Leyani ducking through the door of their home, never wearing her cascade of blonde hair up in any style that exposed her ears, her lack of woodcraft, and her finesse at haggling with human traders. Leyani had been tall for an elf, but seeing her as a human—Khiri realized her mother was actually quite petite. And more disturbingly, Khiri could see the family resemblance to the assassin uncle who had hunted her across the face of

Arra, and was at least partially responsible for Genovar's demise. "I've been keeping watch over the Life Trees. Your father told me to convince as many as I could to seek refuge last season. I've been running escorts as often as I could ever since. I was on my way to see if anyone else was coming when I saw the smoke a few days ago."

Khiri barked out a sound somewhere between a scoff and a laugh. "The Flayer Mage seeks to punish me for my father's death, and somehow—even dead—my father is a better rival than I am."

"Oh, my sweetest girl!" Before Khiri could protest, her mother's arms were wrapped around her like a constrictor snake, squeezing an embarrassing chirp through her lungs. But once she was wrapped in the blanket of Leyani's love, Khiri's tears refused to be held back a second longer. She didn't remember starting to talk, but she was midway through her inadvertent waking of the Flayer Mage and discovering so many family secrets when she realized the words were rushing out of her. She told her mother about all of the loss she'd encountered during her travels, how angry she was at her father, and how much she missed him, Kal, and Micah. "And now, I've got to face down Irrellian Thornne, but I don't have my knife or my brother or anything!"

At some point during the deluge of words and emotions, Leyani had guided Khiri over to the roots of the Life Tree, where they sat on a ridge like it was a bench in a tap room. Catapult was keeping watch a short distance away, flicking his tail at non-existent flies. Khiri wasn't sure if he was actually concerned about an attack or was pretending to give her and Leyani a moment of privacy.

"My Starling, you may not have your weapons, but it sounds like you still have a lot of options," Leyani said. She ran a soothing hand through her daughter's hair, combing the tangles out as gently as she could. If Khiri closed her eyes, she could almost see the walls of her childhood home surrounding her instead of the ridges of the single Life Tree's new root structure. "Don't you still have your friends in Jarelton? And Ullen's out there somewhere. He's always been a great friend to our family."

"But my visions have only ever shown me on my way to face Irrellian on my own," Khiri scowled. "Father died because he believed the visions were never wrong. He had way more experience with them than I do. If he couldn't see a way out of his fate, how am I supposed to?"

With a deep sigh of loss, Leyani leaned back against the Life Tree and placed a hand on her heart. "Your father, as skilled as he was, never allowed for any flexibility in the future. If he saw it, he was sure it would happen, but he never had the gift of hindsight. He never saw the ways he ensured the worst outcomes when he tried to change things, so he stopped trying to change them. It was easier for him to assume the vision was inevitable. If I have any major regrets about our life together, it's that I didn't argue with him more. But he was stubborn and I was tired of fighting. With my birth family, all I'd ever known was fighting and I wanted peace. I craved it so badly, I allowed myself too many blindspots when it came to Genovar's flaws. Now, it's too late to gainsay him, but you're still here. Khiri, heed me, please. Just because you can't see the answer, it doesn't mean there isn't one. Talk to your friends. Tell them everything."

"Everything? But, mother—"

"Everything, Khiriellen Fortiva. They can't help you if you don't let them."

Khiri blinked back what tears she had left and swallowed her protest. Leyani had used the voice all mothers seemed to share, passed down from Mother Arra herself. There was no arguing with the Mother's own voice. Even the forest seemed to take a breath to steady itself.

"Are you... Staying here?" Khiri finally asked. Khiri had known her personal journey wasn't over, but it seemed her mother didn't intend to accompany her back to Jarelton. Parting with Leyani so soon, after she'd arrived so unexpectedly, didn't feel right. "Will you not even travel with me to the road?"

Leyani smiled sadly and said, "Would that I could go with you all the way to Jarelton and take your burdens myself, love. I'll accompany you to the edge of the forest. I've got to make my way back to our people and let them know it's safe to return."

Getting to her feet, Khiri offered a hand to pull her mother up. Even through the massive limbs above, the forest seemed brighter now. Catapult fell in behind the two women, continuing to act as though he were an average war horse. Khiri took almost as much comfort in his presence as she did the warmth of her mother beside her. It surprised her how used to companionship she'd become during her travels. There had been a time in her life when hunting was her greatest joy because it was an opportunity to get away from everyone, her parents included.

They spent the rest of the day remembering shared stories about Genovar and Micah, and telling stories about their lives apart. Leyani told Khiri about bits of her past before she'd switched names, and Khiri told Leyani about the encounters with the man who'd claimed to be her uncle. It saddened her mother to hear about her once-brother—the man he became without her softening influence—but she didn't shed any tears over his disappearance.

"I broke ties with that life a long time ago," Leyani said, her voice taking a much harder note than Khiri had ever heard from her mother. "If I could do it over, I'd have made sure loose ends would never have hunted down my daughter."

And over the campfire, Leyani cooked, using herbs and spices as skillfully as she'd taught Micah all those years ago. Khiri reached out mentally to the place Micah had occupied within her for most of her life, first as a name and then as a presence, but there was only the faintest touch of her sibling bond. She'd fulfilled the unspoken promise she'd made, to reunite him with their people. It hurt, but with Leyani smiling at her from across the campfire, Khiri felt some of the broken edges of her heart soften.

Something was healing inside. Starting to, anyway.

47

~Resmine~

DAGAN ARRIVED AS EXPECTED around midday while Resmine was holding court. With him, he had his usual cloud of hangers-on—roughly ten strong. Not enough to challenge the throng always present at The Dusk and Dawn, but he seemed to think they rendered him untouchable. Resmine took a deep breath and clenched her grip around the armrests of her throne.

She wanted to get this over with as quickly as possible. Once it was over, she could turn her full attention to her uncle and the projects already in motion to deal with him.

One ass at a time, Resmine sighed internally.

Shiv was at his usual spot between her and the stairs, while Corianne was casually flipping a rune over her fingers. A few handfuls of the thieves Resmine trusted most were lounging at the tables she kept for her court. In the Pit, Ysinda had kept maybe fifteen chairs total. Resmine had at least that many lurkers on a quiet day.

"Looking as effervescent as always, my queen," Dagan grinned. The cold calculation of his eyes reminded Resmine of a gnorel. His boyish features were only disarming for someone who'd never woken in the wilderness to find themselves staring death in the face.

"I'm about as bright and bubbly as the water standing in a pitcher overnight," Resmine tone was curt. "State your business, Dagan."

"I've come to see if you've seen reason about my offer to take position as your Consort."

"See reason? That's dangerously close to a threat." Resmine fought the urge to look anything other than bored. She couldn't risk Dagan sensing the trap before it was sprung. Only one person would object to what she had planned.

And Estan wasn't back yet.

"You'd like it if I threatened you, wouldn't you? That'd make it real easy for your two tame pups to off me here and now without so much as a hello, right? Just another dip in the road on your way to rule over the whole of Jarelton?" Dagan's smile didn't shift. "But that's not what's going to happen. You're either going to do this the easy way—call me Consort, we do just enough tap to satisfy the magical bonds you hoodwinked, and I get to make the real calls like I was always meant to—or we do this the hard way."

"You seem to misunderstand what a threat is, Dagan. What exactly is the hard way if the easy way is pretending you don't disgust me down to the dregs of my being? Naming you as my Consort would be worse than death."

Dagan's nostrils flared and he gritted his teeth. "As you would have it, Highness. I'm sure I can find a method more to your liking."

"Working with the Venom Guild, perhaps?"

A wave of shock passed over Dagan's face, though he was quick to mask the reaction. Resmine watched as recalculations tried to weave themselves behind the traitor's eyes. His hands drifted toward his weapons.

Shiv repositioned, shifting his feet to remind Dagan's crowd a mountain of muscle was still watching them. His scowl, always present when Dagan was around, was cavernous. Corianne had stopped moving. She was clutching the rune she'd been playing with, its arcane design softly glowing in the tavern's dim light. Several others, content to lounge on their benches until this moment got to their feet. Dagan didn't seem to notice he'd angered more than Resmine's lieutenants. A few of his followers started to slink back toward the stairs only to find the way blocked by more of Resmine's court.

He's been looking for a fight. I think it's time to oblige.

"Abe! You might want to bar the doors!" Resmine shouted so the bartender could hear. She could feel a reckless grin of her own bubbling up from somewhere. Her bond with Locke had changed since he'd left with the rest of the High Ones to take his place within the heavens, but the thrill of battle ignited some of the same channels he'd forged inside of her. "We've got to do some house cleaning."

Making a dash for Resmine, knives leapt into Dagan's hands. He was coming too fast, but Corianne's rune slammed into the floorboards at his feet. Vines erupted from the ground, tangling the would-be assailant's feet and climbing up his legs. Resmine was ready, standing with her new whip in hand, by the time he was free. She blocked and dodged as Dagan growled incomprehensibly.

Shiv bowled into the center of Dagan's crowd. He tossed one man over the balcony rail and picked up another. He was swinging his hostage around as an improvised club. All around him, thieves picked off stragglers. More bodies made desperate attempts to fly as they were pushed from the throne room.

One of Dagan's knives grazed against Resmine's armored-leather bodice. *Praise Locke I wore it today,* Resmine thought as torchlight caught the greenish glint to Dagan's blade.

Poison.

Corianne tagged Dagan with another rune, freezing the traitor in place. Ice crystals ran along his cheekbones and his skin took on a bluish hue. Not sure if he was gone or merely inconvenienced, Resmine pulled her own knife and gave him a Thieves' Smile. Blood trickled down his neck like molasses.

The fight to keep her throne was over almost as quickly as it had started.

While she enjoyed a good fight, there was something truly unnerving about the slow, cold death of Dagan. Turning away to clean her blade, it was a chore to keep her voice steady. "Get this thing out of my sight."

As several people came to retrieve the body, Resmine held up a hand and motioned them to wait. She'd been wearing down the trust between the Venom Guild and her uncle for a few days, but what better way to solidify a rift than to make it look like the other party was taking down their allies? As she explained exactly what she wanted done, many in her guild were grinning with the enthusiasm of Adari.

48

~Holt~

OPENING THE DOOR OF his inner courtyard to find the slowly thawing corpse of the man, one he'd entrusted to take over the Thieves' Guild and crush his irksome niece, had been the last straw.

More accurately, the *letter* attached to the corpse had been the last straw.

> *H,*
>
> *It's been decided our contract is no longer in the best interest of our people.*
>
> *Consider this a contribution to your campaign to 'take back the city.'*
>
> *Don't forget about our severance policy.*
>
> *AR*

Those assassins had been a means to an end—they were supposed to be the evil he overcame to win the hearts of Jarelton and ensure his own succession. But nothing had gone right.

First, they'd spent months trying to oust the Thieves' Guild to no avail. If anything, that endeavor had only led to Orin's short-lived triumph. Nothing about it had gained Holt anything. Then, the estranged niece he'd so carefully buried had become a genuine nuisance. After all the years and funds Holt had sunk into Caspen, the butler had been killed and Araylia had disappeared. And now—

Now...

Holt's teeth ground against each other hard enough he felt something give. Without pausing to wait for the pain to sink in, he plucked a healing rune out of his desk drawer and activated it directly against his jaw. He'd taken to keeping a few handy, but this was likely his last batch given the state of his funds.

Which was the whole problem.

Even with the outlandish fees he'd paid upfront—Arad Rhidel had personally assured him the results would be to his liking—the Venom Guild had drained his accounts. No one was supposed to know when the Venom Guild had a contract, but Holt had heard his name whispered all over the streets of Jarelton. People knew his hand had been tied to the kidnappings of their children. They hissed about him letting the demons into the city. The assassins were basking in the riches of a lord—Holt's personal wealth—while they spread word of his plans, and now he'd been left a message.

It had been suspicious enough when Rhidel stopped attending meetings personally, leaving some hooded figure in his wake. Someone in the guild of assassins was playing Holt for a fool. They wouldn't leave it at a corpse in a courtyard.

Holt didn't waste time considering other enemies. The Thieves' Guild was run by someone as incompetent as his niece. He'd looked into her past as much as he was able, and she'd spent years as a stable hand when she proved too dull-witted for knighthood. Araylia's belief that her daughter would make a good candidate for Ilamar was obviously driven from some misplaced maternal affection—Araylia didn't have the mind of a puppet master. It was beyond reason either of them could pose a true threat.

He had to act. What was left of his personal guard was obviously useless. Whomever he could still pull from the City Guard would have to do. It wasn't common knowledge yet his bribe money was well and truly gone, so he could probably convince an entire contingent to escort him to The Two Beams. They would burn the tavern to ash with the Venom Guild inside.

Holt had to roast them before they came back to tie up loose ends.

CURSING UNDER HIS BREATH, Holt left the Southern Guard House. It was the third he'd visited, and none of the guards had been willing to lift a finger to aid him.

He was in no mood for civility when he came to the Graystone Commons Guard House.

"Got a report you're under investigation, Lord Treag. We've been advised to stay out of your dealings until the matter is settled," the captain on duty informed him. With ageless umber skin and a single long braid, she looked like a child in her uniform.

Rage filled Holt's chest as he raised his arm to backhand her across the mouth like the uncouth wretch she was. But his hand never met her face. The woman had his wrist in a grip like iron and was holding him back with no effort whatsoever. "Lord Holt, did you really just attempt to strike a Guard Captain for telling you no? In her own house?"

"I am owed the respect of my title! You will unhand me and you will be brought lower than you can imagine for this insolence," Holt hissed. He tried to jerk his arm free, but her grip only tightened.

Several of the other guards within the house came to stand at the captain's side. Holt smirked as they approached. Once they saw this farce of a girl laying hands on a true noble, their senses had been shocked into place. After they freed him, they would come to resolve his issue with the assassins, then he'd have their captain dealt with in a very permanent and public fashion.

"You, there!" Pointing with his nose to the largest and most able looking of the men coming to his aid, "Wrap this bitch in chains and then follow me to Two Beams to burn out the assassins that plague our city! I'll see you rewarded! You'll become one of my personal guards, set up in the finest house in the city! Pay raise! Power! I'll even see you given a medal!"

The large man leaned closer, but he didn't pull out a set of cuffs or raise his big hands toward the woman grinding the bones in Holt's wrist even tighter. His brown eyes held Holt's gaze for a silent moment. "We don't take well to them that try to rough our own in front of us. Sir."

It was the way that *Sir* was tacked on to the end of the statement. There was no respect in it. It was a word coated in contempt and seasoned with threat. A sword of fear glided its way down Holt's spine. Looking for a friendly face, Holt attempted to take a step back.

He couldn't even tell his wrist was held by a human hand any more, the captain's grip was so tight. Holt couldn't help but think of a rabbit caught in a snare. For as long as he could remember, he'd been a wolf among sheep. Fear was for peasants and fools. Controlling the game board meant he was never in danger. No one had ever been his match in any way that mattered.

But he'd miscalculated somewhere.

"I've heard of the cover ups and those gone missing after your drunken ruts. You flaunt your power over those you believe lesser and you've unleashed a flood of death and torment upon Jarelton with no regard for those who walk her streets. Now, you've walked into an establishment created to maintain order, attempted to strike the acting captain, and stage a coup. I don't care who you were born to, I don't let filth run free in my city," the woman holding him said. Her voice was low, but held the weight of every stone in Jarelton.

"Nav, Parren, get us a spare uniform and one of those raid helmets. We're going to the Two Beams to smoke out these assassins what's been reported by an anonymous citizen."

For a brief moment, Holt didn't understand. She was giving him what he wanted? Didn't she know what he would do to her, and her whole guard house, once he was free? It was foolish. But then—

Before he could finish the thought, she tossed him into the waiting arms of the other guards. "Get him fitted and then do what you must. Such a shame we're to lose one of our own while burning the Venom Guild scum out of our city."

"Aye, Captain," someone said.

Pain like Holt had never imagined erupted in the back of his skull. He barely had time to register the strike before a helmet was shoved over his face and darkness took him.

49

~Estan~

EMERGING FROM THE HIDDEN arch and back into Jarelton proper, Estan half-expected to find another gathering of Flayers and thieves waiting for him. There was only Loni. She rushed to his side and helped him up the last few steps. She didn't embrace him, but she was as kind and gentle as he'd always known her to be. The basket tucked into the crook of her elbow might also have been impeding displays of affection. Estan tried not to be disappointed.

He also tried—and failed—not to look for Corianne.

She was likely busy with guild happenings. Resmine's needs would obviously come first to her lieutenants. Which was only correct.

But he still experienced a pang of disappointment.

Estan was embarrassed at his weakness as he returned to the world. Though the spirit of the tomb—Mother of Telgan and Mother of Jarelton—had shown him so many things, the knight didn't think he'd been gone for more than a day. The worry-etched lines of Loni's face told him otherwise. He opened his mouth to ask about the state of things when she pushed a water jug into his hands.

"You can take a moment to rest, Estan. This area's one of the first Resmine commissioned runes for when she started getting more of the Flayer repelling enchantments laid down in the city," Loni said. Guiding him over to a blanket spread over an otherwise empty porch, she made sure he was comfortable. Sitting on her knees with her feet tucked under the folds of her skirt, she began rummaging in her basket. "She's always been good about watching your back."

Estan nodded as he made restrained sips from the clay jug. He hadn't realized how parched he was and the urge to chug hammered at his will. But he was a fully trained Knight of the Protective Hand, and even with his temple fallen into Gray Army service, they'd taught their knights well. When he'd sipped almost half the jug, Loni produced a sandwich of cold ham and a mustard almost too spicy for his tender stomach. "I don't suppose there's an apple in there?"

Loni produced a battered and withered fruit. "Not much of one, I'm afraid. Produce is getting harder to come by."

Despite the apple's age, it was one of the best things Estan had ever tasted. On a different day, he may have paid more attention to how mealy and dry it was—but there was some sweetness, at least a little juice, and it eased an ache in his throat in a way the water jug hadn't. "It's perfect. Thank you. But where is everyone? Why are you out here alone?"

"Resmine's fighting a war with assassins and her uncle, not to mention the demon-bound. Her betrothed, Dewin, has been trying to get back to her temple—she says it's like every Flayer still within the city has crowded the streets around Dothernam Square. They're too thick to get in to lay the runes needed to expel them. I don't really know what the rest of them have been up to... I'm concerned for Khiri. Since she went to the Life Trees, there's been a large column of smoke visible in that direction. Another smoke cloud was visible toward Seirane. We've had no news yet from either. Corianne—" Loni's voice broke. A sadness swept across her almost too quickly for Estan to see it, but he'd known Loni for more than half of his life. Before he could interject, she continued, "is a very capable woman. She's doing well."

Tucking worries about Khiri away for later—which was difficult with what he'd learned in the arch—Estan kept his focus on Loni. She had seen him scan the area earlier, looking for Corianne.

Of course she had.

Estan sighed, meeting Loni's hopeful and hurt gaze. "You both deserve so much better than me. I'm an ass that can't seem to make up his mind. I don't recognize half of what's in front of me. And often misinterpret the rest."

Searching his face, whatever Loni saw didn't please her. She sighed and shook her head. "I can't fault you for being self-aware, at least. Estan, I know I left you all those years ago. Assuming I'm not a widow or the gods see fit to hold me to my union vows, I might even still be married. Taymahr knows I'm free in my heart to choose again, but— Sorry, I'm getting way ahead of myself. The point is: I messed up back then. And I never really moved past you. I thought I loved the man I married, but I never really knew him. Not like I knew you. Something which became abundantly clear when he was looking to murder me so they could frame you. I wasn't even a full person in my husband's eyes. You've always seen me. I know in my heart you still feel something. Why am I suddenly in a competition for your affection?"

Estan reached to caress Loni's cheek. She leaned into the touch, and as soon as her smooth skin met his palm a sob escaped her lips. Tears rained from her eyes and while he wanted to reassure her, no words came.

Loni had been his shining light. Even after she'd left him for another man and a less complicated life, the ember he'd held for her never flickered out. He'd jumped from spark to spark ever since, never focusing on any one woman for long enough for something meaningful. Without meaning to, Estan found himself chuckling. "I'm such a dope. Ever since this whole mad dash started, I've been looking for someone to love. First, I got all up in my head about Khiri—"

Loni startled Estan with her own laugh. "Not that she's not wonderful, but while traveling together... And I felt badly for Kal too, because I could tell he wanted to be more to her, but Khiri—"

"I know. She's of the Life Tree clans and was on a quest to find her soul mate," Estan said. "She made it quite clear she wasn't interested when I kissed her like an idiot."

"It's not that," Loni shook her head. "Khiri's not a bedder. She likes romance well enough, but she's not the type to be aroused by a sweetie. If not for the constant attention in that arena, she'd likely never think to take a partner at all."

Blinking at Loni, a thousand interactions with Khiri locked into place and Estan found himself laughing even harder. "By Taymahr, I am a bigger idiot than I realized. Kal, too. I kept telling myself she was shy or inexperienced, but—she met Petora and it didn't even phase her! Blessed High Ones!"

And the realization also made something else lock into place for Estan. Something which had weighed on his heart heavily since he'd learned about Telgan Korsborn's past. The weight of betrayal lifted. Khiri might have been keeping secrets, but it wasn't for some nefarious bride-of-the-enemy plan. More than likely she was scared. Scared her friends would think—

Would think exactly what he'd initially thought.

"Okay, so you're an idiot, and you made a pass at Khiri. Who else?"

If Loni had been asking with anger or reproach, Estan would've moved on without telling her anything. But she seemed to genuinely want to hear about who he'd been involved with since they'd last really spoken. Loni had always been remarkably easy to talk to, so Estan found himself telling her about Ysinda and their doomed romance. He even told her about the peppermint tea and the way the former Thief Queen had kept delicate glass ornaments and stuffed creatures amongst her shelves of weapons. And then he laid out his complicated history with Corianne: from their first meeting where she'd admitted having the intention to rob him, to when he'd been poisoned, to the warnings about Ysinda, to being alone with her in a warehouse when they'd had very adult thoughts, to the repeated instances he'd decided there would be time later to think about her in a real way, and finally, the realization he'd had while trapped in a cage next to his childhood hero.

Adjusting her skirts so her legs were out in front of her, Loni picked through the basket of goodies she'd brought along and pulled out a small mead bottle. Pulling the cork, she saluted Estan and threw her head back. Her blonde curls bounced around her shoulders, and Estan realized he didn't have the urge to stroke them with his fingers.

It seemed wrong somehow. He'd genuinely thought there would never be a time when Loni wasn't second only to Taymahr.

"I think you've realized what I suspected when I arrived," Loni said. She made herself smile, but it was a sad little grin. "Corianne replaced me in your heart a long time ago."

"No!" Estan pulled himself over to Loni and wrapped her in a hug. "Never replaced. No one could replace you. You were my first love, and there will always be a piece of me thinking about you and remembering you. We were great together. But I guess, without me realizing it, my heart got attached to someone else."

"She's a good choice," Loni chuckled even though her eyes were still watery. "No one would think it to look at us, but we're a lot alike. I can tell that once she's in your corner, she'll never let you down."

Passing Estan a bottle of his own, and letting him try again on the sandwich, they spent almost an hour chatting about nothing important. Estan had been underground for nearly a week, and Loni had been coming to wait for him almost daily. Most days, Resmine sent her with an escort in case she happened upon Flayers or rival guild members. This particular day, Loni had left early. Tak had accompanied her most of the way, only to leave her at the stairwell citing an urgent message he needed to see about.

"I haven't given my future plans much thought," Loni admitted. "Since the day Khiri asked if I wanted to come with her to find you, I'm almost ashamed to admit you've been my primary focus. Now, well—I guess it's good we got closure. But it does kind of leave me at a loose end."

Thinking about closure, Estan's mind flashed on Ren and Adela of the Talon Acre Inn. It didn't sit right, not telling them he was alive when so much else was going on. It was time to right a long-standing wrong, and he knew they'd take to Loni immediately.

Assuming they didn't toss him out on his ear.

But Estan had never been a coward. He and Loni would stop by on his way back to The Dusk and Dawn.

After that, he needed to find all of the former avatars of the High Ones he could. They were due for a war council.

IT WAS SATISFYING TO know at least one thing he'd had a hand in had gone exceedingly well. While Ren and Adela weren't overwhelmingly happy with him, they were genuinely relieved he lived and told him to come by more often. As he'd suspected, they'd all but adopted Loni on the spot. She reminded them of the good parts of Ysinda, but Estan didn't think they were in danger of confusing the two women. As soon as they heard her story, Adela offered Loni a job along with room and board.

With his childhood sweetheart taken care of, Estan's heart was lighter.

But his shoulders were now weighed down with the mantle of duty. Knowledge was one of the most important weapons in any war, and his time within the arch had given him a full arsenal.

The knight's thoughts were so immersed in his findings, he wasn't paying any attention to his surroundings. It wasn't until a gentle, familiar nip at his breaches that he noticed the war horse with an elven rider. "Estan! I wasn't expecting to run into you on the streets. Where are you headed?"

"Back to The Dusk and Dawn. I— It's good to see you back. Loni mentioned seeing smoke outside the city," Estan said. Though his romantic fantasies revolving around winning Khiri's heart were firmly in the past, something about the woman still made his thoughts chaotic and awkward—like he was constantly seeking her approval.

Maybe it's still her relation to Genovar. Despite the way everything ended, I still have some residual hero-worship.

Khiri slid off of Catapult's back and gave Estan a firm hug. "It's good to see you, too. We've got a lot to talk about—all of us."

There was no bow at her side or strapped to her back. The words popped out of Estan's mouth before he could stop them. "Where's Micah?"

Her eyes glimmered with unshed tears and her mouth tightened. Estan found himself pleading with Taymahr not to have to comfort another crying woman this soon after Loni's earlier weeping. Two in one day was too many. He never quite knew where to put his hands, and he wanted to say things to fix everything but he only ever seemed to make things worse—the person he was attempting to comfort would cry harder until some unknowable signal transformed the tears into anger.

But Khiri didn't dissolve into a puddle. She blew a sigh out through her nostrils and tilted her head toward the road. "That's definitely part of it, but there's a lot more. So if we could find the others before I start on what will be a very long story..."

Estan nodded. The name *Telgan Korsborn* had hovered in between the two of them before many times when Estan thought he'd been in love with Khiri, but he'd done his best to ignore it then. Now, it was time to address the Flayer Mage in the room.

Almost time.

Back to the tavern first.

RETURNING TO THE DUSK and Dawn, Estan received as many hugs as Khiri did. Resmine and Dewin were sitting together at one of the tables in the throne room. Estan had noticed a few tables mended with fresh lumber in the lower tap room, the floor held a few new stains—not all of which were alcohol—and some splinters which had been missed by brooms. People had been busy while he'd been away.

Corianne kept her distance, though Estan could tell she was pleased to see him. He wanted to march over to her and sweep her up in his arms right then and there, but there was too much to discuss and Estan wasn't sure if he kissed Corianne if he'd ever come up for air. Conveying his feelings through his eyes wasn't working, so he hoped he could make it up to her eventually. Now that he knew who he wanted, he'd spend his whole life trying to convince her how important she was to him.

But he was and always would be Taymahr's knight first.

"We've got to talk," Khiri said. "All of the remaining avatars."

"Cori, Shiv, and Tak, too?" Dewin asked.

Khiri looked like she was about to object and then shrugged. "We could probably use the help. If you trust them, ask them to come."

It took less time than expected to gather everyone into the stable of The Dusk and Dawn. Catapult could have projected himself into the Pit, but Estan was grateful not to be asked to return underground so soon after his ordeal in the arch. Despite the stench of horse and hay, the stable yard was a paradise of light, breezes, and open space. It would probably be a few weeks before Estan voluntarily entered so much as a basement. The protections they had against listening were less impressive than Kal's displays of glittery dome magic but, with the subject being Irrellian Thornne, Estan doubted even his late rival's magic would've kept them entirely safe.

"Those that traveled with me, you know I was looking for Telgan Korsborn—my Destined. I probably should've told you all much sooner, but we found him. I knew him in The Burning Valley. And he recognized me in return. I don't know how or why Irrellian Thornne is also Telgan Korsborn—"

"I have some insight on that, Khiri," Estan interrupted. "The arch below the city... Res, you were right. The Thieves' Guild didn't build it. It's the tomb of Telgan Korsborn's mother. He was the original founder of Jarelton, a hero to his people, and the first human to ascend to godhood."

"Well, dash me 'cross the teeth and call me a squirrel," Corianne said, awe softening her tone. "How's the Flayer Mage got a god inside?"

"That's the thing," Estan sighed. This had been hard for him to stomach, but he'd watched it—all of it—happen. "Telgan Korsborn was a human. He ascended. More humans followed. Less people remembered him. He faded. He descended. He became the first demon. Again, more gods faded, and followed. They took contracts with mortals to try and come back to the living realms of Arra. No one could recall their names, so they consumed their hosts only to return to the hells once the bodies housing them died. Telgan watched them. Rather than offer himself into a bargain, he wore a ring in life—one that followed him into godhood, and remained within the demon lands. He began infusing it with his own essence. Sending it up with one of the lesser Flayer-contract demons, he waited. It passed through many, many hands before Irrellian Thornne came by it during his time in the Mages' College. I didn't understand most of what he did to uncover Telgan's name from the ring's memory, but he called for a binding using the name of the first god. They are bound by a wish, like all other Flayers, but because Irrellian knows the demon he's bound to—"

"He can feed Telgan Korsborn with belief instead of blood," Resmine said. "And that ring, that was the ring Khiri wore on our first trek across Mytana?"

Estan and Khiri both met the other's gaze and nodded together.

"Irrellian lost it during the war. Telgan somehow wiped the loss from his host's mind. From what I witnessed, the host and demon are not always working in complete union," Estan explained.

Eyes distant, Khiri picked up the thread of her original story. "The ring found me at a time when the price of a bargain my father made with the gods came due. Because my mother's soul-name was changed so they could be together, the name of my soulmate was... Malleable. Genovar knew my fate would be touched by something horrible, and he asked for the change anyway. Much like when he knew he'd become a Flayer and I'd be the one to kill him. My father always made the worst possible choice and was treated like some sort of wise benefactor. A protector of Arra," Khiri said, her voice bitter but resigned. "I can't even make myself hate him for it."

A silence fell over the gathering of former avatars and their trusted friends. The only sound was Catapult whipping his tail. Dewin twirled a bit of straw between her fingers and scowled into some nether distance while Resmine leaned her back against her betrothed's shoulder and studied the rafters. Corianne crossed her arms, keeping her eyes trained on Khiri, while Tak looked more pensive than Estan had ever seen him.

"It's definitely a lot to process, but I think we need the full story from each of you before we can start planning," Resmine sighed. "From the beginning, starting with Khiri, and then a full report from Estan. And then, we need to know exactly which one of us is still an avatar."

Khiri started again, not limiting herself to the last few weeks, but from the day Micah brought her the ring as a Name Breathing gift. She told them about the moments within the cave when Irrellian Thornne woke from his crystal prison.

Resmine asked for a brief pause and left the stable only to return with a blank journal and writing supplies to take notes.

When Khiri resumed, she revealed the entire history of her parents that she'd uncovered with Kal while they'd been investigating armor-equipped Flayers in Eerilor. She told them about accidentally plane-shifting and encountering Irrellian within the demon lands. She told them about sacrificing Micah to save the Life Trees and her people. She told them about the talk she'd had with her mother beneath the limbs of the new Life Tree. And she told them about the dream which had plagued her ever since the return of Irrellian Thornne.

After Khiri was finished, Dewin told everyone about what she'd witnessed from the floor of her consecrated temple in Dothernam Square. "He was getting closer to coming through each time, and I hate to think what he's done since I been blocked."

Estan steadied himself and revealed everything he'd learned within the multiple lifetimes he'd witnessed during his time in the Mother's Tomb. He'd already hit most of the broader points, but relaying everything, he could start to see details he'd missed. Laying out as much of Telgan Korsborn's history as he could, Estan described the small child and his rise, and his eventual bargain with Irrellian Thornne. Estan recounted watching the current High Ones take power and how they'd marked certain changes within the Flayers even before Irrellian made his bargain. The High Ones, and all other gods, were aware of the belief cycle and fought to maintain heavenly standing.

"So, they knew who he was from the beginning?" Khiri asked, tension vibrating through her slight form. Anger was coming off of her so strongly, Estan could practically feel the temperature rising inside the stables. "Obviously, they knew who Irrellian Thornne was, helping my father and his generals bind him away from the world for twenty years—but, they knew about Telgan Korsborn, and Imyn never saw fit to say anything?"

"Would it have changed things?"

The source was unexpected, coming from Catapult. It was a little bit of Micah's warmth, and a touch of Kal being rational, but mixed with a third voice Estan couldn't place.

Deflating slightly, Khiri shook her head. "Yes—No—Maybe. I had a right to know who I was tied to. I've been a pawn of these human gods since before I was born, and I'm tired of being treated as though who I am is irrelevant as long as I'm useful. Spirits! It's exhausting and I'm sick of it."

"I think we're all getting a might done with it, love. Not with as much as reason as what you've faced and all. But it's right bothersome, no mistake," Dewin agreed.

Being the only true priestess among them, Estan's chest constricted with the truth behind Dewin's words. Even he felt a bit used, after all he'd learned. Not that it changed his allegiance to Taymahr, but he'd also wondered about the gods' silence in this business.

"Which leaves us with the big question. Which of our heavenly friends is still here?" Resmine asked. "Because I think I have the beginnings of a plan."

50

~Khiri~

SILVER MISTS SWIRLED around Khiri's feet as she moved over the cobblestones. Her father's knife was little more than decoration at her waist. She reached for Micah, but his reassuring weight was no longer at her back. She was alone as she approached the waiting form of Irrellian Thornne.

"Come to me..."

TELGAN KORSBORN, *the name within her practically trilled in excitement. The moment was nearing. Soon she would be united with her father's enemy and—*

"There you are," *Kal said.*

Khiri whipped her head around, searching the mists for the familiar lanky frame.

"Remember what I taught you," *Kal coaxed.* "Sense with your magic, not just your eyes."

Calming her mind, Khiri reached out with the arm she didn't see. There, just beyond the mists and stones, behind the curtain of dreamscapes, she could sense him. He was much like she remembered him, but also distant in a way she couldn't define. His gray hair was less solid, the shimmer of his skin a bit more translucent, and his owl-like eyes were less golden. But he was also more than a phantom. It was as though the magic within Kal had created a ghost.

"What are you doing here?"

"I was an avatar to Shydan, remember? God of Death and Dreams. It took me a while to make it back to you, but we are bound, *laska.* I will always find a way to have your back. I would've been quicker if you still had the staff."

Khiri laughed, though there was bitterness in it. "Are you going to become a weapon for me as my brother did? Will I forever be carrying those I've lost in some other form?"

"Everyone carries the ghosts of those they lost, *laska*. Yours have just been a bit more tangible than most," *Kal chided.* "But that's not why I'm here. Khiri—"

Something shifted within the dream. A deep rumbling shook the cobblestones beneath Khiri's feet. A primal, fierce evil crashed against her meager mental-shields. If not for the shining golden dome of Kal's protection, Khiri was certain either she or the dream she was in would've shattered on impact.

"Khiri, you have a choice coming. One that could change everything. No matter what you decide, know I support you. I can't be the bow at your back, and the rules prevent me from interfering directly—but since when have you and I been great at following rules?"

"What rules?" *Khiri asked.*

"Rules created by Arra herself. Rules to keep her children in check. We of dual nature, we can tap into the gifts of our people—knowing the currents, or immunity to disease. Humans tap into belief the same way, but it's still Arra's gift. And since you and I were born with the ability to wield both kinds of magic, if those channels are opened just a bit wider, we can tap into Arra's own power. Maleck's staff showed me the way. I had hoped to guide you through it. It would've been easier."

"You've been gone almost a week, and all you want to do is chastise me for breaking your staff?"

Kal smirked and gave her one of those suggestive eyebrow raises that made Khiri miss him even harder.

"What?"

"Never change, *laska*," *Kal said. The fabric of the dream quaked and shuttered.* "I can't stay much longer, and I must give you something before I go."

Glittering magical energy flowed from Kal's ethereal form and into Khiri's core. The light she'd witnessed during the single kiss they'd shared blinded her mind's eye as new knowledge awakened within her—and with it, power beyond reason.

Kal's lips brushed her forehead one last time. "Stay safe and good luck, *laska.* Live well."

The evil, unhappy at being blocked, was charging toward them again. Khiri still couldn't see, but she felt Kal move to intercept the entity. With no magic, she didn't see how he would survive impact.

"NO!"

She was still glowing softly through her blankets as her eyes flew open. Throwing her senses as widely open as she could, there was no trace of Kal or the force attacking them. Only the soft motes of magic hanging in the air confirmed it had been more than a dream.

IRRELLIAN THORNNE HAD always told Khiri she would come to him of her own volition. She wasn't thrilled that Resmine's plan actually meant the Flayer Mage was right. Locating her thread of connection to Telgan Korsborn's name, she pulled until there was a ping of recognition. She wanted him to know she was on her way.

Most days, his name had been a dull thing, iron and stagnant but for the occasional flare of excitement or anger. It was different today, as though he could sense victory near at hand. Khiri didn't like this plan, but she couldn't think of anything better. Their path was committed now.

Khiri hadn't wanted to stay at The Dusk and Dawn again. The odd underground rooms were filled with all the sorrows she'd left behind, and she needed her head as clear as possible for what was to come. Instead, Estan had led her to a place called The Talon Acre Inn. It was filled with warmth and a sense of belonging. She exchanged hugs with Loni, pleased to see the woman. Loni seemed content, having found another job. Ren and Adela told Khiri they'd heard all about her and showed her several letters from Ullen. It wasn't as good as seeing Ullen in person, but Khiri's heart was warmed by his praise.

The dream she'd had about Kal, if it could be called a dream, played through her mind once more as she strapped on her armor, including the useless knife hilt at her hip. Khiri wished she liked the gods well enough for prayer to lend her a semblance of comfort, but she had more reason to resent them than speak to them. Well, actually, not all of them—

Petora,

We only met once. Your advice was very cryptic and I have no idea if I've been 'igniting the darkness' or not. Please know I've been doing my best. Elves aren't much for prayer so I don't know if I'm doing it right. I'm mad at your High Council but that doesn't necessarily mean I want to destroy them. Most of my friends want to save them from the cycle of disbelief and demons. Part of me thinks Irrellian might have a point. Change is needed.

Change was needed.

Like the soul names of her people, the ascension-and-descension of gods was broken. It was horrible for people making desperate wishes to be consumed by the monsters they summoned. Someone had wished for Khiri's death, her father had wished for Khiri's safety, and both of the wishers were met with gruesome destruction. Meanwhile, their wishes were unfulfilled.

Creeping down the stairs during the dim twilight, before Arra truly woke, Khiri hoped Loni and the innkeepers forgave her for not saying goodbye. If things went to plan, the other avatars would already be waiting.

Her steps echoed off of Jarelton's bland stone walls as she walked the path Dewin had given her. As a trained hunter, Khiri hated the sound. She fought the urge to quiet her tread. The whole point of this was not to hide. Though the walk seemed to take entire seasons, she also found herself at the entry to Dothernam Square all too soon.

Arra was turning toward spring, and the mists promising morning dew drifted through the streets. Khiri began to recognize the cobblestone beneath her feet. This was it. The beginning of the dream she'd had so many times.

"Come to me, Khiriellen Fortiva," Irrellian Thornne coaxed. "Come, and meet me as your destined."

Swallowing back the urge to launch an attack, or turn and run, Khiri planted one foot in front of the other. She had no idea if the others were where they'd planned to be or not. The power Kal had awakened within her seemed too loud, too obvious. If she tried to sense them, the Flayer Mage might notice.

There hadn't been a waiting ring of Flayers surrounding the temple to Adari. Resmine had guessed Irrellian would make a path if he thought Khiri was on her way. Either Resmine's guess was right, or Khiri had plane-shifted without realizing it.

Kal's gift sent a wave of reassurance through her. If she were to plane-shift, she would definitely know about it. And it certainly wouldn't happen by accident.

Despite herself, Khiri reached for Micah's grip only to clasp at the nothing on her back. She could've used his support as well.

"I told you you would come to me eventually," Irrellian smiled.

"You also told me I would come alone," Khiri said. It was the agreed upon signal. The sign for her friends to emerge from Catapult's veil and attack.

She waited.

Irrellian Thornne was close enough to reach out and touch her if he wanted. Khiri didn't remember closing so much distance.

Seconds rolled by with the gathering mists.

She continued to wait.

Finally, the sounds of fighting drifted through the growing fog. Flashes of Dewin's hatchets and Estan's sword caught the blue light of Irrellian's shield magic as they crunched and slashed their way through Flayers Khiri hadn't been able to see. Resmine took a hit from a Flayer claw and fell back beyond Khiri's sight. Dewin rushed to block the attacking demon-bound. Tak flew through the air, his feet angled like knife-edges as he drove a Flayer into Estan's blade. Corianne blew something up and her muffled cackle barely penetrated the blue dome. Shiv, the giant mountain of a man, lay unmoving across the cobblestones.

"My dear girl," Irrellian said, "you are alone."

Khiri's heart started to sink. The ability to sneak up on the Flayer Mage had always been a long shot, but she'd believed Catapult could do it. After all, Irrellian hadn't seemed to notice the horse when he'd burned down the Life Trees.

"Not quite," the voice came from behind Irrellian.

Time seemed to slow as the mage turned, his hand conjuring a fireball of black flame. Catapult was reaching to grab the Flayer Mage's robes with his teeth. She didn't want to see what would happen to the roan if the fire connected with his flesh.

Throwing herself forward, Khiri's momentum closed the distance between herself, Irrellian, and the war horse. The black flame fizzled out as horse teeth met with the Flayer Mage's body. He yelped in pain and Khiri wondered if that was the first real damage he'd suffered since making his deal with Telgan Korsborn.

As she thought his name, she could feel the god-demon laughing within Irrellian's skin. Something about it made her stomach flip and she fought back the urge to throw up.

"I've got him!"

Despite never having heard Numyri's voice before, Khiri recognized it immediately.

Breaking the Flayer Mage's concentration also broke his shield. Holy energy burst through the clouds, parting the mist. Estan made a relieved groan as everyone in the square began to radiate white light, even Corianne and Tak. The space inside of Khiri where Imyn had dwelled during their shared time when Khiri was acting as an avatar filled with the goddess's presence once more. **"I'm with you,"** Imyn told her fellow goddess.

Irrellian tried to shove Khiri away with his free arm while Catapult had him firmly by the butt-cheek. "It took all seven of you to encase me last time and your powers were much greater then. You can't afford to risk your whole pantheon again, and we all know it. What makes you think this feeble attempt to entrap me will work?"

"We're not trapping you," Khiri said, wrestling back control of her own voice for a few precious seconds. "We're transporting you."

As her fellow avatars all grabbed onto the struggling Flayer Mage, Khiri used her ability to plane-shift to take them back to a grove she'd only visited once during a dream meeting.

UNLIKE THE DREAM, THERE was no gentle separation between the avatars and their host bodies. What had been eight beings was suddenly fifteen tumbling away from each other in the glade that was overwhelmingly perfect. The gods got to their feet faster than their avatars, but Irrellian Thornne was already standing.

Catapult continued to roll in the overly green grass even after everyone else managed to disentangle. Numyri watched him wistfully, as though she were disappointed by the separation.

"Congratulations, you've all successfully brought me to where I aimed to be," Irrellian said dryly. "Now, any last words before I cinder you all and retake what *should have been mine all along*!"

Though he hadn't split into two people when they'd arrived, Khiri could see the seams forming in the Flayer Mage. Irrellian's wish to make a better world didn't seem to align entirely with Telgan Korsborn's own goals anymore. And thanks to Kal's gift, or maybe the talents granted her for being an avatar of the Goddess of Power and Change, Khiri could see the streams of belief flowing to each deity. Irrellian also had a stream of belief, thicker than any of those connected to the High Ones, but Telgan was trying to tear it away from his mortal host.

"Enough of that," Khiri said. She reached out with her new power and placed a shield between the Flayer Mage and his belief stream.

With a shriek of rage, Irrellian turned toward her and let loose a torrent of fire. It wasn't the black flame responsible for eating the Burning Valley or her Life Trees, but it could've caused serious damage if not for the shell of shields cast over her by all seven of the High Ones. The fire ate whatever reserves Irrellian had banked.

"We brought you here, to propose a bargain," Locke said, as though neither the attack nor threats had transpired.

"A place among us, if you agree to share your pool of belief. It's the same bargain all in our council have made. You would become a High One," Taymahr offered.

Irrellian Thornne drew himself up to his full height, looking at the gods with all the disdain he could muster. Being bound to the first god to ever ascend and inhabit the demon planes, it was an impressive display. "Why should I take your non-offer? What do I gain from cowering to your demands to eat my power?"

Tharothet, who'd temporarily ridden within Tak, tapped his long fingers against his lips and studied the Flayer Mage through hooded eyes. His scarred arms flexed, showing more menace than seemed usual for the God of Seeking and Knowledge. "What power do you truly have in this moment? You seem to be capped by a barely-trained mortal."

"You can't be serious?!" Estan shouted. He ran to Taymahr and fell on his knees. "My goddess, please! You can't seriously want to give this man a position on your council! He's personally killed countless people, and he's had even more killed in his name! He schemed his way here, only to be offered a godhood? What about justice? What about what's fair and right for Arra? What about all of the families broken in his wake?"

Resmine and Dewin shared a look. Khiri got the impression they'd anticipated the gods would make this kind of offer. Resmine was pragmatic enough to set aside her principles and rule a guild of thieves, and Dewin was priestess to the Goddess of Greed and Guile. Dewin had sanctified the Jarelton temple by claiming the assassination of a noble as a holy sacrifice. Tak and Corianne were standing to the side, trying their best to fade into the background. The temporary jump made by Tharothet and Shydan into their respective bodies seemingly hadn't lasted long enough for them to have any level of comfort gain-saying the gods' decisions. If they even wanted to.

"He was a god before," Adari pointed out. "We're not so much elevating him as reinstating. And if we all have a share in his power, he won't be able to oust us."

"But—"

"Be at ease, knight," Irrellian growled. "I'll not surrender to this farce. The Fortiva girl can't hold me for much longer. Not when all of you together weren't able to keep me for more than a few decades."

Khiri hadn't been thinking about it, but she was still holding him. It wasn't even difficult. Despite Irrellian's confidence in his coming freedom, Khiri felt strong enough to hold him for as long as she had to. Looking at the barrier she'd cast, she understood. Kal's gift—he'd tapped her directly into the magic of Arra. While the gods bickered and squabbled over the river of belief flowing into their realm, Khiri's power was coming from the riverbed and the landscape surrounding it. She could do so much with this kind of power, but—

She didn't want it. Once Irrellian Thornne was dealt with, she just wanted to be Khiri again. If going back was possible.

But things did have to change.

Looking at the seams of Irrellian Thornne and Telgan Korsborn, Khiri started picking them apart as delicately as she could. The two men started to scream despite her gentleness. They'd been merged for a very long time and not all of their bits were ready to be divided. Finally, they both collapsed as individuals, panting and sweating in agony.

Once they were two beings, Khiri studied Telgan Korsborn. She recognized the malevolence from her dream—the evil force who had attempted to stop Kal from awakening the power of Arra within her. He wasn't much to look at. While strong, his frame was more wiry than muscular and he wasn't even as tall as Estan. He had mousy hair and dusty brown eyes. His skin had gone ashen from so many long decades spent within the underworld. It was as though everything about him had been washed out to make room for more evil. But, he hadn't always been that way. At one time, Telgan had been a hero, a benevolent king, and even a kind god. He was another bear with rabies.

"It's time for you to rest," Khiri told him.

She reached out with the hand of Arra, and dismissed his soul to the afterlife of mortals. The entire heavens seemed to sigh beneath them with relief.

While the rift to the afterlife was open, Khiri searched for her father. Even with the power of Arra behind her, she couldn't bring him back but she wanted to know he still existed somewhere. It was soft, but she sensed an echo of his midnight eyes and fatherly affection. It was enough.

There was a whisper of Kal somewhere, but not within the afterlife. She didn't have time to search now, but she was certain she'd see him in her dreams again someday.

"Khiri? What just happened?" Estan asked. "What did you do?"

The gods behind him had stilled like frightened rabbits, as though they were suddenly aware judgment could easily find them next. Khiri wasn't interested in taking all of the human gods away, but she could change things. "I put someone to rest that was sorely in need of it. It's okay, Estan. The way we've been avatars for the gods—I'm doing it for Arra now."

Irrellian Thornne had crawled back up to his hands and knees. He was looking at her from under his disheveled hair. The glimmer of his glassy, onyx skin was reminiscent of deep waters Khiri had never visited. "Actually, you could be a god. I've removed the demon from you, and you've done horrible things. But there is a group of people that could desperately use someone that understands them—that can lay them to rest when it's their time, and judge if they push too far or make terrible bargains. Irrellian, would you take the position I am offering?"

"You want me to be the God of Flayers?" he asked. "From Flayer Mage to Flayer God?"

Khiri considered. "Maybe the God of Wishes? Or Hope? You'd be in a position to make the world a much better place."

"Khiri!" Estan tried one more time.

She could hear the desperation in his voice, but Khiri shook her head. "Estan, I've lost more than most to this man's machinations. I know what I'm offering, and to whom. Hope shines brightest in the darkness."

Rolling onto the grass with a moan, Irrellian chuckled with ill humor. "All that I have done, only to be offered the chance to rule what I loathed most."

"This is a Council. They make the big decisions together. It's up to you. I could put you to rest as well."

Shaking his head, Irrellian accepted her offered hand and rose to his feet. "I had a feeling when we met you might be able to help me change Arra, you know. We were destined."

There were many more details to iron out before they were all done, but the hardest decisions were already made. Khiri had finally smoothed out the wrinkles in reality left by her parents' decisions. Gods and mortals debated in the clearing long enough for a full day to pass on the face of Arra. While it was hard to say if anyone was truly happy with the decisions made, most parties walked away somewhat satisfied.

Change didn't happen overnight, even with the backing of Arra.

But *Telgan Korsborn* no longer sounded within Khiri's head. Her destiny was fully within her own hands.

It was time to go home.

Epilogue

~Estan~

HE STILL HADN'T FULLY forgiven Khiri for the decision to make the Flayer Mage into a god, but Estan couldn't imagine staying mad at his friend forever. It was hardly different from what his own goddess had been offering, after all.

In some ways, Khiri's offer was much worse for Irrellian Thornne than what the High Council had planned. Khiri had given Irrellian dominion over Hope, a nebulous title at best. While the High Ones hadn't seen fit to tell them what they'd had in mind for the Flayer Mage in the heavenly grove, Numyri had taken the chance of allowed by some shifting stations to demote herself to a minor deity and continue to use Catapult—with the horse's permission—as her avatar. She'd admitted to wanting to make Irrellian the God of Fear.

The thought still made Estan shudder. Arra was a hard enough world for most people. Which might have been why, in addition to adding Irrellian to the pantheon, Khiri suggested Petora be brought forward as the Goddess of Fertility and Light. The Moon would still be considered part of Petora's aspect, though it had been taken out of her title.

"So, now Arra's been saved, are you on to build new temples in Seirane?" Resmine asked. She had her legs swept up over the armrest of the Thieves' Throne and her head dangling over the other side. "Can't imagine you want to hang around here after the wedding. I'm about to be Lady Ilamar and the Queen of Thieves. As open minded as you've proven yourself, can't see you quite stomaching all my changes."

"You're probably right," Estan admitted.

"Corianne was only ever staying on as my second until I was properly settled. Didn't she tell you she resigned today?"

"Cori resigned?" It was the first Estan had heard of Corianne's plan, and a jolt of fear ran through him. He was only sitting in Resmine's Court because he'd intended to finally have a talk with the thief woman about what she meant to him. "Did she say where she was going?"

"Travelling. Had her pack ready to go." Resmine sat up. "She's probably going to the Northern Gate, now that the roads are passable again. You can probably catch her if you hurry."

Giving Resmine a quick brotherly hug, Estan nearly plowed into Dewin on her way up the stairs. "Hold on, love! What's the hurry?"

"Corianne!"

"Oh, right, then. Get on! I want you for a proper brother-in-law 'fore the summer's out! Scoot!" Dewin laughed, phasing through him and patting his butt platonically as she went.

Estan shook his head as he ran out the door and down the street. Catapult caught up with him before the knight had made it a full block and demanded Estan mount up. They flew through streets which were still recovering their former bustle, the war horse not bothering to pretend his ability to sense crowds was anything less than preternatural.

Corianne was within spitting distance of the gate when Estan tumbled off of Catapult to intercept her. "Cori!"

"Essy? Why in Arra are you charging through Jarelton like a gnorrel what's burned his tail?"

"Resmine said you resigned and you were—"

With a sigh, Corianne shifted her backpack from her back to her feet. It had pots and pans, a bedroll, all of the provisions that spoke to a long journey ahead. "I ain't good with goodbyes and I told you, I ain't willing for half. Thought it'd be better to have gone and done. If you—"

Estan didn't wait for her to finish her sentence. He pulled her into an embrace and brought his lips down, giving Corianne just enough space to decide whether or not she wanted this too. When her lips met his, he thought he understood how Khiri had felt when she realized she'd held all the power of Arra at her fingertips.

It felt good.

It felt right.

Estan didn't know where Corianne was planning on going, but he knew he was going with her. It wasn't until they broke away from the kiss—and Estan was trying to figure out how quickly he could get to the apartment and pack—that he noticed Catapult's saddle bags were fully equipped, a pastel mug carefully peeking out of his spare clothes. It seemed his bond-sister had planned for his escape once again.

~Resmine~

Watching her bond-brother dart out of the tavern for what would likely be the last time in many summers, Resmine smiled a bittersweet smile. She would've liked for him to stay for the wedding, and the coronation, but Estan wouldn't be Estan if he stopped to think about things. Hopefully, Corianne would be able to keep him in line.

Looking after the knight wasn't Resmine's job any more.

Sweeping into the Throne Room, Dewin was every bit as beautiful as the first time Resmine saw her. The urge to melt into her betrothed right then and there was intoxicating. Catching the look in Resmine's eyes, Dewin shook her head even though her smile brightened. "None of that now, love. We've got actual plans that need planning. Your mum is all aflutter to give her long-lost daughter and the future Ilamar the biggest to do Jarelton's seen. She's sending invites to nobles all over Arra, and we've got to give her some actual decisions by week's end."

Dewin began spreading blueprints and wedding diagrams and sorting samples all over the tables usually reserved for gambling and Shiv's Knives and Nobles board.

A pang of sadness threaded its way through the happy flutterings of Resmine's heart. Though Shiv had lived through the assault on the Flayer Mage, he hadn't woken yet. The best healers in the city were maintaining a magical comma while they attempted to bring the big man back.

Khiri probably could've done something, but she'd left right after the battle. Resmine sent a messenger to Eerilor to wait for her friend and ask her to return. She owed Shiv every attempt to wake him at her disposal.

Later tonight, I'm going down to the temple and yelling at the High Ones. After all we went through, the least they can do is bring back Shiv.

But that was for later. Right now, between the demands of her people, her city, and her heart, Resmine was going to give her heart priority for a few hours.

~Ullen~

"**D**ratted contraption," Ullen muttered, fiddling with the rune controls for his new moving chair. Rigger had shifted from barrel-walkers to chairs which rolled or hovered, or—his latest—ran around on what looked like massive chicken legs. "Has Vess delivered on that prosthetic yet? Why is it taking her so long to make one leg when her apprentice is drowning me in fancy chairs?"

They were out in the royal runeworking shop—Ullen had replaced several of the troop bunkers with more productive spaces once he'd retaken the palace. As much as he hated all of the memories of the place, it would break Eerilor to try and build a new one. Eventually, after his people had recovered from the civil war and the purging of the Gray Army, Ullen wanted to convert the Taman palace into a University and have a small, more practical building created for governing.

Maybe even one he didn't live in.

Jaspar attempted to hide a chuckle behind her curls as she leaned in to kiss Ullen. They'd had a battlefield marriage while healers had been bandaging what was left of Ullen's leg. Ullen had come so close to dying, he'd decided hell with politics and requested the vows to be sanctioned before he passed out. When he'd come to, he'd been concerned Jaspar would resent him for binding her to him in a field of blood and death. She'd just called him an ass for thinking it mattered, and they proceeded to work on the succession.

The smoke damage in his lungs was still gradually improving. As was his father-in-law's opinion of him. His chopped foot was well gone, but Vess had promised him a master rune-work boot that would fit so well he would supposedly forget the war ever happened.

And in the meantime, Ullen could pretend he was the king of chickens.

"Soon, my love. Masterwork takes more time than experimentation. You're lucky Rigger's got this much energy left after the war."

"Aye, I know. Lad's right set to take over the whole of Eerilor with his ideas. Think we should adopt him and nip his coup in the bud?"

"You finally read the letter that Khiri's on her way to visit, didn't you? You're excited and irritable all at once."

Ullen sighed. "It's one thing to have the people of Eerilor see me like this. It's another to have someone I regard as a daughter see me as less than I was."

Jaspar clasped Ullen's hand and let him mull things over in silence for a while. It was one of the things he loved most about her. She was never pushy when he wanted a moment of quiet, but she always found a way to let him know he wasn't alone.

"Am I interrupting?" Vess asked. "I've brought your new boot."

"Finally!" Ullen stood on his remaining foot and hopped out of the chicken leg chair. He couldn't go very far without a crutch this way, but he was too excited to wait for someone to bring it to him. He hobbled his way over to the bench. Vess helped lift him into a proper seat with one arm while she managed a case in the other hand. There were a few straps that needed buckling, a winch in need of winching, and a leather cuff that slid over his stump like a sock—but once everything was in place, it was indeed as though the ax had never fallen. The new prosthetic was as sturdy and easy to use as his foot had been.

"Now, you can't bathe with this on. It will need recharging every seven days. Once you take it off, it won't go back on for a four hour period. Can't be helped, that's part of the binding process for it to feel as natural as it does. Runes are a touchy business, and I know you're not about to argue with a friend that made you a masterwork attachment out of the goodness of her heart."

Clamping his teeth down around a half-formed argument, Ullen huffed out a laugh. "Thank you, Vess. Truly. And my thanks to that apprentice of yours. It's been a lot to deal with and you've both made things a solid dash easier."

Vess clapped a hand against her king's shoulder and nodded. "Things have been going well with Rigger. Might be time I find a few more apprentices. He's about ready for his journeyman's tests."

All too soon, Ullen found himself heading to the throne room to deal with matters of state—but at least he was able to walk there on his own again.

~Irrellian~

He hadn't been ready for the prayers. A constant barrage of the hopes and wishes of mortals flooded his being constantly. The Fortiva girl had duped him, and duped him well. There was no way he'd be able to take over anything with this constant racket.

Not to mention the braiding of power she'd left him with.

Where the original bond shared by the High Ones had been a single thread of power connecting them beyond their belief tethers, which would've allowed them to break off into individual power bases—the High Ones were now sharing one woven cord. Attempts to undermine the rest of the Council would break the cord for all of them.

"HEY! You up there! I know you're listening, by Locke! You put Shiv in this coma!"

Irrellian recognized the voice. It was one in millions, but it was also the shrewd niece of his once-ally and one of those responsible for his current status. He was tempted to shut out this prayer with all the other voices vying for his attention.

"She's calling from the Jarelton temple," Petora said. She was standing in the doorway of Irrellian's chambers. He hadn't noticed her arrival, and it disconcerted him how much the goddess seemed to see. "Temple and shrine prayers are always loudest."

"Are the others calling for my resignation already?" Irrellian asked. Not that any of them could leave without the rest anymore.

"Just came to see how you're settling in," Petora smiled. It washed over Irrellian like a warm, spring rain. Even other gods weren't immune to the charms of the Goddess of Fertility and Light. Irrellian had been in the dark for what felt like lifetimes.

"Please—I know... I know I'm probably one of the last people you'd ever grant a boon, but, please! He's my second-in-command, and more than that, he's my friend. I owe him—more than I can say. This world needs Shiv. I need Shiv. Please."

Something about that please.

With Petora watching.

Irrellian wasn't sure exactly what came over him, but a spark of his divinity trickled down to Arra's face and touched the nose of a sleeper who wasn't meant to wake. The large man opened his eyes and gasped, startling a room full of healers.

The cord of belief fed Irrellian several droplets of what tasted like pure light.

"Gratitude," Petora explained, also seeming to bask in the drops ecstasy. "That's belief mixed with gratitude."

"Interesting..." Irrellian said. It was time to get a handle on his new power set. "I was trained as a mage. How different is it from being a god?"

Petora granted him another smile. "I'd be happy to teach you."

~Khiri~

Nocking an arrow, Khiri sighted the gnorrel grunting at the base of the tree. She'd sensed the anger of the beast from the edge of the forest and tracked it here. A small silver cat was clinging to the upper branches, hissing as the gnorrel attempted to jar its prey loose.

The kill was swift and clean. Khiri would likely have enough gnorrel meat to make it through the pass to Eerilor.

As she was butchering the gnorrel, the silver cat slunk its way to the ground. On closer inspection, Khiri could see darker bands of gray through the silver fur. It put a pleading paw on Khiri's knee and mewed. Offering it a few bite-sized tidbits, Khiri looked around for any sign of an owner or some sort of dwelling. It seemed an odd place to discover a domestic cat, but this—a quick, discreet check—lad didn't seem in the least bit feral.

"I'm more than happy to have a traveling companion, if you'd like to join me," Khiri told the cat. "I used to travel with a whole band of people, but things have changed. I lost a few, and a few found other paths. But you know, Micah was right. I've never been alone."

The cat blinked up at Khiri with lovely delicate green eyes and begged for a few more scraps with a questing paw. Khiri obliged and watched as the cat daintily picked at his meal.

"What shall I call you?"

Another mew, as though he understood the question.

"I like it. Alright, Leaf it is. We're on our way to Eerilor to see a very dear friend of mine. He's a king," Khiri said.

Climbing up to drape himself on Khiri's backpack and over her shoulder, Leaf began to purr. Khiri wrapped more gnorrel scraps into some waxed bags and stuffed them in her hip pouch. It was always nice to make friends on the road. She wasn't sure if Leaf would come all the way to Eerilor with her or stay at the next inn, but she was glad for the company while she had it.

Also by Christina Dickinson

A Briar Egibi Novel
The Tacomancer and the Cursed Blood Knife

Ashes of the Past Saga
Waking the Burning Valley
Dropping the Keystone
Igniting the Darkness

Standalone
Strange Stars and Stranger Songs
Chance and Change

Watch for more at https://christinadickinsonwrites.com.

About the Author

When she was younger, Christina lived in Michigan, where she earned a black belt and took archery classes. She loved running through the forest, climbing through sand dunes, and swimming in Lake Michigan. She started writing in the fourth grade, with a story about her big, orange tabby cat wanting to be a rock star.

Now that she's older, Christina lives in Texas with her husband and their cats, Dagger and Glyph.

She's worked all kinds of jobs—from retail to waiting tables to warehouse to massage therapy to management. She has earned her Associate Degree with focuses on Creative Writing and History. Through all of it, her dream was to see her work in print on someone's shelf.

Christina's hobbies include playing board games, role-play games, video games— basically all games—reading, and traveling. She's always up for a ren faire, exploring an ancient ruin, or taking a cruise.

Read more at https://christinadickinsonwrites.com.

Milton Keynes UK
Ingram Content Group UK Ltd.
UKHW040402111224
452348UK00004B/379